THE GIRL IN THE TENT

A JOE COURT
NOVEL

BY
CHRIS CULVER
ST. LOUIS, MO

First paperback edition April 2024.

www.indiecrime.com
Facebook.com/ChrisCulverBooks

CONTENTS

PROLOGUE

D ry, brown leaves from a big pin oak tree blanketed the
ground around Brian Dobbs's white Ford SUV. Gray
skies stretched to the horizon. The skeletal arms of leafless
oak, poplar, and ash trees along the roadway swayed, and
the occasional breeze blew through the open windows of his
marked SUV. Brian had written three speeding tickets two
hours ago but hadn't seen another car since.

In the past, it had been easy to find and ticket speeders.
You drove to a stretch of road where drivers exceeded the
speed limit, parked behind a tree or other obstruction, and
waited for them to come to you. But now drivers got alerts
of speed traps on their phones. Already this morning, Brian
had moved twice. He'd have to move again if he wanted to
meet his enforcement goal for the day.

Missouri law prohibited the Highway Patrol from estab-
lishing a policy that required troopers to issue a certain number of tickets each week or month. Instead, the administra-
tion issued its troopers enforcement goals that resembled a

quota but stayed within the confines of the law. At their present rate, Brian wouldn't reach his goal ever again.

He reclined in his cushioned seat and glanced at the laptop that covered the center console. As a trooper, Brian needed immediate access to the department's various databases to verify license information and check for warrants, so every department-issued vehicle had a laptop and 5G internet connection. It made his job much more tolerable.

He sipped his coffee and watched the screen, a half smile on his face as two thugs urinated on a rug owned by an unemployed, lazy pothead portrayed by Jeff Bridges. *The Big Lebowski* was Brian's favorite movie. He watched it once or twice a month, usually while sitting alongside the road. Brian rubbed his eyes and blew a raspberry while considering whether he should move closer to the interstate or the town of St. Augustine when he spotted movement down the road. It was a yellow box truck from a big rental place, and it swayed on loose shocks as it came around a curve. The rear end appeared to fishtail.

His speed gun clocked it at fifty-three in a forty-five-mile-per-hour zone. He would have ignored a smaller vehicle, but a moving truck was dangerous on these curves. He closed his laptop, let the truck pass, flashed his lights, and slipped onto the road behind the vehicle. Immediately, the truck accelerated to fifty-five. Brian sighed.

"Don't do this, buddy," he said, reaching for the switch box on his dashboard to activate the siren. The truck's speed increased to fifty-eight, and Brian reached for his radio to request assistance when the rental vehicle's taillights lit up. Then the driver signaled and slowed to a stop. Brian parked about ten feet behind the truck's bumper and left his cruiser's lights on to alert incoming drivers to slow down.

He tilted his head to the microphone on his shoulder and reported his location, a description of the truck, and the truck's license plate to his dispatcher. His dispatcher informed him that the closest backup was three miles away in the town of St. Augustine and asked if he needed help. He declined but requested they be put on standby. Then he unhooked the strap that held his sidearm in the holster at his side in case he needed to draw it and stepped out of his vehicle.

Traffic stops were nerve-racking. A lot could go wrong. Most people Brian pulled over were solid citizens who just drove too fast. He'd give them a ticket, warn them that most fatal car accidents involved excessive speed, and send them on their way. Sometimes drivers took personal affront that anyone would pull them over. A professional demeanor usually took care of those.

Occasionally, though, a traffic stop became an ambush.

As he walked alongside the truck, Brian watched the truck's side view mirror until the driver came into focus. He was a man, probably thirty or thirty-five. Brian couldn't see his hands. Steps welded to the truck's fuel tank led to the cab. The driver rolled down the window, allowing Brian to see his face. His skin had an almost ghostly pale pallor. A tattoo artist—one in prison, judging by the blotchy ink—had tattooed 1488 on his neck and two teardrops beside his right eye. He had a swastika on his forearm. A marijuana odor wafted out of the vehicle.

"Turn off the vehicle and step out for me."

"I haven't done anything wrong."

Brian nodded and hovered his hand over the holster of his pistol.

"I hear you, but I need you to turn off your truck and step out all the same. It makes it easier to talk."

"That's it?" asked the driver. "You just want to talk?"

"Turn off the vehicle and step outside, sir."

"What if I don't want to?"

Brian's stomach started tightening. His skin almost itched.

"Get out of the vehicle, sir. I can smell marijuana from here."

"Weed's legal, Officer."

"It is, but you can't smoke it while driving," said Brian. "Turn off the engine and step out. If you don't, I will extract you."

The driver reached for the door.

"Slowly, buddy," said Brian. "Open the door with your left hand. Extend your right hand through the open window so I can see it."

"I didn't do anything wrong, Officer."

THE GIRL IN THE TENT

"You're speeding, and I suspect you're driving under the influence. You're going to come out and conduct a field sobriety test. Do you have any weapons on you or inside the vehicle?"

"I'm strapped. There's a Glock on my ankle and a .45 in the glove box."

Brian drew in a slow breath and inhaled the aroma of decaying leaves, damp asphalt, and the lingering odor of marijuana. His heart beat faster than he preferred, but so far, he had the situation under control. It would only take one false step to escalate, though. He leaned his chin toward the microphone on his shoulder and requested an additional unit for a potential felony arrest.

The truck's door swung open, and the driver clambered down.

"Put your hands flat against the side of your truck," said Brian. "I'm going to pat you down and confiscate your weapon. Once we're done, I'll hand it back to you."

"Is this necessary?"

"Yes," said Brian. "Hands against the vehicle, sir."

The driver complied and allowed Brian to search him for weapons or other contraband. He found a knife along the driver's belt, a cigarette lighter in his pocket, and a pistol on his ankle. After disarming the driver, Brian walked him toward his marked SUV, handcuffed him, and sat him on the ground.

"This is bull. I didn't do anything wrong."

"I appreciate your input," said Brian. "I'm going to look through your truck's cab for marijuana."

"Weed's legal."

Brian ignored him, walked to the truck, and stepped up to the cab. The ashtray held only ashes, but there was an empty Ziplock bag on the front passenger seat. He sniffed the bag and noted a prominent marijuana smell. Then he opened the glove box and found a black Colt 1911 pistol with rosewood grips. It was an expensive gun. By the time he stepped out of the cab, a second officer—Trooper Charise Johnson—had arrived. The driver was reiterating his belief that the traffic stop was frivolous. Charise nodded and listened. Finally, she walked to Brian.

"Hey, Sergeant," she said. "Our friend back there is animated."

"Yeah, he's pissed. You want to get his information and field test him? I'm going to look at his cargo."

She hesitated.

"Do we have a warrant?"

"We don't need one if our friend cooperates," he said, already walking toward the driver. "Hey, buddy, Trooper Johnson is going to get your name and information so we can make sure you don't have any outstanding warrants against you. We'd like to look in your truck."

He scowled.

"You've already been inside my truck."

"What are you hauling?" asked Brian.

He said nothing for a moment. Then he shrugged. "Just stuff."

"You seemed in an awful big hurry when I pulled you over," said Brian. "You going anywhere in particular?"

"Home."

"Where's home?" asked Brian.

The driver paused again.

"The Church."

Brian nodded, putting two and two together. Charise furrowed her brow, so he filled her in.

"He means the Church of the White Steeple," he said. "It's in the county."

"That's the racist church that does all those protests, right?" she asked. Brian nodded. "The prison ink makes sense now."

Brian focused on the driver again.

"Can I look at your cargo?"

"You won't find anything. I haven't done anything wrong."

"Terrific," said Brian. "Sit tight with Trooper Johnson. I'll get a search warrant and return in a few hours."

"I've got to get home, man. I don't have hours to waste."

"Then open the back and give me permission to search. We'll be done in ten minutes."

Brian didn't have probable cause to get a search warrant, but he had a reasonable suspicion that he'd find contraband—drugs, most likely—somewhere in the truck. He could bring in a drug-sniffing dog, and he could use that dog's findings to get a warrant. That'd take time, though.

"Knock yourself out," said the driver. "Like I said, you won't find anything."

"Will Trooper Johnson find anything when she runs your name through the system?" asked Brian. "You wanted anywhere?"

"Only by women everywhere."

Brian smiled.

"Good deal, then," he said. "I'm going to search the truck. We'll run your name, make sure you're sober, and get you on your way. Sound good?"

"Sounds like a giant waste of time."

"I hope so," said Brian, already walking toward the truck. The driver hadn't padlocked anything, so he unlatched the door and slid it upward. The truck held pallets loaded with white bags. Brian pulled himself up.

Prilled Ammonium Nitrate. 25 Kilograms.

"It's fertilizer, Officer," said the driver. "It's for the farm's winter wheat."

Brian ignored him and started counting bags. Each pallet held forty bags, and the truck held four pallets. At twenty-five kilograms per bag, it came to something like nine-thousand pounds of fertilizer.

He furrowed his brow and looked at the driver.

"How big is your farm?"

"Pretty damn big," said the driver. "I don't know. Couple hundred acres. I'm just the pickup guy."

Nothing was illegal about transporting fertilizer, and the driver's story seemed plausible. The cab had smelled like marijuana, but Brian hadn't found any drugs. If the driver passed his field sobriety test and didn't have any outstanding warrants, they'd have to let him go. He'd have a pretty hefty speeding ticket, but they couldn't hold him on that. He had sped up a little when Brian flashed his lights, so he could argue the driver had resisted arrest, but he doubted that would hold up.

Still, this felt off. He watched as Charise led him through a field sobriety test—which he passed just fine. An hour after he pulled the truck over, Brian watched as it pulled away. Charise nodded to the truck and then to Brian.

"It sounded like a good stop," she said. "All's well that ends well, right?"

"When do you plant winter wheat?" he asked.

Charise raised her eyebrows, leaned against her cruiser's hood, and crossed her arms.

"During the winter? I don't know," she said, laughing. "I'm a city girl. Why?"

"He was carrying almost nine-thousand pounds of ammonium nitrate to fertilize his winter wheat."

Charise blinked and nodded, considering.

9

"Okay. Sure. That's what he said," she said. "Why is that a problem? I don't know that I'm following your train of thought."

"Ammonium nitrate is one of the primary components of the fuel oil bomb that blew up the federal building in Oklahoma City in 1995."

Charise blew a raspberry.

"Before my time," she said. She paused. "How old are you, anyway, Brian?"

He chuckled.

"Older every day," he said. "And more paranoid, too."

Charise went quiet.

"You think he's making a bomb?"

Brian rubbed his eyes and sighed.

"I think I need to get back to work," he said. "Speeders won't catch themselves."

Charise looked down the empty road and laughed.

"Keep up the good work, boss," she said. "I'm going back to town."

He nodded and watched her leave. Then he got in his cruiser. For a few minutes, he sat still. Then he pulled his laptop toward him and wrote a report about the traffic stop and his suspicions. If his superiors thought anything of it, they'd run it up the chain of command and visit the farm. More than likely, though, he was just paranoid.

Finally, he got back to his movie and settled into his cruiser, wondering if anybody would miss him if he just went home for the day.

CHAPTER 1

The Attorney General's Office in Jefferson City was three hours from home. Roy, my Chesapeake Bay retriever, and I left our rental house yesterday afternoon and drove straight there. In Jefferson City, we walked around, ate dinner at an outdoor café, and stayed the night at a cheap motel. Roy was a certified cadaver dog and the closest thing I had to a partner. He was also my friend.

This morning, I dressed in a suit jacket and slacks and slipped Roy's harness over his shoulders and chest. The harness had a badge identical to my own sewn onto the chest, allowing him to enter most places I could. Roy was a little too lazy to be a dedicated K9 officer, but he loved me, and I loved him. I couldn't ask for a better friend.

And I had needed one that morning.

My meeting with the Attorney General had lasted an hour and a half. I shook hands and was promised all the support I needed. Then an intern escorted Roy and me out. For half an hour after that, we had walked around, allowing the contents of the meeting to settle into my gut before we drove back to St. Augustine.

Now, as Roy and I walked into the appellate courtroom at the St. Augustine County Courthouse, I wished we had stayed away. Roy seemed content to walk beside me, but my knees felt shaky, and my chest felt tight.

This was a meeting of the St. Augustine County Charter Commission. For years, the St. Augustine County government had been spectacularly corrupt. That corruption had mostly ended with the murder of our former county executive, Darren Rogers, and the arrest of several members of the previous County Council, but there were still shady elements hovering about. Because Rogers and his cronies had illegally pushed through changes to the county charter, we threw it out. We were starting fresh, which meant a new charter and government—one elected by the citizens of the county.

The Charter Commission had been tasked with creating that charter. Composed of community members representing local businesses, the school system, and various other constituencies around town, the Commission had held open meetings with the public, commissioned help from good governance groups, debated, talked, and argued for months. We did everything we could so that the charter we created embodied the values of our community. It took a lot of work, but we had endured and finished the job. Now, we just needed the community to vote on it. A couple more weeks, and we'd be done.

As Roy and I entered the courtroom, the commission members looked at us. Some smiled. A few waved. Others gave me blank expressions. Brian Mayhew, the commission's head, stood and nodded.

"Okay, now that our law enforcement rep has arrived, we can start. I assume you have some news, Joe?"

I tried to say I did, but I couldn't get the words out. Instead, I just nodded and took a breath. The county courthouse had several courtrooms, but the Charter Commission held its meetings in the largest—the appellate courtroom.

Roy and I walked to the podium. The somber atmosphere seemed fitting considering the address I was about to give. I swallowed hard and felt my stomach flutter before leaning forward and adjusting the microphone.

"Are we ready to go?"

The PA system amplified my voice, including the catch in my throat as I spoke. I turned my head and coughed.

"You need some water or anything, Joe?"

The voice belonged to Jerry Baker, and he picked up a glass pitcher from the judge's dais. Jerry was probably fifty and taught at the high school. He was a good football coach and an even better math teacher. I forced myself to smile and nod, and he poured me a glass of water and even thought well enough of me to deliver it. Once he stepped closer, he lowered his voice.

"You're doing fine," he whispered. "Take deep breaths. It'll be over soon."

Then he smiled. I nodded, drank, and stepped back. Once everyone settled, I leaned forward.

"Roy and I just got back from our meeting with the attorney general," I said, my fingers trembling as I spoke. I balled them into fists at my side. "As the committee knows, I recently investigated a case that resulted in the arrest of Officer Dave Skelton and the resignations of Detective Marcus Washington and Sergeant Bob Reitz. Dave, Marcus, and Bob were three of the most senior members of our department. With their departures, our department was reduced to twenty-four full-time sworn officers.

"Very shortly after Dave's arrest, five additional officers announced their retirements. Within a week of those departures, two more officers accepted positions at departments in neighboring counties. Those departures took us down to seventeen officers. Given the size of the county, I determined we couldn't safely and effectively operate.

"With the blessing of this Commission, I contacted the attorney general's office for emergency assistance. Our neighbors have rendered aid where possible, but resources are tight everywhere."

I paused so they could process my remarks.

"This morning, I had a meeting with the attorney general in Jefferson City. At twenty after eight, the AG signed paperwork dissolving the St. Augustine County Sheriff's

Department due to our inability to maintain a minimum safe staffing level. Troopers from the Highway Patrol have already cleared out the station's armory for safekeeping, and an armored truck has come down from St. Louis to clear our evidence vault of drugs, guns, and other dangerous or valuable items. The remaining evidence has been stored pending future litigation."

I paused and coughed to clear the growing catch in my throat. That didn't quite do it, though, so I took a deep drink of the water Jerry had given me earlier.

"At that same meeting, I turned in my badge. You guys should just call me Joe now. I'm not Detective Court anymore." I focused on the lectern. "So that's that."

The room went quiet until Fred Ogletree sighed.

"Any word about the prosecutor's office?"

I shifted and looked down at my dog. He seemed to grin at me. I wanted to tell Ogletree to read my written reports, but I held back.

"Not directly, but as you know, Shaun Deveraux and his entire staff resigned a month ago. Mr. Deveraux and the other attorneys have all received offers from the prosecuting attorney's office in St. Louis County. They took their support staffs, too. Any arrests made in St. Augustine County will be prosecuted in neighboring courthouses."

I paused again.

"If anybody's curious, I've talked with most of my colleagues. Everyone who's sought another job in law enforcement has received one. They're working in Jefferson, Perry, St. Francois, and St. Louis County now. Darlene McEvoy, our lead forensic scientist, put in her papers for retirement. Kevius Reed, our junior forensic scientist, has received interview requests in St. Louis, Chicago, Kansas City, Indianapolis, and Nashville. He hasn't accepted a new job offer yet, but he'll get a job. He's good."

"What about you?" asked Jerry.

I looked down at the podium.

"The Missouri State Highway Patrol has offered me a temporary position in St. Augustine. I'm a reserve officer, but my duties will be those of a civilian. The sheriff's department headquarters building will become a Highway Patrol substation. My job is to keep the place running until we pass a charter and elect a new sheriff."

"Who's going to provide police services?"

I looked at Helen Krause, the speaker. Helen had been on the county school board since before I was born and had worked tirelessly to prevent the infiltration of pornography and other filth from entering the hallowed eyesight of our youth. Had she ever seen the average teenager's phone, I suspect she'd quit and realize her life's mission had been for naught.

"The highway patrol. If we need additional help, several neighboring departments have offered to send officers for emergency calls, but without local first responders, things are going to be tough. Six highway patrol troopers live in

St. Augustine County, so they're going to field a lot of our calls. We'll have help for emergencies, but less pressing calls for service might be low priority."

The commission considered. Then Brian Mayhew leaned toward his microphone, smiling.

"So, if we call 911 about a car accident, you'll dispatch officers, but if we call for a noise complaint, we'll have to take a number."

I considered my response before answering.

"We'll dispatch officers for emergency calls. So if you call and tell us you're being carjacked by a masked man with a gun, we'll send everybody we can. It might take them fifteen or twenty minutes to arrive, but they'll come. If you call us about a stolen car, we'll take a report over the phone and mail you a copy for your insurance. Car accidents without injury and noise complaints will be low priority. Our residents will have to take responsibility for themselves."

"Unacceptable," said Helen. "If I call 911, I expect a response."

I looked at her and nodded.

"Okay."

She narrowed her eyes.

"What does that mean?"

"It means okay. I acknowledge what you said," I responded. "Your expectations are noted but will not be accommodated."

She raised a hand and started pointing at me as she sputtered through an answer. For the first time since I left the AG's office, I felt the heat of anger flush my cheeks and enter my voice.

"Whatever you planned to say, keep it to yourself," I said. "My department did the best we could in an impossible situation. I've worked eighteen-hour days without a break for weeks. I'm exhausted, my dog is exhausted, and my former colleagues are exhausted.

"Your personal squabbles with your neighbor, Helen, don't matter. If his kids retrieve their Frisbee from your yard, I don't care. If his dog takes a dump in your yard, I don't care. If you go to the high school library and find a book you don't like, I don't care. Unless your life is in danger, solve your problems like an adult."

Roy whined and shuffled so his shoulder leaned against my leg. I reached down and stroked his neck so he would know I wasn't mad at him. The room went quiet. Helen's face went red, but Fred spoke before she could.

"You're under a lot of stress. We understand, and we're sympathetic," he said. "The situation is unfair. What can we do to help?"

Some of the heat left my face, and my chest loosened as a helpless, heavy feeling began filling me.

"Be kind to each other, I guess."

"My neighborhood had a neighborhood watch years ago," said Jerry. "We can restart. We'll watch our own neighborhoods."

It was a fine idea, so I thanked him. Gina Ellington, another commission member, suggested encouraging business owners to form their own neighborhood watches. They could watch the commercial districts. With enough eyes and cameras on the streets, the thought was criminals would stay away. The discussion went on for a few minutes, but I tuned it out. I felt sick. Then the room went quiet, and Brett Mayhew, the commission's chair, focused on me.

"The present moment is hard. Our mandate is to focus on the future. Once we pass our charter, we'll elect a new sheriff. He or she'll have a lot of resources. We've got a state-of-the-art building, we've got cruisers, a great forensics lab, and everything you could want, right? How long will it take our new sheriff to reconstitute the office? Are we talking weeks, or are we talking months?"

I looked at Brett. Then I looked down. When I spoke, my voice was soft.

"This is a backbreaker. We've got equipment and a building, and we'll hire new people, but we can't replace what we've lost. The police academy teaches cadets how and when to use a firearm, it teaches them the rules of evidence, and it teaches them how to write a report. If a cadet shows aptitude, he might even learn a little criminal investigation. The academy can't teach instincts, though. It doesn't teach anyone how to de-escalate a conflict with his fellow officer. It doesn't teach judgment. The academy teaches the hard skills, but soft skills take years to develop.

"For the first year on patrol, every officer is a liability. That's why we support them with field training officers. Unfortunately, we just lost every FTO we had on staff. Even with the budget to hire new recruits, we don't have veterans to train them, and we'll have a hard time hiring veteran officers because so few seek new jobs—especially in counties facing the problems we have."

Brett nodded.

"So what do we do? How do we get back up after this?"

I squeezed my jaw shut, feeling some of my anger rise once more as I shrugged.

"I don't know. We weren't just pushed down here. A truck hit us. Then the driver backed over us for good measure, got out of the cab, and shot us until we stopped moving. The department we had before... that's gone. It's not coming back. We need to be honest."

"So what do we do?" asked Brett.

"The best we can," I said.

Chapter 2

Hunter's anemometer indicated that the wind blew from the west at five miles an hour. The sun had begun to peek through the previously overcast sky. His rifle was a Remington 700 SPS Tactical with a twenty-inch threaded barrel and suppressor. Its butt rested against his chest. As a kid, Hunter had been taught to place the butt of his weapon in the pocket of his shoulder and to angle his body toward it. That position led to problems, though. Upon squeezing the trigger, the butt would kick to the right and the barrel would kick to the left, preventing him from seeing if he had hit his target.

Instead, Hunter now taught his students to put their rear end behind the rifle and to lean into it. The position eliminated that angle and kept the barrel straight after firing. It allowed him to see whether he had hit his target and to reorient in case he had to fire again.

He looked at his students. None could even shave yet, but each could shoot and kill a white-tailed deer at 500 yards.

Then, they could butcher it and harvest the meat for their families.

For some, hunting was a hobby. For the boys at the farm, it was a survival skill. It put food on the table. Self-sufficiency was always the goal. If you relied on others for your means of survival, they had power over you. It was as simple as that.

Hunter had no illusions about the world. The government hated him and everyone like him. One day, they'd come for him. Their storm troopers wouldn't be able to overtake the farm, so they'd surround it and cut them off from the outside world. So Hunter and his people prepared. They stored food—which they grew—they trained each other in the skills they would need, they built the structures necessary for their survival, and they watched and waited.

"You boys know what to do. Take turns shooting and spotting. Every shot counts. You might shoot deer today. Tomorrow, it could be an opponent who shoots back. You can't afford to miss. If you're not shooting or spotting, I want you to watch. If somebody's got bad form, I want you to call them on it. We are here to learn how to survive and feed our families. You make each other better. If that doesn't interest you, we'll use you in the garden. Everybody on this farm has a job, and every job is important. Are we clear?"

Though they were young, the boys understood. They got to work. Hunter left them there and stepped out of the open-air shooter's cabin. Within moments, he heard the first shots and then the telltale sound of rounds striking metal

23

targets downrange. It made him proud. The Church of the White Steeple owned or controlled almost a thousand acres of pristine property in St. Augustine County. Until recently, it had been smaller, but a trust controlled by the Church's Elders had recently made surreptitious acquisitions of land once owned by a prominent St. Augustine family. The rifle range was far from the gardens, fields, and children's play areas. Most of the farm's residents had never even seen it. Hunter preferred it that way. This was his domain, and he didn't need civilians getting in the way.

It struck him oddly, then, when he saw a middle-aged woman hurrying down a trail toward the cabin. He squinted in the sunlight as she drew near.

"Donna?" he asked. The woman glared at him and closed the distance between them before speaking. Donna Wright lived with her family on a farm about ten miles away from the Church's property. She and her crew were assets to the Church's survival as much as the boys in that cabin were, but Hunter rarely saw the Wright family on the property except for Sunday services. He smiled despite her glare. "My boys are in the range right now, but if you can wait, we'll set you up to practice."

"I'm not here to shoot," she said, her voice strident and her face red. "I'm here because we've got a problem."

He stepped closer to her and lowered his voice.

"This about Jeremy? The highway patrol pulled him over, but he got away with a speeding ticket."

"Jeremy's fine," she said. "Material's in the barn, and it's high and dry. Jeremy's off doing whatever the hell he does when he's not driving. The problem is a phone call I got this morning about my family's work at Nuevo Pueblo."

Nuevo Pueblo was a small company town built by Ross Kelly Farms, a local poultry processing company. The company's workforce consisted of Latin American immigrants, both legal and illegal. They worked long hours for little pay and few benefits. Donna Wright and her family provided food, blankets, toiletries...everything the company didn't. She and her kin made those immigrants feel as if they deserved respect and dignity.

It made them easier to exploit.

"Who was the caller?"

"I don't know. They used some kind of app to disguise their voice," she said. "They demanded fifty-thousand dollars cash, or they'd expose us. I assume that meant the Church as well."

He considered before nodding.

"Did you record the call?"

"No. It came in on my burner phone. I thought it was you. Who'd you give that number to? Because I didn't give it to anybody."

He furrowed his brow.

"They called you on the phone I gave you?"

She nodded. Nobody should have had that number. He exhaled a slow breath and crossed his arms.

"What'd they say, exactly?"

"They wanted fifty-thousand cash in a duffel bag, or they'd publish an exposé on everything we were doing at Nuevo Pueblo. They mentioned the clinic."

Hunter straightened.

"How would they know about the clinic?"

"I don't know," she said.

"When do they want the money?"

"Now. They didn't give me any time."

That was another problem. It meant they knew enough about the Wright family's operation to know they'd have cash available on short notice.

"You got the cash?"

"In my truck. The handoff location is a campground. Connor, the kids, and I go there a couple of times a year because they stock their lake with bass. Connor already set up a campsite. You can hide in it."

Hunter nodded and thought.

"Go to the drop-off spot, follow their directions, and we'll take care of the rest. I'll bring some shooters. We'll find out who's messing with us and set them right."

"You're going to blow their heads off, right?"

He considered.

"I'll ask them some questions first, but that's the idea."

"Good."

Donna described the location, a public campsite. Ideally, Hunter would have scouted the location and noted potential escape routes. Today, they'd just have to wing it. He walked into the range cabin to find the boys cleaning their rifles.

"Ryan, David, you come with me and bring your weapons. You other boys, keep doing what you're doing."

They nodded and agreed. Then they followed Donna about a quarter mile through the woods. The trail ended at a recently tilled fifty-acre field that would eventually hold winter wheat. They walked on the grass that grew on the outskirts of the field until they reached the settlement proper. As the world fell apart, the Church of the White Steeple grew. Almost two hundred people lived, worshipped, and trained on those thousand acres. It was a town and community unto itself. Hunter was proud to call it home.

They walked past the newly constructed bachelor barracks and an old farmhouse that held the single women of the community before reaching a parking lot. Within moments, they were on the road and within twenty minutes, they were at the campsite. It looked like a pretty place. A gate and fence surrounded the grounds, limiting access. The property had multiple spots to camp with varying levels of amenities. Donna parked in the lot closest to the most primitive sites. Hunter parked at the other end.

The primitive campsites were spots amidst trees that had been cleared of debris and vegetation. Presumably, campers could hike to the toilets, but Hunter guessed that most just dug holes in the ground or peed on tree trunks. As Donna had said, someone had erected a tent on one campsite.

He, Ryan, and David exited their vehicle. The boys each had a rifle, while Hunter carried a .45-caliber 1911 manufactured by Sig Sauer. It was a big weapon with ample stopping power. They'd be just fine.

"Boys, we're going to get into position in the woods. This isn't a test. This is the real deal. Our job today is to protect Mrs. Wright. You all know her from Church. She's a nice lady. Somebody threatened her family, and she's out here to meet him. We're going to hide in the woods. Find a spot and hide. You guys are my backup.

"Mrs. Wright is going to meet a bad guy. They're going to talk. I'm going to assess the situation, and then I'm going to introduce myself to this bad guy and take him into custody. We'll interrogate him at the farm. If this bad guy pulls a gun on me, you boys are to drop him. Kill shots. You remember the golden triangle? Corners of the mouth to the tip of the nose. You hit that, you will sever his spine, and his body will go limp before he can fire at me. That's where you're aiming. There's no wrong in this. You boys are soldiers, and you're here to do a job."

"Yes, sir," said Ryan. David nodded along.

"No matter what happens, I'm proud of you two. Now get set up."

They nodded and disappeared into the woods. Hunter watched Donna for a moment. She sat on a navy-blue camping chair that could fold up on itself for easy transport. Outwardly, she didn't look concerned, but Hunter knew how nervous she was. Donna was a civilian, a good woman. Aside from her family's good work at Nuevo Pueblo, she had a counseling degree and helped an awful lot of people, both within the Church and without. Losing her or her family would be a problem. That wouldn't happen, though.

For fifteen minutes, Hunter waited in the woods and leaned against the trunk of a big silver maple. Then, a blue Honda pulled into the parking lot about a hundred yards from where Hunter stood. The driver was a kid in his late teens or early twenties. He had black hair and olive-colored skin and reminded Hunter of a Greek kid he had played with when he was a boy.

Hunter gripped his pistol as the Greek man looked around. After orienting himself to the area, the Greek started walking again. Hunter shadowed him in the woods but tried to keep his distance. Donna stood as the Greek approached. She crossed her arms, looking pissed. Hunter couldn't blame her. He'd be pissed, too, given her situation.

The Greek stopped and said something, but Hunter couldn't hear what. Then Donna walked right to him and grabbed his arm. The Greek ripped his arm from her grip and gave her a bewildered, angry look, like an animal caught in a snare. Donna cupped her hands around her mouth and shouted toward the woods.

"He's right here! Get him!"

Hunter squeezed his jaw. This wasn't the plan. The apprehension was his job, something he had trained for. Donna was a middle-aged therapist.

The Greek unholstered a pistol. Hunter swore to himself and started running. Donna lunged toward her quarry, probably hoping to surprise and overpower him. Hunter made it three steps before the pistol fired. Donna went down.

"No," said Hunter, sprinting now. The Greek guy must have seen Hunter coming because he raised his pistol, fired in Hunter's direction, and started running toward the parking lot. Then a shot echoed from the woods. It must have been Ryan or David. A round slammed into a tree about a foot behind the Greek. The boys didn't have as much practice shooting moving targets and hadn't given their shot enough lead. The second boy fired as well. This time, Hunter couldn't see or hear the round hit anything.

The Greek fired into the woods. Hunter ducked. With their heavy, bolt-action rifles, the boys didn't have time to return fire before the Greek crossed the remaining ten yards to his vehicle. He dove inside. Within a second, the car shot backward. Hunter memorized the front license plate and then pulled out his phone as the car's tires sprayed gravel and rocketed out of the lot.

He recited the plate number into a text message box and sent it to one of his soldiers before sprinting back toward the campsite.

"David, Ryan, emergency evac. Get in the truck."

The boys came running. The Greek had shot Donna right in the chest. Hunter didn't bother checking for a pulse. Her dead, brown eyes, and the growing puddle of blood told him everything he needed to know. At least she didn't suffer.

He pulled her into the tent and zipped it shut, kicked the dirt around to cover the drag marks, and then ran back to the truck. The boys had already stowed their gear in the bed and were waiting for him.

"Sorry," said Ryan. "I tried to get him, but he was moving."

"Me, too," said David. "I should have had him."

"Not your fault," said Hunter, putting the truck in reverse. He didn't floor the accelerator, but he hurried out of the campsite. "This went bad from the start. You'll get your shot again, but right now, we regroup and figure out what happened."

CHAPTER 3

M y report had sapped the room's energy, but the Charter Commission still had an agenda full of tasks to complete. When the county formed the Charter Commission, they had required a law enforcement representative to start and adjourn every meeting. Theoretically, any sworn officer would do, but I had had the highest profile and most public speaking experience of anyone in my department, so the responsibility had fallen to me. Now, with the sheriff's department closed, I didn't even know if I fit the statute's criteria.

An hour after I finished my report, the meeting adjourned, and Roy and I went back to my station so I could inventory the contents of the first-floor storage closet and he could take a nap. In Missouri, a popular vote elected the attorney general. I loved living in a democracy, and I loved being able to vote for those who wrote the laws I enforced and lived under. At the same time, certain fields were best left to actual professionals.

The attorney general wasn't stupid—far from it, in fact—but that didn't mean he was qualified to lead the law enforcement community in Missouri. He was a politician. He didn't understand the needs of modern law enforcement and thought the sheriff's department in St. Augustine would bounce right back upon the passage of a new county charter and the appointment of a new sheriff. We wouldn't, though. We'd feel the repercussions of that meeting for years. That was assuming we tried to reconstitute a sheriff's department at all. The more I considered it, the more it made sense to roll our operations into another department.

For two hours, until lunchtime, I worked with a bar-code printer, scanner, and laptop. The closet held forty-three reams of copy paper, seven Swingline staplers, two hundred and eight cartons of staples, an unassembled desk chair still in its packaging, four dozen boxes of pens, and eighteen pairs of scissors. It also had a lot of dust and dozens of storage boxes I had yet to open.

I took a break at 11:30. The St. Augustine County Sheriff's Department had operated for years out of an old Masonic temple. I loved the architecture of the building, and I loved the space it gave us. We had twenty thousand square feet spread over three floors and a basement. For most of my career, those twenty thousand square feet were inaccessible and disgusting. The pipes had leaked, the heating and air had rarely worked, and the structure had been held together by a prayer and duct tape.

That all changed with a huge top-to-bottom renovation paid for by a bond initiative. Now, we had a modern police station that looked historic. We had a gym in the basement, a modern crime lab, spacious locker rooms, private offices for detectives and supervisors, modern evidence storage facilities, an armory, clean holding cells, state-of-the-art surveillance systems in the interrogation rooms...everything an officer or court system could want.

And it was all wasted on a former detective and her dog.

The building had power and water, but the crime lab was locked tight; no one had touched the gym or locker rooms in weeks, and we had cleaned out the armory. My office had a desk, two chairs, and a bookcase, but I had cleaned it out otherwise and rarely entered. Other offices held furniture, but the detectives and supervisory officers who once inhabited them had departed weeks ago when it became apparent that the department could no longer function.

Roy and I stood in the entryway beside a desk once occupied by Trisha Marshall, our longtime dispatcher. The phones and computers remained, but the pictures of Trisha's family, her houseplants... even the brown, earthenware coffee mug she filled every morning were gone. It felt like a tomb.

I reached down and scratched Roy's ear. He leaned into my hand and made a throaty, contented growl.

"What are we doing here, buddy?" I asked.

Roy's tail thumped into the side of the desk. I sighed and wondered, not for the first time, if the highway patrol had stuck me here alone so I'd quit and they'd be done with me permanently. The attorney general said he had wanted me to stay so there'd be an institutional memory in St. Augustine. I'd be that link to the past when we recreated our department. Some history, though, was overvalued.

I looked down at the dog.

"Let's eat lunch and take a walk."

Roy's body went rigid, and he seemed to grin. We walked to my office, where I had left his leash, and we sauntered outside into the early fall air. In years past, there had been half a dozen cafés, restaurants, and bars open for lunch near my station. Most had gone bankrupt in the past year, leaving blank storefronts on once-thriving streets.

I could have driven to Able's Diner—they still had good food and were kept in business by drunken college students from Waterford College—but I didn't want to drive anywhere. Instead, Roy and I walked two blocks to the little bungalow I had rented two months ago. I had signed a six-month lease but hadn't intended to stay until the end. Now, I suspected I'd be here for the long haul.

The housing market in St. Augustine was a mess. The town had families from every social class, wealthy to dirt poor. Those wealthy families had once owned significant portions of St. Augustine, none more so than the family of Darren Rogers. Upon Rogers's death, his real estate assets had passed to his children who had auctioned them off to the highest bidder—almost none of whom lived anywhere near St. Augustine. Those absentee landlords let their properties go to pot, or they jacked up the rent to maximize their return on their investments, or—as was common—they turned them into short-term vacation rentals. It was hard to find a decent rental property, and for the first time in its history, St. Augustine now had a homeless problem. The landlords from California or New York didn't care, but it made things difficult in town.

I was lucky enough to have money, but the place I had rented stank. Literally. It was a three-bedroom, single-story house with a fenced backyard. The previous renter smoked inside, and nicotine had stained the walls a dull yellow. The carpets stunk, too. Before I signed the lease, the landlord had assured me—in writing—that he had shampooed the carpets and covered the walls with a primer and paint that would eliminate the smell and nicotine color.

He lied.

If I had spare time, I would have taken him to court. Instead, I hired a handyman to paint the place while his adult son-in-law and daughter-in-law used a rented carpet steamer to clean the carpets. They did a good job, and I paid them well for their services. I was glad to give them the work. They had needed it.

I got lunch and ate in the kitchen while Roy sunned himself in the backyard. He was a good dog. I had considered dozens of rental places, and many were open to small dogs and cats, but only one had a yard big enough to accommodate Roy and a landlord amenable to housing an oversized Chesapeake Bay retriever. I just wished it had smelled a little better.

Twenty minutes after I arrived, my cell phone rang. The number belonged to the public safety office at Waterford College. Waterford was a private college that owned thousands of acres of rolling central Missouri property. It was a beautiful place that charged a premium to educate the sons and daughters of wealthy doctors, lawyers, and accountants. I had briefly looked at it years ago when I was researching colleges but had ended up at a public school in St. Louis. I graduated without debt. Had I gone to Waterford, I suspected I'd still owe hundreds of thousands.

I answered before the phone rang a second time.

"Joe Court," I said. "What can I do for you?"

"Hey, Detective," said a familiar man's voice. "This is Austin Reich at Waterford College. I need some law enforcement help."

The public safety officers at Waterford were licensed sworn police officers who had attended the same police academy I had, but the college didn't have the facilities to handle serious crimes. Those, they outsourced. I slipped a stray lock of hair behind my ear and cleared my throat.

"I don't know what you've heard, but the law enforcement situation in St. Augustine is tricky right now. The sheriff's department's closed. I'm not Detective Court any-more. If you need help, you might have to call the highway patrol."

He paused.

"You still have a badge?"

I grimaced.

"Sort of," I said. "I'm a reserve highway patrol trooper, but I'm working as a civilian."

He paused again.

"That's a problem," he said. "We need somebody to eval-uate a situation on campus."

I sighed and considered.

"Let me call my new boss and see what she says. Can I call you back?"

Reich agreed, and I called the lieutenant who, theoretical-ly, supervised my work. She answered right away. The high-way patrol had a few detectives, but they were tasked with keeping the roadways safe. Lieutenant Cognata requested that I figure out what was going on at Waterford and deter-mine if we had an actual emergency. I agreed, called Reich back, and got the dog.

The drive to the college was easy. It was a beautiful place with rolling hills and big, Federalist-style brick buildings. Trees, now in brilliant fall colors, dotted the landscape. I parked in the small lot beside the building that held the public safety office and stepped inside. Two men stood in the lobby. One was Austin Reich, the Assistant Director of

Public Safety, while the other was Rusty Peterson, Austin's boss. I shook both their hands. Roy sat beside me and panted.

"Okay," I said. "What have you got?"

"A young man came in about twenty minutes ago. He had blood on his shirt," said Rusty. "He was armed, but he gave up his firearm."

I straightened and drew in a breath.

"Okay," I said, nodding. "Is he a student?"

"He is," said Austin. "Just starting his senior year. Never been in trouble here. Clean record, no outstanding warrants. Name is Wyatt Caparaso. He's twenty-two and lives off campus with a couple of other students. We've already checked them out, and they're fine. I've got Wyatt's shirt bagged in an evidence bag. It had a considerable amount of blood spatter on it. I gave him a sweatshirt to cover himself up. He walked through the door and said he needed help. I made sure he wasn't bleeding and then called you."

I swore to myself and grabbed a notepad from my purse to jot down some notes. Then I glanced up.

"You have him in custody?"

Austin looked at Peterson.

"He's in my office," said Peterson. I followed him toward a small private office behind the front desk. There, I found a young man sitting in a chair in front of Rusty's desk. He had black hair. His pale skin had an almost greenish hue. I suspected it was olive-colored most of the time. Now, he

39

looked sick. Peterson and I stayed near the doorway. The kid turned around. His eyes were glassy and streaked with red.

"You're Mr. Caparaso?" I asked. He nodded. "You doing okay? You look like you're going to vomit."

"I killed a lady. I didn't even know her."

Skin all over my body tingled, and I nodded.

"Okay," I said. "You sit tight. Mr. Peterson here is going to stay with you. Keep your hands on the arms of your chair so we know you're not trying to hurt anybody or yourself."

Caparaso didn't react, so I leaned into Peterson and lowered my voice.

"He's in shock. If he moves, cuff his arms to the chair."

Peterson nodded, and I stepped past him and into the lobby again, already taking out my cell phone. Austin perked up when he saw me. I gave him a tight smile and called Lieutenant Cognata.

"Hey," I said, "This is Joe Court in St. Augustine again. I need a detective for a homicide investigation."

CHAPTER 4

Had Hunter been in the Army or in law enforcement, he would have had hours of paperwork to complete after Donna Wright's death. Investigators would then read through his reports, interview him, and then go to the campgrounds, where they'd try to figure out whether the physical evidence fit his recollection of events. They'd look at his phone, they'd talk to Ryan and David, and they'd talk to Donna's family. The whole process would take weeks, and ultimately, they'd come to the truth—or at least an approximation of it as close as they could get. Then they'd ignore the truth entirely and concoct a story that furthered their aims.

Hunter hadn't been in the Army for a very long time. He wasn't a police officer, either. He was a man tasked with protecting those he loved, and he had done his best to protect Donna. It hurt that he had failed.

Upon arriving at the farm, Hunter had left Ryan and David with their mothers before walking to the meeting-house, where he had hoped to deliver an address to the Elders and the boys' fathers. When he got there, he had instead found Connor Wright, Donna's husband, standing outside.

"Where's my wife?"

Hunter's eyes flicked up and down Connor's torso. He was probably fifty, maybe a little younger, and he likely weighed a little over two hundred pounds. In a straight fight, Hunter could easily outmatch him, but a fistfight at the Church would create its own problems. He wore jeans and a baggy brown sweater that overlapped his belt and could have easily concealed a pistol. Hunter hesitated before speaking. Elder Damon Burke exited the meetinghouse and stood behind Connor but said nothing. Hunter pretended that he hadn't seen his mentor and friend. Instead, he focused on Connor.

"We should go inside," he said. "We can sit and talk."

"Where's my wife? She went with you to the campsite. She still there?"

Hunter swallowed and considered the best tactic to use. The Wrights were important to the Church. If Connor accused Hunter of dereliction of duty, there'd be consequences, the ramifications of which he couldn't foresee. The Church had procedures in place to resolve disagreements between members, but the Wrights had enough influence to stir up a lot of trouble. Normally, Hunter wouldn't mind a little trouble. Even healthy trees needed pruning. Disputes, properly addressed, allowed the community to vent frustration and come to understandings.

Hunter had too much work to deal with to handle Connor, though. He needed to shut this down.

"I need you to tell me what's going on, Connor," he said. "Donna came to me this morning with an emergency. She said someone was blackmailing her, and that she needed help. I took two shooters with me, but she was ambushed. You set up the campsite before we arrived to make it look as if she had been out there for a while. We were fired upon. My boys did their best, but we didn't know we'd be stepping into an ambush. You want to tell me what happened?"

"You tell me, Hunter. Where's my wife?"

Hunter stepped forward and infused his voice with menace.

"At the campsite you set up. She was shot. Didn't even have a chance. Then we were fired upon. If I had known we'd be walking into a firefight, I would have been prepared. I thought we were there to help a congregant with a personal problem. So I'm going to ask again: what happened at the campsite you set up, and who knew you were out there?"

Donna wasn't ambushed, but that didn't matter. The fight left Connor's eyes. His shoulders fell.

"You left her there?"

"She was gone. I'm sorry. My boys and I had to leave so we wouldn't be shot ourselves."

Connor blinked and looked down. Damon Burke stepped forward and put a hand on his shoulder.

"Let's go inside, son," he said, his voice soft. "Let's talk this through. You are not alone."

Connor nodded but said nothing as he turned and walked toward the meetinghouse. Hunter started to follow, but Burke shook his head.

"You have work," he said. "Secure the Wright's homestead. Bring the kids here. If there's a threat to any member of our Church, we will protect them with the full weight of our fury and righteousness."

"Of course," he said. Burke and Connor shut the meetinghouse's door. Hunter wasn't sure whether the order was genuine or whether it was for Connor's ears, but it made sense to secure the Wright's property. The family owned several hundred acres of farmland near the Mississippi River. Every few years, the Mississippi would swell under spring rains and spill over its banks to flood the Wright family's fields, leaving behind rich silt. On wet years, you couldn't plant much, but the fertile, constantly replenished soil always made up for the loss. The property was worth millions, but its true value lay elsewhere.

Hunter got in his truck and headed toward the family's compound. Where most of the property had been cleared of trees decades prior, the parcel that contained the family's homes was still heavily wooded. Hunter flicked on his turn signal before slowing his heavy truck and turning onto a meandering gravel driveway cut through the woods. After approximately two hundred yards, he arrived in a clearing, shockingly bright after the dim woods. An older man with a shotgun slung over his shoulder sauntered toward the truck.

Hunter opened his door, stepped out, and nodded to the older man.

"William."

"What are you doing here, Hunter, and where's my son?"

"Connor's meeting with the Elders," he said. "I'm here to bring your family to the farm."

William was over seventy and had buzzed white hair and a rawboned jawline. The sun had baked his skin into a golden color, while a lifetime of physical labor on the farm had left him lean and fit. Though he rarely spoke of it, William had spent much of his early life in the Army. He had fought in Vietnam and served his country with distinction. Afterward, he took over the family farm, married the love of his life, and helped found the Church of the White Steeple. He had fought the good fight his entire life. He was a good man.

"How's Donna?" he asked.

"Gone," said Hunter. "We were ambushed and came under fire."

William snorted and spat. It landed near Hunter's feet.

"You were supposed to protect her," he said. "Now my son's lost his wife, and my grandkids have lost their mom. You been shot?"

"We were shot at."

He grunted.

"If the bishop were alive, he would have strung you up and had you strapped. Donna was like a daughter to me. What makes you think you're going to walk away from this farm alive?"

"With all due respect to Bishop Clarke, he would have been wrong to string me up. I'm here to take your family to the farm where we can keep you safe until we figure out what's going on."

William snickered and glanced around him.

"You think we're defenseless here?"

"No, sir," said Hunter. "I'm sure you're well armed, but that doesn't change the facts. Protective work is tough. You've got to be on duty twenty-four hours a day, seven days a week. Your attacker only has to get lucky once to put a bullet in your back."

"There are two rifles pointed at your back right now," said William. "I give the signal, my grandsons will drop you where you stand."

Hunter nodded.

"I don't doubt that."

William raised his eyebrows.

"That's all you've got to say?"

Hunter shrugged.

"If you feel safe here, I won't drag you out," he said. "Donna contacted me with information about a threat. She was dead before I even had time to follow up. The Elders sent me out here to help, but if you want to do this on your own, do it on your own. You shoot me, there'll be repercussions. Nobody needs that. This is a time for our community to come together and deal with a threat."

William's expression remained neutral.

"I think we'll be just fine here. This is a family matter now. If my son doesn't come back within the hour, there's going to be a problem."

Hunter considered before nodding.

"If that's how you want to do this."

William said nothing. Hunter flicked his eyes left and right, memorizing the terrain in case he had to return. Then he climbed into his truck and left. By the time he reached the farm, the Elders had finished speaking to Connor Wright. He sat on a bench outside the meetinghouse, his elbows on his knees, and his head low. He looked broken.

Had Hunter seen almost any other member of the community in a similar state, he would have sat beside him. Because that's what you did when you were part of a community. Connor's family, though, had made it clear what they thought of his help. They wanted to be apart from the community, at least for the moment. Maybe their disaffection had been brewing for a while, or perhaps it was new. It didn't matter. They had their own problems. Hunter could only help if they asked.

He walked into the meetinghouse. The entryway and community rooms were empty, so Hunter followed the sound of voices to the kitchen and dining room in the back.

Most of the families who lived on the farm cooked and ate in their own homes, but those who couldn't cook their own meals ate in the dining room together. The meals cost money, but no one with an empty belly would ever be turned away. The Church provided dignity and security to those who couldn't afford it on their own. Hunter was proud to be a part of that.

Elder Burke sat alone at a table, eating a bowl of Cheerios, but he motioned Hunter over when he saw him.

"You hungry?"

Hunter shook his head.

"I'm fine."

Burke ate for another moment before pushing his bowl away.

"You go to the Wright's farm?"

"Yep," said Hunter. "Talked to William. He wasn't pleased about his daughter-in-law and told me to leave. Didn't order his grandsons to shoot me, though, so that was something."

Burke snickered and shook his head.

"William's always been a curmudgeon, but he's had a real bug up his ass since Richard died."

Though many people had contributed to the Church's founding, Richard Clarke had provided its spiritual core. He had been a good man and was taken too early. Michael Clarke, Richard's son, had tried to step into his father's shoes and play the same role in the community his father had, but he didn't have his daddy's backbone.

"Curmudgeon or not, the Wright's farm is important," said Hunter. "I don't know if we can lose the family."

"We lost them the day Richard died and his son took over," said Burke. "This Church needs a leader to step up to hold us together. The community's becoming fragmented."

"You're preaching to the converted, boss," said Hunter, lowering his chin. "You know where I stand."

"I do," said Burke, nodding. "That's why I want to talk to you. We're moving up our plans. We can't wait any longer. You and your boys have been training. It's time to put that training into practice. Your boys are going to be our Church's last line of defense. I just heard the state dissolved the county sheriff's department."

Hunter straightened and tilted his head to the side.

"How'd that happen?"

"Doesn't matter how. This is God's work. Where the government fails, the Church will step in. I want our CAP teams out on the streets, keeping order. Your boys will become a symbol for our community to rally behind, and you'll keep the wolves at bay."

It made sense, so Hunter nodded.

"Not a problem," he said. "How about our special project?"

"That's moving up, too."

"When?"

"Soon," said Burke. "A truckload of supplies just came in this morning, but our courier was pulled over by the highway patrol. It probably isn't anything to worry about, but I want us to move while we still can, just in case."

"I heard about Jeremy," said Hunter. "We'll move things up. My team's been drilling. We'll be ready. The world won't ignore us anymore."

CHAPTER 5

L ieutenant Cognata agreed to send an officer to the campus, but it'd take her an hour and a half to arrive. I had investigated an awful lot of homicides over the years. Twelve hours ago, this would have been my case without question. It should have been mine now.

I respected the chain of command. At its heart, it was a chain of accountability. As a detective, I had been responsible for my actions and the actions of everyone I supervised. If I had ordered a uniformed officer to collect evidence and that uniformed officer had screwed up, we both would have taken the blame—as would my boss. That incentivized us to review each other's work and hold each other accountable.

When you were uncertain about your duties and the duties of your colleagues, that chain of accountability would break down. In most circumstances, I would have walked my dog around campus, enjoyed the afternoon, and maybe even gotten a snack in the campus center. Wyatt Caparaso, though, wanted to talk to somebody. He had already admitted to killing a woman. If we waited too long, his common sense and better judgment could overcome his cooperative spirit and shut him up.

Chain of command be damned. I didn't want to lose Caparaso, so I asked Austin Reich to get me a video camera, which we set up in the public safety office's conference room. Caparaso was led to one side of an oval table. I sat on the other, facing him with a clean notepad on the table in front of me. Rusty Peterson, the Director of Public Safety, sat on the end, while Austin Reich, the Assistant Director, stood behind the camera and made sure it was working. I was a reserve officer, so I still had a badge. Both Reich and Peterson were licensed, sworn officers, too. Our findings would be admissible in court—even if I'd get my ass chewed out. The pros outweighed the cons.

Reich nodded to me to let me know he was filming. I focused on Caparaso.

"Hello, Mr. Caparaso, I'm Joe Court. Until 8:00 AM this morning, I was a detective with the St. Augustine County Sheriff's Department. Now, I work for the Missouri State Highway Patrol. With me in the room is Rusty Peterson and Austin Reich. They work for Waterford College, but they're both sworn and licensed police officers. That means they've both taken oaths to follow the constitution and protect the men and women within their jurisdiction. That also means they have the power to make arrests. I do as well. Do you understand that?"

Caparaso hesitated before nodding.

"I need you to answer aloud," I said, smiling.

"Yeah. I get it," he said, his voice. "What are we doing?"

"We're going to talk," I said. "You made a statement earlier. We'll return to that, but I need to clarify our situation first. You are under arrest, which means you can't go anywhere until we talk and I clear you to leave. I'm going to ask you some questions. You have the right to remain silent. If you choose to talk to me, I can use the things you tell me against you in court. You have the right to an attorney who can offer you advice. If you can't afford one, the court system will provide one for you for free. Do you understand that?"

He nodded, and I reminded him, again, to answer verbally. He agreed, so I slid a rights waiver form across the table for him to sign.

"Read this and sign it. It says you understand the situation you're in and still would like to talk to me."

He did as I asked without hesitating. Then I leaned back and put my forearms on the arms of my chair. My heart beat just a little faster than usual, as it always did during pivotal moments of an investigation. Roy sat beside my chair. He had exercised enough today that he'd be calm for a while. The room smelled like lemon furniture polish. The conference table had a sheen to it that reflected the overhead light. A clock ticked somewhere behind me. I said nothing. Caparaso flicked his eyes left and right nervously. Finally, I smiled at him.

"Are you feeling okay, Mr. Caparaso? I can get you a drink or something to eat if you'd like. Bathroom breaks are always fine."

He shook his head and looked at the table.

"I want to get this over with. I killed a lady."

"Okay," I said, nodding. "Tell me about that. Who was she?"

He shrugged and fidgeted.

"I don't know. She showed up and tried to kill me. I barely made it. Then there were these kids. And they were dressed like hunters, but they were aiming at me. I shot at them, too."

"I hear you," I said, my chest tightening just a little. "Kids with guns are dangerous. Did you shoot a child?"

"No," he said. "They shot at me, though. If I hadn't gotten in my car, they would have killed me."

Good. Hopefully, I wouldn't have to investigate a dead child. I jotted down notes and glanced up.

"Let's step back," I said. "You said a woman showed up and tried to kill you. You defended yourself. Is that right?"

He nodded but then stopped.

"Do I have to answer verbally still, or can I nod?"

"You can nod," I said, the corners of my lips curling upward, hoping a smile would disarm him and make him feel more at ease. "Where did this occur?"

He gave me the name of a campground popular with hikers, fishermen, and Cub Scouts.

"That campground is huge. Where were you, exactly?"

THE GIRL IN THE TENT

He shrugged.

"I don't know. There was a tent."

"Were there RVs or cabins?"

"Maybe. Yeah. I think so. There were cabins."

The campground didn't have cabins. I wondered if there were private vacation rentals in the woods nearby. I'd have to look it up later.

"You go to Waterford, right?" I asked. He said yes, so I continued. "As I understand it, you live off campus with friends. Why were you at the campground?"

He furrowed his brow as if he were confused.

"The note told me to go there."

I nodded and smiled, hoping he'd continue. Finally, I leaned forward a little.

"Tell me about this note."

He said something but then stopped himself.

"It was just a note."

I kept the smile on my mouth.

"How'd you get it? Did it come in the mail? Did someone hand it to you? Was it an email?"

"It was in my campus mailbox, but I already threw it away."

I jotted the information down. Whoever gave him this note, if he existed, understood how Waterford's internal mail system worked. That limited my suspect pool.

"The woman you shot... did you recognize her from campus?"

"No. I've never seen her before."

"Could she have been a student?"

"No. I mean, maybe, but not, like, a traditional student. She was older than you."

"That's helpful," I said, nodding and raising my eyebrows. "What'd the note say?"

"That somebody had information about Erik Hoyle, and if I wanted it, I should meet them at the campground."

I recognized the name Erik Hoyle, but I didn't know why a college student would care about a man convicted of rape and murder almost a decade ago. Still, I wrote the information down and waited for Caparaso to continue. He seemed content to be quiet.

"Putting this together, you received an anonymous note through campus mail promising you information about Erik Hoyle. You then went to this campground to meet this anonymous person. You were attacked by multiple people—including children—and defended yourself. In the process, you killed a woman. Is that right?"

He nodded.

"Did you bring the gun, or did she?"

He said nothing, so I repeated the question. Again, he said nothing.

"By your silence, can I take it you brought the weapon?"

"She attacked me," he said, leaning forward. "I didn't do anything wrong."

"I hear you," I said, nodding, "but I'm trying to get my facts straight. After shooting her, you ran. Did you call 911?"

He said nothing.

"Did you tell anybody at the campgrounds that you had shot someone? They shot at you, too. This is a stand-your-ground state. If you were defending yourself from armed gunmen, we legally can't charge you with anything."

That was stretching things a little, but I needed him to talk. Unfortunately, he stayed quiet. Then he rubbed his eyes and sighed.

"I've already told you everything you need to hear."

"You've told me a lot, and I appreciate that," I said. "It sounds like you were in a stressful situation and that you did the best you could given the circumstances. My job as a police officer is to contextualize the facts. I need to understand your thinking and feelings. I'll also try to figure out how the woman you met felt and what she was thinking. If she ambushed you, she did it for a reason. Why would she do that?"

He straightened. "I'm asserting my Fifth Amendment right to remain silent."

I sighed internally.

"That is your right," I said. "You're going to stay here. I'm going to do some work."

He didn't acknowledge me, so I stood and looked toward Reich.

"You can stop recording," I said. He nodded and touched a button on the video camera. Then I looked at Rusty Peterson and motioned with my head toward the door. He and Reich both followed me outside. "You guys mind hosting Mr. Caparaso for a little while?"

"Not a problem," said Rusty. "I've got his pistol in a safe in my office."

"How about his shirt?" I asked. Rusty looked at Reich.

"I bagged it. It's in the safe, too."

"What kind of bag did you use?" I asked.

Reich looked perplexed at first. Then he blinked and looked thoughtful.

"Just a plastic bag," he said. "A Ziplock, I guess."

"I appreciate your work," I said. "Can I see it?"

"Sure," he said. I thanked him, and we walked to Peterson's office, where the older officer opened a safe behind his desk. He offered me the pistol, but I didn't need to see that. The shirt, though, needed some help. I pulled a pair of blue polypropylene gloves from my purse and snapped them on my hands. Roy's tail thumped on the ground as Reich patted his head.

"I think you've got a new friend, Austin," I said, smiling.

"He's a good dog."

"He is," I said, nodding. "He's also a certified and licensed cadaver dog, so the smell of human blood makes him excited. He probably thinks we're going to run and play in the woods. If there's a field nearby, you can take him out and throw him a ball."

Peterson cleared his throat.

"You can play with your new friend later, Austin," he said. "We're going to work for now."

I opened the bag and looked up.

"Can you guys get me some sheets of paper? The bigger the better."

Austin said he'd see what he could find. I examined the shirt. It was a gray T-shirt with a few dark spots. If Caparaso had stabbed his victim, I'd likely find blood everywhere. Having shot her, though, we had minimal spatter. It was enough to preserve, though. Reich returned about fifteen minutes later with big sheets of thick paper he said he had procured from the art department.

I put one sheet flat down on the desk, and then I put the shirt flat on top. I then put a second sheet of paper inside the shirt to prevent the stains from transferring across the folds. Then I folded the shirt with paper between each fold. Finally, I put the folded shirt in a paper bag so the blood could dry.

"You look like you've done this a few times," said Peterson. "We don't have the opportunity to collect blood evidence often."

"Mostly, we collect vomit in the back seats of our cars," said Austin. "Drunk college kids can be gross."

I snickered and felt my lips curl upward.

"Yeah, we collect a lot of vomit, too," I said. "At least we used to when we had an actual department. Thanks, guys. I'm going to head out. I've got a body to find."

CHAPTER 6

Roy and I headed toward the campgrounds. The area was wooded and pretty. A creek had cut through the property eons ago and slowly eaten away at the limestone to create a valley with jagged peaks and trails that ran alongside the cliff. Missouri was lucky enough to have beautiful state parks. If the state had owned and used this property as a park, it would have been among the prettiest in the system. I appreciated that its present owner had turned it into a campground instead of a private retreat for the rich.

The gatehouse was closed, but a sign on the window gave me a phone number to call for service. I waited through three rings before someone answered.

"Hey, my name is..."

I stopped before introducing myself as Detective Joe Court. That was no longer my title. Now I was Ms. Court or Joe. My body suddenly felt heavy, and my throat felt dry.

"Are you there?"

I cleared my throat.

"Yeah, sorry," I said. "Frog in my throat, I guess. I'm... Joe Court. I work for the state highway patrol." I gathered my thoughts and tried to clear away that fog that had just taken up residence in my mind. "I interviewed a man this morning who reported a shooting at your campground."

The campground employee didn't respond. I repeated myself. Finally, a hesitant voice spoke.

"Are you sure?" she asked.

"I'm sure he reported it," I said, my voice growing stronger and more certain the longer I spoke. "I'm a police officer. Whether a shooting actually occurred, I can't say. People lie to me every day. It's the only certainty in my life."

The campground worker paused again.

"That's the most cynical worldview I've ever heard."

"Life is what it is," I said. "I'm at the campground now, and I have a cadaver dog. Do you mind if we look around?"

"You go right ahead," she said. "Keep us in the loop. Do you need me out there? I'm not far away."

"No, I should be okay unless I find signs of a shooting," I said, before pausing and thinking. "Do you have cabins on the property?"

"No, but the neighbors do."

"Then I guess the dog and I will be taking a hike."

She wished us luck and hung up. I wrapped Roy's leash around my hand and petted his cheek before bending down.

"Find the blood, buddy," I said. "Find it."

He stuck his nose in the air. When Roy smelled a body, his entire torso would go rigid, his tail would rise, and he'd lower his head. Instead, he sniffed, turned around, and then looked at me, panting.

I petted his side.

"Good boy," I said. "You smell something, you let me know."

He didn't understand what I said, but he'd react if he smelled a corpse all the same. We walked for about half an hour before my phone rang. The number was blocked. It could have been spam, but I doubted it. I answered before it finished ringing once.

"Hey, this is...Joe Court."

Again, I almost introduced myself as Detective Court. By this point, it was reflex. It was almost funny how much my job had defined me.

"Thanks for taking my call," said a terse, female voice. "I'm Detective Heather Atherton, and you seem to be working on my murder investigation."

"Yeah. Sorry about that. You were a hundred miles away. The investigation needed to get moving. So far, I've spoken with Wyatt Caparaso, and..."

"I'm going to interrupt you right there, Ms. Court," said Atherton. "I don't care what you have to tell me. Everything you've done, I have to redo. The problem is Wyatt Caparaso isn't talking."

"You don't have to redo anything, ma'am. I'm a licensed, sworn officer, the same as you, and I've worked the case in a methodical, professional manner."

"Gonna stop you right there again. I have a detective's badge. You have...whatever badge you have. You knowingly interfered with my case, and now it's irrevocably damaged. Wyatt Caparaso refuses to talk to me. So thanks."

I looked down at the grass. Roy and I stood on the outskirts of a field. There were cabins in the distance—on the neighbor's property—and numbered campsites ahead of me. No tents were pitched, no fires burned, no campers greeted us.

"Detective," I said. I paused and counted to five so I wouldn't snap at her. "I get that you're angry and upset. In your position, I'd be snippy too. I'd also recognize that there might be extenuating circumstances. Do you want to ask about those extenuating circumstances or continue with your assumptions?"

I could almost hear her teeth gnash.

"I'm not interested in this conversation or your investigation," said Atherton. "Did you bother looking Caparaso up before calling me?"

My back was straight.

"We had him in custody, and he confessed to shooting someone. We needed to find his victim. If she's alive, and there's a chance we can get her to a hospital and save her life, that's worth doing."

"Have you found her?"

"Not yet. My dog and I are still looking."

"Does your dog help you find a lot of bodies?"

I forced myself to smile.

"He's a cadaver dog. That's his job."

She paused and sighed.

"The kid's a YouTuber, honey," said Atherton. "He does pranks for publicity, and now he's convinced a gullible former detective that he killed a woman."

I shook my head and closed my eyes, ignoring her condescension.

"Even if he has a YouTube channel, he had blood on his shirt. I didn't test his hands, but I suspect they're covered in GSR."

"He was arrested two years ago for throwing money from a pickup at the Brentwood Promenade in Brentwood, Missouri. Have you ever been there?"

The shopping center sounded familiar. I narrowed my eyes, thinking.

"Isn't there a Target and Trader Joe's there? My parents lived nearby."

"Yes. It's the worst shopping center on the planet. He knew that too. He advertised on his channel that he planned to share a hundred thousand dollars cash in the parking lot. Thousands of people came. He almost started a riot."

I nodded and closed my eyes.

"That was reckless, sure, but that doesn't mean he lied to me today."

"It adds to the probability that he's lying. Have you found the victim?"

I looked at the empty field around me and shook my head. "No."

"Did anybody else see or hear about this supposed shooting?"

"No, but it's deer season. There are lots of gunshots in the area."

She sighed.

"Is your dog a real cadaver dog? The trained kind?"

I squeezed my jaw tight before forcing the biggest smile I could muster to my lips.

"Yes, ma'am. I'm a real police officer, too. The trained and experienced kind."

"If he's a cadaver dog, he should have found her. It doesn't take a body long to decompose."

I closed my eyes.

"Detective Atherton, I did my job professionally. I apologize if I stepped on your toes, but I was doing my job."

I counted to five, and then ten, waiting for her to respond. At the thirty-second mark, she cleared her throat.

"I swabbed his hands, and they were positive for GSR. I don't have a particulate count, though. Gunshot residue transfers easily. He could have gotten GSR on his hands after touching a doorknob in that little station."

"That's possible," I said. "He brought a firearm to the station. Even if he didn't shoot it today, he could have shot it in the recent past and transferred material to his skin."

"The college rent-a-cops have the gun still. I haven't seen it."

"They're sworn officers, and they know what they're doing. They're not rent-a-cops."

"I'll take your word for that," said Atherton. "Caparaso has worked hard if this is a prank."

She was inviting me to second-guess her opinion. At the very least, she wanted me to offer an opinion. I could do that.

"I find Caparaso credible, but he held back on me, and I haven't found his victim. If this is a prank, it's elaborate. That's well within his wheelhouse, though, if he spent a hundred grand to start a riot in Brentwood."

She snickered.

"The little shit didn't even use real money. It was all fake. It had his picture on it as well as a QR code that linked to his YouTube channel. He and a bunch of his followers were arrested and pled guilty to unlawful assembly. The video got eight million views and probably made him twenty thousand bucks. The local PD spent more than that cleaning up the mess."

I paused.

"What do you want to do?"

"I'm an hour and a half from home, and it's almost five. I want to go home, have dinner, and put my kids to bed."

I smiled to myself.

"What do you want to do about Caparaso?"

"Without a body, we don't have enough to arrest him for murder, and we can't arrest him for filing a false police report because we can't prove his story is false. We can hold him for twenty-four hours and keep working, but he's probably got a camera shoved up his ass that he plans to take out in jail. We know where he lives. He's a college student, so he's got ties to the community. Let him go for the night. You, meanwhile, are going to investigate this woman he supposedly shot. Find out if anybody with a matching description has been reported missing. Consider it a late-night penance for working the case without consulting me first."

I nodded and sighed.

"That sounds like a plan," I said.

"You got a better one?"

I looked around the empty field again and shook my head.

"No."

She wished me luck and hung up. I looked down at Roy.

"I think our adventure's over for the night."

He licked his nose, and I petted his cheek. His tail thumped on the ground as he panted and looked into my eyes. A good scratch on the cheek, and Roy's world was fine. I wished mine were so easy. I drove back to my station and spent the next hour combing through missing persons' reports. I found lots of missing people that matched my supposed victim, but none had gone missing in the past few days anywhere in St. Augustine.

Then, I looked up Wyatt Caparaso on YouTube. His channel had a hundred thousand subscribers, making it medium-sized. I browsed his uploads until I found the video from Brentwood. People thanked him profusely on camera, as if he were some kind of folk hero. One guy said he had just lost his job and needed help paying the rent. A young woman said any money she found would go to buy her kids' school clothes.

It was all fake, though. Wyatt didn't give those people anything but grief.

What an asshole.

Before this was through, I hoped I'd get to send him to prison. Maybe I could even film him walking in. I wondered how many views that would receive.

CHAPTER 7

Roy and I stayed in our station until almost eight. Then we walked home. My rental in town was convenient, but I missed my old house in the woods. It hadn't been beautiful, but it would have been one day. The county took it from me in an eminent domain proceeding and paid me a pittance. Darren Rogers planned to turn the property over to the Parks Department and allow people to pitch tents on the front lawn. The house, he had promised, would be converted into toilets.

Rogers could have proposed his park on property the county already owned, but he took my place because he could. He had wanted to show me he had power, and I didn't. The entire process had been dirty. To add insult to injury, a crazy person then burned the house to its foundation. Now it was an empty field. The county owned it, but they couldn't afford to develop it, and I rented a crappy house at an inflated rent. It was a waste all around.

At home, I fed the dog and boiled some pasta and defrosted some spaghetti sauce from my freezer. Dinner was simple.

Roy napped, snored, and drooled on his bed in the living room, and I browsed pictures my adoptive sister had posted on Instagram. Later, I walked Roy through the neighborhood before settling in for the night. Life wasn't perfect, but Roy and I were safe and well. I considered myself lucky.

As I closed my eyes that night, I reflected on my day. My entire life, if I had picked up the phone and called 911, a stranger would race to my house, risking their own life to make sure I was okay. It was an amazing thing. Three hundred years ago, if your house had burned down, nobody would come to help you get your kids out. Now, you placed a call, and dozens of strangers would race toward you, risking their lives to save yours.

At least they would in other cities.

If I called 911 right now, I didn't know who'd answer. It made me feel sick. If a ten-year-old called 911 to say his drunken mother just locked his screaming, drunken father in the basement, would a police officer come? Who'd respond if a woman called to say her violent husband had threatened to kill her? The highway patrol might send somebody, but they wouldn't send me. Several troopers lived in the county, but they might still be twenty or thirty minutes from the caller. A lot could happen in the time it took them to arrive. People would get hurt.

And it was my fault. I broke my department.

A few weeks ago, Sergeant Bob Reitz and Detective Marcus Washington had lied to me during a case to protect a friend, and I forced them to quit. Unknown to me—and to them—Bob and Marcus were the last support beams holding the house together. With them gone, the entire edifice fell in on itself. I had wanted to do the right thing. Bob and Marcus lied to keep a guilty man out of jail and send an innocent volunteer in his place. They had reasons—good ones. They had wanted to do the right thing, too. The guy they had been protecting had killed someone, but he, too, had thought he was doing the right thing.

So who was right? I couldn't say. I did the best I could, and I had to live with the consequences. Maybe that's all anyone could do.

I tossed and turned all night, forcing Roy to sleep on the floor. When I woke, I felt more tired than I had felt before lying down. It didn't matter, though. I had a job to do. I showered and dressed, walked Roy, and drove to work.

My supervisor with the highway patrol had given me a laundry list of tasks to accomplish in the building, but she hadn't given me a deadline or even any guidance about what she wanted done first or how I was to notify her once I finished things. Realistically, if the highway patrol needed my projects completed, they'd send a team of civilians to my station to do them. They gave me a list of tasks because they didn't know what else to do with me and because the attorney general told them to keep me on staff. This was busy work, but that didn't matter. I'd do the best I could—even if it meant weeks of mind-numbing boredom.

Once I reached my building, I cleaned the break room, made a pot of coffee, and dragged Roy's bed to the lobby so he could see me while I continued inventorying the first-floor supply closet. For about an hour, I worked and drank coffee and listened to music broadcast over the building's intercom system. Then I heard a woman's voice call my name. Roy barked, but it wasn't an unhappy, protective bark. He sounded excited.

I hurried out to find a middle-aged woman in a cream-colored sweater and blue jeans, holding up her hands as if to ward off my dog. By the way his tail wagged and his mouth hung open, Roy thought she was playing a game. I called him to me, and he disengaged from her and padded toward me. I petted his cheek.

"I know you," I said, nodding. "You're from the casino company trying to build a convention center downtown."

She nodded and stepped toward me. Roy hopped a little. I patted his backside to get his attention. Then I told him to sit. My guest drew in a breath.

"Thank you. I'm Loraine Fisk, and I work for Columbia Holdings. Sorry to arrive unannounced, but I didn't have your phone number."

"That's okay," I said. "What can I do for you, Ms. Fisk?"

She looked down.

"Two things, I guess," she said. "I heard about your department, and I wanted to express my condolences for you.

I've never been in your exact situation, but I once worked for a tight-knit company that had to close. It was hard."

I forced myself to smile.

"Thank you," I said. "I'll miss my colleagues, but everyone who wanted a job got a new one elsewhere in the state. A lot of people retired as well."

"That is good," she said. We lapsed into an awkward silence before she cleared her throat. "That was my personal bit. As you know, the company for which I work is interested in developing St. Augustine's riverfront. We are believers in community development, and we can see that St. Augustine County is a community struggling. We want to help get your department back on its feet. What can we do? Our pockets aren't limitless, but we can help with bridge funding if necessary. We'd be happy to donate equipment, too."

I held my eyes on her for a moment, trying to get a read. She looked sincere. I wondered if she had taken acting classes.

"The last time I saw you, you and your partner had conspired with Brian Mayhew to force a measure through the Charter Commission that would make it easier to take property at bargain prices from the community you claim to be interested in helping."

She cleared her throat. Her concerned gaze slipped.

"We regret any appearance of impropriety..."

"You wanted to rip people off but couldn't get the entire Charter Commission to pass your bill. Instead, you worked with Mayhew to call a sham meeting with only those members you could buy off," I said. "This isn't a wealthy community. People here don't have much. Still, you tried to take their homes so you could build a casino with a riverfront view."

She smiled, but the look was cold.

"We're here to create a business that will provide jobs and revenue to a county that needs it. We'll also turn a profit. If you have a problem with that, you've got a problem with capitalism."

My eyes flicked up and to the right as I considered my response.

"My objection has nothing to do with ideology or capitalism," I said. "I don't trust you, and I don't trust that you have my county's best interests in mind at all. You haven't earned my trust. This place has been cheated enough."

"I see," she said. "If that's how you see us, then I guess I'll be leaving."

I smiled.

"Have a nice day, ma'am," I said. "If you need police help in the future, be sure to call 911. No need to come back."

She nodded and left. Roy's tail thumped the ground. I looked at him.

"I think it's time for a break," I said. "You want to go out?"

He shot to his feet and seemed to hold his breath. I smiled and walked to my office for his leash. We had a nice time and even walked to a park nearby. After school, kids would flock to the playground, but it was empty now. I took advantage of it by unhooking Roy's leash and throwing him a stick, which he retrieved. We hadn't played fetch for a while, so I think he liked it.

After about ten minutes, my arm grew tired, and Roy started slowing down. I put his leash back on, and we started walking back to work. Along the way, my phone rang, but I didn't recognize the number. Hopefully, it wasn't a civilian in need of service. I answered and the caller identified himself as Cecil Bache and claimed to be Wyatt Caparaso's attorney. He informed me that Wyatt had no interest in speaking with me and advised that if I needed to communicate with Wyatt in the future, I should contact his office. I thanked him and texted Heather Atherton to inform her that Caparaso had legal representation.

Just as Roy and I returned to my station, Atherton called. I answered the phone with a sigh.

"Good morning, Detective Atherton," I said. "Did you get my text?"

"I did, but that's not why I'm calling. You at your station?"

"Yep," I said.

"I'm in St. Augustine right now. We got a call from a resident named Connor Wright this morning. I'm at his family farm. His wife, Donna, is missing. She is a 34-year-old Caucasian woman who went camping yesterday. She was supposed to return this morning, but she hasn't. Her husband has been trying to reach her, but she's not answering her phone."

I felt a knot tighten in my stomach as I straightened.

"Oh."

"Yeah," responded Atherton. "I may have acted too quickly in calling you off from the campground yesterday. Mr. Wright mentioned that his wife has an orange half-dome tent."

I tried to recall if I had seen an orange tent during my time at the campground, but I couldn't remember. Still, I nodded and wrapped Roy's leash around my hand.

"Roy and I will head to the campsite now," I said. "Do you want to meet us there or stay with the Wrights?"

"I'll stay here," she said. "We'll have to find Wyatt Caparaso, as well."

"Sounds good. We'll keep you updated."

Atherton thanked me and hung up. I checked to make sure the station's front door was locked before making my way toward the campsite. This time, I avoided the areas Roy and I had already covered and headed toward the more primitive campsites. I parked on a gravel lot beside a minivan.

Almost the instant Roy's feet touched the ground, his body went rigid, and he lunged forward to run. I held onto his collar and told him to sit. He whined but complied. Already, my limbs felt heavy, knowing we'd likely be finding a body any moment. The instant I had his leash secured, he stood up and started pulling.

"Alright, buddy," I said. "Find it."

He pulled hard, and we ran toward the woods. Sure enough, I found an orange tent at a numbered campsite. Roy wanted to continue his search for the body, but I wrapped his leash around my hand and made him walk beside me so that I could document the scene. The tent was zipped shut, and the firepit appeared unused. There were no footprints as best I could see, but I snapped a couple dozen pictures anyway. Then, I looked at Roy and instructed him to lie down. He whined but eventually complied. I wouldn't have trusted most dogs to stay, but I knew Roy's limits and abilities. He'd be fine.

With my hands free, I unzipped the tent but did my best to touch only the edges of the zipper's pull tab so I wouldn't smear any fingerprints. Roy stayed on his belly but barked as I revealed a woman's body. A significant quantity of blood had pooled inside the tent, soaking a sleeping bag and pillow.

I snapped pictures but then backed away. Roy followed me as I pulled out my phone and called Detective Atherton. She answered immediately.

"I found Mrs. Wright's body," I said. "Wyatt Caparaso wasn't lying to us. He shot a woman."

"Secure the scene. I'll notify the family and be out there as soon as I can."

I hung up, wishing Caparaso had pranked us after all.

Chapter 8

I sent Atherton as clean a photo of the victim's face as I could. Ideally, I'd get a picture of Wright that made it look as if she were asleep so we wouldn't traumatize her family, but in this case, she had died with her eyes open, and she had lain in the tent overnight, causing her blood to settle closer to the ground, leaving her skin pale and sick-looking. She was clearly dead, but we still needed a relative to identify her.

Once I had the photograph, I backed off. Trained forensic technicians would search the tent and surrounding grounds for evidence, which we'd use to bolster our case against Wyatt Caparaso. Once we had him in custody, we'd question him, compare his story to the physical evidence we had found, and figure out what the hell had made him shoot a middle-aged mom.

I took Roy's leash and walked back to my Volvo, where I searched the back for my evidence kit. Though I could collect evidence, my training was minimal compared to the highway patrol's dedicated technicians. Instead, I grabbed a spool of crime scene tape and wound it around trees near the tents to keep hikers and other civilians away from the scene.

As I worked, a highway patrol SUV arrived, and a trooper stepped out. She was forty or forty-five and had brown hair pulled back from her face. I nodded to her and showed her my badge. She squinted at it.

"You're a reserve," she said.

"It's a long story," I said. "Detective Heather Atherton is the lead detective on the case, but she's with the victim's family right now. I need you to work crowd control. Nobody's here yet, but we'll have a coroner and evidence technicians soon enough. You'll need to tell them where to park. I've cordoned the crime scene with tape, so let's keep everybody out of that. I'll need you to start a logbook, too. I'll be your first entry. You'll be the second. Have you ever worked a homicide?"

She narrowed her eyes and drew in a breath.

"You're a reserve," she repeated. "Where's the body? I'll take over. You and your dog can get back to whatever you're supposed to be doing."

I closed my eyes and sighed.

"I'm a reserve officer with the highway patrol. Until yesterday morning, I was a detective with the St. Augustine County Sheriff's Department. This is my county, and I'm securing the crime scene. I've worked dozens of murders. If you have a problem with that, you can talk to Detective Atherton or my supervisor."

Her eyes flicked up and down me.

"That badge you carry might impress drunks at a bar, but you're a civilian who can be called up in times of emergency. I'm done having this conversation," she said. "I'm going to walk around and check the scene. You can go home. The real cops have this."

I looked toward her vehicle, crossed my arms, and looked back at her.

"You're a commercial vehicle enforcement officer," I said. "This is a murder scene. I'm guessing you were called because you were the officer closest to the scene. Have you ever worked a homicide?"

She snorted, shook her head, and then walked to the crime scene tape I had strung up.

"Don't go under there," I said. "You could disturb footprints, smear fingerprints, or contaminate the scene."

"I'm going to make sure your victim's dead," she said. "If you interfere, I'll arrest you and put you in handcuffs. Are you armed right now?"

"Of course," I said. "Is that a problem, too, now?"

She walked toward me and pointed to the badge on her chest.

"Do you see this?"

I forced myself to smile.

"Yep."

"I'm an actual police officer," she said. "And I don't like your attitude. I don't feel safe with you here. You're going to walk toward my vehicle and place your hands on the hood. Then I'm going to pat you down and confiscate your weapon until I can get some backup. If you refuse, I will use force. That includes the use of deadly force if necessary. You told me you were armed. That puts my life in danger. Do you understand the situation, miss?"

I gritted my teeth before speaking.

"Is your body cam on?"

She reached to her shoulder and flicked something on the body camera mounted to her uniform, but I couldn't tell if she turned it on or off.

"I won't ask again," she said. "Walk toward my vehicle, place your hands on the hood, and I will pat you down. I will then place handcuffs on your wrists and take you into custody pending an investigation into your conduct."

"Fine," I said. "Everything you do here will go into my report and the formal complaint I plan to file against you."

"Sure thing, hon," she said. "Just start walking. Does your dog bite?"

"Only on command," I said, walking toward the vehicle.

"Good. I'll call Animal Control to take custody of him in a moment."

I straightened and stopped walking.

"You will not," I said. "He is a licensed cadaver dog. This is ridiculous. I'm a sworn officer doing my job. Call your commanding officer. I want her out here because you clearly need supervision."

"I will convey your request. Do you plan to continue re-sisting arrest? I can always Tase you."

As she spoke, a second highway patrol vehicle, this time a white cruiser, arrived. I ordered Roy to lie down. He did. Then I walked toward the officer's SUV and put my hands on the hood. She patted me down and removed my pistol from the holster at my waist. Then she put me in handcuffs before conferring with the newly arrived trooper. The two of them then walked toward the tent. I sat on the ground beside the officer's SUV. Roy eventually sauntered over to me while the two uniformed officers did...whatever they were doing.

About fifteen minutes later, a van from the St. Augustine County Animal Control Office arrived. Though I didn't work with him directly, I had known Gary for years. He looked at me and furrowed his brow.

"You all right, Detective?"

I looked at the two uniformed highway patrol officers.

"Ask them," I said. "They're in charge."

The woman shifted and crossed her arms.

"She's not a detective," she said. "Don't call her that."

Gary, the Animal Control officer, held up his hands.

"I'm just here to do a job, ma'am," he said. "What do you want me to do?"

"Impound her dog."

"Impound Roy?" asked Gary. "He's a K9 officer. Are you sure you want me to impound him?"

"Ms. Court is under arrest. I can't care for her dog and the crime scene."

Gary looked at me.

"You want me to call somebody, Joe?"

"What is with you people?" asked the highway patrol trooper, throwing up her hands. "I told you what to do. Just do it."

I nodded to Gary, and he walked to Roy. The dog thumped his tail on the ground and licked his nose. Then he sprang to his feet as Gary hooked a leash to his collar.

"You going to be out of commission for a while, Joe?" he asked. "Either way, I'll take care of Roy. He's a good boy."

"He is, and no, this should be short," I said. "I'll be out of here as soon as a supervisory officer arrives."

Gary looked at the troopers.

"You guys got an ETA for your supervisor?"

"She's on the way."

Gary looked at me again and smiled.

"Since it won't be long, I'm going to take him for a walk. No need to fill out useless paperwork. We'll be okay."

I thanked him and told Roy to behave—not that he understood me. Gary and the dog walked away. I sat and waited. Almost an hour after the first trooper arrived, a gray Dodge Charger pulled into the lot. Detective Atherton stepped out. When she saw me, she quirked an eyebrow and walked toward me.

"Making friends, Ms. Court?"

I blinked.

"What kind of response do you expect to that question?"

Atherton rolled her eyes and walked away. A few minutes later, she and the female trooper walked toward me. The trooper told me to stand before unlocking my handcuffs and walking away. Atherton squinted in the sunlight.

"The family confirmed that our victim is Donna Wright," she said. "Our forensics van was held up at another crime scene, but they're on their way now. They should get here in fifteen or twenty minutes. We've got a coroner coming as well to take the body. The front office was locked when I drove past, but have you talked to anybody from the campgrounds yet?"

I rubbed my wrists.

"Haven't had the chance since your colleague arrested me. I'd like my pistol back as well."

"Later," she said. "Donna came here last night after a rough week. She's a licensed therapist, and she had to have one of her clients committed after he threatened to kill himself and his parents. She was pretty stressed out."

"We going to talk about my arrest?"

"You're not under arrest, and there's no paperwork saying you ever were," said Atherton. "I'd like you to ask the campground's staff for a list of other registered campers. Once you talk to the staff, I want you to pick up Wyatt Caparaso. We'll be charging him with murder. We'll close this case by five tonight."

I considered Atherton before speaking.

"Sure. You're in charge."

"I am," she said. "But you wish I weren't."

"No," I said, shaking my head. "This is your case, but it's a mistake to set a deadline without knowing where the evidence will lead you."

She drew in a breath and closed her eyes before speaking.

"Wyatt Caparaso has already confessed. He came to the campsite and shot her. Donna Wright was unarmed and innocent. She's a middle-aged mom who stepped out of her house because she needed time to herself. Any way you cut it, this is murder."

"Caparaso says she attacked him," I said.

"I saw the video of your interrogation," said Atherton. "He also said he fired a weapon at children."

"He said they shot at him," I said. "If he was telling the truth, we'll find shell casings. We can get metal detectors and search the woods."

"Do you have a metal detector?"

"Somewhere in my station," I said, nodding. "I don't have the inventory memorized."

Atherton nodded.

"Come back in your free time. I don't care," she said. "I've got a dead mom and a college kid who admitted shooting her. Our victim's a civilian who's spent her entire adult life helping people. Our shooter is a dirtbag who's spent his life hurting people on camera for money. A jury will find him guilty."

"Even without knowing all the facts?" I asked. "This is a remote campground. Caparaso came here for a reason. He said he got a note that promised him information about Erik Hoyle. Hoyle's a convicted rapist and murderer. Aren't you the least bit curious about that? Why would someone send him a note?"

She shrugged.

"No one sent him anything. This kid is a professional prankster. I'd bet the house this was a prank that got out of hand. Maybe he thought his gun held blanks, or maybe he was just here to scare her. It doesn't matter. He came here and shot her. I don't need to know his life story to send him to prison. He murdered an innocent woman."

I sighed and shook my head.

"Okay."

Atherton rolled her eyes again.

"You're not going to argue with me?"

"No. I'm done. I've said my piece," I said. "I'll write a report and come back later to do the job you should be doing now."

"That's your choice. In the meantime, you've got an assignment. Get in touch with the camp's manager and send him to me. I'll question him. Then find Caparaso. Bring him in, but don't question him."

"Yes, ma'am," I said, nodding. "I'm going to find my dog first."

"You do that, Ms. Court," said Atherton. She started walking toward the tent but then stopped and cleared her throat. I looked at her expectantly. "Try to avoid getting arrested again."

I wanted to tell her that I was placed under arrest because she didn't notify the officers she called to the crime scene to expect me, and because those officers behaved in an arrogant, unprofessional manner. Instead, I forced myself to smile.

"Sure. Good luck, ma'am."

CHAPTER 9

I got my pistol from the troopers with minimal fuss and then called Gary from Animal Control. He and Roy came back to the parking lot a few minutes later. Roy was carrying a stick as thick as my thumb and as long as my arm. Gary said Roy had picked it up and refused to drop it. I respected that.

"I wish all my calls were for animals like Roy," he said. "If your life changes, and you can't care for him, call me. I'll give him a great home."

He meant it too, I thought. But Roy wasn't going anywhere. He was mine.

"If my life changes that much, Roy and I'll buy a cabin by a lake and retire," I said. "He's with me for the long haul. Thank you, though. I appreciate the thought."

"Sounds like you're both lucky," he said. "If you need me, you know where to reach me."

"I do. Thanks, Gary."

He headed back to his truck, and I called the camp staff member I had spoken to the day before. As soon as she heard about Donna Wright, she agreed to come out and talk to Detective Atherton. That left me looking for Wyatt Caparaso.

I got in my car and headed to Waterford College. As always, the grounds were beautiful. The maintenance staff had mowed the lawn, cleared the sidewalks of leaves, and pulled the weeds from the planting beds. It felt peaceful until a pair of naked male undergraduates sprinted from between a pair of trees and across the road directly in front of my car. I sighed, braked, and waved while the two ran toward a row of fraternity houses. It was cold for streaking, but if they wanted to freeze their balls off, they certainly could. I wasn't in a hurry.

Once they passed, I sped up again and drove to the public safety office. Rusty Peterson sat behind the front desk, drinking a cup of coffee and watching a video on a monitor. When he saw me, he nodded and smiled.

"That your Volvo I saw a minute ago on Campus Drive?"

"Yep," I said.

"You want to press charges against our naked idiots, or do you think I should let them go?"

I shook my head and chuckled.

"Oh, just let them go," I said. "They want to embarrass themselves by running around naked, they can embarrass themselves."

He looked back at his monitor.

"They were running from the campus center to their fraternity, but it looks like their fraternity brothers have locked the doors. Now they're hunched over, naked, and hiding in the bushes. I'm going to have to let them inside."

"Serves them right," I said. "Before you go out, I'm here on business. I need to pick up Wyatt Caparaso. We're arresting him for murder."

Peterson grimaced and leaned back.

"That's a shame," he said. "You find the woman he shot?"

I nodded.

"Yep. Detective Atherton thinks he's good for it, so we're picking him up."

Peterson paused and tilted his head to the side.

"You disagree?"

"I think he probably shot her, but there are open questions: Was he lured out there as he said? Did his victim attack him? What's his mental state? Was he sober? Is he on drugs? An arrest is justified, but I need some answers."

Peterson minimized the video and typed.

"I can't help with much, but I can pick him up with you," he said. "I'll send Austin and Lance after the streakers."

That sounded just fine with me. We left the building and got into separate cars—me in my Volvo and Rusty in a white public safety SUV. Presumably, he called his team as we drove to a two-story rental home just off campus. Dark gray siding clad the building. A big oak tree loomed over the front porch and likely provided a nice bit of shade in the spring and summer. Now that fall was upon us, its leaves had turned brown and fallen in a thick layer over the soil.

Rusty and I parked in front of the home. The leaves crunched as we walked up a brick paver walkway to the front porch. A young woman answered my knock. She had blonde hair with brunette roots. Time had yet to impart wrinkles to her skin or wisdom to her sleepy green eyes. No makeup adorned her cheeks, but she didn't need it. She was beautiful. When she saw us, she furrowed her eyebrows.

"Mr. Peterson?" she asked, looking at Rusty. He gave her a tight smile and nodded.

"Hi, Lily," he said, looking from the young woman to me. "This is Ms. Joe Court. She works for the highway patrol and was a detective with the St. Augustine County Sheriff's Department. Ms. Court, this is Lily Tidwell. We need to talk to Wyatt."

Lily swallowed and looked down.

"He's, uhm..." she paused before looking at me. "What'd Wyatt do?"

I smiled and cleared my throat before Rusty could speak.

"You look worried," I said. "Are you all right?"

"I'm fine," she said.

"Are you close to Wyatt?" I asked.

Her eyes locked on mine. Her chin quivered as she blinked.

"He's my...boyfriend," she said. "I love him. Please don't hurt him."

"I'm not going to hurt him, but I do need to see him. Is he in?"

She blinked again before shaking her head.

"No. He left."

Internally, I swore, but I tried to keep my voice even.

"When did he leave?"

"Last night," she said. "We had a fight, and then he ran out."

"What'd you fight about?" I asked.

She crossed her arms.

"Nothing important," she said, tilting her head to the side. "It was just a fight. You know?"

I nodded as if I understood.

"Do you guys fight a lot?"

She blinked and looked away.

"Everybody fights."

"Your fights ever turn violent?"

Her eyes shot back to mine, her brow furrowed.

"Of course not," she said. "Wyatt doesn't have a mean bone in his body."

I said nothing, hoping she'd continue.

"I'm glad to hear that," I said. "Do you know why I'm here?"

She licked her lips and nodded.

"He didn't hurt that woman," she said.

I raised my eyebrows.

"Did he talk to you about what he did?"

CHRIS CULVER

She shook her head.

"I'm done talking."

"I understand," I said, nodding. "And you're sure he's not inside?"

"I'd know if he were here."

I nodded and tried to look serious.

"This is your home, obviously, so you know it well. I'm a police officer, and I've got a dog. His name is Roy, and he's got a great nose. Is it possible Wyatt is hiding inside? If so, Roy can help me find him before anybody gets hurt. I want Wyatt—and you—safe."

Lily tightened her arms and narrowed her eyes.

"You think he murdered that woman, don't you?"

"Wyatt admitted shooting her, but that doesn't mean he murdered her," I said. "The victim was a mom. She was a therapist who spent her life helping people. She was unarmed when he shot her. Did you know that?"

Lily said nothing, so I continued.

"You shoot an unarmed person, nine times out of ten, that's murder. I need Wyatt to help me understand what happened. The best thing he can do is turn himself in and talk to me. If he doesn't talk to me, we'll continue investigating without his input. When we interpret evidence, we may not do it accurately. We might think the worst of him, even if he did nothing wrong. Only Wyatt can tell us what really happened. He needs to help himself and talk with me. Can you help him do that?"

She stepped back.

"I want you two to leave," she said. "This isn't campus property. You have no right to be here."

"You're not going to help your boyfriend?"

"Get out," she said, her voice sharp. "Don't come back."

She shut the door hard enough that the house shuddered. I waited a moment and listened for footsteps. When I didn't hear any, I looked at Rusty and raised my voice.

"I want your campus locked down. That means officers on every entrance and exit. Classroom doors are to be blocked, and students are directed to hide in place. I want active shooter protocols enacted. We are looking for a student accused of murder. I want every building checked. Work in pairs and arm yourselves. Wyatt shot an innocent woman. He won't hesitate to shoot a staff member or fellow student. Consider him armed and dangerous. If you see him and he makes any sudden moves...if he reaches into a bag, into his pocket, his jacket, or anything that could hide a weapon, put him down. I want center of mass shots, and I want you to keep firing until your magazine runs dry. Don't hesitate or he could kill you. Clear?"

"Yes, ma'am."

"Good. Let's go."

I left the porch and walked toward my car. Rusty followed a moment later. When we reached my car, he stepped closer to me, his voice low.

"Lily's crying inside. I could hear it through the door."

I looked toward the house and nodded.

"Good. She needed a kick in the ass. Hopefully she'll turn him in now."

"You really want me to lock the school down?"

"Oh, yeah," I said. "I wasn't kidding about that. And I want you and your team armed. I know you don't carry weapons, but this is a special circumstance. Wyatt Caparaso is wanted for murder. If he's on campus, I want him found."

"I can set that up," he said, nodding. "Let me make some calls."

"Hold on a second. You said Wyatt lived with two people. I've met Lily. Who's the third?"

"Parker Jeffries. You saw some of their fraternity brothers earlier."

I rubbed my eyes and sighed.

"Delightful. Let's hope they've put on some pants by now."

Rusty wished me luck before getting in his SUV and making the calls to lock the campus down. The students would know what to do. Everybody there had grown up in the era of mass shootings and lockdown drills at school.

I parked in front of the fraternity and walked to the front door. It was unlocked, but I knocked anyway until an elderly woman answered the door. She introduced herself as the housemother and led me into the lobby where I found two young men with towels around their waists.

"Hey," said one, looking at me and winking. "How you doing?"

"Dude," said the second, patting his buddy on the arm. "What are you doing? She's old."

I snickered, and they looked at me.

"No offense, ma'am."

I laughed again.

"None taken," I said. "We're cool. You guys live here?"

"Yeah," said the first guy. "And I like mature women. You see anything you like?"

I reached into my purse for a notepad and turned pages until I found a clean one.

"Saw you two running outside earlier. You looked cold. You sure you don't want to get dressed before talking to me?"

Before they could respond, I heard a chorus of alarms throughout the building. Probably cell phones. The housemother pulled out her phone, read the screen, and hurriedly locked the front door.

"What's going on?" asked the first guy.

"We're locked down," said the housemother. "No details except that it's not a drill."

The boys looked at me again.

"Are you supposed to be here?"

I reached into my purse for my highway patrol badge.

"Yep. You two seen Parker Jeffries lately?"

"He's gone," said the second boy. "I think he went to Disney World."

I lowered my notepad.

"The theme park in Florida?"

"I don't know, man," he said. "That's just what I heard. He's gone, though. I haven't seen him since yesterday, and he slept on my couch most nights so he didn't have to hear Lily and Wyatt bone."

"Have you seen Wyatt lately?"

The first kid walked to the back window and peered out.

"His car's gone," he said. "Maybe he went with Parker."

"Were they close?" I asked.

"Yeah," said the first kid. "You should ask Lily these questions. Wyatt doesn't do anything without telling her first."

Unfortunately, Lily didn't seem too interested in talking to me. It didn't matter. Detective Atherton had enough for an arrest warrant. Once we showed that to Wyatt's lawyer, I suspected he'd show up. I put my notepad in my purse.

"Okay, guys, thanks," I said. "Good luck with your streaking. Hope it warms up."

"With you here, it's already hot," said the first guy.

"Glad to hear it," I said. I started toward the door but stopped when the second kid called out.

"Hey," he said. "You said we looked cold earlier. How'd you know?"

I shook my head and unlocked the door but said nothing.

"You think she was making a penis joke?" asked the first kid, his voice soft. "It wasn't that cold."

"Were you making a penis joke?" called out the second kid, his voice much louder. "Because shrinkage is real. My penis is bigger than it looks."

"I'm sure it is," I said. "Lock this door behind me. And keep your clothes on if you go jogging."

I left the two streakers inside, walked Roy to my Volvo, and called Detective Atherton. The campus around our vehicle was almost eerily empty. The detective answered on the second ring.

"Hey, it's Joe Court. I'm at Waterford College. Wyatt Caparaso and his roommate have disappeared, but I've got campus security looking for them now. They've locked the university down and shut the entrances and exits. If they're on campus, we'll find them."

Atherton sighed.

"And if they're not?"

"Then we'll find them elsewhere," I said. "It's kind of what we do."

Chapter 10

Atherton and I continued speaking, but she had learned little new about her case. Donna Wright had reserved her camp spot the day she was murdered and pitched her tent without anyone noticing. There had been reports of gunfire in the area all morning, so the camp's manager had advised guests to wear orange or bright yellow gear so hunters wouldn't mistake them for game.

"Wyatt said people fired at him," I said. "You find evidence for that?"

"No," she said. "And I refuse to traipse through the woods to find shell casings. This is deer season. There are hunters everywhere. If we find shell casings, they'll complicate the case and confuse a jury. He's already confessed to shooting a woman. That's all I need to hear."

I paused for a moment.

"Did your evidence technicians examine the tent?"

"It had a lot of blood in it."

I nodded.

"It was zipped when I arrived. I took pictures. Roy indicated that there was a body inside, so I had to unzip it. When I did, I only touched the edges of the zipper pull, not the flat parts. Mrs. Wright did not zip herself inside there. You should document it."

Atherton cleared her throat.

"We considered that. My technician found smudges on the top and bottom but no clear fingerprints. Are you sure you only touched the edges?"

I clenched my teeth and nodded.

"Yep."

"The lack of clear fingerprints might indicate that Caparaso wore gloves. This could be premeditated murder."

I shook my head.

"Or it indicates a highway patrol trooper touched things she shouldn't have, despite my explicit request for her not to. You can't assume Caparaso tampered with the evidence just because there is damaged evidence. Incompetence is just as likely an explanation."

She paused.

"You really don't like us, do you?"

I tightened my jaw.

"Personally, I'm sure you're a lovely person. Professionally, I don't believe you're best suited for this assignment, and you're overlooking things that a more experienced homicide investigator would find significant. You're also making connections between pieces of evidence that other investigators would consider weak."

"An investigator like you," she said.

I clenched my jaw for a count of five.

"A more experienced homicide investigator," I said. "You asked for my opinion, and I gave it. Do what you want with it."

She sighed.

"I guess I did ask for it," she said. "Thank you for your work. I'll take over from here. We'll find Wyatt Caparaso. If I need anything else from you, I'll let you know."

"Sure, thanks," I said. She hung up, and I rubbed my eyes. They were going to railroad this kid. He killed Donna Wright. Of that, I had no doubt. His reasoning mattered, though. A mentally ill person didn't deserve to spend the rest of his life in prison.

It may have even been a weird accident. If someone had shot at him believing he was a deer, he could have freaked out and shot Donna, believing she was trying to kill him. We needed more information. It was too early to close the case, but that was Atherton's call.

Roy and I drove to our rental house, where I had leftover spaghetti and marinara sauce for lunch. Then we walked around the block. I stopped and said hello to a neighbor who was out cutting off the yellow and brown leaves of her hostas. We didn't know each other's names, but that didn't matter. We were acquaintances and content to keep it that way. After our conversation, Roy and I continued and eventually made it back to the house. That jaunt around the neighborhood had revitalized me.

My station was quiet upon my arrival—as it always was now. A week ago, I would have found Trisha Marshall behind the front desk. Likely, a couple of uniformed officers would have been in the lobby, chatting about their days. I hadn't always gotten along with my colleagues, but I missed them all the same, especially Trisha. She was a licensed, sworn officer, but she had such a soothing, calm voice that she made an excellent dispatcher and 911 operator. More than that, she was my friend.

Now, instead of working the front desk and greeting everyone who came into the building, Trisha and her husband were touring the country in an RV. Every couple of days, she'd post a picture of somewhere new on Facebook. She looked happy. She deserved her retirement.

Everything in my station gleamed. It was state-of-the-art. Safe, clean, and efficient. At times, I could even smell the adhesives the contractors had used to secure the countertops to the front desk, and I found drywall dust in the corners of underutilized rooms. Despite its newness, that station held ghosts in every corner. Everybody had a favorite spot in that building. Some people liked the commotion and camaraderie found in the busiest public spaces. Others liked things quieter and stayed at their desks or in the break room. Marcus Washington should have been in his office, sitting behind a desk laden with pictures of his wife and kids. Bob Reitz should have been leaning against the front counter, making sure the patrol officers understood their assignments and had what they needed before they began their shifts. Katie Martelle should have been in the bullpen, avoiding the cacophony of noise and conversation elsewhere.

My colleagues had all moved on with their lives. I hadn't. My dad had been a firefighter and described his workplace as a family. His colleagues supported each other—even as they bitched and complained about each other's idiosyncrasies. Mom said similar things about the police department where she had worked.

My department hadn't been a family, but we had been a community. Some days, my job had robbed me of hope, but other days, it showed me humanity at its best. I had seen families draw together after the death of a loved one. I had seen a community dig itself out after a tornado that destroyed buildings and killed several people. I had seen a colleague risk his life to save mine.

My job and my department had given me an identity when I wasn't strong enough to give one to myself. It became a retreat from the world. Some kids grew up and created lives that were identical to those of their parents. They became families of teachers, doctors, carpenters, or HVAC technicians. They were born fully formed, it seemed.

Other kids rebelled against their parents. The sons and daughters of plumbers became artists. The children of wealthy lawyers or businesspersons became international aid workers who'd never be able to afford a home of their own. They rebelled, though, because they had something to rebel from. I never did.

Families provided structure, but I never had one. My adoptive parents were wonderful, but I was a teenager when I met them. My biological mom lost me after selling herself to some asshole with more money than morals. The older I got, and the less my life made sense, I wondered if I was supposed to follow in my biological mother's footsteps and somehow, I had ruined the universe's plans by escaping.

I had tried to leave St. Augustine before. A friend had accused me of running away. I hadn't been running away, though. I had been searching for something that would help me become happy. I returned to St. Augustine because I thought it needed me. It had taken care of me for so long, I thought I needed to return the favor. As I walked through that empty station, though, and I drew from its silence, I realized that St. Augustine and I were even. I had done my part.

I didn't want to get back to the storage closets right away, so I unhooked Roy's leash and started walking. He followed along beside me, the steadiest presence in my life. For about ten minutes, we walked through the building, and I noted all the rooms, closets, and storage areas I'd have to inventory next. Then I heard a thud from downstairs. Roy stopped and cocked his head to the side. Then he barked. I patted his side.

"It's okay, dude," I said. "Somebody forgot to lock the front door, apparently."

We walked downstairs, a little quicker than we had a moment earlier. When we reached the lobby, I found a tall, fit man a little older than me standing beside the front desk. He had short brown hair parted on the right side and round, metal-rimmed glasses. People interested in movie stars and underwear models would say he was handsome. I reserved judgment.

"Can I help you?"

"Maybe," he said, flashing me a smile and revealing a mouth full of white, even teeth. "I'm looking for Joe Court."

I crossed my arms and nodded.

"What do you want with her?"

His smile slipped just a little, and he hesitated before answering.

"It's kind of personal. I'd rather not get into it."

"I see," I said, nodding. "Do you know her?"

"I know of her, but we've never met," he said. "It's a long story. If she's around, I'd like to speak to her."

I drew in a long breath and sighed before looking at Roy.

"Ms. Court isn't available," I said. "If you need the police, I'd be happy to put you in touch with the state highway patrol. I know somebody there."

He looked down and raised his eyebrows.

"I don't need the police," he said. "When will she be around?"

"She won't be," I said.

He nodded and stepped back.

"Okay. Sorry to bother you," he said. Then he paused. "This place is empty."

I nodded and raised my eyebrows.

"You're not local, are you?"

"No. I just flew in."

I lowered my chin.

"You flew in to see Joe Court?"

He paused, presumably to think.

"She's one reason."

I rubbed my eyes and then pinched the bridge of my nose.

"Are you a long-lost brother? If so, she's not interested in meeting you. No offense. She's done enough of that."

His lips curled into a curious sort of smile.

"No, I'm not a sibling," he said. "She knew my Great-Aunt Susanne."

"Susanne Pennington?"

He nodded. Before she died, Susanne Pennington had been my neighbor. She had also been a wonderful friend, probably the best human friend I've ever had. My throat felt tight.

"If you're Susanne's nephew, we can talk."

"You're Joe Court?" he asked.

I nodded. He crossed his arms and stepped forward. It was an aggressive posture. My back stiffened without my conscious thought. I lowered my hand over the pistol on my hip and dropped my right leg back, putting the bulk of my body between Pennington and my weapon. My instructors at the police academy had drilled the practice into me. That, combined with other small, seemingly inconsequential practices, had kept me alive.

"We've got a lot to talk about, Ms. Court."

The muscles in my back and shoulders relaxed, and the tight feeling left my throat. He was trying to intimidate me. If he had common sense, he would have seen my posture and left.

Even years after Susanne died, I had difficulty dealing with the loss of my friend. I didn't know what to feel. I didn't want to share that with her nephew Pennington—or anyone. He wasn't interested in sharing my grief, though. He came with an agenda. By the way he stepped toward me, he wanted me to feel insignificant, to fear him.

People had done that to me my entire life. I didn't fall for it anymore. Mr. Pennington was going to have a bad afternoon.

Chapter 11

"**S**tep back and place your hands flat on the desk where I can see them."

Pennington's mouth fell open just a little, and he stopped mid-stride. He didn't do as I asked, so I repeated the command. Then he opened his eyes wide as the situation dawned on him. He stepped back and held his hands in front of him, palms toward me in a defensive posture.

"I came here to talk to you."

"That's fine, sir. I don't know you, and when I identified myself, you crossed your arms and stepped toward me so that you could stand over me. Your face is red, your breathing is quick and shallow, and your expression is tight and angry.

"I am alone in this building. If I screamed for help, no one would hear me. Physically, you outweigh me by sixty to eighty pounds. Very likely, you could outrun me as well. My dog would protect me if you attacked, but I'd rather he not get hurt. Unfortunately for you, that leaves me with few options. Even worse for you, I am an armed, licensed police officer doing her job. Carefully consider your next move. I'd suggest you do as I ask and place your hands flat on the desk."

"I understand. No one needs to get hurt," he said, his voice conciliatory now. He lowered his hands to the desk. "I never intended to intimidate you. I'm sorry if I did."

"Terrific," I said, my voice still hard. "Are you armed, Mr. Pennington?"

He didn't respond, so I repeated the question.

"No. Of course not," he said. "Let's just take a step back and de-escalate the situation. Can we start over?"

"Nope. Some bells you can't unring," I said. "And I'm already de-escalating the situation. Once I determine the level of threat you pose to me, we'll talk. Clear?"

"I'm not a threat to anyone."

"I'm going to pat you down for weapons," I said. "Then I will take your license, confirm your ID, and check for outstanding warrants for your arrest. Will I find any?"

"Of course not."

I nodded and forced myself to smile.

"Great. That'll make this easy. Keep your hands on the desk. I'm going to start at your ankles and pat your legs down. Then I'll pat down your chest. Anything in your pockets that can hurt me? Knives, needles, anything like that?"

"I'm not a drug user or some kind of thug," he said. "I'm an engineer."

I nodded and stepped around him before patting him down. His pockets held keys and a wallet, but he had nothing else on him. I placed both on the counter near his hands, walked around the desk, and logged into the computer.

"Hand me your driver's license so I can confirm your ID," I said. "This will only take a moment."

He flicked his wallet open and glanced at me.

"Is this necessary?"

"If I had walked into your office, demanded to speak to you, and then stood over you at your desk, what would have happened?"

He looked away but said nothing, so I answered for him.

"You would have called the police or a security team to escort me from the building. You wouldn't have invited me to chat," I said. "Neither my badge nor my position here gives you the right to treat me differently."

"Sorry," he said, his voice soft as he slid his ID across the desktop.

"Me, too," I said, searching our databases for his information. Pennington lived in Montecito, California, and was thirty-three years old. His license said he was six foot one and two hundred pounds. He had no criminal record. I slid his ID back toward him.

"Okay, Mr. Pennington," I said. "You want to talk about your Aunt Susanne. That's fine. You will speak to me in a polite, measured manner. Clearly, you're angry. As long as you are in my station, you will keep yourself under control.

You will neither raise your voice nor your hands toward me. I will answer your questions for as long as necessary. If you're nice, I'll even get you a cup of coffee. It'll taste like shit, but a former colleague of mine bought a hundred and twenty pounds of it for the station, so it's what we drink.

"If you raise your voice or scare me, I will ask you to leave. If you attack me, my dog will attack you. He weighs a hundred and ten pounds, he can sprint at well over twenty-five miles per hour, and his bite force is at least as strong as a German shepherd. He will tear you apart, and then I will shoot you. You will die on this floor, writhing in pain. Do you still want to talk?"

He straightened and held my gaze before shaking his head.

"I feel like I should call my lawyer."

"That's your right."

He looked down and drummed his fingers on the desk.

"How did you know my aunt?"

"She was my neighbor. My dog used to visit her while I was at work. He kept the animals out of her garden and sat with her on the porch. A couple of times a week, we had dinner together."

He looked at me, his gaze intent and almost flinty.

"You were friends."

My throat grew tighter.

"We were."

"You were with her when she died."

I nodded but then reconsidered.

"I wasn't in the room, but I drove her to the hospital. She was in the ER. The doctors took her back. I was in the waiting room."

He balled his hands into fists and squeezed his jaw tight.

"Explain something to me, Joe," he said, his voice hard. "You're, what, twenty-five? Thirty?"

"Closer to the latter," I said.

"Why would you befriend an elderly woman who lived alone?" he asked. "You were neighbors. I get that. You can pay each other visits. That makes sense. You drink coffee together every now and then and gossip about the neighborhood. That's great, but you made yourself part of my aunt's life. You made her depend on you. You lied to her and made her think you were her friend. What did you even have in common? She retired before you were born."

"Those are fine questions," I said, nodding. "You're not done, though. Get it all out while you can."

"Fine. My aunt was a lonely, wealthy widow. Did you know that when you bought that crappy house next door? Did you know that when you let your dog run roughshod over her garden? Was that the plan? Let your dog crap all over her garden, so you could fix it and show her what a good friend you could be? I want to understand how this worked. It's too late to change things now. I talked to the lawyers. My wealthy, single aunt put you in her will. Within a year, she died. That's quite a coincidence, don't you think?"

Grief was a funny thing. At one moment, it could press down on you with a crushing weight of sadness that you could barely withstand, but then, in an instant, it could shift into a cold, furious rage. My hands trembled, and I could feel my heartbeat quicken. My muscles felt twitchy.

"Continue," I said, leaning forward. "You're really worked up now. Keep going."

He hesitated and almost looked unsure of himself. Then he cleared his throat.

"You're picking a fight," he said. "I came here to talk."

"You came here to confront me," I said. "Do it."

He stayed quiet, so I leaned forward and spoke.

"Susanne was my friend, maybe the only real friend I've ever had. She killed herself by overdosing on opioids and sleeping pills. I rushed her to the hospital hoping I could save her life. I couldn't. She never told me she put me in her will."

He nodded.

"Her lawyer told us that, too," he said. "Why'd she kill herself? Nobody could tell us that. As her friend, maybe you can."

"That's a long story, and you may not like to hear it. It may change how you view your family."

"I think I can take it," he said.

So I told him the truth: that his Great-Uncle Stanley, Susanne's husband, founded a chain of hotels, which made him wealthy and powerful. In 1971, Stanley raped and murdered a young woman named Helen Saunders at a summer camp sponsored by Pennington Hotels. Instead of arresting Stanley, the county sheriff covered things up. Stanley got away with it—at least until he told Susanne.

She drew him a bath one night. Stanley climbed in, and Susanne plugged in a hairdryer, turned it on, and dropped it in the tub. His official cause of death was heart failure, but he was electrocuted. The county covered that up too. In payment, an ambitious young County Council member named Darren Rogers extorted millions from Susanne.

That money became seed capital that turned St. Augustine from a depressed rural county to a wealthy tourist destination with expensive restaurants, hotels, and even a massive Spring Fair. Susanne later told me she had planted a poison tree the day she gave that money up. Everyone partook of that poisoned tree's fruit and spread its black curse. This entire county was built on lies and pain.

"So she killed herself because she felt guilty," said Pennington. I shook my head.

"She killed herself because I was arresting her for Stanley Pennington's murder," I said. "She didn't want the story known because she thought it would destroy St. Augustine. The story got out anyway, and we're paying the consequences."

He swallowed, his gaze distant.

"I don't know how to respond," he said.

"Then don't," I said. "Susanne was my friend. We spent Thanksgiving and Christmas together. I didn't even know she had any living family members. She never mentioned you. When she spoke of her family, she spoke of her grand-parents, parents, and deceased cousins. If I had known about you, I would have called after she died. And if she had meant anything at all to you, you wouldn't have let her die alone.

"Now please get out of my station. We're not open to the public. Whatever you're doing in town, I hope you finish and move on. St. Augustine isn't the place you think it is. Not anymore, at least."

"How do you know that?"

I looked down. My entire body felt heavy.

"Because if you understood this place, you never would have come. And your aunt and I had a lot in common. We were both hurt by people who should have protected us. That made us sisters, and I loved her like one. I would have protected her with everything I could, but I couldn't protect her from herself. You should leave while you can."

He didn't move, but he did start to say something. Then he closed his mouth. Finally, he sighed.

"I'm sorry if I bothered you, Ms. Court. Thank you for telling me about my aunt."

He turned and left. I looked at Roy.

"Let's get out of this dump. There's a tennis ball at home with your name on it."

CHAPTER 12

The dog and I walked home. Usually, my walks with Roy made me feel better. Today, though, I was tired. It wasn't the kind of exhaustion one could sleep away, either. It was a weariness that ate at me like an infection. Alcohol would help the symptoms abate for a time, but booze wouldn't touch the disease. It was a malaise driven by life itself.

I couldn't point to a particular event in my life that left me feeling tired. It was more an accumulation of ordinary losses that became acute. My friends had moved on with their lives, and I rarely saw them. My job had changed, and my employer no longer existed. My mom and dad had moved to Chicago to be closer to my pregnant sister. My idiot brother had slept his way through most of the female student population at his present college and was contemplating transferring to a school in Chicago.

Most of those ordinary, pedestrian losses stayed at the periphery of my consciousness. I recognized them, but I had other things going on that demanded my attention. I hadn't worried about those friends with whom I had lost touch because I had a house to fix, a family, a job that demanded I be available twenty-four hours a day. Now that my department had closed and I had lost my house, those distractions that prevented me from feeling everything at once also disappeared.

And so I walked aimlessly with my dog.

For about twenty minutes, Roy and I played with a tennis ball in the backyard. He was tired after that, so I put him inside in his crate so he could sleep, and I walked back to work alone. For half an hour, I dove back into my spreadsheet and took an inventory of a different supply closet that held nearly identical crap as the first one.

Then my phone rang. The number was restricted, which probably meant it was Detective Atherton or somebody else from the highway patrol. I wanted to send the call to voice mail, but I answered in case this was an emergency.

"Yeah," I said, my eyes closed and my chest tight and heavy. "This is Joe Court."

"Ms. Court, thanks for taking my call," said a now-familiar female voice. "This is Heather Atherton. Are you still at work?"

I sighed and closed my eyes.

"All day," I said. "What can I do for you?"

"I just got a call from Connor Wright. He is...or was married to Donna Wright. He said his nephew's dog found something in the woods by their house."

I straightened and felt some of the tightness leave my chest.

"Any idea what?"

"He wouldn't say," she said. "He just wants us to come."

I started toward my office so I could pick up my pistol, which I had removed from its holster while I took inventory.

"The Wrights live way out on River Road, don't they?" I asked. "I saw some of your reports earlier, but I don't have the exact address memorized." She paused and then read out an address. I didn't know the house number, but I recognized the area. It was pretty river bottoms land that flooded every couple of years. I wouldn't have wanted to live there, but they would have had a great view of the water. Of course, the mosquitoes probably flourished as well, making it a less-than-ideal homesite.

"I'm fifteen minutes out," I said. "I've not met the family yet, so if you want to call ahead and let them know I'm on the way, I'd appreciate it. How far out are you?"

"I'm not going," she said. "Officially, the Donna Wright murder is on hold until we find Wyatt Caparaso. There are open questions in the case, but I'm confident Wyatt can answer them. Wyatt's attorney, parents, and girlfriend have tried to contact him, but he's not responded so far. We've also got every highway patrol trooper in the state looking for him and his car. He's a kid. He can't hide forever. Meanwhile, I'm working a vehicular homicide in Johnson County. A semi driver seems to have fallen asleep at the wheel. His truck hit and killed a civilian."

I stared up the steps toward the second floor.

"It sounds like you've got a pretty good understanding of your case," I said.

"I guess," she said. "Trucker had a dash cam in his cab, so I've seen the accident. Now, I've got to work to assign blame. I'll go through his logs and see how much he's been working lately. We'll run drug tests on him, too. It's a tragedy, but nobody woke up this morning wanting to kill somebody else."

"Yeah, I guess so," I said. I drew in a breath. "Unless there's anything else, I'll head out to the Wright's farm. You want me to keep in touch?"

"Not really," she said. "I'll read your report. And if you find Wyatt Caparaso's body, I'll request somebody else work the case. Maybe Lieutenant Cognata will even let you play detective. I don't know or care. That won't be my call."

It sounded like I'd be ending this partnership with little love lost, but I could live with that.

"All right. Thanks for the call," I said. "If you need me, you've got my number."

I hung up before she could respond. Then I trekked the rest of the way to my office for my firearm, wondering whether I should go back to my house and get Roy. I liked having him along when I did next-of-kin notifications be-cause he tended to have a calming effect on people, particularly children. Atherton had already spoken to the family, though, so they knew Donna was dead. This call was...something else.

I slipped my pistol into a holster at my waist and a sub-compact pistol into my purse as a backup before heading to my Volvo. As much as St. Augustine's government frustrated me, its countryside thrilled me in equal measures. Maple, oak, and poplar trees, resplendent in their fall colors, stretched across an undulating landscape, looking like nothing so much as a beloved family quilt draped across the landscape. If someone could take the parts of the county I loved and isolate them from the parts that left me scratching my eyes out, I'd be thrilled. Since I couldn't do that, my feelings were always more mixed.

I put the Wright's address into my phone and drove. The sky was overcast, and the leaves blew behind me as I drove. I opened my windows to draw in the scent of decaying leaves, damp soil, and the nearby Mississippi River. For better or worse, this was home. I needed to make peace with that.

I reached the Wright's compound about twenty minutes after leaving my station. Judging by the barbed wire fence lines that stretched in either direction from the cattle guard in their driveway, the family owned a significant amount of property. Parts looked wooded, but most looked like farm fields. I didn't know if that information would help, but it couldn't hurt.

I drove over the cattle guard, down a gravel driveway, and parked beside a two-story, white clapboard farmhouse. Other houses and structures lay deeper in the woods. A canvas hammock swayed between two big oak trees in the front lawn. There were muddy shoes, including a lot of children's shoes, strewn over the front porch beside the front door. A middle-aged man wearing light brown overalls and a green hooded sweatshirt emerged from the house as I stepped out of my car.

"You the police officer Detective Atherton sent?"

I nodded.

"I'm Joe Court," I said. "Until a couple of days ago, I was a detective with the St. Augustine County Sheriff's Department. Now I work for the highway patrol."

I wondered how long I'd have to say that before it felt normal. Probably a while. He nodded.

"I'm Connor Wright. We've got it on the table."

"Okay," I said, nodding, hoping he'd continue. He didn't. Instead, he turned and walked inside. On the plus side, I doubted he would have dragged Wyatt Caparaso's body into the house and put it on the table. Of course, that still left a wide range of possibilities.

I stepped onto the porch and felt the old, wooden slats creak and move beneath me. Connor Wright hadn't taken off his shoes, so I left mine on and stepped inside the house. Gleaming oak hardwood floors drew my eye from the front door, down a hallway, and to a kitchen in the rear of the home. Stairs led to the second floor, while cased openings led left and right to various rooms. The house was clean and neat. The walls were painted a creamy yellow color, and the woodwork was crisp and white. It smelled like cinnamon.

"This way, Officer," said Wright, beckoning me deeper into the home.

We walked down the center hallway to the kitchen. While the front rooms looked original to the house, the kitchen area was clearly an addition. White shiplap covered the walls, while oak beams in the ceiling crisscrossed the room. The kitchen was big enough for three or four people to prepare meals simultaneously. A cased opening led to a living space with a couch, TV, and a dining table. Wright directed me toward the table. On it, I found a trail camera, the kind a hunter might place to spot game.

My shoulders drooped a little, and I nodded.

"The camera?" I asked. He nodded.

"Yep. The kids were walking to the bus stop, and the dog ran after them. The boys chased after it and found the camera. They brought it here."

I nodded, considering.

"How many people live on the property?" I asked.

He paused.

"Why is that relevant?"

I raised my eyebrows.

"Because the camera could belong to a family member. It's deer season, and if you've got hunters in the family, they might have put the camera there to track game without telling you."

Connor nodded.

"The camera doesn't belong to anybody here."

"Is it possible a hunter stumbled onto your property and put it up without realizing he was trespassing?"

"Why would he point it at the driveway? Wouldn't he have pointed it into the woods? And how could he have missed the fences? Somebody came onto this property and put that camera there specifically to watch us. With my wife dead, I'm just worried. That's all."

"I understand," I said. "And I'm sorry."

"Could her killer have put this up?"

I considered what to say.

"I think her killer's fled," I said. "Detective Atherton has sworn out a warrant for his arrest, and we're working with his family and his attorney to find him. Every highway patrol trooper in the state is on the lookout for him, as are police officers in neighboring states. If he pulls money from an ATM, we'll track him. If he uses a credit card, we'll have officers arrest him immediately. Thousands of police officers across the region know his name and what he looks like."

Connor drew in a breath.

"What if somebody's helping him?"

"Then they'll be arrested for harboring a fugitive," I said. "We've spoken to his friends and girlfriend. They understand that if they help him, we will send them to prison.

124

There aren't many scenarios that would worry me about his capture. He's a college student who's never wanted for anything in his life. Once he blows through whatever cash he's got in his wallet, he's going to use a credit card or contact a friend for money. As soon as that happens, we'll locate and arrest him."

Connor looked at me out of the corner of his eye.

"You sound confident."

"I am," I said. "We're throwing a lot of resources at his capture. It's in his best interest to come in on his own. If he doesn't, it might not end well for him. He knows that."

Connor's eyes flicked to the table. His chin trembled.

"My wife didn't deserve to die. She helped people her whole life. She was a good woman."

"None of you deserve what's happened," I said. "I can't promise much, but I will do everything in my power to bring her murderer to justice."

He nodded.

"Okay."

I hesitated, wanting to give him time to say anything he needed to say. He stayed quiet, though, so I picked up the trail camera.

"I'll examine this and see what I can discover."

He nodded but said nothing. I started to leave but then stopped myself and considered.

"Does the name Erik Hoyle mean anything to you?"

He blinked a few times. Then he furrowed his brow and shook his head.

"No, should it?"

I shook my head. Wyatt told me someone had lured him to the campgrounds by promising him information on Erik Hoyle. It was a long shot, but I figured someone ought to ask the Wrights about him.

"Thank you for your time. And I'm sorry again about Mrs. Wright."

He swallowed and nodded. I left him in the kitchen to grieve and walked to my car. My arms and legs felt heavy and sluggish. The Wrights seemed like a decent family. Even if we arrested Wyatt Caparaso, Donna Wright wouldn't come back. This family would feel the loss of his actions for the rest of their lives. Even if I could figure out Wyatt's motive, it wouldn't make anybody feel better.

This was a tragedy all around.

CHAPTER 13

I drove back to my station, put the camera on my desk, and snapped pictures. Then I wrote a report in my office about my trip to the Wright's home. Ideally, the Wrights would have left the camera where they found it so I could document its position, but it probably didn't matter that the kids had brought it home.

From Connor Wright's description, it did sound as if someone was monitoring traffic into and out of the farm. That didn't mean someone was spying on the family, though. If this camera didn't belong to a hunter, it probably belonged to a family member suspicious that his or her spouse was having an affair and wanted video evidence of clandestine meetings. In that case, we'd find more cameras throughout the compound.

I sighed, blew a raspberry, and examined the device. A removable plastic panel covered the back, while an antenna protruded from the top. According to my phone, it was emitting a wireless signal that I could connect to, presumably to download the video. Hopefully it recorded video as well as broadcasting it. I popped off the back with a screwdriver to reveal a battery pack and something else: A sticker with a QR code, serial number, and ownership mark.

Property of US Government.

I closed my eyes, rested both of my hands on the desk, and let my head dip low.

"Damn."

The United States government had the Wright farm under surveillance, which meant there was a federal warrant—probably sealed—granting the government the right to enter the property and film.

I swore under my breath again. The camera had a USB port that I could connect to my computer to download pictures and video. Had I not seen that sticker, I would have done just that. Instead, I plopped down on my chair and sighed. Then I called Atherton. She answered right away.

"Detective, this is Joe Court. I went by the Wright's home. They found a trail camera."

"Next time, email instead of calling."

"Fine," I said, nodding. "I called because I figured you'd want to know that the camera was placed there by the US government."

She paused.

"What agency?"

"I don't know yet," I said. "The sticker doesn't say."

"Jesus," said Atherton, sighing. "You're calling me because you found a sticker?"

THE GIRL IN THE TENT

I forced a smile to my lips so I wouldn't snap at her.

"A sticker that identifies the camera as US government property, which means the federal government is conducting surveillance at property owned by a murder victim. As the detective investigating that crime, you should be interested."

Atherton went quiet.

"Donna Wright was murdered by Wyatt Caparaso. I don't care about this camera, I don't care about any intuitions you might have, and I don't care about you. I was called to St. Augustine to do a job, and I did it. Wyatt Caparaso confessed. Case closed. We're looking for him. When I find him, we'll arrest and prosecute him. End of story. The camera was probably government surplus. They auction that kind of crap off every day. Look on eBay."

"Okay," I said. "You sent me to the farm, so I just thought I'd keep you in the loop. Have a good day, Detective."

I put the phone down and rubbed my temples. People sucked. After a moment, I searched my address book for the number of the US Attorney's Office in St. Louis. A receptionist answered and transferred me to a paralegal, who asked a bunch of questions about my investigation into Donna Wright's death and about the trail camera. She knew nothing about the Wrights, but she promised to investigate and return my call. I thanked her and hung up.

Then I leaned back in my chair. It was too early to drink, but I wanted one anyway. When I looked at Facebook or

Instagram or any other social media site, women my age frequently posted about alcohol. They joked that as soon as the kids went to school, it became wine o' clock; that there was always time for wine; or that if life gave you lemons, you should sell them and buy wine. They seemed happy in those pictures.

Alcohol didn't make me happy. It just made the world dimmer. Sometimes I needed that.

I drummed my fingers on my desk, considering my next move. If I took the rest of the afternoon off, I'd probably get drunk. I didn't want that. I had assignments, but even my supervisor didn't care if I completed them.

For a while, I sat and looked at real estate listings in St. Augustine. A few places looked interesting, but nothing compelled me to call a realtor to set up viewings. I needed a kick in the ass. I had paused my life long enough. I needed to hit the play button and start moving again, so I broadened my real estate search to include counties around St. Augustine. Then I stopped looking at rural properties and looked in St. Louis. There I found lots of properties, some gorgeous—and even in my price range.

I could get a job in St. Louis. My old colleagues had all moved on from our department. Maybe it was time I did, too. I saved a couple of links, stretched, and walked to the locker room. It was time somebody put the equipment in our gym to use. I changed into some workout clothes and spent half an hour on a treadmill. It lifted my mood a little. Afterward, I showered and went back to my office.

I could have gone back to my inventory assignment, but my mind kept going back to Wyatt Caparaso. Why would the promise of information about Erik Hoyle lure him to a campsite? We sent Hoyle to prison eight years ago. Caparaso would have been a young teenager, and he had lived in Kansas City. Hoyle's conviction made the front page of the local newspaper, but the *St. Louis Post Dispatch* didn't pick up the story, and neither did any of the TV stations in St. Louis.

So I looked Hoyle up. Within two minutes, I found my connection. Caparaso wrote for the *Waterford College Blade*, the college's newspaper. Mostly, they covered events on campus and news pertinent to the campus community, but occasionally they ran stories of wider interest. Caparaso, according to his biography on the paper's website, was a journalism major who hoped to go to graduate school.

As a seminar project his junior year, he wrote a series of articles about Erik Hoyle in the hopes that he could get enough interest to free him from prison. Caparaso believed Hoyle was innocent and that the evidence against him was circumstantial. Some of the evidence clearly was circumstantial, but we had hard facts, too. In addition, Hoyle had confessed. Somehow that fact had escaped Caparaso's notice.

I read a few articles but stopped when they started repeating themselves. Caparaso was a student journalist, relying on facts when convenient and conjecture everywhere else. I understood his interest in Erik Hoyle, but I also could see why professional journalists from major newspapers had ignored the story. There was nothing there.

Still, I couldn't help but wonder why he shot Donna Wright. She was a middle-aged mom trying to relax on a camping trip. Over and over again, I kept thinking about mental illness. That happened in men in their early twenties sometimes. They would develop depression or anxiety due to changing hormone levels. Schizophrenia was another consideration. I didn't have a ton of experience with it, but I had taken a continuing education seminar on mental health that taught schizophrenia could start manifesting in young people in their late teens to early twenties.

If Wyatt was in the midst of a mental health emergency, or if he had some kind of undiagnosed brain injury, it was all the more important that we found him quickly before he killed himself or someone else.

If he wasn't mentally ill, we had a whole other set of problems. Usually, prosecutors didn't care much about motive. They'd present one to a jury if possible, but nothing trumped hard evidence. If a ballistics lab matched the striations on the bullet retrieved from Donna Wright to rounds fired by Wyatt Caparaso's pistol, we'd have him.

Caparaso, though, claimed that someone—presumably Donna—lured him to the campsite via a note sent through the campus mail, which he then destroyed. I didn't believe it, but if he credibly claimed someone had set him up, he might be able to establish reasonable doubt in a jury's mind. All of that meant I had to show he was a liar.

I didn't know how the campus's mail system was set up, so I called Rusty Peterson in the campus's public safety office.

"Hey, this is Joe Court," I said. "I'm going over a few things related to Wyatt Caparaso. You haven't received any reports of him on campus, have you?"

"Not a one," he said. "We've been listening, too."

"Tell me about your campus mail system," I said. "If I wanted to send a letter to Lily Tidwell, could I do it?"

He paused.

"Sure. Just type it up and email it to me, and I'll make sure she gets it."

"That's not what I mean," I said. "Could someone without a connection to Waterford send something to her through the campus mail system?"

"Of course," he said. "Students get mail from home every day."

"How about if I didn't want to go through the postal service? Does your campus mail center have a drop box?"

He paused again and drew a breath.

"We have campus mail baskets all over the place," he said. "A lot of professors don't like handing exams or papers back in class because they don't like talking to angry students, so they put them in the campus mail. The papers go right to the student mailboxes, giving them some time to cool off before confronting their professors about their bad grades."

I smiled a little.

"Are bad grades a problem at Waterford?"

"We had a math professor assaulted with a desk about ten years ago," he said. "Split her skull open. It almost killed her."

I lowered my chin and opened my eyes wide.

"That's awful," I said, pausing to think. "So it's possible for someone to drop off a letter and have it delivered. She wouldn't have to show a campus ID or anything."

"No. It's not a secure mail service. We've never had a problem with people off campus abusing it."

So it was possible that someone had sent Caparaso an anonymous note that lured him to the campground. The bare possibility didn't make his story true, but it did add marginally to its credibility. Hopefully, we'd find him soon, though. It was a lot easier to question a crappy journalist than a corpse.

CHAPTER 14

I thanked Peterson, hung up, and wrote a report that indicated the time of my call, who I spoke to, and what I learned. Many civilians would have called my report a waste of time. It wasn't. Transparency mattered. Caparaso deserved to know that I had investigated his claims. Very likely, we were going to send him to prison—or possibly a mental health facility—for the rest of his life. The least we could do was contextualize Donna Wright's death. Was it murder, or was it self-defense? One would send Caparaso to prison for the rest of his life. One would allow him to walk.

It was a little after five when I finished my report. I saved the document, locked up the building, and headed out. The moment I got into my rental, Roy barked happily from his crate. I let him out, and he raced outside to the backyard, where he sprinted along the fence line for a few minutes before finding a stick to chew. It did my heart well to see his carefree exuberance.

Once he settled, I hooked a leash to his collar, and we walked for half an hour. Afterward, we went home. I checked my text messages and responded to one from my sister. She and my mom had gone out wedding dress shopping. Audrey was pregnant with her first child. They wouldn't buy a dress until Audrey had the baby, but she was enjoying trying them on. She sent me pictures of a few. I said she looked beautiful. Within a minute of my text, she texted back.

The second is my favorite because it has the lowest neckline. My boobs are gigantic.

I smiled and responded that she'd look great in anything. Then I told her I loved her and wished her a good night. Audrey replied, but I didn't look at the message. Instead, I went to the freezer and pulled out a bottle of vodka.

Nothing I did would help Donna Wright's family feel better or bring her back to life. Knowing that I'd eventually send a bad guy to prison usually made me feel better, but here, I didn't even know whether Wyatt Caparaso was evil, mentally ill, or a target of someone else. Almost before our investigation began, Detective Atherton shut it down.

As a police officer, I could ruin someone's entire life with an accusation. That power came with responsibility. We had to get things right. People got hurt when we screwed up. Atherton, though, had half-assed her entire investigation. That didn't sit right with me, but I couldn't change anything.

And so, I stared at my bottle of vodka and contemplated whether I should drink. Even before taking a drink, I knew that I wouldn't stop at one. It'd feel too good. Most people could drink without issue. Alcohol helped them relax and have fun with friends. I didn't drink to have fun, though.

When I was a teenager, my foster father, a man named Christopher Hughes, drugged and assaulted me on the sofa in the living room of our home. My biological mother had been in rehab, so I didn't have anyone to protect me. No one comforted me afterward. No one held me and made me feel safe. I'd never forget how I felt that night.

Even almost fifteen years later, I still cleared my house and checked the closets every time I came home. I told myself that it was a standard safety procedure, one every single woman should do. In my heart, though, I knew the truth: I did it because I was still scared. Christopher was dead now, but he still gave me nightmares. Objectively, I knew I was safe. My doors were locked, my house was empty, and I had a dog that would die to protect me. At the very least, Roy would slow an attacker while I got my pistol.

Despite Roy, I sat in the same seat every night, my back to a wall, my eyes facing the front door so no one could surprise me. For a brief while, I wanted to forget my day, my department, my old friends... my entire life. Five or six drinks would make that happen, guaranteed. I'd relax, maybe even put on some music. I'd feel human again.

Which was why I returned the bottle to the freezer un-opened. I didn't want to relax. I didn't want to forget the pain. Because no matter how much I drank, I'd never leave my past behind. It made me who I was. Some things, you just can't outrun.

I petted my dog. His tongue stuck out as he wagged his tail.

"Hey, dude," I said. "Let's get some dinner."

I fed Roy, ate a burrito from my freezer, and settled in for the night. I watched TV while Roy snored. Afterward, I went to bed. I knew I wouldn't sleep well with so much weighing on my mind, so I took a sleeping pill and slept the restless slumber of one whose anxieties carried on even in her dreams.

Roy woke me up the next morning at a little after six by stretching before licking my face. I pushed him away, rubbed my eyes, and swung my legs off the bed to let him outside. Then I stretched, changed into athletic clothes, and took the dog for a jog.

It was a cold, crisp fall morning, and the exertion felt good. For half an hour, I focused on the road and my dog. It was a welcome break. Unfortunately, the world came crashing back shortly after we arrived home.

I was starting to get undressed to take a shower when my phone screeched. It was an unfamiliar sound. I hurried through the house and grabbed the phone from the table beside the front door. It was the dispatcher for the state highway patrol alerting reserve officers of an emergency callout. Then the app started dinging as assignments came through.

The instant I read the first message, the muscles across my back and shoulders tightened.

We had reports of armed individuals at every public school in St. Augustine. I was ordered to drive to the elementary school and call my dispatcher upon arrival. Additional officers were on their way. I threw on some clothes, grabbed my pistol, and hooked a leash to Roy's collar before running to the car. The elementary school wasn't far. Cars lined the roads as moms and dads waited to drop off their kids at school. The sidewalks were empty.

I flashed my lights, honked my horn, and hurried, unsure what I was going to walk into. Buses should have been lined up to drop students off, but none awaited me. I parked in the fire lane and hopped out. The principal, a woman about ten or fifteen years older than me, hurried toward my car from the front door, a black walkie-talkie in hand.

"Are you a police officer?" she asked.

I nodded and opened my rear door to let Roy out.

"I am. What's going on? My dispatcher just told me to get here ASAP."

She drew in a slow breath and looked around.

"There are four men with rifles in pickup trucks half a block away. They're trying to direct traffic as if they're police officers, but they won't tell me who they are, and they're scaring our parents. People started calling 911, thinking we had a shooter. I called a colleague at the middle school, and they've got a similar situation there. The district put every school on lockdown, and we've sent messages to moms and dads to keep their kids away."

I exhaled a slow breath, nodded, and felt some of the adrenaline flooding my body wane.

"Where are these men now?"

She pointed to intersections to the northwest and northeast. I thanked her, wrapped Roy's leash around my hand, and called the highway patrol's dispatcher. We didn't have an active shooter, but we did have idiots with firearms outside a school. This was a mess.

I walked to the nearest intersection and found two middle-aged men standing beside a pickup. Both carried rifles, and both wore bright yellow T-shirts with the word CAP emblazoned on the chest. One man carried an AR-15, while the other carried a hunting rifle with a wooden stock. My footsteps slowed as I neared. The two men stopped talking. One ran a finger across his phone. I scowled at the other.

"Hey, Shane," I said. "Haven't seen you for a while. How have you been?"

"Good. How about you?"

"Just dandy," I said, forcing myself to smile in the early-morning glare. Until a couple of weeks ago, Shane Fox had been an officer in my department. He quit alongside everyone else. He wasn't old enough to retire and draw a pension, but, unlike most of my colleagues, he hadn't sought another law enforcement job.

We settled into silence. I kept my eyes on Shane. He and his companion kept their eyes on me. I waited for them to say something, but they didn't.

"I know it's deer season, but I'm not sure you guys are going to find anything in town," I said finally.

A minivan at the intersection backed up, tried to turn, hit a car parked alongside the road, and then sideswiped another car as the driver tried to pull a U-turn. Then she drove away. My heart pounded against my breastbone, but I tried to keep my growing sense of unease out of my voice.

Neither Shane nor the other dude spoke.

"What the hell are you doing, Shane?" I asked, finally. "You're a bright guy. You know what happens when people carry AR-15s outside elementary schools. Moms and dads see guns at school, and they get jumpy. Like that minivan driver there."

He looked over his shoulder.

"You really ought to do something about that, Joe," he said. "That's a hit and run."

"I'd love to, but my hands are full dealing with another matter."

Shane nodded. He was probably forty and had black hair, pale skin, and several days' worth of growth on his chin.

"And that's the problem. Without a full-time police force, this town just isn't safe. We stepped up."

I smiled and nodded.

"And who do you mean by 'we'?"

"The Church."

I nodded again. In St. Augustine, *The Church* referred to the Church of the White Steeple. It had been founded years ago by a group of St. Augustine residents intent on keeping the world segregated. Its founder, Richard Clarke, had even run for state office on a pro-segregation platform. He hadn't won, but it was close.

"I didn't know you were a racist," I said. "Learn something new every day. I'll have to write that one down."

"I don't like that word racist."

I nodded as a pickup truck approached the intersection. This one hung a yellow flag with CAP written on it in bold, black letters. More new guests. Terrific. I leaned forward.

"Just between the two of us, I don't enjoy calling you one," I said, "but if you're a Church member, the name fits."

He grunted but said nothing as the pickup pulled to the curb. Its passenger window rolled down.

"Anything to report?"

The speaker was probably in his early thirties. He had thick, sandy blond hair and blue eyes. He was thin and fit. Very likely, the truck held weapons, but I couldn't see any. I walked toward him.

"You in charge of this group?"

He narrowed his eyes.

"Yeah. Who are you?"

I reached into my purse for my badge and held it out.

"I'm Officer Joe Court. Step out of the truck and keep your hands where I can see them. If we all cooperate, nobody needs to get hurt."

CHAPTER 15

H unter had expected a response. But he hadn't expected to find a cop who was so...attractive. The officer had shoulder-length blonde hair and a trim figure. She wore a white blouse, jeans, and a green cardigan that nearly matched the color of her eyes. He couldn't see any jewelry, and if she wore makeup, it was subtle. If she could keep her mouth under control, he suspected she'd make somebody a good wife someday.

"Joe Court," he said. "I've heard of you. I've even seen pictures. They don't do you justice."

She said nothing. Her dog sat down. He had a big, blocky head and curly fur. He was a big boy, well over a hundred pounds. If Hunter went after Joe, the dog would be a problem, but he looked content for the moment.

"It's nice to meet you," he said. "I'm Hunter Collins."

"I've requested that you get out of the vehicle, Mr. Collins," she said. "If you make me say it again, I'll call backup, and they'll drag you out."

He smiled and opened his door, knowing that if she called for backup, they'd be fifteen minutes out at least. She and her dog would be long dead by the time they arrived. He hoped he didn't have to kill her, though.

Richard Clarke, the now deceased founder of the Church of the White Steeple, had placed Ms. Court under his personal protection. Since Richard's death, his son Michael had extended the courtesy. The Clarke family wanted to convert her. Hunter doubted that would happen, but it'd be quite a coup if they could. The Church could use every police officer they could get—especially one like her.

"It's nice to meet you, Mr. Collins," she said. "Care to tell me what you and your friends are doing here?"

"We're exercising our Second Amendment rights and standing around."

She smiled, but she didn't look happy.

"You've scared people. Your right to carry and bear arms is important, but you're scaring children. They had to lock the school down."

Hunter nodded and matched her humorless smile.

"I'm sorry to hear that," he said. "We're a thousand feet from school property, and we're here to keep people safe. This town's falling apart. We don't even have a sheriff anymore. Now, if I call 911, I don't know what would happen. Would anyone even pick up?"

She nodded and stepped her right leg back just a little. It almost looked as if she were stepping into a shooter's stance.

"People called 911, and I showed up. Doesn't that tell you enough about our emergency services?"

"You're just one person, honey. How would you stop a real shooter at the school? Or thugs from East St. Louis who start carjacking people?" he asked. "I've seen what happens when order breaks down. It's not pretty. If we let the lawless savages see that we're weak, they'll swarm this town like locusts. You won't be able to walk down the street without stepping on dirty needles and broken glass. If my boys and I are violating a city ordinance, we'll adjust our watch. Otherwise, we're here for the long haul. So what do you say? We breaking the law?"

Hunter smiled. Joe was easy to smile at. Pretty girls usually were. She looked over her shoulder and sighed.

"Missouri law is pretty clear. Armed or not, it's your right to stand here," she said. "What is CAP?"

"It's the Citizen's Action Patrol," he said. "We're a group of citizens interested in keeping our town safe now that our police force has been disbanded. We'll never take your job, obviously, but we need criminals to know this town's not up for grabs. There are good people here. We refuse to sit back and let anyone take advantage of them. That counts double for our kids."

She nodded, her pouty lips pursed. Her eyes and posture shifted, and her expression softened. Hunter had convinced her. She just needed somebody to tell her how the world worked.

"I appreciate your position," she said, "but you are scaring children. Put the guns away. You can keep them in easy reach—that's your right—but don't openly carry a rifle. You keep wearing your shirts, word'll get out about who you are and what you're doing. You don't need to display the firearms around children who aren't used to seeing guns."

He considered her. Kids were women's work, so she probably understood them innately. Hunter and his boys could live with that compromise.

"It's a deal," he said. "We'll keep the streets safe. Don't you worry."

She flicked her eyes toward the other men. Hunter told them to stow the long guns in their truck but keep their pistols at hand. They did as he asked. Joe thanked him and walked away, giving Hunter an opportunity to see her from behind. It was worth getting up in the morning for.

Then he walked toward Shane Fox.

"Response time?"

"Eleven minutes, twenty-four seconds."

Hunter sighed and shook his head. The Church had members everywhere, including in the neighborhood around the school. One of them had called 911 before Hunter and his men even took position. In years past, the first responder would have taken five minutes. Eleven and a half minutes was slow. Whether or not St. Augustine realized it, they needed Hunter and his men. It didn't matter, though. The county couldn't stop them.

"We'll keep watch for another half hour, and then we'll head home."

Shane nodded, and Hunter climbed into his truck and started driving toward the middle school to ensure his team there was doing okay. About halfway there, his phone rang. It was Damon Burke, so Hunter had to take the call.

"Hey," he said, answering after the second ring. "Joe Court—she's the pretty blonde the Clarkes like so much—came out, but it took her over eleven minutes."

Burke grunted.

"Never understood what Clarke saw in her."

"I take it you've never seen her from behind, then," said Hunter. "It's a view worth savoring."

Burke paused and then laughed.

"Maybe she has some redeeming qualities," he said. He paused. "This town's falling apart. It'll take time to put it back together, but we will. It shouldn't be long before we're running this place."

"I look forward to the day."

The conversation quieted, and Hunter focused on the road.

"We found Wyatt Caparaso," said Burke. "He made a run for his mom and dad's house. We picked him up before they even knew he was in town."

"What's the plan?"

"Connor Wright asked us to find out why this little shit stain murdered Donna. So that's what we're doing. You and Shane can interrogate him. Then you'll dispose of him. We've got him at a congregant's farm near Kansas City. I'll give you the address when I see you in person."

Hunter drew in a breath.

"Are Connor and family doing okay? Or do we need to make alternative arrangements?"

"We're on schedule," said Burke. "We're set up in their barn."

The conversation quieted again. Hunter cleared his throat.

"I hate this plan," he said. "My people are going to die."

"You have made your objections clear," said Burke. "And you're right. We're going to lose people. That happens in war—as you know."

"Yes, but you don't throw away your soldiers. We need a better plan."

"We can't afford to give our enemies time to get their act together and raid us," said Burke. "We are on a time crunch here. We do this right, in one swoop, we will stab all our enemies in the heart before they can respond. I watched you and your CAP team grow up, and I love you boys like you were my own. Don't you forget that. I don't."

"I know," said Hunter.

Burke sighed.

"You're a good man, Hunter. Don't let your kind nature impede your duty. We are going to strike our enemy, and we are going to strike so hard and fast that they won't recover. That's our God-given duty."

Hunter nodded even though Burke couldn't see.

"My CAP team'll pack up, and we'll head home. Then Shane and I will deal with Caparaso."

"Good boy," said Burke. "You make me proud every day."

"Thank you," said Hunter, a heavy feeling beginning to fill his gut. "We're going to wrap up here. Then Shane and I'll head out."

Burke said he'd be there waiting. Then he hung up. Hunter rubbed his eyes. No matter what happened, he would lose friends, men he respected, soon. Burke was right: they'd deliver a heavy blow to their opponents, but it'd come at a cost of blood. Hunter would pay that cost, but he wouldn't forget. His people would owe him after this.

And he planned to collect.

CHAPTER 16

Roy and I walked back to my Volvo where I met the school's principal. I was honest with her. I didn't like having armed men near the school, but there was little we could do until those men broke a law. Our best option, as I saw it, was to let the kids inside and lock the doors. The kids could have recess in the gym to expend energy but would otherwise stay in their classrooms. Pickup would have to be regimented as well to minimize exposure outside. If possible, I planned to come back that afternoon to watch Hunter Collins and his team of racists during pickup to make sure they didn't do anything stupid.

The plan wasn't sustainable long term, but eventually, we'd have a county charter and a working police force. Until then, we'd do the best we could with the resources we had.

At nine, Roy and I drove to work. As always, the place was empty. I made a pot of coffee, sipped my drink, and walked through the building to make sure everything was still closed tight. Then I went to my office and checked my messages. Wyatt Caparaso was still in the wind, but a highway patrol trooper thought he had seen his car near Kansas City. The kid's parents lived there, so it made sense he'd be in the area. Hopefully, we'd find him soon before he got hurt.

With that done, my investigative work was complete. I drummed my fingers on the desk. Then I sighed and looked at Roy.

"I think it's back to the closet for us," I said. "Sorry, dude."

He tilted his head left and right before barking.

"I don't like it, either, but it's our job."

He said nothing. That was his way. So I grabbed a clipboard, a pen, and a flashlight and headed to the second-floor supply closet. For an hour, I worked. Then my cell rang. I didn't recognize the number, but the caller ID identified it as belonging to the St. Louis County Prosecutor's Office. I wondered if they had found Caparaso in the city. I answered before it rang a third time.

"Hey, this is Joe Court."

"Joe, it's good to hear from you. This is Shaun Deveraux."

Deveraux had been St. Augustine County's prosecutor for a number of years. He was a good lawyer and had done his best in a difficult situation. Now, he and his entire staff had been hired by St. Louis County. It was a shrewd move. The county acquired three talented, experienced prosecutors and a support staff accustomed to a constantly high workload without having to train anybody or go through the expense of a nationwide job hunt. Everybody won.

"It's nice to hear from you, too. How's life in the big city treating you?"

We exchanged pleasantries for a few minutes. Deveraux and his staff seemed to be doing well in St. Louis. I was glad for them all.

"I doubt you called to catch up," I said. "What's shaking?"

"I hear you're looking for somebody named Wyatt Caparaso."

"I sure am," I said, my voice perking up. "You haven't got him, have you?"

"No, unfortunately," he said. "His name has been mentioned in a case I'm working on, though, and I wanted to give you a call. You remember Erik Hoyle? He was convicted of murdering Brittany Ashbury. Hoyle was Ashbury's supervisor at a hardware store. We prosecuted him for rape and murder."

I stepped out of the closet. Roy was lying on the carpet beside the door, but he lifted his head when he saw me. I clicked my tongue for him to follow me and started walking toward my office.

"I remember the case vaguely, and I think I know what you're going to say," I said. "Caparaso's articles are conjecture at best. Erik Hoyle raped and killed a woman. He confessed. That's all there is to it."

"I hear you, but I've been assigned to the conviction integrity unit here in St. Louis County. Because Hoyle was prosecuted in St. Louis County, his conviction falls into our jurisdiction. My office has been working on his case since well before I arrived."

My stomach started growing a little fluttery as I sat down behind my desk.

"He was St. Augustine's case. How did St. Louis County get it?"

"Judge granted Hoyle a change of venue. He didn't think he could get an unbiased jury in St. Augustine."

I had worked on the case as a uniformed officer but hadn't kept up with it after we arrested Hoyle. Given the sensational murder and the ill will it generated, I could see why Hoyle had wanted a trial elsewhere.

"It sounds like you're working yourself up to something, Shaun."

"I am. An appeals court recently granted Hoyle a retrial due to shaky evidence. We've decided to withdraw the charges against him."

I blinked, sure that I had misunderstood something.

"He's guilty. He confessed."

"How well do you remember the case?"

"I worked it," I said. "It's familiar."

Deveraux paused.

"You were a twenty-two-year-old rookie," he said. "It was George Delgado's case."

"His name may have been on the forms, but I was the first responder. I found her body."

Deveraux went quiet.

"You still there, Shaun?" I asked eventually.

"I am," he said, his voice softer than I had expected. He sighed. "Go back and examine the evidence. You're the best detective St. Augustine's ever had. Go through the case as if you're reviewing a young colleague's work. Then tell me what you think."

I closed my eyes and squeezed my jaw tight before answering.

"Fine. I'll do that. Afterward, I want to hear how you justify allowing a confessed rapist and murderer to go free."

"We'll talk," said Deveraux. "I'll be here. You can call me at this number."

I said I would. Then I hung up and squeezed the arms of my chair hard enough for my knuckles to turn white. Deveraux and I hadn't always agreed on everything, but I respected him and his judgment. He was making a mistake, but it sounded like the situation was out of his control. If I studied the evidence, maybe I could see what the prosecutors in St. Louis missed.

I took a couple of breaths and called up the case file. We had the physical evidence in our vault. The paperwork was digital. I'd find something.

For half an hour, I read through the paperwork. The initial 911 call came at 8:10 AM I had just started my shift as a patrol officer. Since I was close to the hardware store, Trisha dispatched me to evaluate the situation. I drove out and found Brittany Ashbury on the ground behind the dumpster. Her shirt had been ripped open, her lips were blue, and a purplish ligature mark was visible on her neck. The buttons on her skirt were torn, and her underwear had been removed, but the skirt itself had been pulled down to cover her. She was quite clearly dead.

I secured the scene and called George Delgado. He did the bulk of the work.

Brittany wasn't the first body I had seen, but she was close to my age. That she had been raped before she died made it all the harder. My reports detailed my sense impressions and what I had done from the moment I arrived. They didn't mention that I had cried in my car for almost an hour after finding her.

That was a hard day, probably the hardest of my career at that point. I didn't know the victim, but I understood what she had gone through.

From the start, George focused on Erik Hoyle. He managed the hardware store where Brittany worked and he had known her for years. Brittany's colleagues said they were close. She spent a lot of time in Hoyle's office, and several of her colleagues recounted incidents where the two flirted with one another.

Hoyle, a thirty-two-year-old father of two, had worked in the hardware store since he was sixteen and had managed it for five years. He hired Brittany when she was sixteen and seemed to give her favorable treatment from the start. When she graduated from high school, he promoted her to assistant manager. Her colleagues thought she'd stay there forever, just like him.

Then her life changed.

She worked at the hardware store full-time for a few years, but then she decided she wanted a different life. She applied to and was accepted by the University of Missouri-St. Louis. Her mom said she wanted to become a teacher. It had been her dream since she was a child, and she was finally making it happen. On her last day of work, her colleagues threw her a party. Hoyle even brought in a cake. Brittany's colleagues had described the night as joyous and carefree. Everybody was excited for her.

Afterward, Hoyle was left to clean up—but he wasn't alone. Brittany, his right-hand employee, stayed behind, too. Nobody questioned it because everyone knew Hoyle and Brittany had a special relationship. I found Brittany's body the next day.

Hoyle claimed he hugged her goodbye, promised to keep in touch, and then drove home, where he slipped inside through a basement door and slept in the guest room so as not to wake up his spouse or the kids.

A board-certified forensic pathologist autopsied Brittany within twenty-four hours of her death and found ligature marks on her wrists, significant vaginal bruising, and a bite mark on her shoulder. Importantly, he didn't find defensive wounds or DNA inside her. It indicated that she likely knew her attacker and didn't think to fight back before he incapacitated her, put on a condom, and raped her. Then he shot her in the heart.

Delgado talked to Brittany's friends and coworkers. Two of her coworkers said they thought Hoyle and Brittany had a sexual relationship, and several recounted times in which they heard sexual noises coming from Hoyle's office while the two of them were inside. When confronted, Hoyle denied everything and claimed he wasn't even in the building during their supposed trysts. We knew they were having an affair, though, because one of Brittany's friends told Delgado in confidence.

To defuse the situation, Hoyle even allowed us to search his cell phone for text messages or emails. Brittany's mother did likewise. We spent days reading through their texts, and while we found a significant number of messages between them, none were openly sexual. The two were definitely close, though. They talked more often than I talk to my mother or sister.

The case was strong. A forensic odontologist even took a casting of Hoyle's teeth, which he was able to match to the bite on Brittany's shoulder. We had Hoyle dead to rights, so we picked him up. Delgado interrogated him while I watched. Then he gave me an opportunity. Jasper Martin, Delgado's partner at the time, told him that was a bad idea, but Delgado trusted me. The victim was my age and body type. Hoyle cared about Brittany. He might have even loved her. When he looked at me, we knew he'd see someone just like her.

And I broke him.

I didn't threaten Hoyle or call him names. I was honest. In slow, methodical steps, I laid out our case. It was cold, almost clinical. Never once did I lose control or raise my voice, but every word I spoke held anger, pain, maybe even a little menace. I had never met Brittany Ashbury, but we were sisters. I knew what she had felt, I knew how scared she had been, how disgusted she had felt for not fighting back, how helpless she had felt when she realized she couldn't trust the people in her life she should have trusted most. I had been in Brittany's place, assaulted by someone who pretended to care about me.

For one hour in an interrogation room, I let go of the bonds that held my simmering rage in control. I became something more than a police officer. Years later, my colleagues would joke that I was an ice queen, that I didn't feel anything. That was wrong, though. I felt the same things everyone did. Everything, though, was tempered by rage. Sometimes, it was almost blinding. Even as a rookie police officer, I had known I couldn't show that to anyone and keep my badge.

So I held it in check. I embraced that cold persona. I became the person they claimed I already was. For an hour, I became that mean, cold-hearted bitch they wanted me to be.

And then he spoke.

"I guess I did it."

Five words uttered after an hour in a room with me. The moment Hoyle closed his mouth, Delgado hustled in and handcuffed our suspect. He even shook my hand. Neither he nor his partner had ever paid me a lick of notice before, but everyone knew what I had done in that room. That night, Hoyle slept in a jail cell because of me. I got drunk alone in my living room because it was easier than allowing myself to feel what I felt.

Looking back, I wasn't proud of the person I had been, but I was proud of the work I had done. Hoyle was a shit bag. Deveraux may now want to let him go, but I wasn't going to let that happen without a fight.

CHAPTER 17

After reviewing the case, I took Roy for a walk. The air outside was brisk but not yet cold. It smelled sweet. Roy sniffed every fire hydrant, lamppost, and street sign we passed, and an elderly man stopped and introduced himself. He said he had once owned a dog just like Roy and had taken him hunting every weekend. Roy loved the attention, and I appreciated the distraction.

Afterward, we walked back to my station, and I sat in my desk chair, my chest and legs feeling heavy. I felt... sick. It shouldn't have been like this. Erik Hoyle had the same rights anybody did, and he deserved every appeal permitted to him under the law, but he also deserved to rot in prison. Why the hell was the prosecutor's office in St. Louis letting him go? I already went through the file. The case was tight. I didn't miss anything.

I grabbed a cup of coffee from the break room, sat at my desk, and breathed in deeply before calling Shaun back. I tried to keep my voice even, but it was a challenge. My hands nearly trembled.

"Shaun, hey," I said. "This is Joe Court again. You got a minute?"

He paused.

"You're angry."

I drew in a breath so I wouldn't snap at him. Then I swallowed hard and closed my eyes.

"I'm doing my best to keep an open mind," I said. "The evidence against Hoyle is overwhelming. What am I missing?"

"Before I say, I want to be clear: you're a good cop. No one in my office thinks otherwise."

I paused again.

"Was my competency in doubt?"

Deveraux paused, presumably to think.

"Yours? No. But this case shouldn't have gone to trial. George mishandled things. Jasper Martin, George's partner, wouldn't sign off on the final reports."

A knot began to form in my stomach, and I leaned forward.

"I didn't know that."

"George removed Jasper from the paperwork," he said. "We interviewed Jasper. He set us straight."

I squeezed my jaw tight.

"Did George threaten Hoyle?"

"No," said Deveraux.

I nodded.

"Okay," I said. "Did George plant evidence?"

"No."

I nodded again.

"Okay," I said, drawing the word out. "So George wrote his partner out of his reports because Jasper didn't like the way George handled the case. What was he hiding?"

"You."

I squeezed my jaw tight and shook my head.

"No," I said. "I didn't do anything wrong. I worked the case in a professional, fair manner. I did my job. Hoyle raped and murdered a young woman barely old enough to buy a drink. He stole her life and her future. He stole her parents' lives and futures. He robbed her siblings of a loved one and left a gaping hole in their lives where she should have been. He ruined those people. He's a monster."

Deveraux drew in a breath.

"He's not a monster."

I shot to my feet hard enough that my chair fell backward. Roy jumped to his feet, surprised. I squeezed my jaw tight before speaking.

"He raped and murdered a girl. He admitted it."

"You're right. He also recanted that confession."

I slammed my hand on the desk.

"He's lying. That's what rapists do. You've done this long enough to understand."

Deveraux went quiet. I counted to five.

"Say something," I said.

"Are you okay, Detective?"

"I'm not a detective anymore," I said. "They took the title from me when they shut this place down."

Deveraux kept his voice calm, but I could hear the strain when he spoke.

"You were a young woman when Brittany was murdered. She was twenty-one. You were twenty-two."

"I was," I said, nodding. "And that's important. I knew the world Brittany lived in. When I was in high school, I worked in a movie theater. Perverts hit on me all the time. When I was sixteen, forty-year-old men would tell me they wanted to ride me like a bucking bronco. A man old enough to have grandkids asked me what color my nipples were. I didn't have anybody to protect me. She didn't, either."

"I'm sorry that happened to you."

"Me, too. It shouldn't have happened, but it taught me lessons. I learned to carry my car keys with me at all times so I could slip into my car right away. I learned that I needed to carry pepper spray in case someone tried to hurt me. I learned to avoid men if I was alone.

"Brittany lived in that same world. She experienced the same things. She would have had her ass and boobs grabbed by handsy customers—who you can't even tell off because you're afraid your boss will fire you. If I'm protective of her, it's because I know her, and I know what she went through. And it's wrong. Don't assume I can't be objective because I was too close to the victim. It's that closeness that made me understand her."

Deveraux drew in a slow breath.

"Again, I'm sorry. I wish none of that happened to you. It's appalling. We can't hold Hoyle accountable for the sins of other men, though."

"Apparently we can't even hold him accountable for his own actions."

Deveraux sighed. I forced myself to sit down.

"You've looked through the case file. What hard evidence did you have tying Hoyle to Ashbury's death?"

"George Delgado had heard they were having an affair. We theorized that she tried to break it off and go to college. In a jealous rage, he raped and strangled her behind the hardware store. He had motive, means and opportunity, and he had no alibi. What else do you want?"

"That's circumstantial, and we found no evidence of an affair. In fact, their relationship was more like family. Hoyle wrote her a letter of recommendation for college, he taught her how to change a tire, and he scolded her when she was caught drinking and driving."

I squeezed my jaw tight.

"You investigated almost a decade after the fact. Time distorts perceptions. He was paternalistic. Maybe he even loved her in some sick way, but he still killed her."

"George used you, Joe. He didn't have a tip about an affair. He told you that because he knew it'd make you go after Hoyle harder. That's why Jasper Martin didn't want you anywhere near the case. George thought you'd unnerve

Hoyle, being roughly the same size and age as the dead woman. It biased you."

I closed my eyes. Unfortunately, that sounded like something George would have done. At the same time, it didn't materially change the situation. I counted to five, giving myself a moment to breathe and cool off. Roy shifted so that he was closer to my chair. I patted his shoulder to let him know I wasn't angry at him.

"Even if you're right, Hoyle still confessed."

"After an eleven-hour interrogation, and only after you and George both told him you had supposedly irrefutable bite mark evidence against him. You remember the last time you used bite marks in a case?"

I shook my head.

"I don't run into that many bite marks on cases. If it was needed, and the county had the funds, I'm sure we'd use it more often."

"Bite mark analysis is utter nonsense."

I pushed back from my desk.

"What does that even mean?"

"We don't use bite mark analysis because the entire field has been discredited. Skin shifts too much upon death to be a reliable medium to compare to someone's teeth. In controlled tests, forensic odontologists were wrong 63 percent of the time. You'd be better off asking their opinion and then doing the exact opposite of what they suggest. That some states still use bite mark analysis as evidence is mind-boggling."

I rolled my eyes.

"I didn't realize you had become a defense attorney after moving."

"Don't go there," said Deveraux. "You're angry. The situation's unfair. You did nothing wrong, but I can't say the same for George. He and Jasper Martin tag teamed Hoyle in an interrogation booth for ten hours. He didn't break for ten hours. Then you came in. Hoyle saw you and realized it wasn't going to end unless he gave George what he wanted. I know you've read papers about false confessions. You know they happen. George used you to railroad an innocent man."

My arms and chest started to feel heavy as the situation pierced my anger.

"George told me he did it. He said we had the evidence. My job was to get a confession."

"That wasn't your job," said Deveraux. "George knew he couldn't get a conviction based on the evidence he had. He used you."

My eyes felt glassy, and my throat grew tight. I coughed to clear it.

"You're telling me I abused my position and sent an innocent man to prison for eight years."

"I'm telling you George used you to put an innocent man in prison for eight years."

I leaned my head back and squeezed my jaw so tight I thought my teeth would crack.

"I ruined a man's life. I don't know how to react."

"You move on and learn. And you reopen Brittany Ashbury's murder investigation."

A new weight began pressing down on me. I brought my hand to my face and swore to myself. It'd take time to process everything Deveraux had said, but already I felt sick. I swallowed it down as much as I could.

"This is real," I said. "This isn't just some bad joke."

"It's not," said Deveraux.

I wanted to throw up. Instead, I swallowed hard and drew in a breath.

"So how does this work?" I asked. "Logistically, I mean. Do I have to give a deposition or testify?"

"No," said Deveraux. "My office is working with the AGs office, the Bureau of Prisons, and Hoyle's attorney. We've been working for months. As soon as we get the paperwork signed, he'll be free to go. It's not going to be long."

"And you don't need me to testify?"

"Not yet. Hoyle's got the best defense attorney in the state. For now, his lawyer hasn't requested to talk to you, but he will."

I covered my mouth and processed the statement.

"His lawyer's Brian Carlisle, isn't it? You said he was the best defense attorney in Missouri."

"I didn't realize you paid that much attention to the legal market."

I rubbed my eyes and swore under my breath.

"Carlisle's representing Hoyle, though, right?"

"Yes," said Deveraux.

"Carlisle has declined to speak to me so far because he's weighing his options and considering his best course of action," I said. I paused. "He's my biological father. I found out a couple of months ago."

"Oh."

"Has anybody told Brittany Ashbury's family that Hoyle's going free?" I asked.

Deveraux cleared his throat.

"My boss called. It didn't go well."

I nodded.

"Yeah, I bet it didn't," I said, sighing. "Thank you for taking my call. Apparently, I've got an old murder to work."

I hung up. For a few moments, I just stared into space. Then I squeezed the arms of my chair hard and leaned forward.

"Damn."

CHAPTER 18

I needed a break, so I went to the locker room in the basement, changed, and jogged on the treadmill for about twenty minutes as my adrenaline faded. If Delgado had been alive, I probably would have driven to his house and screamed at him. Since he was dead, though, I didn't have anyone with whom to share my guilt.

After my brief run, I showered until the locker room filled with steam. I had sent an innocent man to prison. He had missed watching his children grow up, he missed anniversaries with his wife, he missed all those things he loved and that made his life worth living. I had locked him in a cage and patted myself on the back.

And I was wrong.

The water was nearly scalding hot, but I deserved it. I would have stayed in there for a while, but Roy started barking when my phone rang. I turned off the shower, wrapped a towel around my torso, and looked at the screen. The number was restricted, which meant it was probably either a scam artist or somebody important. I braced myself for either.

"Hey," I said. "This is Joe Court."

"Ms. Court, this is Rashaad Moore. I'm an Assistant US attorney in St. Louis. Are you in your station right now?"

I paused and forced myself to focus.

"I am, and thank you for calling. This isn't about Erik Hoyle, is it? If so, I've already talked to Shaun Deveraux."

Moore didn't pause before answering.

"Are you in your station, Ms. Court?"

I wrapped the towel tighter around my chest as if that would protect me.

"I am."

"We're at the front door. We need to talk."

This didn't bode well for me.

"I'll be there as soon as I can."

I hung up before the lawyer could respond. Then I looked at Roy as I toweled off.

"This might get ugly, dude."

I dressed and unlocked the front door. Two men and a woman stood outside. The two men wore suits, while the woman wore dark jeans and a cream-colored sweater. All three were middle-aged. The woman flashed me a gold badge. I had only seen that badge a few times, and I furrowed my brow as they glared at me.

"Homeland Security?" I asked. "What are you doing here?"

"Nice to see you, too, Ms. Court," said one of the men. He was slight of build and had black hair and dark skin. His black suit was cut to hug his torso. He was unarmed, which meant he wasn't law enforcement.

"Rashaad Moore?" I asked, my eyebrows raised. He nodded. "Come on in. We can go to the conference room."

Roy stood beside me, took a shuffle step forward, and then yawned.

"Oh, this is Roy," I said, glancing down. "He's a cadaver dog, so he works with me."

Moore's lips curled into a smile, but he didn't look thrilled.

"Great."

I let them in and led them to the second-floor conference room, where we sat facing each other. Roy stayed beside me.

"So...." I said. "How are you guys?"

"We want our camera," said the male Homeland Security special agent. I looked at him.

"And you are?"

"None of your business."

I glanced at Moore and raised my eyebrows.

"It'd be helpful if I knew who I was talking to," I said. "Otherwise, I have to start giving you nicknames for my own internal monologue."

"This is Special Agent Frank McNair," said Mr. Moore. "His partner is Special Agent Ashley Jensen."

I smiled at them both.

"Great. I'm Joe Court. I work for the highway patrol. I used to be Detective Joe Court, but then my station shut down. It's a long story. I'd offer to share it with you, but I suspect you don't plan to stay that long. I'll refrain from offering you coffee for the same reason, but just between us, that's all for the best anyway. The coffee's terrible."

"Ms. Court, you called the US Attorney's Office in St. Louis after you discovered a hidden surveillance camera," said Jensen. "We'd like that camera back."

I narrowed my eyes at her.

"It was a trail camera," I said. "The kind hunters use to track game. It wasn't hidden, either. It was secured to a tree trunk and pointed at a private citizen's driveway."

She smiled, her face exhibiting all the warmth and merriment of the north wind.

"We'd like it back. If you can just give it back to us, we won't need to worry about stolen government property."

I looked at the attorney.

"A private citizen's children found the camera on his property. He called me because his wife had just been murdered. I examined the camera and found a sticker beneath the back panel that said it was US government property. I promptly called the US Attorney's Office. Does that sound stolen to you?"

He held up his hands defensively.

"I'm here as an adviser and mediator," he said. "I'm not getting into the middle of this."

"Great job mediating, dude," I said, glancing from him to the HSI agents. "So you guys work for Homeland Security.

You investigate transnational criminal gangs that smuggle humans and goods across the border."

They said nothing.

"Why are you investigating the Wrights?" I asked.

"Have you watched the video the camera shot?" asked McNair.

"No. Never got the chance," I said. "I saw the sticker and called the US Attorney's Office."

"Good," said McNair, nodding. "You don't need to know. Give us the camera, and we'll go."

I bit my lip, pretending to think, before shaking my head.

"No. That doesn't work for me. How about you tell me why you're interested in the Wright family, and then I'll give it to you. Donna Wright was murdered a couple of days ago. We have a suspect, but why are you watching her family? I'd hate to arrest the wrong person because you held back on us."

Moore reached into his jacket and pulled out a typed piece of paper.

"This is a court order compelling you to release the video camera to us. I've already spoken to Lieutenant Colonel Shelby. He expects your cooperation."

Shelby was the second-highest ranking member of the highway patrol. I had never met him and likely never would, but he far outranked me and my boss. I stood without saying a word and got the camera from my office. When I handed it to Moore, he immediately stood.

"Thank you, Ms. Court."

The two special agents stood to leave, but I shook my head.

"This is stupid," I said. "I'm investigating the murder of a woman who lived at the farm you're surveilling. What's the probability that Donna Wright's death is unconnected to whatever you're investigating?"

They ignored me and started to leave. I followed them to the front door, where I repeated my question. The two men stepped outside, but Jensen stopped and turned to me.

"Your case is closed," she said. "You've got your suspect. Leave this one alone."

She was partially right, at least. We did have a suspect, one whose actions still made little sense.

"You're not going to even give me a clue about what you're investigating?" I asked. "I could be putting my life in danger every time I step foot on their farm. Are they trafficking drugs?"

"No."

I nodded and considered.

"So you think they're trafficking human beings. That's the other half of your mandate."

She held up a hand.

"I didn't say that. Have a nice day, Ms. Court. Thank you for your cooperation."

Jensen, Moore, and McNair got into two separate cars and drove away. I wrapped Roy's leash around my hand and glanced at him.

"Come on, dude. We're going to a farm."

Roy wagged his tail as I turned and locked the front door. Then we piled into my Volvo and headed out to the Wright's farm. The drive was easy, and I called Connor Wright on the way. He didn't seem too thrilled about talking to me, but he agreed to a meeting when I mentioned I had news about the trail camera.

I parked and met Connor on the front porch, just as before. He led me inside, where the two of us sat in the front room.

"First, I gave the trail camera back to its owners. Second, I wanted to ask you about farm labor."

Connor leaned forward, a confused look on his face.

"What do you want to know?" he asked. "It's me and the family."

"You don't bring in seasonal labor? Perhaps those of Hispanic descent."

He barked a laugh.

"A little extra help would be nice, but it's just us."

I leaned forward.

"I'm not interested in illegal immigration," I said. "If you pick up laborers from the parking lot at the hardware store, I don't care. My interest is murder, and the more I know about your world, the better I can investigate your spouse's murder. So I'm going to ask you again, and I want you to be honest: are you bringing in Hispanic employees to work your property?"

He started to say no when an older, gruff voice called out.

"Just tell him the truth, Connor."

The hardwood floors creaked as an older man with buzzed white hair walked down the hallway toward the front room. Connor stood.

"Dad, you don't need to be part—"

"You won't be honest, I will," said the older man. "I'm William Wright. Donna was my daughter-in-law. She was a good woman. My farm doesn't hire seasonal labor. I rescue men and women in distress and help them get to safety."

Connor sighed. I looked at him, and he covered his eyes with his hands.

"Stop talking, Dad," he said. "This woman's going to send you to jail if you keep talking."

"Kind of wish she would," he said. "It'd be a whole lot cheaper than that goddamn retirement village you and Donna wanted to send me to."

"You'd be happy there, Dad. You wouldn't have to do anything. There'd be people to cook your meals, clean your apartment, and do your laundry."

"Let's just try to focus, if we could," I said. "Mr. Wright—William—what do you mean you rescue people in distress?"

He looked at me.

"People are human beings. People in distress are human beings in some kind of peril. By rescue, I mean I remove them from that peril so that they may live another day."

I forced myself to smile.

"I see," I said. "Who do you rescue and from what peril?"

"Mostly Mexicans, but we occasionally run across families from Central America, too," he said. "They're human beings, and they're treated like rotting garbage by those assholes at Ross Kelly Farms."

Connor said something, but I ignored him. This made sense now. The Wrights owned a large piece of property that bordered Ross Kelly Farms, a poultry processing outfit that housed its largely migrant workforce at a dilapidated company town called Nuevo Pueblo. Even when St. Augustine had a police force, we rarely ventured into the area because Ross Kelly Farms policed its own. If the Wrights helped migrants in the US illegally, I could see why they'd draw interest from Homeland Security's investigators.

"Thank you for your honesty," I said. "I'm not sending you to jail, but we need to have a long talk."

CHAPTER 19

I sat and talked with the Wrights for about half an hour. According to William Wright, they hadn't planned to aid the migrant community but had stumbled into the role when migrants took refuge on their property. Ross Kelly Farms overworked its employees and charged them exorbitant prices to rent crappy homes. When workers spoke out, the company's security personnel intimidated them into silence.

The Wright family lived beside the company, so they had a much closer view of the conditions at Nuevo Pueblo and the factory than the sheriff's department. In William Wright's eyes, their workers were more indentured servants than employees. If a family didn't meet their work quotas, a security team would remove them from their home and relocate them to a dirty barracks-style building, where the kids and family were afforded little to no privacy. If they complained, a security team would handcuff the adults and separate the family members. They'd place the kids in foster families and lock the adults in veritable prison cells with a bucket for a toilet.

Eventually, they'd reunite the family. Nobody would even tell them what they did wrong. They were expected to know. If they continued complaining or tried to organize, entire families, along with their possessions, would disappear..

It didn't happen often, but workers sometimes just left. They abandoned their home and possessions because they knew they'd die if they stayed at the farm. Ross Kelly Farms would then send teams to find them and bring them back.

The Wrights, at first, had given care packages with blankets, soap, and other supplies to the workers they ran across. Then, they started sheltering those same workers so the security teams wouldn't find them. Eventually, they realized that even that wasn't enough. So they became organized.

They started giving prepaid cell phones to workers. During an emergency, the workers could call the Wrights for pick up. Ross Kelly Farms had security cameras and fences, but it wasn't a prison. The Wrights would drive the workers to a shelter in St. Louis. If the family was stable and had legal paperwork, the shelter and its staff would help them get jobs and integrate into the community. If they were in the US illegally, the shelter staff would help them disappear.

Those emergency calls used to come once or twice a year. Since St. Augustine fell apart, though, the calls have accelerated. As William spoke, I jotted down notes and occasionally asked questions.

Each person the Wrights had helped disappear represented a monetary loss to Ross Kelly Farms. I always knew the company was shady. Their head of security had once openly threatened his workforce in front of me, believing—correctly—that I couldn't speak Spanish. He didn't count on my partner at the time having taken Spanish in high school. It was a big step from threats to murder, but if the Wrights had cost Ross Kelly enough money, I could see them stepping up to the plate.

Wyatt Caparaso may have shot Donna Wright, but she had enemies galore.

"When did you last receive a call to pick up a family?"

Connor looked at his father. The older man shrugged.

"I'm not sure. Donna usually took care of that. She spoke better Spanish than any of us."

I looked at Connor. He leaned forward and rested his elbows on his knees.

"The day she died," he said, his head low.

I lowered my notepad and tilted my head to the side.

"Is that why she visited the campground?"

He nodded, and I squeezed my jaw tight to keep from snapping at him. Then I drew in a breath through my nose.

"Did she know Wyatt Caparaso?"

He shook his head.

"No. We didn't know who she was picking up, but they were Spanish speakers."

I rubbed my eyes. This changed things. Wyatt said he was lured to the campgrounds. Apparently, Donna was as well.

"You're telling me your spouse went to a campground by herself to pick up strangers?"

He nodded.

"We've never had a problem before."

They certainly did now, but I kept that to myself. I was starting to form a new theory. Somebody had lured both Wyatt and Donna to the campsite. When Donna saw a Caucasian man instead of the Hispanic family she expected, she panicked and attacked him. He fought back and shot her.

Wyatt was a student journalist who wrote about topics of note in St. Augustine County. Recently, he had written articles about Erik Hoyle. I wondered if he had ever written anything about conditions at Nuevo Pueblo. If he did, he and Donna Wright might have had an enemy in common.

"Who knew you were involved in these rescue operations?" I asked.

"We don't hide, Ms. Court," said William. "We try to make it so that everyone at Nuevo Pueblo knows they can call us when they need a friend."

If the residents of Nuevo Pueblo knew the Wrights, so did the security team at Ross Kelly Farms. This could get ugly.

I wrote some notes and stood.

"Thank you for meeting me," I said. "I'll take it from here."

I started toward the door. William stayed put, but his son followed me to the front porch.

"My dad gives blankets and food to the working poor, and he gives rides to the homeless," he said. "He's not breaking the law."

"I'm investigating a homicide," I said. "I don't police charity work. Other people might, though. Be careful. You never know who's watching."

He hesitated before nodding.

"Thank you."

I drove away, wondering how many Homeland Security trail cameras had filmed our conversation. Then I realized I didn't care. I had my own priorities, and they didn't involve sending an old man who gave away blankets to prison.

Nuevo Pueblo was five minutes away. The town had packed gravel roads placed in a grid pattern. The buildings had exposed pier-and-beam foundations. Typically, a builder would install skirting to prevent wind from whipping beneath the house, but they hadn't done that here. As best I could tell, they hadn't added insulation beneath the house, either. The homes were glorified sheds. They should have housed lawn equipment. I wouldn't have even put paint inside, for fear of it freezing over winter.

Instead, Ross Kelly Farms' migrant workforce lived there, sometimes ten people to a building that should have housed two. That never sat well with me, especially when compared to the company's gargantuan—and nearly empty—headquarters building. Their corporate offices had every modern amenity one could ask for, including biometric door locks to keep the riffraff out. Their head of security had locked a uniformed officer and me inside once. He claimed it was an accident, but it wasn't. I hated this place.

I parked in a gravel lot beside a field that had once held a Catholic church. Most of Ross Kelly's workers had children, many of whom attended public school in St. Augustine County. The younger kids attended a company-sponsored preschool in town. On previous visits, I had found those kids outside playing. Now, the entire town looked empty. It was almost eerie.

For half an hour, I knocked on residential doors. Not a single person answered. Then I went to the laundromat. It was open but empty. Half a block away was a convenience store. It was closed. Next to that was a bar. It, too, was closed. The entire town seemed abandoned.

I hadn't heard anything about Ross Kelly Farms shutting down, but every business in St. Augustine had been under strain lately. The only employer in town to escape unscathed lately was Waterford College. With a multi-billion-dollar endowment and a seemingly endless supply of students willing to pay fifty or sixty grand a year for tuition, its future was bright. The rest of the county faced poorer prospects.

I started walking back to my car when I heard an engine. A moment later, two pickup trucks came toward me and parked on the roadside. Ross Kelly Farms had a security team, but they drove big black SUVs with light bars similar to those we installed on our cruisers. These were late model trucks with small beds but big cabs. They were useful for moving people if not cargo. Five men emerged from the two vehicles. All five men looked Hispanic, and they stared at me. I waved.

"Hey," I called. "I'm Joe Court. I work for the Missouri State Highway Patrol. Can you guys talk for a minute?"

Instead of answering, three walked to their left. Two walked to the right. They were surrounding me. My heart started beating a little faster. I hovered my hand over my pistol.

"I don't like it when you guys are behind me where I can't see you," I said, trying to see to my left, right, and straight ahead simultaneously. They kept positioning themselves in a circle around me. I tried to backpedal toward a gap, but they closed it. I looked at a lamppost, knowing Ross Kelly Farms had security cameras everywhere. Hopefully, a security officer was seeing this because I didn't have any backup.

"What are you doing here, lady?" asked a guy in front of me. He had black hair, and he wore a blue and black flannel shirt and tan pants. "This place isn't for you."

"I'll take your word for that," I said, stepping to my left. My Volvo was about 200 yards away. Roy was at my side. "I'm on my way out."

"It's too late for that. You've got to pay the toll."

I glanced down at Roy. I had a lot of experience with dogs. The vast majority, when their handler was threatened, would run away. Very few dogs without training could deal with the stress of a violent attack. Roy, though, was a trained service animal.

My dog could be lazy, but almost from birth, he had an unusually high prey drive. As he grew older, he had developed a defensive drive. It was a genetic disposition. Most avoid fights; Roy didn't. His trainers utilized both those drives to help him develop a fight drive.

If forced, Roy would protect me with his life. That was his job, and it was ingrained into him at a young age. If I gave him the command, Roy would run straight at a target at twenty-five miles an hour, forcefully bite his arm, and drag him to the ground. It'd give me time to escape—or at least get to my weapon. But considering there were five men here, and they were likely armed, I'd lose my dog if I did that.

I didn't want that to happen, so I kept stepping to my left. As two men tried to step in my way, I pulled my pistol from its holster but kept my finger outside the trigger guard. Then I stopped moving and focused on the two dunces to my left. Both wore hooded sweatshirts and heavy utility pants. I couldn't see any weapons, but their outfits were bulky enough that they could easily conceal a pistol.

"You're positioning yourselves to cut off my retreat," I said. "That's a bad idea. If you don't move, I will shoot you both. My dog will then attack a third. I will then shoot the other two. In total, it'll take, maybe, five or six seconds. My Glock 19 holds fifteen rounds in the magazine plus one in the chamber. That means four of you will get three rounds in the chest. One lucky asshole's going to get four. Either way, unless you get out of my way, you'll go home in a body bag. Consider that your toll."

I stepped to the left and slipped my finger from the trigger guard to the trigger. My legs burned as adrenaline coursed through me. Muscles all over my body practically screamed at me to run. I squeezed my left hand into a ball, hoping they wouldn't see me trembling. The speech had held some truth but a lot of bravado. Realistically, I could kill the thugs to my left, and Roy could probably distract a third, but the remaining two could shoot before I could respond. This was a bad position.

Two of the men spoke to each other in Spanish. Then they stepped aside and held up their hands as if to show me they weren't a threat. My lungs loosened immediately, and the muscles in my shoulders relaxed, but I couldn't let them see my relief. They were backing off because I had forced them to. If I showed them weakness now, they'd pounce.

I slowly walked to my car but kept my eyes on my opponents. As Roy and I drove off, I glanced in my rearview mirror to make sure they hadn't jumped in their trucks to follow me. Only when I saw them standing did I suck in great gulps of air and allow myself to calm down. Then I squeezed my steering wheel and clenched my jaw as the adrenaline waned.

Muscles all over my body trembled. A year ago, I would have driven to safety, called for backup, and then returned in force. We'd arrest everybody. Now I couldn't. Whatever those men were doing and to whomever they were doing it, I couldn't stop them. I could barely escape alive.

My county needed its own sheriff's office. I couldn't do this solo. If I kept going on my own, there was a good chance I'd end up as dead as Donna Wright.

CHAPTER 20

Hunter gripped the truck's steering wheel with both hands and focused on the road. The weight of the work he and Shane had ahead of them pressed him into his seat, while the monotonous roar of his tires on the asphalt gave him an excuse to stay silent. Hunter hadn't asked for his current position. He wanted kids, a farm, and a spouse. His wife would be a teacher or a nurse—something that made her happy. His kids would be healthy and happy, too. Maybe they'd play sports. Or maybe they'd be into robots and math. He didn't care. He just wanted a healthy family.

Unfortunately, the world was a broken place. Hunter had seen that from a young age when his father would turn on the news. Every day, politicians fought about something new, stupid, and pointless instead of solving genuine problems. It was worse when the idiots agreed on things. Usually, that meant the country was going to war.

Hunter had been twenty when he first saw a friend die. They had been in Afghanistan. Hunter couldn't even remember whether the country was officially at war at the time, but it didn't matter either way to those men and women deployed at forward operating bases. The rounds fired at them and the explosives hidden along the roadside still killed people no matter what Congress said.

When the Army pulled out of Afghanistan a few years later, and when the Taliban seized control of everything he had fought for, Hunter realized how pointless his sacrifice had been. He had wasted his adult life fighting for causes and believing in things that didn't matter. Republicans, Democrats...they all lied and cheated and schemed with lives that weren't their own. None deserved his loyalty or respect. He was done with them all.

Hunter believed in the Church of the White Steeple, though. Its mission made sense to him. The Church's founders hoped to create a better world. The founders were honest, too. When Richard Clarke wrote the Church's first set of bylaws, he did so knowing some rifts could never be repaired. He created a haven for his own people, one where they could live as a community and help one another.

Outsiders didn't understand. They vilified the Church and its mission. They called them racists and bigots. They weren't, though. Hunter and men and women like him simply had their eyes open.

Finally, he glanced at Shane.

"Tell me about that cop this morning," he said. "Joe Court. Is she a threat?"

Shane considered.

"She's smart, and she puts in the hours," he said. "If she thinks you're up to no good, she can be vicious. I wouldn't want her as an enemy."

"So she's a good cop. That's not exactly what I wanted to hear."

Shane shrugged.

"I didn't say she was a good cop," he said. "I said she's vicious if she thinks you're up to no good. The key with Joe is to keep her busy. You give her a rape to investigate or a missing kid to find, and she'll focus for weeks. She won't even go home. You leave her to her own devices, and she'll find things to keep herself busy. People will get hurt."

Hunter sighed and nodded. They could find her a job. There are plenty of women and kids at the Church. If they gave her a phantom to chase, she'd follow it to hell and back.

"Good. Thank you."

For the next twenty minutes, he focused on the drive. Then he pulled off the interstate near Odessa and headed north. Two hundred yards from the highway, the road turned to gravel. Flat fields surrounded him as far as he could see. No other cars moved. The landscape was forlorn.

Hunter drove for another fifteen minutes before turning down a gravel driveway. A cattle guard and barbed wire fence separated the private property from the public road. Otherwise, little changed. He drove slowly for another ten minutes before coming to a white, two-story farmhouse and beige pole barn. There were three cars in the driveway. A middle-aged couple sat on rocking chairs on the farmhouse's front porch and drank sodas straight from the can. The scene was almost idyllic in its rural simplicity. Hunter and Shane parked and walked toward the porch. The couple both stood.

"You guys thirsty?" asked the woman. She had red hair, and she wore jeans and a green sweater. Her husband was about her age—maybe forty or forty-five—and had wiry brown hair and skin cooked into an even deep tan by long hours in the sun. A chilly breeze blew.

"No, ma'am," said Hunter. "I'm Hunter Collins. My partner today is Shane Fox. A friend of mine said you were hosting a young man named Wyatt Caparaso."

The woman looked down and went inside. Her husband put his hands in his pockets.

"Damon Burke's your friend?"

Hunter nodded.

"Yeah. He's a good man."

The farmer nodded and looked down, just as his spouse had done.

"Damon is a good man, and I trust his judgment," he said. "I don't know what that boy did, but he's in the barn. My wife and I are going to go inside. You need anything, knock. Otherwise, this is your show. I'm not a part of it."

"Understood," said Hunter, nodding. "Thank you."

The farmer left. Shane cleared his throat.

"What's the plan?"

"We talk to him and solve a problem."

Shane raised his eyebrows and lowered his chin.

"What if he won't talk?"

"That's why you're here," said Hunter. "You were a cop. You've talked to uncooperative suspects before."

He looked toward the barn.

"I had a slightly different set of rules back then."

"I'm sure you can adapt," said Hunter, already leaving the porch. He crossed the gravel driveway. The pole barn had two big garage doors for trucks, tractors, and other farm equipment, as well as a normal entry door for humans. There were no windows or other exits. As long as they kept those doors shut, Wyatt would have nowhere to go.

Hunter pulled open the door and stepped inside. The cavernous interior had a rough concrete floor and spray foam insulation on the walls and ceiling. The farmer must have built furniture because he had an entire woodshop complete with a table saw, planer, jointer, and other heavy equipment. A young man sat on a white, plastic chair. He was breathing heavily. His arms and legs were secured to the chair, while duct tape kept his mouth shut. A sleeping mask covered his eyes.

"Hey, Wyatt," said Hunter, crossing the room. The kid wiggled but couldn't otherwise move. Hunter removed the mask, and Wyatt shuffled in his seat, his nostrils flaring as he breathed. Hunter held up his hands. "Easy, buddy. We're not here to hurt you. If I take this tape off, will you start screaming?"

Wyatt didn't shake his head, nod, or otherwise acknowledge the question, so Hunter waited another minute for him to calm down. Then he leaned closer.

"My name's Hunter Collins. I'm not here to hurt you. My partner is Shane Fox. He's a police officer. We're here to figure out what the hell's going on. You shot a friend of ours, and we want to know why. Can I remove the tape now?"

The kid's hands balled into fists. Slowly, he nodded, so Hunter reached to his face and peeled the tape back. To his credit, the kid didn't scream. Instead, he looked at Shane.

"You're a police officer?"

"I was," said Shane. "It's a long story. My department closed. I'm between jobs right now."

Wyatt's breath was shallow and quick.

"Breathe, kid," said Hunter, reaching into his pocket for a packet of gummy candies. "Have some of these. You'll feel better. You might have low blood sugar."

Before Wyatt could respond, Hunter pressed three into his mouth. He made a face but swallowed.

"Those tasted like weed," he said. Hunter nodded.

"They were," he said. "Like I said, they're going to make you feel better."

"How much did I take?"

Hunter raised his eyebrows and blew a raspberry, thinking.

"A hundred and twenty milligrams of THC," he said. "Like I said, you're going to feel better soon. You're a college student at Waterford, so I figured you had a tolerance built up."

"I don't smoke."

Hunter chuckled a little.

"This should be interesting, then," he said. He glanced at Shane. "My partner and I will step outside for a little while. When we return, you'll either be feeling pretty good or crying. We'll see which."

He didn't wait for Wyatt to respond before leaving the barn. Outside, Shane put his hands on his hips.

"I wish you had told me the plan was to get this kid high," he said. "I would have told you it was a bad idea. You ever interviewed a drunk before? It's not fun."

Hunter shrugged.

"We'll talk to him, but I'm not overly interested in what he has to say," he said. "The candy will keep him docile. Our job is to kill him and dump his body."

"Burke told me we were going to interrogate him."

"And we will," said Hunter. "I just don't give a shit about his answers. What's done is done. He killed Donna Wright. I don't know why the police released him. It doesn't matter. We're going to take care of him, and then we're going to pay our respects to the Wright family."

Shane agreed, and for half an hour, the two men sat in their truck while the drugs worked their way through Wy-

CHRIS CULVER

att's system. When they returned, his pupils were slightly dilated, and he had stopped fighting.

"Hey kid," said Hunter. "Why can't you ever trust trees? Because they're so shady."

Shane shook his head. Caparaso burst out laughing. Hunter looked at his partner.

"The drugs are working," he said. Shane nodded. The two men focused on Wyatt. "Why'd you kill Donna Wright?"

Wyatt narrowed his eyes and drew in a breath.

"Was that her name?"

"Yep. She was a therapist," said Hunter. "She dedicated her life to helping other people. She had two kids, too. They don't have a mom anymore."

Wyatt looked down.

"I didn't mean to kill her," he said, his voice soft. "Are her kids okay?"

"Well, you didn't kill them, so yeah," said Hunter. "Other than the fact that their mom's dead."

"Their mom's dead?"

"We established that, yes," said Hunter. "You shot her."

Wyatt didn't respond at first. Then he started sniffling.

"I didn't want to kill anybody. She tried to kill me."

"No," said Hunter. "You called her and demanded cash. If she didn't give it, you said you'd go to the police and say she trafficked in human beings."

He looked up, his eyes red.

"I didn't do that."

"Yeah, you did," said Shane. "You set up the meeting, you went to the campground, and you shot her. It's time to come clean and tell us the truth."

"No," he said, shaking his head so hard Hunter thought he might hurt himself. "I didn't set up anything. She sent me a letter and said she wanted to talk about Erik Hoyle."

Hunter furrowed his brow.

"Who's Erik Hoyle?"

"A prisoner. The cops arrested him eight years ago for raping and murdering Brittany Ashbury, but he didn't do it. I've been writing about it for the school paper."

Shane glanced at Hunter. Hunter blinked, considering.

"So you're a reporter?"

"Yeah," said Wyatt, now tears streaming down his face. "I was just trying to get into graduate school."

Shane crossed his arms.

"Why would Donna Wright know anything about Erik Hoyle?"

"I don't know, man," he said, his voice growing frantic as the drugs hit him harder. "I don't even know who Donna Wright is."

"She's the woman you murdered," said Hunter.

"I didn't murder her. She tried to kill me. What's happening?"

Hunter straightened, looked at Shane, and then nodded toward the exit. The two men left the barn. Wyatt cried inside.

"So what do you think?" asked Shane.

Hunter blinked and looked toward the barn before shaking his head.

"I don't think he's lying."

"If he didn't lure Donna Wright to the campsite, who did?"

"I don't know," said Hunter. "It doesn't matter, though. Donna had an enemy. That's her problem. Our job isn't to answer the questions. It's to keep people from asking them in the first place. We've got what we needed from him. It's time to shut this circus down."

CHAPTER 21

When I got back to my station, I went to my office and called Detective Atherton. My call went directly to voice mail. Then I called my supervisor, Lieutenant Cognata. She, at least, answered.

"Hey, this is Joe Court in St. Augustine. I need some help. I was just at Nuevo Pueblo. It's a company town in St. Augustine County, owned by Ross Kelly Farms. While there, five men surrounded me, menaced me, and told me I needed to pay a toll. To escape, I was forced to unholster my weapon and threaten to kill them."

"Okay," said Cognata, her voice sharp. "First, are you physically unharmed?"

"Physically, I'm fine. If I'm honest, though, they scared me, and I don't scare easily. They surrounded me and refused to let me leave until I threatened to use deadly force."

"Were they armed?"

"I couldn't tell," I said. "They were all wearing bulky clothing that could have concealed firearms. None of them pulled a weapon on me, but they had me outnumbered five to one. When I tried to leave, they blocked my exit."

"Did they threaten anyone else?"

"No," I said, shaking my head. "There was no one else to threaten. The town looked abandoned."

Cognata paused.

"I don't know your area, but is it usually that empty?"

"I've never seen it that empty."

She drew in a breath and paused.

"How would your department have handled this?"

I leaned back in my chair.

"The policy when making felony arrests was to utilize overwhelming numbers to reduce the chance the suspect would resist arrest and to minimize risk. In this particular case, we'd probably work with the security team at Ross Kelly Farms to monitor the situation. They've got surveillance cameras all over their property and know their workforce very well."

"Why were you there?"

I told her about my meeting with the US Attorney and my discussion with the Wrights. She already knew about the Donna Wright murder, so I didn't delve too deeply into that. When I finished speaking, she paused before speaking.

"What does Detective Atherton say?"

"She considers the investigation into Donna Wright's death closed," I said. "I've tried to contact her, but she's not taking my phone calls."

Cognata went quiet.

"That's a problem," she said, finally. "If we sent officers, what would we gain, and what are the risks?"

"I can't say with certainty," I said. "I went to Nuevo Pueblo for information. Instead, I found the entire town empty. Before I could leave, some thugs showed up and threatened me. That's all I know."

Cognata clicked her tongue a few times.

"Given the circumstances, I'm not sure that organizing a team to respond immediately would yield benefits that outweigh the risks. As you said, the company has a surveillance system that monitors the town, so their security team will know who harassed you. They'll be able to identify them for future arrest and interrogation. Does that work for you?"

It was a sensible, balanced approach that would keep people from getting hurt.

"That sounds just fine."

"Good. Make sure you write down everything you've told me and put it in a report. I want Heather Atherton to see it."

"Yes, ma'am," I said. Cognata wished me luck and told me to call if I had further questions. I thanked her and hung up. Then I got to work. I wrote a four-page report, outlining everything I had done, who I had spoken to, why I had spoken to them, and what I had hoped to do in the future. Atherton might look at it, but I doubted it. She was done with St. Augustine and with me. After that, I walked Roy.

When we got back to our station, I tried to work, but my brain felt fried. I wanted to drive home, and since I lived in a bizarro world where my badge came without duties or assignments, I could. Many people would have loved my position, but I hated it. For good or ill, my work gave my life meaning. Now I had lost that.

At least I had time to figure things out.

**

Hunter didn't like waiting, but Caparaso's parents were still awake. Caparaso was alive, but he wouldn't be for much longer. After interrogating him, Hunter and Shane had driven in separate cars to a farm owned by Caparaso's parents on the outskirts of Kansas City. It was a pretty place. The Caparasos had a big barn and a couple of pastures. Hunter would have loved a similar farm. Of course, he couldn't have afforded its multi-million-dollar price tag.

For almost two hours, Shane and Hunter had waited. The two men probably could have finished their work without Wyatt's parents noticing them, but it was better safe than sorry. Wyatt wasn't going anywhere. They had injected him with enough ketamine to keep a horse sedated. In the off chance the police ran a toxicology screen on him after his death, they'd find the drugs in his system, but both marijuana and ketamine had recreational uses. The coroner wouldn't think anything of finding them in a college kid's blood. Hunter and Shane would be just fine.

Hunter had parked a quarter mile from the Caparaso's home. Shane had driven Wyatt's Honda Accord and parked in the shadows cast by the family's barn. Thick rows of trees planted as a wind block separated the house from the rest of the farm. Tonight, they'd pull double duty and block sight-lines, too, and prevent the Caparaso's from seeing anything they ought not see.

At ten after ten, the lights in the Caparaso's home finally went out. Hunter waited a few additional minutes before sending Shane a text message.

Lights out. We're on.

He turned on his truck but kept the lights off and drove toward the barn. Caparaso's sedan was parked beside the structure. Hunter parked behind it on the gravel driveway. The barn had a rustic, wooden exterior, a sliding door for vehicles, and a regular door sized for human beings. Shane opened the smaller human-sized door and glanced around. A scintilla of light spilled outside, but Shane had smartly avoided turning on most of the barn's overhead lights.

"We're good?" he asked.

Hunter nodded and stepped inside.

"Family's out. Nobody's watching. Let's get this over with."

Hunter cast his eyes around the interior. Where a modern pole barn would have had a ceiling supported by steel trusses, the Caparaso family's timber-framed barn had thick wooden beams and even thicker wooden support poles. The hayloft held no hay, the stalls held no animals, and an old green tractor looked freshly painted and never used. This was not a working barn; this was a barn a family used a few times a year to throw parties for their dentist and doctor friends.

"You have the rope?" asked Hunter. "We can hang him from the hayloft."

Shane looked at the loft and nodded.

"The hayloft is sixteen or seventeen feet off the ground. Figure Wyatt's about six feet and two hundred pounds, we're looking at a six-foot drop. That'll give us plenty of clearance."

Hunter furrowed his brow.

"What are you talking about?"

"Hangman's table," said Shane. "It tells you how long the hanging rope should be to break the condemned man's neck instead of choking him to death."

"You've done your research," said Hunter. "You set it up. I'll write the suicide note." He had brought a notepad and pen for the occasion. He paused. "What should I say?"

Shane had already started climbing a ladder to get into the hayloft. How they would get a comatose two-hundred-pound college student up there, Hunter couldn't say, but they'd figure it out. Once he reached the top, Shane peered over the edge but quickly stepped back.

"That's a big drop."

"Yeah, so don't fall."

Shane peered over again, presumably looking for something he could tie their noose to.

"Suicide notes come in a couple of flavors," said Shane. "Some take the blame for everything wrong in their lives. Others blame everybody else. Sometimes they apologize. Sometimes they lash out. Just depends on the person."

Hunter nodded to himself.

"Wyatt's going to be apologetic, I think."

"Short and simple," said Shane, climbing down the ladder. He repositioned it in front of the hayloft to tie the rope to a support beam. Once he finished, he tugged on the knot before giving Hunter a thumbs-up. Hunter scribbled a note apologizing for what he did and saying he couldn't go on. It seemed sad enough.

The next ten minutes passed quickly. They tied a rope around Wyatt's shoulders and pulled him up the ladder as if he were a bucket of paint. He stirred but didn't have the strength to fight back. When they reached the landing, both men stood and breathed, their hands on their knees.

"I'm getting old," said Hunter.

"You and me both," said Shane, securing a noose around Wyatt's neck. "You ready?"

"Sure," said Hunter. Wyatt stirred again as the two men lifted him to his feet. The kid's eyes fluttered. He said something, but Hunter couldn't understand what. "Sorry, dude. This isn't personal."

He pushed Wyatt backward. The kid fell straight down. The rope popped. Then there was a thump. Hunter peered over the side and found a growing puddle of blood. The rope had held, but the kid's body hadn't. Instead of breaking his neck, the rope had decapitated him.

Hunter covered his eyes. Shane looked over the edge. For a moment, neither man spoke. Then Hunter sighed.

"On the plus side, he's definitely dead now," said Shane.

Hunter rubbed his eyes, nodded, and sighed again.

"Don't step in the blood. We don't want to leave any footprints," he said. "We'll wipe the ladder on our way down."

Shane agreed. Within five minutes of Wyatt's death, the two men left the barn, closed the door behind them, and started cleaning Wyatt's Honda. They couldn't leave anything identifiable behind, so they scrubbed it with the cleaning products they had brought and got in their truck. Shane drove, and Hunter called Damon Burke, his superior in the Church. The older man answered quickly.

"It's done," said Hunter. "The scene's messier than we wanted, but we didn't leave anything behind.'

"Good," said Burke. "Jeremy needs some reassurances about the operation in St. Louis. He's worried."

Jeremy had good reason to feel worried.

"I'll see him when we get home," he said. "We're about four hours out."

"He won't be here if you wait," said Burke. "Call him."

Hunter sighed. Jeremy was a lot easier to deal with before he got sober. Then, if you needed to calm him down, you handed him a bottle of cheap vodka and went on your merry way. He sighed again.

"I'll call him. If I need to, I'll visit him when we get home."

Burke hung up. Shane glanced at Hunter and started to ask something, but Hunter held up a hand, stopping him. Then he called Jeremy. The former convict answered a few minutes later.

"Hey, buddy," said Hunter, his voice soft. "What's going on? Damon told me to give you a call. You feeling okay?"

"I'm not going to jail."

Hunter forced himself to smile and hoped a little levity could brighten Jeremy's mood.

"Good. I don't want you in jail."

Jeremy scoffed.

"Don't give me that, Hunter. I've known you a long time. I know when you're talking, and I know when Burke's talking through you. This plan sucks. We're going to get caught."

"I have known you since we were kids, and I won't let you walk into something without protection," said Hunter. "And this wasn't Burke's plan. This was my plan. I've got the kinks worked out. You're going to drive an armored car, park it in a designated area, and walk away. That's it. You'll be wearing a hat, sunglasses, and a big fake beard. I will pick you up personally. Even if somebody sees you on a video camera, they're not going to recognize you. If they do, we'll get you out of the country. We have friends in Mexico. You'll live out your days on the beach. You might even meet a pretty local girl."

"I still don't like it."

Hunter drew in a breath and sighed.

"I hear you, buddy," he said, his voice still soft. "We're asking you to take a risk. I don't like it, either, but it's necessary. People think we're a joke. They think they can chew us up and spit us out. We're going to show them otherwise. Just look at our own damn county. They want our votes, but they ignore us. We'll teach them the folly of their misjudgment."

"Yeah. Then they'll come after us."

"And then they'll die," said Hunter. "This isn't a playground argument we're in. We are fighting for our survival. Make no mistake about it. Those nitwits in Jefferson City and DC would murder us in our sleep if they could. We think for ourselves. We're the enemy. They want drones, mindless idiots who eat when they say to eat and crap when they say to crap. They want to replace us. You've seen it as much as I have. We have to stop them and show them the cost of their ignorance."

Jeremy paused and sighed.

"I know, but I'm just nervous."

"That's okay," said Hunter. "I've got your back. I won't let anything happen to you. And if you can't drive, I'll use you somewhere else. You can guard the home front with my boys. You just let me know. I want volunteers, not hostages."

Jeremy went quiet for a moment.

"No. I'll drive."

"Good. We'll go over the plan tomorrow. You play one of the most important roles we've got in this whole thing. Without your truck, nothing else matters. If we do our jobs, everybody walks away a winner."

"I know," said Jeremy.

Hunter wished him well and hung up. Then he rubbed his cheek and sighed. He hated lying, especially about this. Jeremy was about to be sacrificed by some of his oldest friends. Even though it was necessary, it made Hunter feel sick.

Chapter 22

I liked my bed, but I had never loved wallowing in bed. My little sister could lounge in bed all day. It wasn't because she was depressed or sick. She just liked it. She could sit around, alone with her thoughts, for hours. I had tried it a few times, but my brain never shut down long enough for it to become enjoyable. I'd always think about paperwork I needed to complete or the yard I needed to mow or the kitchen I needed to clean.

Relaxing was hard. As a child, if I had relaxed, we wouldn't have had food in the house. My biological mother could go days, seemingly, without food. I had to beg for it from restaurants and food banks. My mother drank most of her calories and took vitamins. It wasn't a healthy lifestyle, but she didn't care. I didn't realize it at the time, but my mother had only truly lived in those few moments after she returned from an extended period in jail or rehab. Then, she could be kind and thoughtful. She had given me hugs then.

My biological mother could never step away from drugs. Heroin, marijuana, cocaine, alcohol... I had seen my mother use them all. When she was using, she didn't really live, she just took up space. She was there, but only physically. On those days, I had to become the parent. It was a lot for a child to handle. Then, she lost me for good.

For years, I had bounced from foster home to foster home, and for years, I had taken care of myself. You couldn't tell a good foster home from a bad foster home from the outside, so you never knew when your foster dad would "accidentally" walk in on you in the shower or when your foster brother would try to grope you in the garage. So, I remained on guard and looked for work. In my experience, the harder I worked, the better people treated me. I had never become part of the family—until my adoptive parents made me so—but if I volunteered to do the dishes or fold the laundry, sometimes my foster mother would look out for me.

Audrey, my sister, was sweet, kind, and fun. She knew how to relax. Her entire life, Audrey had been loved and protected. She was pregnant now, and she would love and protect her child so that he or she could learn to relax. Her little girl or little boy could learn to be comfortable with their quiet thoughts. I already envied them.

As I rolled around in bed and tried to laze my way through the morning, my dog lifted his head and furrowed his brow at me. He couldn't speak, obviously, but his confused look said enough: I was doing it wrong. Roy knew how to relax. Sometimes that involved rolling around, but usually it meant sitting in one spot and watching the world pass.

Finally, I sighed and kicked my legs off the side of the bed. It was 8:30. I should have been at work. Barring that, Roy and I should have been exercising outside. Instead, I wore flannel pajama pants and a T-shirt. Roy tilted his head to the side.

"This is our life, dude," I said. "Get used to it. I am now a woman of leisure."

Even Roy didn't believe that. He lowered his head and closed his eyes while I showered and made coffee. Before I could even get dressed, my phone rang. The number belonged to Detective Atherton. I groaned and rubbed my eyes.

"Oh, what fresh hell is this?" I asked Roy.

I answered and held the phone to my ear.

"This is Joe Court," I said. "What can I do for you?"

"Wyatt Caparaso is dead."

It took a moment to process her words. Then I sat down heavily on the bed.

"Oh."

"It's ugly," said Atherton. "He committed suicide in his parents' barn. Since you worked Donna Wright's murder, I thought I'd let you know."

I exhaled slowly.

"Do we have officers on-site?"

"The Blue Springs Police Department does," she said. "It's their jurisdiction, and they haven't asked us for help."

I nodded, stood, and grabbed a blouse from my closet.

"Are you there already?"

She chortled.

"No," she said. "It's a suicide. I'm calling you as a courtesy to let you know the Donna Wright case is closed and to tell you to stop looking into it. Her murderer is dead." Atherton paused. "What would I even do there?"

"Thank you for your call," I said before hanging up. Blue Springs was a little over four hours from my house. When I investigated a suspicious death case, I'd probably keep a team at the death scene for most of a day, but I didn't know how meticulous the officers at Blue Springs would be over a suspected suicide. It meant I needed to get there sooner rather than later.

I grabbed Roy's leash, and headed out to my station. My Volvo was a fine vehicle, but today, I needed something that could move through traffic faster, so I signed out a marked SUV and headed out. Roy sat on the back seat, his harness secured to the seat belt. Usually, I liked having him on a hammock, but he seemed content on a bench seat.

With my marked SUV, traffic parted in front of me, allowing me to make good time. About halfway to the Caparaso's house, I called the Blue Springs Police Department to let them know I was on my way and that I could have information pertinent to their investigation into Caparaso's death. The deputy chief wished me well and told me she'd call the detectives on scene to let them know to expect me.

A little over an hour after my call, I slowed as I neared the farm. The Caparaso's lived on a picturesque stretch of wooded property southeast of town. Blue Springs was twenty miles east of Kansas City, so a significant portion of its population likely commuted into the city for work. Still, it felt rural. The houses had big lawns, and swaths of trees and fields stretched to the horizon. It was a pretty place.

I turned into the gravel driveway. A uniformed officer stood on the grass. I slowed and opened my window.

"You the detective from St. Louis?"

"St. Augustine," I said. "I'm Joe Court. I hear you have a body."

"We do," he said, nodding and handing me a clipboard with a log sheet. I signed my name and gave them my badge number with the highway patrol. He looked it over and nodded. "The scene's gory, just to let you know. I almost lost my breakfast when I saw it."

If it was gory, he must have shot himself.

"Who found him?" I asked.

The officer raised his eyebrows.

"His dad," he said. "We took him to the ER afterward because we thought he had a heart attack."

"That poor man," I said, sighing. "Thank you. Where's the barn? I'd like to see the scene."

He pointed down a gravel road to the right. I thanked him and put the SUV in gear. I couldn't see the barn from my position, so I followed the gravel road through the woods to a clearing. There, I found two white SUVs and a minivan from the Jackson County Coroner's office. I parked near the SUVs and hung my badge on a lanyard around my neck. A thin, tall man in gray slacks, a white shirt, and a striped tie stepped out of the barn. He wore a pistol on his hip and a gold badge on a chain around his neck. The sun glinted off his bald head. As he walked toward me, he extended a hand.

"James Hawthorne," he said. "Deputy Chief said somebody named Joe was coming by. Is that you?"

"It is," I said, shaking his hand. "Joe Court. I'm with the highway patrol."

His eyes flicked over my shoulder to my St. Augustine SUV as he raised his eyebrows.

"How does the St. Augustine Sheriff's Department fit into this?"

I tilted my head to the side.

"It's a long story," I said. "The short of it is that the St. Augustine County Sheriff's Department no longer exists. When it's reconstituted, I'll be its first employee. It's complicated and not particularly interesting."

"I'll take your word for that," he said. "What do you know about Mr. Caparaso?"

"Before he died, we had an arrest warrant out for him," I said. "He killed a woman named Donna Wright in St. Augustine." I nodded toward the barn. "You mind if I take a look?"

"Have at it," he said. "Our coroner's already taken the body, but we've got pictures."

I told him I appreciated that. Then we walked inside. The barn was cavernous and pretty. It had thick timbers and a loft. A noose hung from a beam beneath the hayloft. Beneath it, a puddle of blood had stained the wooden floor. A young woman and an older man walked toward us. Both wore windbreakers that indicated they worked in the coroner's office. A uniformed officer stood in the loft. He had a flashlight, which made me think he was looking for trace evidence.

I nodded to the two civilians from the coroner's office.

"Caparaso hanged himself, right?" I asked. The older man nodded. "Where'd the blood come from, then?"

The young woman looked down. The older man shuffled.

"My guess is that the victim placed the noose around his neck and jumped from the hayloft. The force of impact when the rope grew taut separated his head from his body."

"Whoa," I said. "I didn't realize that was possible."

"A weight dropped from a height can generate an awful lot of force," said the coroner.

"Any signs of a struggle? Bruises, scratch marks, skin cells beneath his fingers?"

The coroner clicked his tongue and looked at his assistant. She stepped forward.

"He had ligature marks on his wrists, but they looked as if they had been partially healed."

I nodded.

"We arrested him in St. Augustine a few days ago, so we had him in handcuffs. That could have come from them."

"We'll take a look at him in the lab and run a full tox screen on his blood," said the coroner. "With more information, we'll decide our next move."

I thanked them and gave them my card so they could forward me their report. Then the two of them left. I looked at Hawthorne.

"My theory was that Caparaso had a mental breakdown when he shot Donna Wright. I've got audio of him confessing to shooting her, I've got the gun he used, and I've got his shirt. It had blood on it, which, I think, we'll match to her. He had gunshot residue on his hands as well. If he were alive, we'd have him dead to rights."

Hawthorne blinked and drew in a breath. Then he narrowed his eyes.

"Maybe I'm confused, but if he confessed to shooting a woman, why wasn't he in custody?"

"That's another long story," I said. "We've been looking for him."

Hawthorne looked toward the loft.

"You think he was depressed?"

"I don't know," I said. "I haven't had a lot of cooperation. Have you talked to his parents?"

Hawthorne grunted.

"Yeah. They're angry and blame us. The only thing they've told me is that they plan to sue me for everything I've got. They'll also sue my boss, and my department."

I looked toward the exit.

"You mind if I talk to them?"

"I don't know if they'll be interested, but good luck."

I thanked him and left the barn. Then I walked down the gravel driveway, past the entrance, to a sprawling single-story brick home with a fountain in the front lawn. A uniformed officer stood on the front porch. As I introduced myself to him, the front door opened and a middle-aged couple stepped out. They looked at me, and their eyes narrowed. I shifted awkwardly.

"Mr. and Mrs. Caparaso, I'm Joe Court and I work for the—"

Before I could finish speaking, Mrs. Caparaso stepped forward and slapped me hard enough that stars briefly shone in my eyes. I could taste blood. I staggered backward, and the uniformed officer immediately grabbed me before I could stumble off the porch.

"Whoa, whoa, whoa," he said, holding up a hand toward the Caparasos. "That's enough. Back off right now."

I stood and blinked, surprised.

"You need to sit down?" asked the officer, removing his arm from my shoulder. I shook my head. "I'm going to call my CO and see how he wants to handle this."

I swallowed and shook my head again.

"That's unnecessary," I said. "I'm not pressing charges. I'm here for information."

"We're not talking to you," said Mrs. Caparaso, her nostrils flaring. "You murdered our son."

I focused on the couple. I hadn't expected anyone to hit me and hadn't braced myself at all. My head felt light, but my vision was clear. My initial dizziness passed quickly. I hoped I didn't have a concussion.

"I'm very sorry for your loss, but I assure you that I did not kill your son," I said. "I was in St. Augustine until recently. Have you seen the note Wyatt left?"

Mrs. Caparaso looked away. Her husband nodded before looking down.

"We did," he said. "Detective Hawthorne showed it to us."

"Did it look like your son's handwriting?"

He hesitated.

"Who else's handwriting would it be?"

"I'm not speculating," I said, shaking my head. "I'm asking whether it looked like his handwriting."

"Of course it was his," said Mrs. Caparaso. I nodded, already planning to swing by Waterford College and see if I could get a sample of his handwriting.

"Has he seemed depressed lately?"

"My son was fine until he met you," said Mrs. Caparaso. "He was a good man. I hope someone ruins your life the way you've ruined ours."

I nodded and stepped back.

"Thank you for your time, ma'am."

Mrs. Caparaso said something, but I ignored her and walked back to the barn. Detective Hawthorne's eyes zeroed in on my cheek, and he quirked an eyebrow.

"You all right?"

"Yeah, I'm fine. Thank you," I said. "Mrs. Caparaso wasn't cooperative. I'll take pictures and drive home. There's nothing for me here."

"I appreciate you coming by, but I think we've got a suicide. It's a tragedy, but I don't see anything nefarious."

I nodded and sighed.

"You're probably right. I'll make this quick."

Chapter 23

By all appearances, Wyatt Caparaso drove home, hid in his barn, wrote a suicide note, and hanged himself—ostensibly because he was driven to it by the investigation into Donna Wright's death. He didn't check in with his parents, lawyer, girlfriend, or roommates. Instead, he disappeared for at least twenty-four hours. Then he killed himself.

As the primary suspect in a murder investigation, Wyatt was under stress, but he had resources, family, and a lawyer. Moreover, he had a very strong defense. He claimed someone had lured him to the campsite where he shot Donna Wright and that she had attacked him unprovoked. If true, he would have walked. Missouri had a stand-your-ground law. We would have let him go.

I suspected he was mentally ill, but no one would confirm it. He had a bright future. He was preparing applications to go to graduate school and working to create the best application he could by writing articles for his college newspaper.

Those were acts of hope, not desperation. None of this sat well with me.

Detective Hawthorne saw a young man's body, a noose, and a suicide letter. He drew the obvious conclusion that Wyatt had killed himself. He may have been right, but I wasn't willing to close this yet.

I looked at Detective Hawthorne.

"How'd Caparaso get here?"

He pointed toward a gravel parking pad near the barn.

"He's got the Honda," he said. "We already searched it, but there wasn't much to see."

I nodded and walked across the drive to the parking pad. There, I pulled a pair of polypropylene gloves from my purse and snapped them onto my fingers before peering into the windows. The interior was immaculate. I looked over at Hawthorne.

"You guys checked the doors for fingerprints?"

He hesitated and crossed his arms.

"I didn't see the need."

I nodded.

"Would you like me to?"

He scowled and called his uniformed officer from inside the barn. He came out a few moments later with a finger-print kit. I watched over his shoulder as he worked, but I didn't pay much attention until he grunted.

"I'm not getting anything. You didn't touch the door handle, did you, miss?"

"I did not," I said. "Try the other doors and the trunk."

He agreed and moved on to the other doors. Hawthorne crossed the gravel, an intrigued expression replacing his annoyed one. We watched the uniformed officer once more fail to find a single print.

"Was it cold enough here to wear gloves recently?" I asked. Hawthorne shook his head.

"It's been chilly but not that cold," he said.

"This is a college kid's car. We should find prints from roommates, girlfriends, strangers, fraternity brothers, everybody on campus," I said, looking at the car. "Did you open the trunk?"

He nodded.

"We found a jack, a little shovel, a ten-pound bag of sand, and a blanket. I put a similar winter kit in my kid's car in case she got stuck in the snow."

"You find any organic matter? Blood, feces, anything like that?"

Hawthorne blinked a few times and then shook his head.

"It looked like a suicide," he said, already walking to his SUV. He removed a filled evidence bag from the back. Inside, he had Wyatt's keys and key fob. The trunk popped open as soon as he touched the button. Like the car's interior, the trunk was clean. I wrinkled my nose.

"Do you smell that?"

Hawthorne took a whiff.

"Smells like a swimming pool."

I agreed and asked him if he had any luminol. He sighed once more and returned to his SUV. A moment later, he returned with a clear spray bottle and a UV light. He sprayed the interior with a liquid and popped the light on. The carpet lit up in a uniform bluish green. Hawthorne glanced at me.

"This is luminol," he said. "It's only supposed to show blood. This must be a bad batch."

"Your luminol is fine," I said. "This isn't blood. Somebody cleaned the entire trunk with bleach. In the presence of luminol, the bleach oxidizes. The electrons get excited and release energy as a photon. That's what we're seeing. I'm guessing we'd see the same thing on the car's interior if we sprayed it."

Hawthorne put his hands on his hips.

"So somebody cleaned the entire interior with bleach. They wouldn't do that at the car wash, would they?"

I shook my head.

"Bleach is caustic, and it'll change the color of too many fabrics," I said. "You should consider taking the car to a controlled environment where a forensics team can search it more thoroughly. This isn't right."

Hawthorne nodded but said nothing.

"Did you find gloves in the barn?"

Hawthorne sighed.

"No."

I nodded and started walking toward the building. Hawthorne followed. I stopped just inside the door and surveyed the interior.

"So walk me through your thoughts here," I said. "You walked in and found Wyatt's body and a noose. It looked like a suicide, right?"

Hawthorne nodded.

"That's right."

I pointed toward a long aluminum ladder on the ground.

"And where was that?"

"Right where it is now," said Hawthorne. "We didn't touch it."

I furrowed my brow.

"You had an officer in the hayloft earlier. How'd he get up there?"

"There are stairs along the back wall," he said. "You can't see them from here."

"Why would the ladder be there, then?" I asked, my voice soft.

Hawthorne walked toward the ladder and then walked its length.

"It's eight of my steps long," he said. "That's about twenty feet. If you put it up, I bet it would get you into the hayloft."

I considered, but the details weren't making sense just yet. Years ago, I had painted the exterior of my house, and I had dreaded every day of it because I, being an idiot, had purchased a heavy, professional-grade ladder that came with a lifetime warranty. It must have weighed seventy pounds and had a pulley system on it that would allow a roofer to pull boxes of shingles to the roof. The Caparaso's had a similar model. Why would Wyatt set up a heavy ladder if there were stairs?

"How long was the rope he used to hang himself?"

"About six feet," said Hawthorne.

"Would a six-foot drop tear his head off?"

Hawthorne said nothing for a moment.

"You'd have to ask the coroner," he said.

I nodded, thinking.

"The rope is six feet. Could someone have pushed Wyatt from the hayloft while he was standing? If he jumped off the ladder, he'd drop just the six feet of the rope. If he jumped or was pushed from the hayloft while standing, the drop would be considerably longer. It'd develop more force."

Hawthorne crossed his arms.

"That'd explain why his head popped off, maybe."

"It wouldn't explain the ladder, though," I said, my voice so soft it was almost a whisper. I covered my mouth with my hand as my mind made connections. "So here's what I'm thinking. We were supposed to walk in here and see Wyatt's car outside and his body hanging from the hayloft. We were supposed to find a ladder on the ground and believe Wyatt had driven himself here, climbed that ladder, tied the noose around a support beam and his neck, and then kicked the ladder away. We'd find the suicide note, feel bad for his family, and move on.

"Wyatt's murderers botched it, though. They carried him to the hayloft and pushed him over the edge, which added height to the drop. Instead of merely breaking his neck, the force ripped his head completely off. They kicked the ladder over anyway, hoping we'd believe Wyatt kicked it over on his way down. They didn't know there were stairs along the back wall. Wyatt, having lived here, obviously would.

"They cleaned Wyatt's car because they drove it and didn't want to leave trace evidence inside. He was probably tied up in the trunk. They had to drive it, though, so it would seem plausible that he hanged himself. I don't think they expected us to examine it closely."

Hawthorne looked down and shifted his weight.

"We wouldn't have had a reason to look at it closely," he said. "This looked like a suicide. We had a note. His parents confirmed that it was his handwriting. He was a confessed murderer. Suicide fit the profile and evidence."

"Except that he wasn't a murderer," I said. "He claimed he shot Donna Wright in self-defense."

Hawthorne sighed.

"So who killed Caparaso?"

I glanced at him and shook my head.

"I have no idea."

CHAPTER 24

L isa was beautiful. Hunter had known her since she was fourteen. Then, he had been eighteen and a senior in high school. He had felt like her older brother. When the Army shipped him to Afghanistan, she had cried. He told her he'd miss her but that he'd return. He had thought she was worried for a friend. Later, he learned her worries had run deeper than that.

She wrote to him and called when she could. He wrote her long, almost embarrassingly sentimental letters back. He opened up to her. Hunter had loved another girl, but he had lost her. Lisa was different. In his letters to Lisa, Hunter had been honest. He allowed himself to be vulnerable. He had allowed her to become family.

They'd see each other when he visited, but they were just friends. When the Army finally finished with him and Hunter returned home for good, Lisa had stopped looking like a friend or a sister. She had grown. She kissed him, and he kissed her. From that moment, he had loved her and would do anything for her. He thought she felt the same.

Today, they were sitting on her parents' porch on the farm. Lisa's father—Elder Damon Burke—and her mother were inside, washing the lunch dishes. Hunter held Lisa's hand and felt the swing sway in the crisp fall breeze and realized that this was his perfect day. Lisa leaned her full weight against him.

"My roommate is visiting her parents," said Lisa. "How about you stay over tonight? Assuming you and Daddy aren't busy."

Lisa and another girl rented a house in town. It wasn't a nice house, but it was clean and safe. One day, he'd build them both a house on the farm, where they could raise their kids. He tilted his head down and inhaled the sweet, clean scent of her hair. Then he squeezed her hand.

"I'd like that," he said.

She went quiet.

"Are you and Dad okay?" she asked.

He didn't say anything, and she shifted and sat upright.

"What do you mean?" he asked, finally. She looked him in the eye.

"Some days, you spend more time with my dad than my mom does. You didn't come home last night until late. I was worried."

He sighed and gently squeezed her hand.

"Shane and I were out near Kansas City visiting some Church members on their farm. They were worried about something in their barn. We took care of it for them."

Lisa raised her eyebrows.

"You sure you weren't visiting a girl?"

He smiled.

"I like to think I would have remembered that," he said, winking. "And I'm pretty sure I wouldn't have taken Shane."

She laughed and leaned against him once more and sighed contentedly.

"Did Daddy send you?"

He almost didn't answer.

"Yeah," he said.

He could almost feel the tension pass through her. She squeezed his hand tighter.

"This project you two are doing, are you going to get hurt?"

"No, ma'am," he said.

"People are going to die, though."

It wasn't a question, so he said nothing. She nodded.

"That's what I thought," she said. "Are you free this afternoon? I was thinking of driving you to the courthouse and marrying you before you, Shane, and Daddy run off into the sunset together and do something stupid."

His smile turned bemused.

"Don't worry. Neither Shane nor your dad are my type. I'm all yours."

"We should do it soon," she said, nodding. She smiled, but he could feel her trembling. "Otherwise, I'm going to start showing. People tend to judge when they see a pregnant bride."

Hunter's breath caught in his throat. She looked at him and blinked. He could feel her body shake.

"Please say something, sweetheart," she whispered.

He hugged her tight.

"I'm going to build you a house. It'll have a yard and swings and a big porch. We're going to grow old together, and we're going to be happy. You think our kids'll want a dog? I bet they will. I'll build a doghouse, too."

"You mean that?" she asked.

"I do," he said. "I'm going to be a dad."

"And I'll be a mom."

She settled against him once more. Her trembling subsided. He squeezed her tight and whispered that he loved her. She said the same. For twenty minutes, their lives were perfect.

Then Damon Burke walked out.

"Am I interrupting something?" he asked.

"I just asked Hunter to marry me," said Lisa. "We're going to run off together and elope."

"Sounds fun," said Burke. "Before you go, Hunter and I have a project to finish."

Lisa sat upright.

"I wasn't kidding, Daddy," she said. "We're going to get married. Soon. Maybe today or tomorrow."

Burke looked at Hunter.

"Hunter's a fine man," he said, "but we've got work." Burke straightened. "Would have been nice if somebody told me you two planned to get married. We could have planned a party."

"There'll be time for that," said Lisa. "We've got our whole lives."

"You do, sweetie," said Burke. "I'm happy for you, but your fiancé and I have an appointment this afternoon. We can't miss it."

Lisa sighed and gripped Hunter's hand tighter.

"Daddy, tell me you're not going to get hurt."

Burke considered his daughter. Then he looked at Hunter.

"We'll do our best," he said. "Beyond that, I can't make promises."

She shook her head.

"I don't like you two sneaking around," said Lisa. "You're not soldiers. You're my family."

"That's where you're wrong," said Burke, his voice soft. "Today, everybody on this farm is a soldier, you included. If we don't fight today, we damn our children and grandchildren to a lifetime of fighting. We all know what happened to Randy Weaver. I refuse to let history repeat itself."

Weaver had been a former soldier who realized he lived within a corrupt, barbaric world and decided he had had enough. He had moved his family to a homestead in Idaho so that he and his wife could raise their children in a safe, nurturing environment. The Weavers had little money, and they didn't live in a fancy house with modern conveniences. They didn't need those things. They had the essentials: food, water, and shelter. They had each other.

The Weavers didn't look like the average American family. They were religious, God-fearing people who wanted to be left alone. The US government, though, is a jealous, scornful thing. She'll turn a blind eye to murder and theft on a grand scale, but the moment you tell the government no, the moment you turn your back on it, she'll strike you and your family down with her full force.

The government came for the Weaver family on August 21, 1992. Three US Marshals trespassed upon the Weaver's property. They had no warrant or permission, but they came anyway. On the property, they came across the Weaver's fourteen-year-old son, Sammy, a family friend, Kevin Harris, and the family dog, Striker. Sammy and Kevin were hunting, trying to put food on the family's table. Those government agents shot Sammy in the back. He wasn't a threat. He wasn't even looking at them. He was a scared child who tried to run from a monster, and they murdered him in cold blood. They killed the family dog and fired on Kevin Harris, too. Harris returned fire and killed one of the Marshals.

Randy and Kevin retrieved Sammy's body and put him in a shed. The government didn't even let the Weavers bury their boy. Instead, they surrounded the property. Hundreds of special agents came, all under the supervision of the FBI.

On August 22, 1992, an FBI sniper shot Randy as he went to see his boy's body. He was unarmed and grieving the death of his child. That same sniper then shot Vicki Weaver in her home. She was holding her ten-month-old child. She wasn't a threat to anybody. She was a mom, trying to do her best, and an FBI sniper murdered her with a weapon of war. That sniper was charged with manslaughter, but the government refused to send one of its own to prison. There was no justice for Vicki Weaver.

On August 21, 1992, the US government declared war on the Weaver family. They fired the first shots, they congregated at Ruby Ridge, and they murdered innocent people. Unknown to them, they woke up a sleeping dragon that day. Hunter's parents had told him the story. When he and Lisa had children, they'd tell them the same story. The events of that day seared themselves into Hunter's consciousness and made him the person he was.

The world was a brutal place. The men and women who were supposed to protect the innocent were savage murderers. No one could reason with a monster. Like a rabid dog, you couldn't trust it. Monsters never ceased being a threat until you slayed them. This was a fight for survival against a superior, malignant force. In that kind of fight, tactics mattered more than morality.

"Your daddy's right," said Hunter, looking at his fiancé. "I wish he weren't, but we're all soldiers today, and we have a mission."

"What's your appointment this afternoon?" asked Lisa. "You said you two were doing something."

Hunter glanced at Burke. The older man shrugged. Lisa would be his wife soon. She deserved the truth.

"A test," said Hunter. "The boys are mixing ANFO in a cave on Connor Wright's farm. We want to get the mixture right. We just got in a couple of barrels of racing fuel, too. Our chemist says it'll produce a stronger shockwave. I don't know the chemistry of it, myself."

Lisa furrowed her brow.

"What's ANFO?"

"Ammonium nitrate and fuel oil," said Burke. "It's an explosive device."

Lisa crossed her arms.

"What are you going to blow up?"

"The one thing the US government cares about most," said Burke. "Their money."

Lisa chuckled and shook her head.

"Is that all?" she asked.

"It's a start," said Burke. "You two lovebirds spend some time together while you can. We don't have many carefree afternoons left."

Chapter 25

I spent an hour in the Caparaso's barn and another half hour looking at pictures. My conviction only grew stronger: Wyatt was murdered. It took some prodding, but Detective Hawthorne seemed to agree with me. Unfortunately, Caparaso wasn't the only murder victim I had to contend with. Donna Wright was murdered, too, but not directly. Her killer used Wyatt as a weapon and aimed him right at her.

But why?

I stood outside the Caparaso's barn and flipped through my notepad as I tried to put my thoughts in order. According to Wyatt, he was lured to a campground in St. Augustine. So was Donna Wright. Donna then attacked Wyatt, and he responded by killing her. Then two children dressed as hunters—those were Wyatt's words—shot at him. The story got me thinking. What if Wyatt was the target? Or what if there was no target? What if this was a random mess?

I had two dead people, and neither of their deaths made sense. Donna Wright's family helped illegal migrants disappear. They might have made enemies with the resources to kill her, but would those motivated, resourceful enemies lure her to a campground on the off chance that Wyatt Caparaso would shoot her? That made absolutely no sense.

And Wyatt Caparaso...who would want him dead? He was just a college student. If someone wanted him dead, they could have shot him at home. Instead, they lured him to a campground, where he shot Donna Wright. Why? Was he supposed to die there? If so, why would our mastermind lure Donna and Wyatt both to the campground? It added uncertainty and risk. Once again, none of this made sense.

Our killer was either incredibly stupid or far smarter than me. Given that we had two bodies on the ground and had spent considerable resources to little avail, I leaned toward the latter.

I squeezed my jaw tight and forced myself to focus on those things we did know. First, Caparaso's killer knew what he was doing...sort of. He screwed up the hanging, but he wiped down the ladder and Caparaso's car to keep us from discovering his identity. All considered, he was a talented amateur.

Second, the killer knew Caparaso and Donna Wright well enough to lure them to the campground. That was significant.

Third....I didn't have a third yet. I had investigated these cases for days, and I barely knew more than I did when I started. Worse, Detective Atherton had already closed the murder investigation into Donna Wright's death, so realistically, I had no business even being in Blue Springs.

Roy and I walked around the barn to give me some time to think. I had a dead college student and a dead mom, and I couldn't do a damn thing about either. Worse, I didn't know my next move. That wouldn't change by walking around the barn aimlessly, so I found Detective Hawthorne and handed him my business card.

"I'm going to head out. You've got my number if you need anything. If you solve this one, give me a call."

He nodded, thanked me, and wished me well. I said likewise before getting Roy in the car. We took our time going home and stopped at a rest area for a quick walk. It was fully dark by the time we reached St. Augustine, and I was tired. I dropped off the marked SUV, picked up my Volvo, and drove home, done for the day.

The next morning, I walked Roy, got dressed, and drove to the office. By 8:30, I had brewed coffee and surveyed the building to make sure it was secure, thereby completing my to-do list. I wanted to dive into my cases and get my hands dirty. I wanted to investigate and knock on doors. I wanted to put the world right. Donna Wright should have hugged her kids that morning and kissed her husband. Instead, she was dead. Wyatt Caparaso should have been in class. Barring that, he should have been sleeping off a hangover.

These people mattered. We knew Donna Wright's killer, but that didn't mean we understood her death. The murder of a loved one could never be put right with information, but it could be understood, and that understanding could provide comfort. We had too many open questions to close Donna's investigation. Her family deserved better. Wyatt Caparaso's family did, too.

My job as a police officer gave me power civilians didn't have. That power wasn't mine to own; it was given to me in trust in the expectation that I would use it to the best of my ability to keep people safe and to send bad guys to jail. If I didn't do those things, I didn't deserve my badge. Detective Atherton did the bare minimum to investigate Donna Wright's death. That wasn't good enough.

Unfortunately, I no longer had the authority to do anything about it. It made me feel sick.

I grabbed a clipboard, my cell phone, and a label maker, but couldn't force myself to go to yet another storage closet. For a few minutes, I just sat in my office chair. Then I kicked back from my desk as hard as I could. The carpet kept me from rolling too far, so I put my clipboard and label maker down and went to the lobby.

The terrazzo marble floor was slick and expansive. I grabbed a chair from the front desk and pushed off as hard as I could from the receptionist's desk. I didn't exactly rocket across the floor, but I got some speed up, and I didn't fall over. It was silly and childish but weirdly fun. The government had taken everything important from me but left me with a gigantic building with slick, level floors, and dozens of office chairs. My job was pointless. Maybe it was time to have some fun at work.

For twenty minutes, I raced my office chair across the lobby. At first, Roy looked at me as if I were crazy, but then he started chasing me and barking playfully. My lips curled upward as a weight started lifting from me. I laughed and held my arms out as if I were flying. Then I hit the front desk and fell over. Roy licked my face and danced around my body, clearly agitated. I laughed again and sat up and took his head between my hands.

"What are you looking at, Roy?"

He licked his nose and looked away from me. I stroked the fur on his neck.

"You're a good boy," I said.

"He is a good boy," came a familiar, southern drawl from near the building's front door. "You okay on the floor?"

I slowly stood and dusted myself off. Sophie Marie Hitler had entered my station. Sophie was... well, I really didn't know how to characterize her. She was my age, and she lived at the Church of the White Steeple. She had a child with the Church's elderly and now deceased founder, Richard Clarke. Even though she lived in a church full of racists, I had never heard her speak ill of anyone of any race, creed, or ideology. Sophie accepted her world and her place in it. Her blonde hair was always swept back from her face in a pony-tail, and her clothes—while not always fashionable—were always neat and clean. In all the times I had seen her, I had never seen bruises or injuries anywhere on her, and in every meeting, she had been unfailingly kind.

"Hey, Sophie," I said. "I was just testing out my office chair."

"I see," she said, smiling. "And how did it perform?"

"Well, I think," I said. "I don't have a lot to compare it to."

"Got another chair, then? Together, we can whip up some of that comparative performance data you need."

I kept the smile on my face but shook my head.

"You didn't come here to race me on office chairs," I said. "What can I do for you?"

She looked into my eyes, her expression soft.

"I didn't come here to race you on chairs, but it looked like you were having fun," she said. "I suspect office chair racing is even more fun with a friend."

I considered her and then drew a breath before speaking. Sophie was naive and kind. I liked her, but she lived on the grounds of a church that protested at funerals, that demanded we segregate our school system, that treated people like animals because of the color of their skin. We'd never be friends. It was best to nip that possibility early.

"I visit you when I need information about your church. You visit me when you or your church needs help with something in St. Augustine. We're friendly, but we're not friends."

Sophie almost looked hurt. I cleared my throat.

"What can I help you with?" I asked.

She blinked and looked away.

"There aren't many women in town our age. I'm sorry. I guess I overstepped and presumed something that wasn't true."

"It's for the best," I said. "I won't be here too much longer anyway."

"Must be exciting," she said, nodding. "Moving on from all this."

I lowered my chin and my voice.

"I lost my job. It's not exciting," I said. "My entire department fell apart. I lost everything that mattered to me. This isn't something I wanted. This was forced on me."

She nodded.

"I'm sorry," she said.

"Me, too," I said. I almost left the conversation there, but I could feel something welling up in me. "You're here because you want something. Nobody comes here just to see me. So just tell me what you want."

She straightened.

"I didn't think you'd be angry to see me."

I forced myself to smile.

"Sorry. Maybe I'm just angry today."

She hesitated but then shook her head.

"You're not mean," she said. "This isn't you talking. What's really going on?"

I squeezed my jaw tight and held my breath, expecting her to get the hint and leave. When she didn't, I shrugged.

"Okay. Sure. Fine," I said. "You want to hear what's really bothering me? You want to pretend we're friends? Fine. I'm angry and I'm hurt. I love my job, and I lost it. Nothing I do is ever good enough. Somebody always screws it up. I put the bad guys in jail and even tried cleaning this shithole up. Dave Skelton, one of my former colleagues, is in prison now for murdering a guy named Mannie Gutierrez. He confessed. He even had the murder weapon. Skelton didn't murder anybody, though. He was covering for his son. Dave took the fall because he was a shitty father and hoped a grand gesture could put years of neglect right. Marcus Washington and Bob Reitz, two of my colleagues, two of my friends, tried to cover it up."

My lower lip quivered, and my vision grew watery. Sophie just stood there.

"They stacked up the evidence in front of me and pointed at it as if I were some kind of robot."

I went quiet for a moment. Sophie said nothing.

"They used me. My own friends, people I respected... they used me. When I found out, I forced them to resign. I didn't have the evidence to arrest them, but they didn't deserve to have a badge. I did the right thing. Then everybody else quit, too. They knew me. They knew what it'd be like if I were in charge. And they left. All of them. My friends. They abandoned me."

I squeezed my jaw tight, hoping she'd snap at me. I wanted an excuse to scream. I wanted someone to hurt like I did. Sophie considered me. Then she looked down.

"That's unfair. Your friends shouldn't have treated you like that."

The bitter, rancorous edge of my anger left me. I shook my head.

"You shouldn't be here. Just go, Sophie."

She raised her eyebrows.

"Is that what you really want?"

"I want you to call me an asshole and storm out. I want to be alone. Please."

She shook her head.

"You're not an asshole. You were kind of acting like one, but there's a big difference between acting like an asshole and actually being one. Trust me. I know assholes. Since you're leaving town, where are you going to go?"

I shrugged and sighed.

"Nowhere fast."

Sophie nodded and walked toward me. I quirked an eyebrow, unsure what she was going to do, but then she plopped down in my office chair and white-knuckled the arms.

"Since you're not going anywhere, how about you push me as fast as you can down the hallway? Let's see what this bad boy can do with a determined woman behind it."

I chuckled and shook my head.

"You still want to race on my office chair?"

"It's either that or we find an open liquor store and buy some wine," she said. "I'm up for either, but day care closes at four, and I've got to watch my kid afterward."

I gripped the back of the chair and gave it a shove. It was harder to move than I expected.

"You're heavier than you look."

She looked over her shoulder at me.

"I am a mom," she said. "I carry the weight of the world. Now get a speed gun and put your back into it. Let's see if we can break ten miles an hour. Pretty sure you'll feel better."

CHAPTER 26

I spent well over an hour with Sophie. We didn't push each other on office chairs. Instead, we sat and drank coffee in the break room. Sophie and I had spoken dozens of times, but we had never sat down for an actual conversation. It was different than I had expected. Every previous time we had a conversation, it had invariably ended with her saying something so outlandish and crazy that it left me flummoxed. Now, she seemed so...normal.

Eventually, the pauses in our conversation grew longer, and I cleared my throat.

"Can I ask you a personal question, Sophie?" I asked.

"Only if I can ask you one in return," she said. I nodded. "Go ahead."

"Your church has a reputation. I want to know if it's justified," I said. She quirked her eyebrow. I held up a hand so I could clarify. "I investigated the murder of a church member months back. He had almost run over a little Hispanic girl. He shouted terrible things at her and her mom."

Sophie's eyes flicked upward and to the right as she considered.

"You're referring to Laughton Kenrick," she said. I nodded, and she considered again. "You're worried that I secretly want to run little girls over with a truck and then call their families racial slurs."

"I need to know what I'm getting into if I become your friend."

Sophie smiled.

"Part of me feels like I should be offended by the question, but another part of me appreciates your candor," she said. "The Church is a big place. An awful lot of us think Laughton was a vile human being. I won't say he deserved to die, but every now and then, the world becomes a better place through strategic population reduction."

"Your last name is Hitler."

She chuckled.

"My last name is Collins. I tell people my surname is Hitler so they leave me alone."

"What do you believe, then, Sophie?"

She blinked a few times and looked thoughtful.

"I believe the world's a complicated place. Most people can't handle that. They need simplicity. They don't want to hear that their present condition is the result of a chain of events, mostly outside their control. When questioned, I provide the answers people need to hear. So, if you want honesty, Laughton represented the more vile part of my community. I'm glad he's dead."

I sipped my coffee, unsure what to make of my new friend.

"How did you end up here?"

"I was born into the Church," she said, her eyes wistful. "I tried to leave when I was younger. I went to college and then graduate school. I lived with a good man and planned a life. We were going to finish our PhDs and have kids and a house and a white picket fence. Then I heard things about my old Church, and I realized it needed me home more than I needed a life without it. So here I am."

"Are you happy?"

Her eyes flicked up and down me.

"Are you?" she asked.

I didn't answer, mostly because she knew the answer. Sophie and I worked so that the people we cared about could live better lives than us. We settled into an easy silence.

"You met my brother," she said. "His name's Hunter. He teaches the boys at the Church how to hunt deer. He was a soldier."

I recognized the name and felt myself grow colder.

"Your brother's in charge of the Citizen Action Patrol. He took a rifle to an elementary school."

She exhaled through her nose.

"He'd never intentionally hurt a child," she said. "Unintentionally, though, he's an idiot who listens to the wrong people. My community finds itself in a precarious position right now. That's why I'm here. On the one side, you've got people like my brother. They're angry and feel like they're victims of government overreach and tyranny. Hunter doesn't care about race at all, but he takes his allies where he can get them. Then, you've got people like Michael Clarke. I think you know him. He's a genuine racist with delusions of grandeur. He wants to grow the Church and become a televangelist. Mostly, he wants fancy cars and a private jet, and he's willing to sacrifice his followers to get them. The two sides don't get along, leaving us in the midst of a cold war. It wouldn't take much for that cold war to grow hot."

I crossed my arms and nodded.

"What side are you on?"

"I'm a mom. I don't have the luxury of taking sides."

I picked up my coffee cup and sipped, hoping to sound nonchalant.

"Are you, your baby, and other kids and moms at that church safe?"

Her lips curled upward.

"For the moment, everybody's fine. In the future, I'm not sure."

I blinked, considering.

"Get your baby and bring her here. I'll find you a safe place to lay low."

She shook her head.

CHRIS CULVER

"You're sweet, but there are over two hundred people living at my farm. You can't make us all disappear. I came here because my brother and his buddies are planning something. I don't know what."

I nodded.

"You think they're going to stage a coup and kill Michael Clarke?"

"I suspect their ambitions are broader than a coup, but I don't know what they're doing. They've got a lot of firearms, though. Hunter won't talk to me."

The warning was ominous, but it was legal to own firearms. I couldn't act on a tip without specific details. Still, Hunter had an entire team of well-armed CAP members behind him, including a former police officer—Shane Fox. Shane had pretty extensive weapons training. I suspected Sophie's brother did, too.

"Keep your eyes open," I said. "If you hear anything specific, let me know. I'll do what I can."

"You just watch yourself," she said. "I'm not going to suggest you get out of town. You wouldn't listen to that, anyway, so I'll just be honest with you: my brother was deployed five times to Afghanistan and Iraq. He's a combat veteran, and he's taught his team how to function as a small tactical unit. Don't go Lone Ranger on them. They'll kill you. I couldn't bear that."

"Fair warning, thank you," I said. Sophie smiled and stood.

"I've got to go," she said. "My housemate thinks I'm at the grocery. She gets nosy if I'm gone too long. I think she reports my whereabouts to my brother and the Elders."

I stood but hesitated before speaking.

"I've told you this before, but it's worth repeating: if you're not safe, I'll get you out," I said. "You and your daughter. And anybody else who wants to go. Give me some time. I can get vans, buses, whatever you need for however many families you can get."

She patted my shoulder.

"This isn't your fight, and I won't let you step into it," she said. "I grew up in this Church, and I've watched it change. It is my responsibility to put it right—even if that takes my entire life."

"Just don't get hurt. I don't have too many friends," I said, pausing. "You might be the only one, actually. If that's what we are."

"We are friends," said Sophie. "Good luck, Joe. Stay safe."

"You, too, Sophie."

I escorted her out of the station, after which Roy and I walked to my office. Sophie hadn't come to snitch on her brother, so I didn't know how to classify her visit. If her brother was doing something dangerous, though, I wanted a record of her report. I considered how to respond and then wrote an anonymous tip about an unspecified threat from the Church. It was vague, but at least it was in the system.

Once I had my report written, I pushed back from my desk. Officially, I didn't have anything to do other than complete the list of pointless assignments Lieutenant Cognata had given me. Unofficially, Erik Hoyle was getting out of prison today. There wouldn't be a big ceremony. A judge would sign an order, which a clerk would deliver to the Bureau of Prisons. Within hours, a prison official would hand Hoyle twenty bucks and escort him to a bus stop near the prison grounds. More than likely, Hoyle's lawyer—my biological father—would meet him and drive him wherever he needed to go.

A lot of people would say the system had worked. George Delgado and I investigated him and found evidence that implicated him in the crime. We looked for an alibi; we looked for plausible, alternative suspects; we sought out evidence. Everything pointed to him. He even confessed...sort of. At trial, the prosecutor presented the best case he could. Likewise, Hoyle's attorney defended him to the best of his ability. A jury found him guilty, and a judge sentenced him to prison. I patted myself on the back and moved on with my life.

But he didn't do it.

Eventually, a college kid wrote articles about him, and a big-shot lawyer from St. Louis rode to Hoyle's defense. He'd walk out of prison, but what parts of himself would he leave behind? I had met a lot of former prisoners. Prison was a horrible crucible that burned away the soft edges of those inside. Hoyle had to fight every day to survive. He'd probably have PTSD for the rest of his life. The state had funds set aside for men and women wrongly convicted, but it'd never make him whole.

Maybe even worse, Brittany Ashbury's real murderer was still out there. He might have killed other people. Delgado shared blame, but he wasn't around to take his lumps. They fell to me.

I couldn't give Hoyle his time back, but maybe I could find Brittany's real killer. The work would be my penance. I certainly deserved it. I started by calling up the case files on my computer. When Shaun Deveraux told me about St. Louis County's plans, I had been incensed. I had read through the files, but I had sought confirmation of my conclusions. I hadn't been looking for errors or new investigative leads. This time, I did.

George Delgado and Jasper Martin, his partner, had interviewed dozens of people who knew Brittany, but their interview notes were clipped and included mostly biographical information with little content. I wrote their names down, intending to reinterview them all. Then, I read through the autopsy report. The coroner had found indications that Brittany had had sex before she died, but he hadn't found seminal fluid or other DNA-bearing fluids in or on her body. However, he had found traces of lubricant, which indicated that she and her partner had used a condom. That might have indicated intentionality—or maybe her attacker simply carried condoms with him. A lot of men did.

The toxicology report had found hallucinogenic mushrooms and Rohypnol in her system. Rohypnol was a central nervous system depressant that, when taken, made its user feel dizzy and confused. Oftentimes, people drugged with it feel clumsy. Their vision may grow wavy. A significant portion of the time, they black out. Brittany wouldn't have taken Rohypnol for recreational purposes. She was drugged.

The murder happened sometime after the hardware store where she worked closed for the evening. Hoyle claimed he locked the store up with her, wished her luck, and asked that she keep in touch. Then he drove off. When he arrived home, his spouse and children were asleep.

He claimed that he went into the basement and watched CNN for half an hour, but he couldn't remember any of the news stories. He later said he had a few drinks. He claimed he fell asleep at 12:30 or 1:00. His spouse woke when he came into their room, but it was dark. She didn't remember the time. None of his kids heard him come in. They didn't have an alarm or camera system to confirm his arrival or departure time. He had a phone, but it didn't have a GPS chip in it. We could see which towers he was connected to, but that merely gave us an approximate location within several miles.

After zeroing in on Hoyle as a suspect, Delgado had secured a search warrant for his home, car, and office but didn't find mushrooms, Rohypnol, rope, condoms, or anything used in the assault. Delgado and Martin checked out his phone while at the house. Hoyle and Brittany had exchanged texts in which they joked around, but there was nothing suggestive. They talked about work and closing up the store. Delgado surmised that they were speaking in code in case his wife found out.

I found no indications at all that they were having an affair. Delgado apparently had read more into the evidence than I did.

During an examination, the coroner found a possible bite mark on Brittany's shoulder, so he brought in a forensic dentist. The dentist claimed teeth were like fingerprints, and everyone's teeth were unique because everyone's life experiences were unique. The combination of chips, ridges, and other natural features of Hoyle's mouth created a unique imprint on Brittany's shoulder. He used a lot of scientific jargon, and it sounded impressive. His report gave us enough for an arrest warrant.

After hours in an interrogation booth, Hoyle had broken. I had been proud of myself. I had thought I had brought Brittany justice. The world had made sense. I thought I had been in control. I wasn't, though; instead, I had been a pinball ricocheting from one obstacle to another, oblivious to the damage I had done. I had screwed up and ruined multiple lives.

And now I had to face the consequences.

CHAPTER 27

I closed the documents on my computer and looked at Roy. He licked his nose and then panted, almost seeming to grin at me.

"I've got to do something, and it won't be fun," I said. "You want to go?"

He tilted his head to the left and right, his eyebrows quirked in confusion. Then, his tail thumped against the ground, and he barked happily. I figured that was assent to stay with me, so I petted his cheek before standing. We got in my Volvo and headed out. Before she died, Brittany Ashbury had lived with her parents in town. I drove to their neighborhood and parked in front of the family's single-story brick home. It was cool outside. Gray clouds stretched across the skyline. Vibrant yellow and red mums popped over the tops of big terra pots on the front porch, brightening an otherwise dreary day. In the spring and summer, a big sycamore tree would have provided shade, but now its bare limbs and white and light brown trunk looked almost skeletal.

Roy and I stepped out of the car, and I swallowed hard before walking up the walkway. A woman with short, curly brown hair and honey-colored skin answered the door. She didn't recognize me at first, but then her eyes widened. She blinked and stepped back.

"You're a police officer," she said. "I know you."

"We've met," I said. "I'm Joe Court. I was a uniformed officer eight years ago when your daughter died."

She crossed her arms. Her chest rose as she drew in a breath.

"My daughter was murdered."

"I know," I said. "Do you have some time to talk?"

For a few moments, she said nothing. Then she looked at Roy.

"What about him?"

"Roy is my partner," I said. "He's well trained. He won't stray from my side. Where I go, he goes. We're a package deal."

She considered and then stepped back.

"Come in, then," she said. I wound Roy's leash around my hand just so she'd know I was in control, and then the dog and I walked inside. The entryway had a glazed red brick floor. I suspected it'd become slick when wet, but it gave the entryway character. The walls were light gray, and the white paint on the woodwork had a glossy finish that reflected the overhead lights. The scent of something spicy and rich flowed from the kitchen. It could have been herbal tea, but it almost smelled like a curry.

Brittany's mother—Whitney, my notes said—shut the door.

"As I said, I'm Joe Court," I said. "Do you have a table we can talk at?"

She stepped past me without saying a word. We walked down a short hallway to an immaculate kitchen and then to a breakfast table overlooking the backyard. A stainless-steel kettle still steamed on the cooktop. Whitney grabbed a mug from the counter near the stove and gestured toward the breakfast table. I sat. Roy lay down beside my feet and watched the scene as Whitney sat across from me at the small table.

"Thanks for talking to me," I said. "Eight years ago, I helped investigate your daughter's murder. Then, I worked for the St. Augustine County Sheriff's Department. Now, I'm temporarily assigned to the Missouri State Highway Patrol. Has anyone from the St. Louis County Prosecutor's Office spoken to you lately?"

She squeezed her jaw tight and looked away. Her nostrils flared. I let her process the question, but her pained reaction told me everything I needed to know.

"They're letting him go," she said, her voice soft. "The man who murdered my daughter. How could they do that?"

Shaun Deveraux had extensive experience talking to the families of murder victims, and I suspected he had told Whitney everything he could.

"We didn't realize it at the time, but our case against Mr. Hoyle was flawed," I said. "As science has shifted, we've been forced to reevaluate certain kinds of forensic evidence, including the evidence used to convict Mr. Hoyle. I'm reopening the case and starting from scratch. I can't promise results, but I will do my best for Brittany."

Her eyes shifted upward to mine.

"That wasn't much last time."

I squeezed my jaw and looked down as a heavy, gnawing feeling began growing in my gut.

"My plan is to reinterview Brittany's friends and coworkers," I said. "Is there anyone in particular you think I should talk to?"

"I used to keep up with her friends, but time creates distance. I don't know my daughter's world anymore. Her friends have moved on. I can't help you."

"Can you think of anyone who could?"

She blinked.

"I just told you no."

"Did she keep a diary or journal?"

She swallowed and looked down.

"I don't remember," she said, her voice soft. Her eyes blinked rapidly. She brought a hand to her mouth. "A mom should remember, but I don't anymore. Maybe she did. I just don't know anymore." She drew in a breath as a tear slid down her cheek. "I miss my baby."

"Does she still have a room here?"

Whitney nodded and stood but said nothing. Roy and I followed her down a hallway strewn with pictures to a plain brown door. Before opening it, she turned to me and pointed to Roy.

"He stays outside."

I nodded.

"He will."

She hesitated before opening the door and revealing a room that I suspected hadn't changed a bit since Brittany's death. It was a pretty room with a queen-sized bed with a padded headboard, white walls, and a pink rug over a hardwood floor. The furniture might have originally looked dated, but someone had painted it an off-white and installed crystal knobs, leaving it almost chic looking. Brittany had had good taste.

"Thank you," I said. "I'll look around. If I find anything, I'll tell you."

"Do that," she said before turning away. I told Roy to lay down and stay. He whined a little but complied. When I first investigated Brittany Ashbury's death, I hadn't even considered asking Delgado to let me see her room. I hadn't known how to investigate a case. Looking back, Delgado's investigation should have raised red flags with everyone. I wished I had known enough to say something.

The floor creaked as I walked inside. The surfaces held no dust, the bed was neat, and the clothes hamper was empty. Brittany's mom spent time in this room. She cleaned it. If it ever held drugs or anything else illicit, I doubted it did anymore. I snapped pictures of the room. She had two framed pictures on her desk. In one, Brittany wore a prom dress and danced with a group of girls. I snapped a picture, intending to ask Whitney about the young people later. The second picture was of her family.

The desk drawers were completely empty. The closet held dresses, jeans, and skirts on hangers, but nothing pertinent to my investigation. I lifted her mattress, hoping I'd find a journal or diary, but I didn't find anything. It didn't surprise me. Whitney Ashbury had probably scoured that room for things to remember her daughter by.

I left the bedroom. Roy followed me to the kitchen, where I found Whitney at the breakfast table, her gaze distant. She didn't seem to notice I was there, so I cleared my throat. She turned, but her eyes were unfocused. It was as if she didn't want to leave the memory she had been reliving. Then she drew in a breath and closed her eyes.

"Did you get what you needed?"

"I did, thank you," I said, flicking through the pictures on my phone until I found the shot of the photograph on Brittany's desk. "Who were the girls in the picture?"

Whitney focused on my phone for just a minute. Then she sighed.

"That's Jane Hammond on the left. She was Brittany's best friend. She died in a car accident two years ago. The girl with the black hair is Nancy Lynn. I think she lives in town, but I haven't talked to her in years. The girl with the red hair is Mary Curtis now. She used to be Mary Barnes. I think she lives in Chicago."

I jotted the information down. It'd be nice to talk to everybody, but I'd take one real friend over interviews with a dozen acquaintances.

"Did she date?"

Whitney straightened.

"Brittany lived with me and her father, but she was an adult. Her love life was her business. I didn't pry."

I looked at my notepad.

"You think she would have confided in Mary Barnes or Nancy Lynn?"

She hesitated and softened her voice.

"Probably," she said. "Jane was her best friend, but all the girls were close."

Delgado had interviewed them, but he had focused on Brittany's death. Once he learned that none of her friends had spoken to her on the day she died, he lost all interest. Someone needed to do this right. I thanked Whitney for her time and gave her my card in case she had questions. Then Roy and I headed out.

At first, I drove toward my station, intending to look up Nancy Lynn and Mary Barnes. The further I drove, though, I realized I had another stop first. When Brittany died, George Delgado had asked me to stake out her funeral. He didn't explain why, just that he wanted a surreptitious police presence there. I was young enough that I could blend in.

I didn't go to the wake or the burial, but I stayed nearby. Afterward, he showed me a picture of Erik Hoyle and asked if I had seen him. Sure enough, I recognized him because he had been one of the pallbearers. George thought his presence confirmed something, and I knew so little about homicide investigations that I didn't call him on his narrow-minded assumptions.

Roy and I parked beside the main gate and walked. Brittany had a simple headstone that listed her name and years of life. Her father was buried beside her. Before I knew what I was doing, I knelt on the grass beside her.

"Hey," I said. "My name's Joe. We never met, but I'm the police officer investigating your case."

I paused. Roy panted beside me, but I ignored him for the moment.

"I know what happened to you, and I'm sorry," I said. "You didn't deserve any of that."

I paused.

"Maybe you can hear me, maybe you can't. I don't know how life and death work, but if you can hear me, I won't abandon you. You deserved a long, happy life with someone you loved. I'm sorry you didn't get that. I can't bring you back or return what was taken from you, but you mattered. You deserved better than you got. I just wanted you to know that."

The dog and I stayed there for about ten or fifteen minutes, but I didn't experience an epiphany, and the universe didn't reveal anything. I didn't learn anything new about my case. I felt sick for a murdered woman I didn't know, a mom who lost her daughter, and a wrongly imprisoned man who lost everything.

Pain was a part of life. That was drilled into me from a young age. Sometimes, I wished it were easier to take, even if just for a little while.

CHAPTER 28

Roy and I left the cemetery and drove back to our station. Friends were tricky. I had a lot of acquaintances in my life. I liked and respected them but hadn't ever felt compelled to ask them out for coffee. I liked hearing about their families and loved ones and future plans, but we kept a cordial distance. You wouldn't be hurt by people you kept at a distance. That was how I preferred most of my relationships.

Then I had pseudo-friends. These were people I genuinely liked and cared about. They included Trisha Marshall, my station's old dispatcher, and Sasquatch, a colleague who left the department after being shot in the chest. I'd gladly meet them for coffee or a drink at a bar. They saw aspects of me others didn't, but they didn't see everything. I had almost allowed Trisha Marshall in, but that hadn't worked out. It was probably for the best that she left town when she did. Sasquatch was busy with his own life. One day soon, I suspected, he and his wife would have kids. They'd forget about me, but I'd always think fondly of them.

My list of real friends was smaller. My sister, Audrey, was my friend. I loved her dearly and would do anything for her, but she and I had such different lives, I wasn't ever sure how much she understood me. We had a great time together, and we called each other on bad days. Our relationship hadn't always been that strong, though.

For years, I hadn't understood why she called me on Sundays to tell me about her love life, the parties she went to, and her classes at school. Trisha reminded me that she was my sister and was trying to connect with me. I hadn't even considered that she cared enough to connect with me even when I couldn't drive her to tennis practice or talk her through her math homework. I was lucky to have her.

Susanne Pennington had been my friend. She understood me in a way no one else did. Powerful people had hurt and exploited her. Afterward, she withdrew from the world. I knew that temptation all too well.

If I could believe Brittany Ashbury's mother, Brittany had three genuine friends in high school. One had died in a car accident, but two others still lived. If they were like my sister or Susanne, they would understand Brittany better even than her mother. Delgado should have spent hours with them. He should have sought to understand his victim instead of focusing on her death. Had he done that, my investigation might look very different today.

Since I couldn't change the past, I drove to my station and looked up Mary Barnes and Nancy Lynn. As Whitney had said, Mary lived in Chicago now. She was a pediatrician with a thriving practice. Good for her. I could call her office to get in touch with her. Nancy Lynn lived in town, as best I could tell, and she worked at Waterford College in the career center. I called Rusty Peterson and asked for Nancy's number. He wasn't supposed to give out the personal information of college staff without a court order, but I promised to keep his name out of any reports. Besides that, I had her address. If he didn't give me her number, I'd just show up at her house. This was far less invasive.

He gave me what I needed. After thanking him, I called her office phone. She answered with a hesitant hello.

"Hey, my name is Joe Court," I said. "I'm with the Missouri State Highway Patrol. How are you today?"

She paused.

"Fine."

A lot of people became guarded around the police. It was my job to sidestep those walls they put up.

"Glad to hear it," I said, forcing myself to smile. "I'm calling because I need to talk to you about something difficult. Neither you nor anyone else is in any trouble, but this might be a tough conversation. Are you free for a few minutes?"

She said nothing. Her breath was faint. Then she cleared her throat.

"What's this about?"

"Brittany Ashbury," I said. "I'm reopening her death investigation."

"What does that mean?"

Then it was my turn to pause awkwardly.

"Eight years ago, we arrested Erik Hoyle for Brittany's murder, but we've since learned the evidence against Mr. Hoyle was considerably weaker than we believed. We're re-examining everything."

"So you screwed up and ruined a man's life for nothing."

I grimaced and closed my eyes.

"We made a mistake—a big one," I said. "We're trying to put it right. I'm investigating Brittany's death, and I'm hoping you can help me out."

"What if I refuse?"

I leaned back in my chair.

"I'd call Mary Barnes and hope she'd talk to me. If she refused, I'd go to the library and check out the high school yearbook from the time you were all in school, and I'd search for pictures of Brittany. I'd see what she was involved with at school and talk to her classmates. Cold cases are tough, but I'll do my best to find out what happened to your friend—with or without your help."

She went quiet.

"I don't know what I can tell you," she said, finally. "She was murdered at a work party. I wasn't there."

"We think she was murdered after the party," I said. "And I'm not making any presumptions about her murderer. It may have been a coworker, but it could have been someone else. The evidence indicates that she knew her attacker. I don't think it was a random event. You and Brittany were friends. Did she have any problems with men?"

"Like, getting a date?"

I shook my head.

"No, sorry. I wasn't clear. Did men harass her?"

"She was a pretty girl. Of course men harassed her. They're men," she said. "Everybody gets catcalled at the pool. It's gross, but it happens."

I nodded and leaned forward.

"Anybody do more than that? Did she ever mention somebody, maybe, following her home or calling her?"

"No."

I jotted down a few notes and nodded.

"How about Erik Hoyle? He ever harass her?"

"I thought you said he didn't kill her."

I leaned back again.

"I'm just trying to understand the situation," I said. "Like I said, I'm reworking everything. The detective who investigated this case originally thought Brittany and Hoyle had an intimate relationship."

Nancy snorted.

"Brittany didn't date old men," she said. "He was her boss. That was it."

I wrote that down.

"They exchanged an awful lot of text messages if he was just her boss," I said. "They seemed friendly."

"Brittany's dad died when she was in elementary school. Her boss was...he wasn't, like, a father figure, but he was nice to her. We got arrested in high school for drinking at a party. It was stupid, but none of us were drunk. Brittany called him instead of her mom from the police station. He took her home and made her tell her mom. They weren't related, but he treated her like she was family."

Nancy paused.

"Before she died, Brittany was planning to go to college. She was nervous about her mom, but Mr. Hoyle encouraged her. He wanted her to go."

I squeezed my jaw tight. None of that was in a single report Delgado filed. If he had done the least bit of background work, he would have seen Hoyle was a lousy suspect. Instead, he ruined a man's life. It wasn't Delgado's fault alone, though. His partner, Jasper Martin, should have raised a stink instead of just removing his name from the case files. The sheriff should have read over the reports and recognized how thin they were. I should have seen the truth, too. There was plenty of blame here.

"So she wasn't dating her boss," I said. "That's great. Here's the thing, though: multiple people said they heard sexual noises coming from Mr. Hoyle's office while they knew Brittany was inside. Who was she with?"

She paused.

"Brittany had a boyfriend. We went to high school with him. His name was Joaquin Herrera. It could have been him."

I wrote the name down and planned to look him up.

"That's very helpful," I said. "Can we go back just a second? You said something interesting. You said it could have been Joaquin with her in the office. To me, that implies that it could have been someone else."

She said nothing.

"Did you have someone in mind?" I asked.

"I don't know," she said, sighing. "Brittany liked Joaquin. He was a good guy, but she didn't love him. In school, we always thought he was gay."

"Did she love anybody else?"

"Hunter Collins," she said. "He took her virginity after prom."

I doubted that fact would help my case, but it ably described their relationship.

"Is this the same Hunter Collins who lives at the Church of the White Steeple?"

"Yeah," she said. "They were in love in high school. Brittany didn't like Hunter's church. None of us did. She wanted him to leave it, but he wouldn't, so they broke up. Then he went into the Army. Before he left, they had a lot of sex. It wouldn't surprise me if they hooked up at work."

So now I had two viable suspects. This was going somewhere.

"Did either Joaquin or Hunter get violent with her?"

"No," said Nancy. "Brittany wouldn't tolerate it. She was stronger than any of us."

I jotted down a few notes.

"Okay," I said. "Did she keep up with Hunter while she dated Joaquin?"

Nancy hesitated.

"I don't think she ever stopped loving Hunter. Joaquin was just a fling."

I wrote that down and nodded.

"This has been very helpful. Is this a good number for you? I might have to call again."

"Call my cell," she said. I wrote down the number she recited and thanked her again. "I'm taking the rest of the day off. If you call, just leave a message. I'm going to turn off my phone."

"I understand," I said, "thank you."

She hung up, and I drew in a quick breath, feeling energized. Hunter Collins I knew, but Joaquin Herrera, I had never heard of. I looked him up on the FBI's National Criminal Information Center database to see any records for him. I found none, so I moved on to more local databases and instantly felt the buzzed jolt leave my body. Joaquin Herrera had died eight years earlier. His body was found in St. Louis two days after Brittany Ashbury's death. His official cause of death was an accidental overdose.

And there was our case.

I had two suspects, both more plausible than Erik Hoyle. I even had an obvious, plausible theory: Joaquin drugged, raped, and murdered his girlfriend. Then, feeling guilty, he went to St. Louis, where he shot himself up with enough black tar heroin to kill someone twice his size. He even had a pistol on him.

If Delgado had done his job, he would have talked to Brittany's friends and found out about Joaquin. He would have tracked him down and interviewed him. He might have even been able to prevent his death. At the very least, he could have provided the St. Louis police context for their investigation. They would have tested rounds fired from Herrera's gun to see if they matched rounds from Brittany. It could have eliminated a suspect. Or confirmed he was our killer.

But that opportunity was gone. If the police had suspected Joaquin's gun had been used in a murder, they would have kept it forever. Since they had no reason to think that, they would have either destroyed it or returned it to Herrera's next-of-kin. Eight years later, it'd be gone.

The more I learned about this case, the more disgusted I felt. We had sent Erik Hoyle to prison for eight years because George Delgado had been too lazy to do his job. Maybe it was for the best that the attorney general had dissolved our department.

After this mess, we didn't deserve to be around.

CHAPTER 29

I called the detective who had worked Joaquin Herrera's death, but she didn't remember the case. I couldn't blame her. If her caseload had been anything like mine, she had probably worked half a dozen accidental overdoses that month alone. Our country was awash in pills, powders, and injectables, some legally prescribed, some not. Without context, Herrera's death probably looked no different from any other accidental overdose.

I thanked the detective for her time and hung up. Then I swore a lot and wrote a report, unsure how best to continue. Herrera had family and loved ones still living, but I highly doubted they'd talk to me once they learned I was investigating his former girlfriend's death.

Hunter Collins was a suspect, too, but he didn't feel right for the murder. Brittany may have loved him, but he seemed out of the picture. He had joined the Army and moved on with his life. Maybe, though, he found her with Joaquin and became jealous. Jealousy was a powerful motive. Then again, according to Nancy, Brittany had loved Hunter. If he

274

returned from the Army and tried to rekindle their relationship, she would have broken it off with Joaquin. Jealousy would have been a nonfactor.

All told, Herrera felt like a better suspect. The odds were good that he was our murderer. The pieces fit. How I'd prove anything, though, I couldn't say yet.

I needed time to put my thoughts in order, so I took Roy for a quick walk around the block. The sky was overcast, and it felt cold. Soon, I'd have to start wearing a coat over my sweater. That was life, though. It was always changing.

Once I got back to my station, I sat at my desk and typed a report that outlined my thoughts and included summaries of my conversations with Nancy and the detective in St. Louis. My next move would be to confirm Nancy's revelations with Mary Barnes, so I started trying to track her down. Before I could get anywhere, though, my cell phone started screeching. I had heard that same screech earlier when concerned parents started calling 911 about gunmen outside our public schools.

I grabbed my phone and called my dispatcher. There was a report of an armed intruder at a home in St. Augustine. I checked my pistol and badge while grabbing Roy's leash. The dispatcher gave me the address and warned me that backup was inbound but would take ten to fifteen minutes to arrive. I thanked her, hung up, and hurried to a marked St. Augustine County Sheriff's Department SUV.

The caller claimed an armed man had pounded on his door and screamed at his spouse. Feeling his life was in danger, the homeowner shut the door and called us. Domestic situations were amongst the ugliest, most dangerous calls the police took because you never knew what you'd walk into. With families involved, emotions ran hot. People became volatile. This could get ugly fast.

I drove with my lights and siren blaring, so cars parted in front of me, allowing me to make good time across town. I hit the neighborhood in about five minutes and reached my caller's address within a minute of that. My backup was still at least five to ten minutes away, but I had Roy with me. At least that was something. I slammed on the brakes in front of a two-story, split-level home with beige siding and dark brown brick. There was a minivan in the driveway. A red sedan was parked across the street.

Normally, I would have leashed Roy, but today, I left it off. He needed to move in case somebody threatened me.

I threw open my door and stepped out, panning my gaze across the home. Nobody was out. Roy jumped out beside me. His body was stiff, and his tail was up. He was alert and ready.

I unbuttoned the strap that held my pistol in its holster. Nothing had happened yet, but my breath already felt shallow. The air felt thick.

The instant my feet hit the grass, the home's front door opened. Simultaneously, a man stepped out of the red sedan.

I hovered my hand over my pistol and stepped back so I could see both men. The homeowner, I had never seen before. The man in the car, I had.

I swore under my breath. Roy stayed on the grass and sat, his eyes flicking from me to the man walking toward me on the street. I held a hand flat toward him.

"Mr. Hoyle, you stay there. We've got highway patrol officers inbound who can sort this out."

Hoyle kept walking straight toward me. Roy perked up and stood. Then, the home's front door slammed shut. I risked a glance toward it and saw two people walking toward me from the house. It was a couple. Both were in their forties. The woman wore black leggings and a red-and-black plaid flannel shirt. The man beside her wore jeans, a blue Oxford shirt, and a red cardigan. I didn't know him, but I recognized Angela Hoyle beside him. Or at least she had been Angela Hoyle before she divorced Erik. Now, I didn't know what her name was.

This was a problem.

"Everybody stop what you're doing and listen," I said, looking toward Hoyle. "Mr. Hoyle, go back to your vehicle." I looked at the couple. "I'd like you two to stand on your porch. My dispatcher said somebody was armed. Who's got the gun?"

Hoyle stopped walking about twenty feet from me. Roy zeroed in on him, his ears perked up. I told him to stay. Hoyle smirked.

"I'm allowed to carry a gun," he said. "That's not a crime. I'm not a felon. My record was expunged."

My heart started beating faster.

"You're right, but I need you to keep your hands where I can see them," I said. "Nobody needs to get hurt. Everybody, just back up. Go back to your corners. I'll talk to you individually."

I looked toward the homeowners. The man had his hands on Angela's shoulders.

"We're going to go back inside, Officer," he said. "Everything's okay now."

Only, it wasn't okay. This was a home Erik Hoyle had purchased to live in with his wife and kids. Now, his wife and kids lived with another man. His wife thought she had divorced a rapist and murderer only to find her former husband was neither of those things. Unfair didn't begin to describe the situation.

I nodded to the homeowner and focused on Hoyle.

"You're not supposed to be here," he said. "Call my lawyer. I'm not talking to you."

"That's fine," I said. "I'm here in response to a 911 call. I was the closest officer. As soon as another officer arrives, I'll be leaving."

He nodded but didn't move. For almost thirty seconds, he stared straight at me, his face growing redder. I kept my hand over my firearm, hoping he wasn't going to do something stupid. Roy didn't understand what was going on, but he was clearly on alert. He had lowered the front part of his body into a guarded stance. If Hoyle made a sudden move, my dog was going to attack.

"It'd be best if you got into your car," I said.

"You ruined my life, lady," he said. "Don't tell me what to do."

I clenched my jaw and breathed through my nose before speaking.

"I understand your position, and I am sorry for all you've lost. Please go back to your car."

He stepped toward me. Roy growled deep in his throat. Hoyle stepped back and held up his hands.

"No. I'm not going anywhere. You don't get to lecture me. You don't even know me."

"Sir, you were the last person to see Brittany Ashbury alive before she was drugged, raped, and murdered."

He narrowed his eyes.

"You still think I killed her."

"Her case is open," I said. "Somebody slipped her Rohypnol before she died. The drug takes fifteen to twenty minutes to take effect. She was found in the employee parking lot behind your hardware store."

His lips formed a straight line. He said nothing.

"Was anyone with you twenty minutes prior to closing the store?"

He sighed, and his expression softened.

"I don't know. Probably. It was a long time ago."

He hadn't reached for a weapon yet, which I appreciated.

"You need to think hard," I said. "The situation sucks, I know, but I'm trying to find a man who raped and murdered somebody you once cared about."

He closed his eyes.

"There were customers in the store. Blake, one of my cashiers, was there, too. He left about ten minutes before I did when his mom picked him up."

Delgado hadn't included any of that in any of his written reports.

"Did Blake and Brittany know each other?"

"Brittany was his boss. Blake was a good kid. He was just a high school student. We hired kids that age for minimum wage and taught them how to interact with customers. For most of our employees, we were their first employer. Some went to college, others became plumbers or carpenters. Some just left."

I nodded, wishing I trusted him enough to take out a notepad and write notes. I needed to keep my hands free, though, in case he did something stupid. Roy sensed the changing direction of our conversation and sat down. He yawned, panted, and looked at me.

"Brittany stayed well past high school."

"She was moving on, though. I was proud of her. I never would have hurt her. If I had known somebody else had planned to hurt her, I wouldn't have let it happen."

Based on what I had seen so far, that was probably an honest answer.

"Did you have romantic feelings for her?"

He furrowed his brow.

"She was a kid, and I was her boss. I had known her since she was fifteen. She was a child."

"That didn't answer my question," I said, raising my eyebrows and lowering my chin. Roy whined, so I shushed him again.

"No. I had no romantic feelings for her. I was married and in love with my wife. And just for the record, I never had sex with Brittany, never discussed sex with her, never hit on her, never flirted with her...hell, I was never alone with her in my office if I could help it."

I nodded.

"You're angry," I said, nodding. "I get it, but—"

"You don't understand anything," he said. "My wife married another man. My kids barely even know my name. Meanwhile, I'm living out of a bed-and-breakfast. I don't have a job. I don't have clothes. I don't have a car. I barely even know how to use a cell phone. The only job I've ever had was managing a hardware store where my assistant was raped and murdered. For eight years, I've lived in a cage. And that's on you. All of it. How should I feel if not angry?"

I lowered my right hand toward my pistol again and held my left hand in a stop motion.

"It's time to go to your bed-and-breakfast," I said. He stepped forward, his eyes narrowing.

"You know the worst part of this? The guy who put me in prison, Detective Delgado, is dead. Somebody killed him. I hear you found his murderer."

"I did," I said, taking a stutter step back. Roy growled again. We both ignored him. I had an entire yard behind me, so I had room to retreat. None of that would matter if he pulled a gun on me, though.

"Who'd find your murderer if you were killed?"

My eyes popped open wide, and I shook my head.

"Don't do this," I said. "You're making a mistake."

He smirked and shook his head.

"The thing is, you put me in prison, and you knew I was innocent. My lawyer's going to sue you for everything you own. You can't touch me. It'll look like you're trying to intimidate me."

I took another step back. Then I shifted so I could make a run for my car. He kept pressing toward me.

"You don't want to do this, Mr. Hoyle. You've been in prison long enough that you've forgotten the rules outside. Inside, you might have had to intimidate people and threaten violence to survive. Here, if you do those things, I send you away permanently."

"You shouldn't have come to my house, Detective. I don't have anything to lose."

"You've got more to lose than you realize," I said. "Your kids for one. Think about them. I've given you a lot of leeway, but that's running out. Turn around and get in your car."

I stopped backpedaling. Hoyle, apparently, couldn't take a hint because he kept coming forward until he stood about two feet from me.

"If you've got the balls, shoot me. It'll quadruple what this shitty town pays me in the lawsuit. It's the best thing I could do for my kids."

And there we had it: he wanted to commit suicide by cop. I shook my head and reached into my purse for a can of pepper spray.

"Back up right now."

He sneered and reached to his waist.

"Make me."

"Don't do this," I said. He pulled a pistol from behind him. Roy may not have known what a gun was, but he understood the threat. He didn't hesitate, either. Before I could blink, Roy had his teeth on Hoyle's arm and had dragged him to the ground. I stomped on his hand so he'd drop the gun and then kicked it away. Roy held on, but he was just a dog. Hoyle tried to reach for his pistol, so I pepper sprayed him in the face and kicked the gun again, this time so it skittered even further away.

"Out, out!" I shouted, my voice sharp and loud enough to cut through Hoyle's screams. Roy immediately released

Hoyle's arm and backed off, still in a guarded position, the hairs on his back standing. Hoyle rubbed his face and started to push himself up, but I put a foot on his back and forced him down.

"Stay down," I said.

In the distance, I could hear the sirens from my backup. Hoyle writhed on the ground, his arm bleeding, and his entire face bright red.

"You're screwed now, lady," he screamed. "My lawyer's going to take everything you own."

He might have been right.

"You've got the right to remain silent," I said. "Exercise it and shut up."

CHAPTER 30

A uniformed highway patrol trooper I didn't know arrived within just a few moments. He called for paramedics and a supervisor. While waiting for Lieutenant Cognata to arrive, I secured Roy in my SUV and told the trooper what happened and why. The trooper took charge, which, in this situation, mostly meant keeping everybody apart. Paramedics arrived a few minutes after the trooper placed the call.

Hoyle had a pretty deep laceration on his arm from Roy's bite, so they took him to the ER to be patched up. A trooper would meet him there and keep him company. I sat and waited in my SUV for almost half an hour. Roy napped on the backseat. I closed my eyes until Lieutenant Cognata knocked on my window. I unlocked the doors, and she sat in the passenger seat.

"You care if we talk in here?" she asked, looking over her shoulder at Roy. He lifted his head, panted, and seemed to grin.

"I gave a statement to the trooper outside, but fire away," I said. "I did my job."

"The Ortegas have a doorbell camera. Mr. Ortega could hear you shout through the door," she said, nodding. "If our dispatcher had known all the players involved, we would have requested another officer arrive first."

I shook my head.

"Hoyle would have kicked down the door and killed Ortega," I said. "We did the best we could given the situation and the location of available officers."

Cognata nodded and considered me before speaking.

"You showed more restraint than a lot of my people would in your situation," she said. "Thank you. We didn't need a body." Cognata paused. "Mr. Hoyle's attorney is on the way. You should call your union rep for a lawyer."

I shook my head.

"A lawyer's not going to change the facts," I said. "Hours after being released from prison, Hoyle menaced his former wife and her husband. Then he pulled a weapon on me. If I didn't have a dog with me, I would have shot him to protect myself and the civilians on-site. My dog saved his client's life."

Cognata breathed through her nose and blinked.

"I suspect Mr. Hoyle's attorney will disagree with you on that," she said. "Your dog's a licensed cadaver dog, though. He'll be fine. You will, too, based on all I've seen. Given the totality of the circumstances, I'm leaning toward not charging Hoyle with trespassing or harassment. He's paid a pretty significant cost already."

I grimaced and shook my head.

"We should charge him with unlawful use of a weapon. That way we can keep his pistol."

Cognata blinked and drew in a slow breath.

"Mr. Hoyle spent eight years in prison for a crime he evidently didn't commit. If we arrest him for a felony the day of his release, we'll look petty and stupid. He'll argue he was coming home and found a stranger in his house. He'll say he was defending himself."

"He hasn't lived here for eight years."

"The public won't care," said Cognata. "We put him in prison for a crime he didn't do. The optics here matter. You need to think about yourself and your future, Ms. Court. I don't know you, but all I've seen says you're a good cop. If you want to keep that badge, you need to start considering the broader context of your actions and consider alternative courses of conduct that will accomplish your goal while minimizing the collateral damage."

I forced myself to smile.

"And what do you advise, Lieutenant?"

"Talk to his lawyer for a start. We'll work out a schedule for Mr. Hoyle to see his children. He deserves that. We can condition our help and services as intermediaries on his agreement to give us his firearm and a promise not to purchase another firearm until he has a permanent residence of his own."

I straightened and exhaled through my nose.

"That could work," I said. I paused. "That's better advice than most of my superiors give me."

Cognata smiled.

"Be better than your superiors."

"I will."

She nodded and stepped out. Roy and I settled down again, but then he started pawing at the window. I left my SUV and took him for a walk through the neighborhood while a team of highway patrol officers interviewed neighbors and reviewed footage from several nearby homes with doorbell cameras and other surveillance systems. By the time we returned, a gray Land Rover had parked behind my SUV on the street. A middle-aged man in a very finely cut navy suit spoke with Lieutenant Cognata. Even at a glance, I recognized him.

Brian Carlisle was six feet tall and had a thick head of gray hair. His eyes were piercing. I could see why my mother had found him attractive thirty years ago. I didn't know him, but my mother had left an impression on him. He had even named his daughter—my half-sister—after her. He was my biological father, but I had never had a desire to meet him. Now I didn't have a choice.

I wrapped Roy's leash around my hand and continued walking. Cognata and Carlisle looked toward me. For some reason, that made my knees almost feel weak. My stomach rumbled, and my hands trembled. I stopped near my SUV and put Roy inside but opened the windows so he could look out. Carlisle excused himself from his conversation with Cognata and walked to me. His expression was softer than I had expected.

He held his hand toward me. I shook it, hoping he didn't feel my tremble.

"I'm Brian Carlisle," he said. "I didn't expect to meet under these circumstances."

I almost didn't say anything. We both knew each other's names. My throat felt tight. I wanted to walk away. All my life, I had known my biological mother and the painful issues between us. I hadn't considered my biological father. He was just a non-entity. Now that he was standing before me, I didn't know how to feel.

"It's nice to meet you, I guess," I said. "I'm Joe Court."

We both went quiet. As a civilian meeting her father, I had no idea what to say. As a police officer speaking to a lawyer, though, I had experience. I took the opportunity to be honest.

"You did an admirable job getting Hoyle out of prison, but you should have better prepared him for life outside prison. This is his spouse's house. He doesn't live here anymore. You should have warned him against purchasing a gun, too. That was just stupid. He's lucky to be alive."

The softness left Carlisle's expression. I appreciated it. His client didn't need a kind lawyer; he needed one who'd kick him in the ass when required.

"My client was innocent," said Carlisle. "As I suspect you know."

"That doesn't excuse his actions."

Carlisle's lips formed a thin line.

"It certainly doesn't," he said. "Was pepper spraying him business or professional? Your dog had him subdued."

"He was reaching for a firearm," I said. "Again, he's lucky I had pepper spray and a dog. You should also tell him about doorbell cameras and the pervasiveness of surveillance systems in modern suburbia. The world's changed since he went to prison. You can't commit a felony on a suburban street without being filmed nowadays."

Carlisle looked down and shook his head.

"Jesus, you're cold," he said. "If you're angry at me, take it out on me. Don't take it out on my client."

"This isn't about you, Mr. Carlisle," I said, speaking before I fully comprehended what I was saying. "Your client pulled a firearm on me. My CO won't charge him with a crime because she thinks it'd look bad to send him back to prison right away, but I don't care about the optics. Hoyle's suicidal. He wanted me to kill him. I didn't. It won't be hard for him to find someone who will."

Carlisle considered and then held up his hand, palm toward me.

"Let's tone this down," he said. "Let's get a cup of coffee."
I raised my eyebrows and lowered my chin.

"You think it's appropriate for an attorney to have coffee with the police officer who just arrested his client?"
Carlisle smiled, but he didn't look amused.

"Normally, no. In our situation, yes. Erin told me she visited you. I thought we could set some boundaries."
I shook my head and crossed my arms.

"We have all the boundaries we need. I'm a police officer. You're a noted defense attorney. I will treat you with the same deference and respect I'd treat all men and women of your stature and position. I'd expect the same in return."
Carlisle looked down again and sighed.

"You sound like your brother."
I shook my head.

"You haven't met my brothers."
Carlisle looked up. Then he looked away.

"Sorry. I meant Homer. He's my son. He's a detective in St. Louis County. He doesn't like me very much, either."
"Sorry to hear that."
We went quiet. Carlisle stepped back.

"Thank you for your time, Ms. Court," he said, reaching into his jacket. I stiffened at first but then forced myself to relax. He wasn't going for a gun. Instead, he pulled out a business card. "This has my direct line on it."
I took the card and slipped it into my pocket.

"Thank you," I said. "If you need to contact me, reach me through Lieutenant Cognata. I'm not often in the office, so she'll put you in touch with me."

"Okay," he said. "Thank you."

He started to walk away. I almost let him go, but then I cleared my throat.

"Can I ask you one question, Mr. Carlisle?"

He paused and looked at me, a half-smile on his face.

"Sure," he said.

"You know who I am, and you know who my mom is," I said. He nodded. "How long have you known about me?"

"I learned your name when Erin—my daughter—came to my office and told me about you."

I swallowed hard, unsure why I suddenly felt nervous.

"And when was that?"

"The day she met you," he said.

I nodded.

"To be clear, you had no idea who I was when you donated several million dollars to the charity I founded."

"I didn't," he said. "Linda Armus contacted a former colleague of mine as part of a charity drive. Carly contacted me because she remembered your mother. She thought I might have founded the shelter. I wished I had. I donated money because the shelter did good work. If the world had more safe places, it'd need fewer attorneys like me."

I swallowed the lump that threatened to grow in my throat.

"That's a good answer."

"I'm glad you think so," he said. "Good luck, Ms. Court. Stay safe."

"You, too," I said.

He nodded and walked toward Lieutenant Cognata. I looked toward my SUV. Roy poked his head out, panting. I patted his cheek, and he licked my hand. My gut felt both heavy and hollow simultaneously. Roy caught my eye and then stuck his tongue out as he panted happily.

"Let's go home, buddy," I said, my voice soft. "I need a break."

CHAPTER 31

Before leaving, I asked Lieutenant Cognata if she needed anything from me. She didn't, so Roy and I left the scene in her capable hands. We went back to my station, where I sat down and wrote reports. Twenty minutes later, Cognata texted me to let me know she and the rest of her staff had left the Ortega's house without making an arrest. It wasn't necessary, but I appreciated being kept in the loop and told her so.

I hadn't done anything particularly taxing, but I felt completely drained nonetheless. I needed to break out of that funk, so I spent about twenty minutes at a computer before grabbing Roy's leash. He jumped to his feet.

"Let's go find a new home," I said. Roy tilted his head before sticking his tongue out and panting. He was trying to figure out what I meant and then seemed to decide it didn't matter anyway. He was down for whatever I wanted. We left the building, walked around the block, and then climbed into my car. For the next hour, the two of us drove around St. Augustine County, looking at three different houses—none of which truly excited me but all of which could potentially work.

I wanted a yard big enough that Roy could run around, I wanted privacy, and I wanted a decent house—ideally, one with historic charm. With enough money, I could buy a property that met all three criteria, but my budget had limits. The first house had a great yard and ample privacy, but the foundation was sinking, the roofline sagged, and paint over the clapboard siding had begun to bubble, which usually indicated some kind of underlying water damage. I didn't mind a project, but this was a dumpster fire.

The second house we drove by looked great, but the neighbors were really close. I didn't sunbathe naked, but I didn't like the idea of a teenage boy looking out of his second story window and watching me putz around in the backyard. The third house was a new build on fifteen acres of rolling St. Augustine hillside. The pictures on the realtor's website made the property look gorgeous. The house looked nice, too. Unfortunately, the developer had built the house so close to the main road that the homeowner would hear every single car that drove by. The developer had fifteen acres to work with, and he had chosen the worst homesite possible. That didn't speak well for his judgment. The house was a hard pass.

At five, the dog and I went home. The house search was disappointing, but just getting out of the office had lifted my spirits. I made chicken curry for dinner. With so many restaurants in town closed, I had spent the last few months teaching myself how to cook by watching videos on YouTube. I had even bought really expensive knives—most of which I never used. I wasn't a good cook yet, but I was getting better.

After dinner, Roy and I walked through the neighborhood. It was dark, so we stayed on the sidewalk. The weather had cleared up, so I didn't have to worry about rain. Lights from the high school's football field half a mile away drowned out the stars. The marching band was warming up. St. Augustine had faced significant challenges lately. As a police officer, I had focused on changes to my own department. The school system, though, had faced equally grim prospects. There had been talks of canceling the football and band programs to save money, but local businesses and alumni had stepped forward with donations.

A football team and marching band may not have seemed like much, but for our community, they brought a source of normalcy. The school district had gone to a four-day week to save money and had borrowed heavily from the state to stay solvent. Class sizes had ballooned as teachers left for more prosperous districts. Despite those challenges, our young people could still play and relax. For three hours every Friday night, our community could cheer the accomplishments of our young people and live vicariously through their work.

Friday nights had become a time of badly needed respite. I didn't have kids, but I understood how badly needed these Friday nights were for those who did.

About halfway through our walk, my phone screeched a now-familiar screech. My heart sank just as I dialed the dispatcher's number and started jogging home.

"This is Joe Court. I'm a reserve officer in St. Augustine. What's going on?"

"We've received multiple reports of armed persons outside a high school football game. We don't have anyone on the ground, so our information is patchy."

In years past, the sheriff's department would have provided five to ten officers for crowd control and for emergency services. I suspected another group had tried to step in.

"I'm four minutes out," I said. "I'm on my way. What information do we have?"

"Two callers say our gunmen are wearing yellow shirts and carrying flashlights," she said. "It sounds like they're trying to direct traffic."

I swore under my breath.

"They're members of a local church. They tried to do crowd control at schools the other day, too. They're trying to step in and provide services the sheriff's department here used to provide."

The dispatcher hesitated.

"Should I send more officers or..."

Her voice trailed off.

"Send them," I said. "I'll see what's going on and try to defuse the situation. Alert any troopers incoming that I'm in plainclothes and I have a dog. I'll be wearing a highway patrol windbreaker."

"Understood."

The dispatcher wished me luck, and Roy and I ran the rest of the way home. There, I grabbed my pistol, windbreaker, and car keys. We drove toward the high school, got caught in traffic, and had to park alongside the road about two blocks away. Dozens of people were already on the sidewalks, walking toward the stadium.

The high school stadium had seating for about three thousand people. Between St. Augustine residents and fans from other areas, it usually filled up. I hung my badge from a lanyard on my neck, got the dog out of the back seat, and started hurrying toward the main gate. Even from two blocks away, I could hear yelling. It was rhythmic. The nearer we got to the front gate, the louder and more coherent that yelling became.

"Go home, racists, go home."

I swore under my breath. Hunter Collins and his CAP team, it seemed, had taken it upon themselves to patrol the high school football game. The high school had soccer, football, baseball, and softball fields, all surrounded by a tall chain-link fence. A group of boys played with a glow-in-the-dark Frisbee on a nearby soccer field, seemingly oblivious to the chants around them. Roy and I ran until we reached the front gate.

A parking lot stretched toward the football stadium to my right and directly ahead. Dark fields stretched to my left. A crowd had formed inside the chain-link fence, chanting, while five men in bright yellow T-shirts stood outside with flashlights. All five men had rifles slung over their shoulders, and all carried flashlights. They were waving pedestrians inside and telling drivers the parking lot was full while pretending to be oblivious to the two or three dozen protesters standing just inside the fence.

Before I could say anything, Jerry Baker, a math teacher and assistant football coach who happened to sit on the County Charter Commission, stepped out from behind the fence, glared at Hunter Collins and his men, and came toward me, a scowl on his face.

"I'm glad you made it," he said. "We called 911, but I wasn't sure they were going to send anybody."

"They are," I said. "We've got troopers on the way, but I happened to be the closest. What's going on?"

He glared again at Hunter Collins before focusing on me.

"It's Football Friday," he said. "People want to see a game. The Booster Club and I were overseeing the crowds when these bozos showed up with guns. Nearly started a stampede."

"Anybody hurt?"

He grumbled and shook his head.

"No, but my students aren't used to seeing guns at school," he said. "They started getting freaked out, so we moved them into the gymnasium. They're playing basketball now. They're fine. We'll shuffle them outside to the game in just a bit. Meantime, some parents recognized the dirtbags as coming from that racist church and started asking why we had hired racist security guards. I didn't have an answer. I ordered them off school property. Now they're standing outside the gate."

I glanced toward the group. Hunter Collins watched us, but the rest of his CAP members talked amongst themselves. One waved a car past as it tried to turn into the parking lot.

"Have they been directing traffic?"

"Yep," he said. "I told them to stop, but they said I didn't have authority over them. This is going to get ugly, Joe. Our students are good kids, but teenagers do stupid things without thinking through the consequences—especially the boys. What'll happen if a kid throws a rock at them? I don't want a kid getting shot."

I squeezed my jaw tight and swore to myself, considering the situation. Hunter's CAP team was standing on a public sidewalk at least a thousand feet from the school building. This would be iffy at best.

"You said you were directing the crowd with the Booster Club earlier?" I asked. Baker nodded. "Get the crowds away from the gate. I need some room to work."

He hesitated.

"Nobody's going to get hurt, are they?"

"Nah," I said, shaking my head. I paused. "Probably not, at least."

Baker agreed and then typed something on his cell phone. Almost immediately, four men in school jackets came through the gate and started pushing the crowd back. Hunter and his CAP team noticed and started focusing on me. I smiled at them. Hunter walked toward me, scowling.

"We're not trespassing," he said. "What are you doing?"

"You're correct," I said. "You're not trespassing, but I need you and your men to unsling your rifles and place them against the fence. Then I'm going to have you all sit on the curb."

"Excuse me?"

"You're under arrest for impersonating police officers," I said.

Hunter shook his head.

"We are very clear about who we are," he said, pinching his shirt. "You see this? It says CAP. It's bright yellow. Nobody thinks we're cops."

"You're directing traffic on a public street. That's a police action," I said. "I have backup on the way. We're going to take you into custody."

"We're not doing anything wrong," he said. "That old guy you were talking to and his friends were directing traffic, too. We were helping."

I shook my head.

"No, you're scaring people and trying to normalize armed, civilian guards outside our schools," I said. "I'm not allowing that. I have told you that I am placing you under arrest, and you've refused to cooperate. That means you're resisting arrest. That's a felony. At the moment, you have me outgunned five to one. You could shoot me, but there'd be hundreds of witnesses, many of whom have cameras. In fact, given the number of teenagers around us, I can pretty much guarantee somebody's recording us right now. That'd earn you and every single moron you've brought with you the death penalty. If you force me to shoot and kill one of you, every surviving member of your axis of iniquity will be charged with felony murder. How do you want to proceed?"

Hunter considered, drew in a breath, and then unslung his rifle and leaned it against the nearest fence. Then he raised his hands.

"This isn't right," he said. "I didn't do anything wrong."

I looked at the four still-armed men.

"You boys going to cooperate, or should I call the coroner and tell him to start ordering body bags in bulk?"

They looked at Hunter. He glared at me.

"Do as she says," he said.

They leaned the rifles against the fence before raising their hands. I suspected they had rehearsed this. I suspected they also had plans in case an arrest went bad. We waited another few minutes before I heard the first police siren. A marked highway patrol SUV pulled to a stop, and a uni-

formed trooper stepped out. Some of the civilians watching
started cheering. He asked me what was going on. I filled him
in and helped him secure Hunter's team with zip ties.

Another officer arrived a few minutes later. I took the opportunity to step away and call Sophie Collins. She answered
right away.

"Joe, hey," she said. "I am having dinner right now. I wish
you had called earlier. I could have saved you a plate. It's
spaghetti night."

"I wish I had, but this isn't a social call. Is Michael Clarke
around?"

She paused.

"Probably," she said. She paused again. "You all right? You
sound stressed."

"I am stressed," I said. "Get Michael Clarke and tell him
to come to the high school. I'm going to do him a huge favor.
And tell him to bring a crowd."

CHAPTER 32

I told Sophie about my plan. She did the rest. Within fifteen minutes of my call, Reverend Michael Clarke arrived in a convoy of ten vehicles. Unfortunately, they had nowhere to park near the school, so they had to drive a few blocks away and walk. Hunter Collins reiterated his belief that I had no right to hold him or his CAP team. I ignored him.

By the time Michael Clarke's group arrived, we had uniformed highway patrol officers manning every gate and exit to the stadium. They didn't know what I was up to, but it didn't matter. Mostly, their presence alone kept people in line. I had a uniformed officer near me, watching Collins's men. Their rifles were in the back of a marked highway patrol SUV.

Clarke had brought forty or fifty Church members with him. The crowd was a lot bigger than I anticipated, and they looked pissed, making me wonder what Sophie had told them. When Clarke saw me, his eyes caught mine. His look was confused, bemused, and calculating simultaneously. Then he smiled before turning to the crowd of people behind him.

"Behold the queen of Sodom herself," he said. "This vile woman would imprison our men and seduce our women-folk, all for having the audacity to protect people she wants to exploit. Shame on you, Ms. Court. Shame on you."

I had expected Clarke to say something, but I hadn't quite expected that level of vitriol. It took me aback for a moment. I blinked and cleared my throat, giving myself a second to think. Clarke's followers, meanwhile, started shuffling. One, an elderly woman, called me a Jezebel. A few others started chanting *shame* over and over. Hunter Collins followed with a blank expression on his face.

"Everybody just calm down," I said. "This is a legitimate police action."

"This is an overreach of your authority," said Clarke. "You've gone too far."

The uniformed highway patrol trooper eyed the crowd warily and then stepped between them and his SUV, which he had half-parked on the curb. I hadn't talked to him about my plan, mostly because it was half-baked even in my head. I crooked a finger toward Clarke and motioned him toward me.

"Can I see you for a moment..." I paused, searching for the right word. "Reverend?"

Clarke turned and held his hands toward his followers, who were already growing increasingly unruly.

"We're here to talk and peacefully protest. This is not the time to fight. I'll get our boys back, don't worry."

A few members of the crowd kept shouting, but they were shushed in short order. Clarke walked toward me, a smirk on his face.

"How was that, Ms. Court?" he asked. "Sophie told me you wanted a scene in front of the community."

"You succeeded. What the hell did you tell them?"

He considered and then drew in a breath through his nose.

"I believe I may have said you were infested with a demonic entity intent on using your sexuality to lure our young men into a life of sin and slothful waste. If you would like, I can exercise that demon now and restore the high esteem my community holds you in."

I blinked and looked down.

"I'm not sure how to respond."

"Then allow me to smooth things over on your behalf," he said. "Assuming you can make my work worthwhile."

"Hunter Collins and his men are yours. Take them. I'm not charging them with anything. You can tell your people that you negotiated their release. Spin it how you want. I know your community is in the midst of a leadership struggle. Use this to your advantage to cement your place. Show your Church that you outwitted the local police."

He crossed his arms.

"And what do you want in exchange?"

"Keep your CAP team away from the schools," I said. "A wise woman told me that I needed to be better than my former superiors. My old boss would have arrested everybody. I'm trying to find a win-win."

He considered me. Then he covered his mouth as he thought.

"This could help me," he said. "I have to wonder, though: why? My father thought you were a sharp young woman. He liked you. I don't share his sentiments."

"I don't care about your feelings. You're the devil I know. I'd rather have you in charge than the stranger who's giving Hunter Collins orders."

He clicked his tongue a few times.

"I appreciate your honesty, but how do I know you won't try to put me under your foot next?"

"You don't," I said. "I'm giving you a win today. Take it. You walk away without Hunter and his men, you'll look weak. Take them, and you'll look as if you've beaten me. You're not a good man, Mr. Clarke, but you're better than the alternatives. I have to deal with reality."

His eyes flicked up and down me.

"You're more formidable than I expected," he said. "Good for you."

He stepped away and looked at Hunter.

"Stand up, son," he said. "I'm taking you and your boys home. This succubus won't have you on my watch."

Clarke's followers started cheering. Hunter warily stood, eyeing me. I walked behind him and cut his zip ties with a pocketknife. Then I leaned forward.

"This is twice I've caught you with a gun near a school," I whispered. "You do it again, I won't be lenient or kind, and you won't walk away with your minister."

He watched as I cut the zip ties on the other men. The CAP members joined the crowd behind Clarke.

"Thank you kindly, Ms. Court," said the reverend. "One day, I hope you see the light and turn away from your wickedness."

"Sure thing," I said. "Get out of here."

Clarke turned and launched into a speech about evil and the fires of hell that awaited everyone who stood in the righteous path of his followers. Once he left, the uniformed highway patrol trooper nearest me furrowed his brow.

"What the hell just happened?"

"I suspect I made a huge mistake, but that's for hindsight. Everybody's safe, and the assholes with guns are gone. Let's take the win."

The troopers and I stayed for the rest of the game. St. Augustine lost, but it was a good game against a very good team. Two hours after I arrived, the crowds left in good spirits, and neither Hunter nor any of his followers returned.

I probably should have gone to my station to write a report, but I was tired. A report could wait. Roy and I drove home. My house still smelled like coffee from earlier that day.

I closed my eyes and sighed as I shut and locked the front door.

I didn't see Roy drop into a guarded position. Nor did I see the hackles along his back rise. If I had, I probably would have reached for my pistol. My only sign that something was wrong came from his low, throaty growl. My eyes popped open to see movement in the kitchen.

Somebody was in my house.

***

Shane had called Joe Court vicious. He was right. The CAP team was an honest attempt at community outreach. Without a sheriff's department or other law enforcement organization, the town needed volunteers with experience managing crowds and keeping people safe. Hunter and his men had that experience. Some had spent time in the Army. One had even been a cop. Those without law enforcement or military experience, Hunter had trained. A smart woman would have welcomed them. Joe hated them.

Hunter and his team had gone to the high school to watch the football game because he knew how dangerous the world became when emotions ran high and thousands of people were crammed into even the relatively confined space of a football stadium. Instead, she had humiliated them and treated them as if they were criminals.

She was a threat.

According to Shane, Joe had lived in several houses in the past few years. Once, she owned a big property in the country. Then she moved into an apartment above a garage at a battered women's shelter. Then she moved again into a crappy rental house.

Hunter didn't understand it. Joe was a wealthy woman who owned two of the biggest houses in town. Instead of living in those beautiful houses, she rented them to a charity and lived in a dump. It made absolutely no sense.

Hunter believed in charity, but he also recognized the importance of saving for the future and enjoying the present. He had seen too many horrors in Iraq and Afghanistan to squander the present. He owed it to the men and women he had fought beside who didn't make it home to enjoy life. Joe didn't understand the world. She lived a cushy life and had everything handed to her. She was lost and spoiled.

After leaving the high school stadium, he, Shane, and two of his CAP team members drove to Joe's neighborhood to scope the area out. It was depressing and dark. A charity had built the neighborhood twenty years ago, but most of the original homeowners had moved elsewhere. The homes were steppingstones that residents used while they built the foundations of better lives. The houses had few bedrooms and tiny lots. Several had bars over the windows to deter thieves.

It made no sense that Joe Court would live there.

"Pull over," said Hunter, motioning toward the sidewalk. Tyler, the CAP team's newest and youngest member, dutifully complied with the order and pulled his 2005 Mercury to the side of the road in front of a single-story home. They were a block and a half from Joe Court's house and a block from the neighborhood's exit. Hunter looked at his team.

"Tyler's our driver. He'll stay here and wait for us with the car running. Shane and Luke, you're going with me to the house. Luke, you're taking care of the dog. Shane and I will take care of Joe. No guns. We stay silent."

Luke shifted uncomfortably. He was thirty-five and had spent his entire life in the Church. Hunter trusted him implicitly.

"Do we have to hurt the dog?" he asked. "I love dogs."

"We'll do what we have to do," said Shane. "Joe's dog is a cadaver dog, but he's cross-trained to protect her. She'll have a crate. We'll try to shove him into it before he attacks."

Luke agreed. The three men got out. They were so close to the high school that Hunter could hear the marching band and the crowd. Lights from the stadium drowned out the stars. At one time, Joe's neighborhood would have been full of young families and upwardly mobile singles. Now, with massive unemployment, at least half the homes were empty. It made their job easier.

The three men hurried in the shadowed areas between houses until they reached Joe's property. A fence surrounded her backyard, but it barely slowed the three men down.

311

Her back door with its flimsy deadbolt didn't stand a chance, either. Shane picked the lock and then pushed it shut behind them. All three men wore gloves, black clothing, and ski masks to hide their identities and prevent any stray hairs from falling.

Each man carried a pistol, but they'd only draw them in the direst of emergencies. Their primary weapons were friction batons Shane had stolen from his station before departing. The weapons were small enough to fit in a pocket, but their steel construction gave them heft. They were lethal in the right hands.

Once inside, Luke found the dog's crate in the master bedroom while Shane positioned himself in the kitchen and Hunter stood with his back to the wall beside the front door. Then they waited for almost two hours.

Finally, a little before eleven, he heard a key. Muscles all over Hunter's body stiffened, and he extended his baton. He saw Shane do likewise in the kitchen. The door slowly creaked open, and Hunter held his breath while Joe and her dog stepped in. The dog sniffed and shifted his weight. He knew they were there.

Then he growled.

At once, Luke and Shane came sprinting forward, batons in hand. Joe reached for her firearm, and the dog sprinted forward toward the two of them. Nobody saw Hunter in the shadows beside the door.

He swung his baton as hard as he could. The solid steel bulb on the end connected with Joe's skull with a heavy thud, and she dropped straight down. Blood started forming a halo around her head. Hunter's heart pounded as he shut the front door. Joe may have been down, but her dog was still a threat. He bit Luke. Shane grabbed its collar and pulled hard enough to dislodge its bite. Luke was bleeding. He held his firearm against his chest and grimaced but tried to stay quiet.

The dog twisted and snapped at Shane, so Hunter wrapped an arm around its head and a second arm around its waist.

"Where's the crate?" he asked.

Luke, still holding his forearm, ran toward the bedroom. If he dripped any blood on the ground, they'd leave evidence behind they couldn't afford to leave. Shane and Hunter followed their partner to the bedroom, where they found a crate capable of holding a dog. They threw him inside and fastened the door. Even inside, the dog's hackles were high. He growled and charged at the gate, but it held.

"Job's done," said Hunter. "Let's move."

No one hesitated. They hustled through the home. Joe hadn't moved. Hunter would have preferred to check her neck for a pulse, but the dog was barking so ferociously the neighbors would surely hear. They had to get out of there.

Outside, the three men retraced their footsteps to Tyler's Mercury. The instant they had their doors shut, the younger man pulled away. Adrenaline coursed through Shane's system. His hands trembled.

"She dead?" asked Tyler. Shane ignored him.

"Let me see your arm," he said, turning to focus on Luke. Luke held up his forearm. Blood glistened on the fabric of his shirt, but it wasn't dripping. "Pull back your sleeve."

Luke did as he asked and exposed four clear and deep puncture marks. The skin was already growing purple. He'd have a nasty bruise, but they could patch him up at the farm.

"Is she dead?" asked Tyler again. Shane looked at Hunter. Hunter hesitated before speaking.

"I hit her," he said. "If she's not dead, she's hurt and bleeding badly. She's out of the fight. That's all we care about. Now we're going home. We've got work to do."

CHAPTER 33

For a little while, I lost touch with reality. My head throbbed and Roy barked. Somebody—I thought it was my neighbor—tried to wake me up, but I didn't want to wake up. My eyes refused to open, and my body felt heavy. And my brain just wanted to sleep. So I did.

Then some other people came. I recognized they were different because they touched me more. It almost felt like one of them pinched my ear. I think I tried to tell him to stop, but I didn't know if I succeeded. Then they put something behind my head. Finally, they put me on a back brace and carried me outside.

Everything hurt. I remembered that. I couldn't remember the drive to the hospital, but I was pretty sure they took me to the hospital. Somebody held my hand in the ambulance, which was nice except that they had sweaty hands. They ran tests on me in the hospital, but time didn't seem to flow right. I think I got a CT scan. I was sort of in and out. The light hurt, my head throbbed, and my body ached. I shouldn't have been physically exhausted, but I was. I just wanted to sleep.

Eventually, though, they put me in a private room and left me alone. I tried to ask about Roy, but I didn't have enough energy, and I couldn't speak well. My eyes closed, and the world ceased to exist.

I woke up with the worst headache of my life. It was morning. At least I think it was morning. The sun was up. I wore a hospital gown, and I was under three blankets. I wasn't alone in the room, either. Shelby Cain lay on the sofa. She looked asleep. She was married to my friend and former colleague Preston. At work, we had called him Sasquatch. He retired after being severely injured on the job. Shelby and Preston were good people.

I didn't want to wake her up, so I stayed quiet and tried not to move. A bandage pulled my hair. My entire body throbbed, and even though I had just woken up, my brain felt exhausted. It was an odd feeling. I stayed still, trying to become oriented to the room, until a nurse arrived. Shelby stirred and woke. I caught her eye and waved. She stood beside the bed. The nurse checked my blood pressure, temperature, and pulse. Then, before leaving, she told me a doctor wanted to talk to me. That seemed sensible.

"Hey, Joe," said Shelby. "Preston's downstairs with your boss."

"George's down there?"

An almost pained expression passed over her face.

"George Delgado died over a year ago," she said. "It's a highway patrol lieutenant. She brought your purse and phone. There are detectives at your house."

I closed my eyes and tried to shake my head, but that hurt.

"Yeah, sorry," I said. "I'm not thinking right."

"That's okay," she said. "You got hit pretty hard, and you lost a lot of blood. The doctor said amnesia was possible."

I closed my eyes.

"I was bleeding?"

"Yeah," she said. "Head wounds bleed a lot, apparently. It was all external, though, they think. They did a CT scan in the ER. Your skull's not fractured, either. You've got a hard head."

"My mom says the same thing," I said. "I'm really tired. Can I sleep?"

"Yeah. The nurse says we're supposed to let you sleep as much as you want."

I started to drift away, but then I shook my head and tried to sit up. She put a hand on my shoulder.

"You're okay, honey," she said, her voice soft. "I'm still here."

"Where's Roy?"

"He's safe," she said. "Your neighbor heard him barking last night, so she went to your house. When she found you, she called 911. A nurse in the ER recognized you. She called Doug Patricia's wife, and then Doug called Harry Grainger and a few other people. Preston and I picked up Roy. He's at our farm with Cat, our golden retriever."

I closed my eyes and nodded.

"You named your dog Cat."

She chuckled a little.

"Preston did," said Shelby. "He thinks it's funny."

"That sounds like him. He's always thought he was funny."

Shelby may have said something else, but I fell asleep again. This time, when I woke up, I was alone. The window shades were drawn, but the sky felt more subdued. My head didn't hurt quite as much as it had earlier, and I didn't feel dizzy. I wouldn't be running a marathon anytime soon, but I felt okay. For a few minutes, I stayed there. Then I realized how hungry I was, so I called the nurse. She came in and brought me dinner.

A hospitalist came in shortly after dinner. A neurologist in the emergency room had diagnosed me with a traumatic brain injury. They hadn't seen any internal bleeding on a CT scan, and my skull hadn't been fractured—both of which were nice to hear—but this wasn't my first concussion. The doctor warned me that future injuries could kill me. The doctor said I was lucky, but lying in bed with a splitting headache, I didn't feel lucky. They wanted to keep me another night for observation. I didn't like being stuck in the hospital, but I didn't want to move, either, so I agreed.

After our brief conversation, he left, and I fell asleep. A nurse came in periodically to check on me, but mostly the staff left me alone. The next morning, I felt better. My headache had dulled, my stomach felt fine, and I was able to walk around without stumbling.

Because I had been covered in blood, the staff had removed my shirt and pants in the emergency room, and someone from the hospital's housekeeping department had laundered my clothes. The front of my shirt looked fine, but blood had stained the back pink. For a few moments, I just stared at it as the situation sunk in. The doctors were right: I was lucky to be alive.

My hands trembled and my knees wobbled as I dressed, forcing me to sit down again. Some of the weakness in my limbs may have been residual effects of my injury, but it wasn't fully. I had almost died. If Roy hadn't barked and gotten my neighbor's attention, I very well might have bled to death. I didn't know how I should feel, so I focused on my clothes.

As I pulled my shirt over my head, though, another thought struck: someone had hidden in my house and tried to kill me. If they had succeeded, it would have been capital murder. My breath slowed, and I rubbed my eyes.

"Jesus," I said, almost under my breath. I didn't even know if it was safe to go home. I couldn't stay in the hospital, though. They needed the bed, and I needed to get back to work. If my parents had still lived in the area, I would have called them. Since they didn't, I called Preston. The moment I asked for a ride, he and Shelby jumped in their car. I was lucky to have them.

I didn't have anything to pack, so I called the nurse and asked for my discharge paperwork. A doctor came in fifteen minutes later and warned me to take it easy for the next few weeks. I wasn't supposed to exert myself, and I needed to minimize activities that gave me headaches or tired me out. He said I could start taking walks soon. I thanked him, signed half a dozen papers, and left with Shelby and Preston a few minutes later.

We talked for a few minutes, but mostly I stared out the window at the landscape as Preston drove. When we got to my house, Preston parked behind my Volvo in the driveway. My hands trembled as I opened his SUV's door.

"You don't have to go home alone," said Preston. "We've got a guest bedroom with your name on it. You and Roy can stay."

I hesitated before shaking my head.

"Thanks, but no," I said. "I need to get this figured out. Can you watch Roy for a few days, though? My doctor doesn't want me walking too far, and he'd get bored with me cooped up inside."

"Of course," said Shelby. "Cat's living it up with a new friend."

I was pretty sure she was overselling things. Roy was a great dog, but he wasn't playful. When I got him, he didn't know how to play. His previous owner had bred him to be a working dog, and they had begun training him as a very young puppy. Maybe time with a golden retriever half his age was just what Roy needed. Maybe Cat would help break him out of his shell. He deserved it. I thanked them both and stepped out of the car. Shelby and Preston both jumped out.

"I do something wrong?" I asked.

"No," said Shelby. "I thought you'd need a hug."

So I hugged them both, which was nice. When my station had closed, it felt like my community had fallen apart. Maybe it hadn't, though. Maybe my community had always been here.

I waved as they drove away. Then I turned toward my front door. It had an evidentiary seal over the door and framing, which made sense considering someone had tried to kill me. That seal—and a matching one on the back door—secured the crime scene. If they were intact, no one had been inside.

I stepped closer. Lieutenant Cognata and a detective I had never met had signed it. The lieutenant had probably been at the hospital yesterday to interview me. Not that it would have helped anything. I hadn't seen my attacker. For all I knew, it could have been a robbery gone wrong. Half the homes around me had bars over their windows. I had never worked a murder in my neighborhood, but I had investigated a few burglaries.

Maybe Roy and I just scared somebody. Or maybe I was attacked by the same person who killed Wyatt Caparaso. It could have been Erik Hoyle, too. He had just been released from prison. It might have even been Hunter Collins. I doubted he was happy with me after I arrested him and used him to boost Michael Clarke's standing within their community. Or it could have been someone I had arrested years ago. Now that our county didn't have a sheriff's department, maybe it was open season on me. I had given a lot of bad people reason to want me hurt.

As I stood, something warm stirred inside me. I felt agitated. My brain still felt sluggish, but my body was ready to move. Someone had come into my home and tried to kill me. They could have succeeded if not for Roy's barking. I didn't know their identities or what they wanted, but they wouldn't hurt me again.

Now, I was pissed.

CHAPTER 34

My phone said it was twenty to noon. I couldn't stay at home, but it was too early to check into a hotel. I probably should have accepted Shelby and Preston's offer to stay with them, but I didn't want to be a burden. And even if I had somewhere to stay, I had nothing to wear except blood-stained clothing.

St. Augustine used to have a boutique shop that sold expensive but very nice women's clothes, but that had shut down. Instead, I drove half an hour to the nearest department store, where I purchased a week's worth of tops, four pairs of pants, pajamas, a sweater, underclothes, socks, toiletries, and a bag to put everything in. The clothes were comfortable and cute.

After my shopping extravaganza, I drove back to my station, feeling as if I just hiked around a mountain. I was exhausted, and I fell asleep almost the moment I lay down on the couch in my office. About two hours later, my cell phone rang. My head felt fuzzy. I didn't answer. Then my office phone rang, which meant the call was important. I couldn't ignore it, so I grabbed the phone and tried to sound chipper and awake.

"Hey, this is Joe Court's office."

"Ms. Court, I'm glad I found you. This is Lieutenant Elena Cognata. You're in your office, I take it."

I cleared my throat.

"I am," I said. "I'm reading paperwork right now. The doctors haven't cleared me for duty."

"Are you feeling okay enough to be in the office?"

I almost told her I had nowhere else to go, but I held back.

"I'm tired, but I'm okay. The doctors said exhaustion was common."

"I'm glad things weren't worse," she said. "Detective Griffin and I went through your house earlier. We think your attacker came in through the back door. As best we could tell, they didn't steal anything. It didn't look like they were searching for anything, either. It was an attack."

A dull, throbbing pain began growing at the base of my skull, just a few inches below where I was hit.

"Okay," I said. "Did you find prints or anything?"

"Smudges," she said. "Our techs thought they might have worn gloves. We went through your neighborhood as well, hoping we could find surveillance equipment, but we came up empty. We'll be checking red light footage on the off chance they ran a red light. There are a lot of vacant houses in your neighborhood, so witnesses are scarce. They did put your dog in his crate. Would your dog allow a stranger to do that?"

I shook my head.

"Not willingly. If you give him a chance to attack, he'll bite you and hold on, but a big man who understands dogs could overpower him. If you grip him around the neck and under his legs, he can't do much. He's just a dog."

"Your attacker came to kill you. It's interesting they didn't kill him."

I rubbed my eyes.

"Even assholes like dogs."

She laughed.

"That is certainly true," she said. She paused. "When did you last speak to Erik Hoyle?"

I straightened and drew in a breath.

"Do you think Hoyle did this?" I asked.

"I'm asking when you last saw him."

I shook my head.

"Hoyle wouldn't have put Roy back in his crate. He would have just hit him with whatever he hit me with," I said. "Roy bit his arm pretty hard, and I pepper sprayed him in the face. If he had the chance, he would have killed us both."

"You didn't see him after the incident at his former wife's home?"

"Correct. I haven't tried to contact him since then. Like I said, though, I don't think he would have let Roy live. Prison changes a person. I hate to say that, but it's true. He may have been a loving father when he went in, but you could drop Santa Claus in Potosi for eight years, and he'd come out a mean asshole with a short fuse. You can't survive in prison unless you're willing to protect yourself and your reputation for the slightest provocation."

She paused.

"Mr. Hoyle is dead," she said. "The housekeeper at his bed-and-breakfast found him this morning. He seems to have died in bed yesterday or maybe last night. He left a suicide note."

I sat down on my desk chair and put my hand over my face.

"Damn. How'd he die?"

"We're not quite sure, but we found an empty bottle of prescription sleeping pills in his room."

I paused and shook my head.

"Men don't kill themselves with pills. Statistically, they're much more likely to use a gun—which he had access to. What'd his suicide note say?"

Cognata drew in a breath.

"I didn't memorize it, but it said he was tired of our evil world and that he was sorry. You said he was trying to commit suicide by cop when he went to his ex-wife's house. It looked like he chose a different means."

Again, I shook my head.

"He was angry when I saw him, not tired or sad or introspective. He wanted me to shoot him because he thought it would increase his payout in a lawsuit. His kids were important to him. I can't see him abandoning them now."

"Maybe he realized his kids didn't want to see him. They lost him eight years ago."

My head still hurt, but my mind had woken from a nap.

"Did the note use the word evil?"

"It did," she said.

I shook my head and stood.

"Evil is a loaded word," I said, pacing in my small office. "It has theological overtones. It implies malevolence, like something is directing events. He went through serious trauma, so from his point of view, the world sucks. He didn't say that, though. He said it was evil. It's a religious term. Did he become religious in prison?"

"I don't know."

I nodded and considered.

"Can I see the suicide note?"

She paused.

"I understand how close you are to this case, but I didn't call for your investigative assistance. I called as a courtesy."

"Can you send me a picture of the note?"

Cognata sighed.

"I can, but we're going to wait for the medical examiner's report before making broad pronouncements about his cause of death."

"I understand," I said. Lieutenant Cognata agreed and emailed me a picture of the document. I opened it and read through it twice. The text was short.

I'm tired of this evil world. It's never going to get better. Sorry.

The penmanship was familiar. I pulled my cell phone from my purse and flicked through photographs until I found the alleged suicide note found near Wyatt Caparaso's body in Blue Springs. Both notes were handwritten.

People who believed in handwriting analysis thought a person's handwriting could reveal aspects of the writer's character and background. They had long-winded explanations to explain why letters slanted to the left indicated the writer had a repressed emotional state and had likely grown up in a strict, utilitarian household. That was nonsense, but I couldn't help but note the similarities between the letter formations.

I put my phone on speaker.

"Wyatt Caparaso also allegedly committed suicide," I said, "but the coroner in Blue Springs ruled his death a homicide. The police in Blue Springs found a note, too. They're on the same type of paper, and the penmanship looks identical."

Cognata went quiet.

"Did Caparaso and Hoyle know each other?"

"I don't know if they ever met, but Wyatt Caparaso wrote articles about Erik Hoyle. Before he died, Wyatt told me he was lured to a campground by someone who promised him information about Hoyle. At the campground, he ran into Donna Wright and shot her. He claimed it was self-defense."

Cognata went silent for a moment.

"Who lured him there?"

I squeezed my jaw tight before speaking.

"Detective Atherton didn't believe that was pertinent to the murder investigation," I said. "Wyatt claimed someone sent him a note through his campus's mail system, but he also said he had destroyed that note. We couldn't prove anything. Donna Wright's family sheltered illegal migrants and helped them evade capture. Her family says she was lured to the campground by someone claiming to need help."

Cognata considered again.

"I don't understand this," she said. "Why would someone lure Caparaso and Wright to the campsite? If you wanted them dead, you could have lured them to the middle of nowhere alone and shot them. Why would you bring them together?"

"I don't know," I said. "It doesn't make sense to me, either, but if we take them at their word, that's what happened. So far, I haven't found anything to contradict their stories."

She clicked her tongue a few times.

"I will take your observations under advisement."

I stopped pacing and shook my head.

"That's it?"

"Yeah, that's it," she said. "You're proposing a grand conspiracy that combines multiple murders in multiple juris-

CHRIS CULVER

dictions on limited evidence. I have to look at the facts. Erik
Hoyle has been in prison for eight years for a crime he didn't
commit. Upon his release, he went to his former house and
found a stranger living with his wife. He can't see his children, he has no job, and he has no permanent place to live.
He doesn't have anything. He has nothing to hope for. This
is Missouri. Wrongful conviction payout is, what, a hundred
bucks a day? After taxes and his lawyer's fees, he'll be lucky if
he can buy a new Toyota. Facing all that, I bet I'd feel pretty
tired. I'd probably think the world had it against me. I might
even call it evil."

My head hurt. My doctors had warned me against exerting
myself, but they didn't understand the situation. Still, I sat
down again and closed my eyes. The room was spinning, and
my legs felt weak.

"Hoyle's lawyer was Brian Carlisle. He's good. Hoyle had
millions coming his way. He could have sued his wife for
joint custody. No judge would give him sole custody, but
they'd grant him partial custody, at the very least. Life was
hard for him now, but he had better days ahead of him. He
knew that, too. He had resources. His wife divorced him,
but he had family. He had a community. Given what I know
about the victim, I'm not buying this at all."

"You don't know anything about Erik Hoyle. You
couldn't have."

"I put him in prison, Lieutenant."

"No, you didn't," she said. She paused. "You couldn't have. What were you, fifteen, sixteen when he went to prison?"

"I was twenty-two. I was a uniformed officer. It was my first year on the job. George Delgado was the lead detective. His partner was Jasper Martin. George is dead now. I found Brittany Ashbury's body, and I assisted in the interrogation. Hoyle confessed to me."

Lieutenant Cognata's voice softened.

"You didn't put him in prison, Joe," she said. "No matter what happened to this guy, it wasn't your fault. I've been a cop for twenty-eight years. I know how it works. You were a uniformed officer following orders. If Hoyle was wrongfully imprisoned, it's not your fault."

"Thank you," I said. I breathed in and out slowly. "I just need you to consider that this wasn't a suicide."

"We will consider every angle, but the medical examiner will make the final call. If he says it's a suicide, that's it. End of story."

"For your office, maybe."

"For you, too, Ms. Court," she said, her voice sharp. "This case belongs to the highway patrol. The St. Augustine County Sheriff's Department no longer exists. You are my employee, and you will follow my orders. If you fail to do so, you'll find yourself out of a job. Clear?"

"Yes, ma'am," I said before pausing. Cognata drew in a breath, but I spoke before she could. "Has anyone talked to his family yet?"

"We did," she said. "Detective Griffin and I notified Angela. She was going to tell her kids."

"How about Brian Carlisle? He was Hoyle's lawyer."

"I don't know whether anyone called him or not."

I nodded.

"He might have information."

"Even if he does," said Cognata, "he's a defense attorney. As a rule, they don't talk to the police."

"I'm going to talk to him, anyway. My department put Hoyle in prison for eight years. The least I can do now is investigate his death. And you can't fire me. I was appointed by the attorney general. If you've got a problem with me, take it up with him."

She paused before telling me good luck. Her voice sounded resigned. I thanked her and hung up. Then I stood up but kept my hand on the couch in case I felt dizzy again. A drive to St. Louis was going to push me harder than my doctors wanted, but some things were more important than my discomfort. I had a job to do.

CHAPTER 35

Before leaving my office, I looked up Brian Carlisle's firm and called the receptionist. She answered before the phone finished ringing.

"Carlisle and Associates. How can I address your call?"

"Hey," I said. "My name is Joe Court. I work for the state highway patrol. I'm calling to see whether Brian Carlisle is available for a meeting in an hour. I need to see him about one of his clients."

She clicked her tongue a few times.

"Mr. Carlisle is a very busy person. He rarely has time on his schedule for drop-ins."

"Sure," I said, nodding. "I get it. This is about Erik Hoyle. He's a client. Mr. Carlisle needs to hear what I have to say."

"If you were a prosecutor or city attorney, we'd happily fit you into the schedule. We don't routinely meet with police officers, though. If this is pressing, please have an attorney call our office."

I closed my eyes and counted to five so I wouldn't snap at her.

"Okay. Thank you."

She hung up. I swore to myself and then fished Brian Carlisle's business card out of my purse. He said he had given me his direct line, but I wasn't quite sure whether that meant his office line, his receptionist's line, or what. So I dialed. The phone rang three times before a male voice hesitantly answered. By direct line, Carlisle apparently meant his cell phone.

"Mr. Carlisle, this is Joe Court from St. Augustine. I had hoped to speak to you about Erik Hoyle."

He paused and drew in a breath.

"My schedule is tight today. If you need to interview Erik, I can send an associate down."

I grimaced.

"Erik's dead," I said. "Pending word from the medical examiner, we're currently investigating his death as a homicide, but I've noticed some similarities between his death and those of a young man named Wyatt Caparaso. I had hoped to talk to you about it."

He paused again.

"Your other victim was Wyatt Caparaso? And he's dead, too?"

"He is," I said, nodding. "Have you heard of him?"

"Yeah. We should meet in person. Are you on your way?"

"I will be shortly," I said, already standing and grabbing my purse.

"I will see you in my office in one hour. Drive safely."

I thanked him and hung up, wondering whether this was a good idea. It didn't matter, though, because I had already made the appointment. I got in my car and headed north. The drive to St. Louis was usually pretty easy, but today I had to stop halfway because I needed a break. My head hurt, so I stopped at a Starbucks in Festus, a little town about half an hour north of St. Augustine. A quick walk around the building allowed my mind to relax. The caffeine in the coffee I ordered didn't hurt either, and allowed me to make it the rest of the way in relative ease.

Brian Carlisle worked out of a beautiful mid-rise building with a red brick exterior and sheets of glass that stretched forty or fifty stories to the sky. From a distance, the ornate brickwork and carved limestone moldings looked historic, but on closer inspection, the building was clearly modern. I appreciated the aesthetic. I took the elevator to Carlisle's floor and stepped into an expansive, wood-trimmed lobby that smelled like a library. A woman behind the front desk smiled as I walked forward.

"I'm Joe Court," I said. "I have an appointment with Brian Carlisle."

Her smile faltered, and I wondered if she was the person I had spoken to on the phone. She focused on her computer and then tilted her head to the side.

"You do," she said. "I'll let Mr. Carlisle know you're here. Please have a seat."

I thanked her and did as she suggested. A man a few years older than me sat a few seats away, reading something on his phone. There was something almost familiar about his nose and jaw, making me wonder whether I had seen him before. He wore jeans, a blue Oxford shirt, and a blazer. A silver badge hung from his belt, and he wore a pistol in a black holster on his hip. As I sat down, he glanced at me and nodded a hello before focusing on his phone once more.

About ten minutes after I arrived, Brian Carlisle stepped out. He nodded to me but then focused on the detective I was sitting beside. The two shook hands, spoke softly, and then Carlisle handed him an envelope. Afterward, the two stood awkwardly and silently until the detective excused himself. I felt as if I were intruding by watching.

Carlisle watched the detective enter the elevator before turning his attention to me.

"Did you say hello?" he asked.

I pointed toward the elevator.

"To him?"

Carlisle's expression softened. For just a split second, he almost looked wistful.

"That was Homer. He's a detective in St. Louis County. He's my son. I'm trying to convince him to quit his job and join the dark side and work for me."

If he was Carlisle's son, he was my half-brother. I drew in a slow breath, wondering whether I wanted to meet him or not. Carlisle's daughter, Erin, was wonderful and sweet and kind. I liked her, but I wasn't sure if I was ready to welcome other strangers into my life. I'd think about that later; I wasn't here to meet family. Carlisle cleared his throat.

"I would have introduced you, but I don't know how he'd react. He and I have a difficult relationship. You want to meet him, you should meet his wife, Kate, first. I bet you'd like her."

Which meant I had a sister-in-law, too. I swallowed hard.

"Maybe some other time," I said. "We need to talk about Erik."

Carlisle agreed. We left the lobby and walked through a busy—and expansive—suite of offices. Carlisle's name may have been atop the firm's stationary and signage, but his office looked little different from those around him. It had a desk, windows, bookshelves, and chairs. I sat on an upholstered chair.

"Would you like a drink?" he asked. "We usually have coffee."

"Thank you, but no," I said. He sat behind his desk. For a moment, we said nothing. Then he exhaled a slow breath.

"I'm sorry we're meeting under these circumstances."

"Me, too," I said. I looked at his bookshelves. "I kind of expected you to have a nicer office."

"When you pay the bills, you realize the cost of that corner office. It doesn't look as appealing. When I meet clients, we go to the conference room. Tell me about Erik."

"He died at a bed-and-breakfast in St. Augustine. I'm not working the case, but I was briefed. He allegedly left a suicide note. We're waiting for word from the medical examiner, but the initial thought is that he committed suicide."

Carlisle blinked and looked down.

"You used the word allegedly."

"That's right," I said. "They found an empty container of sleeping pills in his room. The theory is that he became overwrought, wrote the note, took the pills, and died in his sleep. I don't believe it. Men don't typically kill themselves with pills—especially if they have access to firearms. They're quicker and more effective."

I paused before continuing.

"And the handwriting on Hoyle's alleged suicide note matches the handwriting on a suicide note found near Wyatt Caparaso's body in Blue Springs, Missouri. He didn't commit suicide, either."

Carlisle brought a hand to his face and rubbed his eyes before leaning forward and grabbing the phone. He dialed somebody.

"Miranda, reschedule my appointments this afternoon. Something's come up."

After a moment, he thanked his assistant and hung up. Then he leaned back.

"From what I've read, you're a good detective. Why aren't you investigating Erik's death?"

My face suddenly felt warm. I gave him a half smile.

"I've been in the hospital recently. Someone attacked me in my house and gave me a pretty significant concussion. Apparently, I lost a lot of blood, too. I'm not cleared for active duty. Truth be told, my home is still a crime scene."

He considered me.

"Do you have a place to stay?"

"Yeah," I said. "I'm fine. That's not why I'm here. Erik Hoyle was your client, so I thought you deserved an update. I don't know what's going to happen with the investigation into Mr. Hoyle's death, but I suspect the situation is more complicated than the reports will indicate."

He sighed and shook his head.

"Thank you for coming," he said. "If I had represented him at the original trial, Erik never would have gone to prison."

"You're that good, huh?" I asked, lowering my chin and allowing my lips to curl into a smile.

He tilted his head to the side and raised his eyebrows.

"Yeah." He paused and blinked. "And his original attorney had such a high caseload he never should have taken Erik on."

I shrugged.

"I worked that case," I said. "Hoyle had no alibi, he was the last person to see Brittany Ashbury alive, we had evidence matching his bite to a bite on the victim's shoulder, and he confessed. Hard to overcome all that."

Carlisle closed his eyes and shook his head.

"Your case was a house of cards. Bite mark evidence is unreliable at best."

"A jury thought otherwise."

"A significant portion of our population believes the earth is flat," said Carlisle. "Scientific literacy is not our society's strong suit."

I crossed my arms.

"That's probably true. It's also why we have expert witnesses who can explain the evidence to a jury."

He considered me. Then he shrugged.

"Okay. Sure. This is an important conversation. You sure you want to have it? You might not like what I say."

I smiled and looked down.

"I'm pretty sure I can take it."

"The forensic odontologist your team brought in is a dedicated professional with a vital role to play in victim identification. He can match a 3D molding of a victim's teeth to X-rays with a high degree of precision and reliability. Bite mark analysis, though, is entirely different. It relies on two premises. First, that human teeth are unique the way a person's DNA is unique. Second, it says that human skin can reliably hold the impression of someone's teeth. We have no evidence to think either is true. In fact, common sense says skin would never work. Skin is constantly changing, especially after death. It gains water, loses water, decomposes, stretches, and heals."

Shaun Deveraux had said similar things. It still rankled me.

"We're not scientists," I said. "We screw up, but we don't put people on the stand to lie."

"That, I believe," said Carlisle. "It's part of the problem, though. Judges aren't scientists, either, but if an appellate judge says some new, unproven but supposedly scientific breakthrough is good science, every other judge follows along. I've been a defense attorney for four decades, and I can think of half a dozen scientific breakthroughs that have been discredited. Bloodstain analysis, 911 call analysis, ear print analysis, lie detector tests, burn pattern analysis...I could go on and on. Prosecutors have put people on death row using these tools, and it's all garbage. A rich defendant can bring in his own experts, but they cost money most people don't have. The system shouldn't work only for the wealthy."

My cheeks were starting to grow warm, and a dull, piercing pain began spreading down my spine. I ignored it.

"I see," I said, nodding. "So prosecutors are liars, cops are liars, and defense attorneys are the lone heroes fighting for the common man. Am I getting that right?"

"Hardly," he said, chuckling. "We all play a role in the system, and we utilize the tools at our disposal. Detective shows like *Law & Order* or *CSI* glorify the criminal justice system. Reality doesn't fit the stories, though. We have systems designed to produce verdicts. The prosecutor's job is to secure a conviction. Mine is to secure an acquittal. Yours is to make an arrest. We hope that through these competing interests, we'll get things right. Four times out of five, that's probably what happens. Even honest cops and lawyers make mistakes, though. The system produces wrong verdicts every day. When that happens, we need to correct our mistakes, but all too often, we double down on stupidity."

I clenched my jaw and shook my head.

"My job is to examine the evidence and arrest the *correct* person. The prosecutor's job is to prosecute the *correct* person. Your job is to defend your client, guilty or otherwise. Two of us are after the truth. One is after a result."

He leaned forward.

"Was George Delgado after the truth when he interrogated Erik Hoyle for ten hours straight? Is that why he removed his partner's name from the final reports? Is that why he brought you, a uniformed officer with less than a year's experience, into the interrogation booth? Delgado used you because he thought you could secure the result he wanted. And you did. You broke Erik Hoyle because you reminded him so much of someone he cared about, someone who was dead on his watch."

I squeezed my jaw tight before speaking.

"I was following the evidence."

"You were following orders, Ms. Court," said Carlisle. "You were doing your job."

He said it softly. It still felt like a dagger. I swallowed.

"George Delgado lied to me and said Brittany and Erik Hoyle were having an affair. George told me Hoyle killed her because she tried to end their relationship. I believed him.

He said one of Brittany's friends had told him. He said he was trying to protect a witness. I didn't realize he had made that witness up."

Carlisle breathed through his nose and nodded.

"That explains a lot, sadly," he said. "You're a good cop. It's a shame you were surrounded by those who weren't."

We settled into an uneasy sort of truce. My headache receded as my heartbeat gradually slowed. I took a few breaths.

"What do we do now?" I asked.

He gave me a tight smile before looking at the ink blotter on his desk.

"We go back to work," he said. "I'm sorry for the circumstances, but I'm glad I got to meet you, Ms. Court. Erin, my daughter, was right about you."

I stood and put my purse over my shoulder.

"What'd she say, if you don't mind me asking?"

"She said I'd like you. And that we'd argue."

I smiled.

"I like Erin. She's a smart woman."

Carlisle wished me luck. I said likewise and stepped out. It was a weird meeting, but somehow pleasant, too. I didn't know if I liked Carlisle, but I had time to decide. I'd see him again. I suspected I'd see Carlisle's son, Homer, again, too. Life had a funny way of putting people together—whether we wanted it or not.

CHAPTER 36

I was too tired to drive all the way back to St. Augustine only to stay in a crappy, overpriced hotel and eat something unhealthy from a diner, and since I hadn't been able to get into my house, the bag of clothes and toiletries I had purchased were still in my Volvo. I checked into a Drury Inn in Brentwood, took an elevator to my floor, and flopped onto a king-size bed in time to see the sun set.

Unfortunately, my empty stomach didn't let me stay in bed long. Restaurants, bars, and shops surrounded my hotel, so I walked across the parking lot to a seafood place and ordered halibut. It was good. The bar was lively, and guests ate, laughed, and conversed at every table around me. I found myself drawing from that energy.

St. Augustine used to feel lively, too. The air itself had seemed to hold possibility. You could listen to live music, meet friends at a restaurant, or lose yourself in the crowds. Now, our restaurants and bars sat empty. Homeless people sat outside in the parks. When I went out, I could feel the ghosts of the past peering over my shoulder. The future there felt bleak. Here, the future seemed more real somehow.

As I waited for the check, I pulled out my phone and looked up law enforcement jobs in the area. Webster Groves, Rock Hill, Crestwood, Ladue, and seemingly every other police department within a five-mile radius needed sworn officers. They'd pay me more than I made in St. Augustine, too. None wanted an experienced detective, but I could go back to patrol. A lot of officers liked being on patrol. There were scary moments, but they didn't happen every day. Mostly, you talked to people. I was good at that. It might be fun.

I paid my bill and headed back to my hotel. My mom and dad had moved to Chicago. My brother Ian was going to college soon, and my brother Dylan was probably going to move to Chicago to pursue new women—and finish his college degree. Most of my friends had left St. Augustine. I could make a life here. It was worth thinking about, at least.

That night, I slept well in a big bed, my mind alight with possibility. When I woke up the next morning, I felt good. The sun didn't seem quite as blinding, and my head didn't hurt. I didn't feel quite as tired, either. I wasn't ready to start running, but I felt more like myself.

The hotel served breakfast, so I ate a bowl of oatmeal and drank coffee. It was relaxing, like a mini vacation. Afterward, I checked out and drove south to St. Augustine, where the world quickly returned.

Lieutenant Cognata called as I unlocked the front door to get into my station. If I didn't know better, I'd say she was watching me.

"Morning," I said. "This is Joe Court."

"Yeah, good morning," she said. "I'm calling to tell you that Detective Griffin and I will be in St. Augustine shortly. We'll need access to your building to store equipment and evidence. The medical examiner hasn't begun Erik Hoyle's autopsy yet, but upon moving him yesterday, a pill fell out of his mouth. A pathologist then looked in Mr. Hoyle's throat and discovered twenty-nine pills lodged inside. The pathologist concluded that someone had jammed them in there after Mr. Hoyle's death to make it look like an accidental overdose."

I nodded.

"The person—or people—who killed Wyatt Caparaso did a poor job, too. The scene was obviously staged, and their rope was too long. It decapitated the victim. I can give you the contact information of the detective in charge of that case."

"Email it to me."

I crossed the lobby's marble floor on my way to the steps and eventually the break room.

"If sleeping pills didn't kill him, what did?"

Cognata sighed.

"We don't know yet. There were no gunshot wounds, no stab wounds, no bruising, no signs of suffocation or strangulation..." She paused and sighed again. "He could have died of natural causes, but I don't know why his killer would then jam pills down his throat."

"That would be peculiar behavior after a heart attack," I said.

"It would be. At the very least, we've got somebody for tampering with evidence and abandoning a corpse. We're going to go back and fingerprint the entire B&B room. We'll see about cameras, too. At the time he died, Hoyle was the B&B's only guest. Nobody else came in all day."

I reached the breakroom and opened the coffeemaker. It smelled like burned toast. Had my home coffeemaker smelled that bad, I would have thought I had shorted something out. Here, it was normal. I started cleaning the pot.

"I'm guessing there was a back door or window," I said, holding my phone between my shoulder and ear.

"There is," said Cognata. "We're going to print the exterior. We might get lucky."

"You should go by the bank on Second Avenue. They're half a block from the bed-and-breakfast, and they've got surveillance cameras. You should also ask at the convenience store on State Street. They're not far, either, and they've got surveillance cameras pointed at their pumps. They get video of every car that drives by."

She paused, hopefully to write that down.

"Thank you," she said. "I'm going to need your help on this. You know St. Augustine. Who would want this guy dead?"

"He's not a St. Augustine resident," I said. "He's been living in Potosi for the past eight years."

"But you've worked this case," said Cognata. "You know the area. Who would want him dead?"

I rubbed my eyes and sighed.

"Brittany Ashbury's mom. She thinks Hoyle killed her daughter. Hoyle's ex-wife didn't seem to like him very much, either. You'll have to interview Angela Hoyle's new husband, too. Those are the obvious suspects. I'd also look at his actions in prison. Some prison gangs have long arms that can reach through walls. If Hoyle owed money to somebody inside, they might have tried to collect at home."

Cognata hesitated.

"You know the locals. You want to interview them?"

"No, but I will if needed," I said. "The elephant in the room is Hoyle's suicide note. The handwriting matches Wyatt Caparaso's suicide note. You should run the prison angle. If you go to Potosi, check their phone and visitor logs. See if Wyatt Caparaso and Erik Hoyle were ever in contact."

Cognata paused again.

"I can do that, but only if you handle the situation in St. Augustine. Somebody needs to interview Hoyle's family and Brittany Ashbury's mom."

"I'm not cleared for full duty, but I can interview people," I said. "You work the prison. I'll tell you if I uncover anything with our suspects."

She thanked me and wished me luck. I said likewise. Then I sighed. I had an assignment, but I needed to check in with Shelby and Preston first, so I called their house. Shelby answered.

"Hey," I said. "This is Joe. I wanted to call and check in and see how the dog's doing."

"Roy's such a good dog," she said. "He and Cat are sitting in the author's office. I dare not disturb them."

"The author?" I asked, quirking an eyebrow.

"Yep," she said. "He hasn't told many people yet, but Preston's an author. He's written a couple of books now."

That tickled a memory. I closed my eyes and thought back.

"Are they detective stories about a police officer hunting a serial killer who murders people and then chops them up in a blender?"

Shelby laughed.

"I see you've met Sir Smoothie," she said.

"Preston introduced me a few years ago when we were still working together," I said. "I didn't realize he actually wrote the book."

"He's written three. They're fascinating character studies of a deeply complex Byronic hero."

"Really?" I asked, furrowing my brow. Shelby laughed again.

"No, but Preston likes writing them, and he's sold a few copies," she said. "Sir Smoothie will be flying us to Greece over Christmas."

"Good for Preston and Sir Smoothie," I said, genuinely impressed. "Since Roy's busy with the author, do you mind if I pick up him this evening? I'd go now, but I'd hate to interrupt Preston's creative process."

"That is just fine," she said. "We'll see you then."

Shelby and I talked for another minute, but we both had work. I hung up and flipped through my notepad until I found the phone number of Whitney Ashbury, Brittany's mom. She answered on the third ring.

Whitney and I didn't speak for long. When I told her Erik Hoyle was dead, she started crying and said no one deserved it more. At this point, it wasn't my job to persuade her of the falsity of that statement. Instead, I asked where she had been the night Hoyle died. Apparently, she had stayed overnight at the house of her significant other. He and his children could vouch for her. That, in my mind, effectively eliminated her from our suspect pool. I thanked her for her time and hung up.

Next, I called Angela Ortiz, Hoyle's former spouse. She took the news of her husband's death stoically, but I could hear the pain in her voice. She may have divorced her husband, but she had feelings for him, too. Like Whitney Ashbury, Angela wasn't alone the night Erik Hoyle died. She was at home with her husband and her three children. Mateo had set the alarm when he went to bed at eleven. Nobody entered or exited the house until a little before eight the next morning. Until I heard otherwise, that, in my mind, eliminated both of them from our suspect pool, too. I thanked her for her time and wished her well before hanging up.

Finally, I called Brian Carlisle with the update. He listened. Then he asked questions. Pointed, insightful questions, the same kind of questions I had been asking my colleagues in the highway patrol since Wyatt Caparaso showed up in the public safety office at Waterford College. After a while, he sighed.

"You have no idea who killed Wyatt or Erik, do you?"

"I don't," I said.

"Eighteen months ago, Wyatt Caparaso called the Attorney General's Office in Jefferson City and said he had information that proved Erik Hoyle was innocent. The lawyers there listened, wrote some reports, and ignored him. He kept at it and wrote his stories. An employee of mine was looking at colleges with her daughter and read the newspaper at Waterford College. She gave me the paper the next day, and I read over the kid's work. It was solid. A week later, I took Erik as a client pro bono. I thought we could get him out of prison and earn some publicity. We did, too, because we got lucky. St. Louis has a reform-minded prosecutor who agreed that the evidence against Erik was shaky. In other jurisdictions, the situation's harder."

I leaned back in my chair.

"I'm sure he was grateful."

"He was," said Carlisle. "When I got this case, I brought in four investigators to work it. I wanted to show that he was innocent. My guys worked three weeks straight. Collectively, they billed me over three hundred hours. My investigators are retired detectives. They were good at their jobs, but we didn't get anywhere. Everybody loved Brittany. She was fun, sweet, and never had a bad word for anybody. Erik was a convenient suspect, not a good one. She had a boyfriend named Joaquin Hererra, but he died shortly after she did. He might have killed her, but we couldn't find anything connecting him to her death."

I nodded and considered.

"Did you come across the name Hunter Collins?"

Carlisle clicked his tongue a few times.

"I don't think so."

"He was Brittany's high school boyfriend," I said. "They were close. They broke up because he was involved in a church she didn't like. He's come up in other investigations around town."

He paused.

"I'll ask one of my paralegals to go through our notes again, but I don't think he came up."

I sighed and rubbed my eyes.

"If Erik was innocent, why would someone kill him now?"

"Nobody's innocent," said Carlisle. "He just didn't kill Brittany Ashbury."

I shook my head and looked at my desktop.

"Thank you, Captain Cynicism," I said. Then I paused and shook my head. "I'm sorry. I shouldn't have said that. It's inappropriate."

"Probably," said Carlisle, chuckling. "You're not wrong, though."

I thanked him for his time, wished him well, and hung up. Then I leaned back. Carlisle was interesting. Clearly, he was bright. He was honest, too, I thought. He represented Erik Hoyle pro bono both to free him from prison and to earn some publicity for his firm. How much publicity he received, I couldn't say, but he had done his job. His daughter, Erin, seemed like a bright, intelligent young woman, too. I liked her.

Still, he had impregnated my mother and left her to fend for herself. Mom probably didn't tell him about her pregnancy, but he still slept with a vulnerable woman. It wasn't a fling though. She had meant something to him. He named his youngest daughter after her and donated millions to a charity simply because it was named after her. Maybe my mom had pushed him away. She had certainly pushed everyone else in her life away. Maybe there was more to him than I had thought.

Hope was a scary thing. To allow yourself to hope for something is to recognize that you may not get your heart's desire. For years, I hadn't allowed myself to hope for anything. I didn't like the sense of vulnerability it entailed. Brian Carlisle would never become my father—I already had the greatest dad in the world. Whether I wanted it or not, though, he and his family were a part of me.

So, for now, I allowed myself to hope for something good, even if history had taught me that was a long shot.

CHAPTER 37

My brain wanted to run in half a dozen directions at once, so I walked down the hall to a storage room and grabbed a rolling whiteboard and some dry erase markers. Since my office was small, I wheeled the board to a conference room and started a timeline of events and my investigation.

Eight years ago, Brittany Ashbury was raped and murdered behind the hardware store where she worked. My department investigated and ultimately arrested Erik Hoyle. As best I could tell, Detective Delgado hadn't considered anyone else. Hoyle confessed but later recanted that confession. Still, he was convicted and sent to prison.

Eighteen months ago, Wyatt Caparaso contacted the Missouri Attorney General's Office with information that he claimed exonerated Erik Hoyle. The AG's office ignored him, and Caparaso wrote a series of articles, at least one of which landed on Brian Carlisle's desk. Carlisle signed Hoyle as a client and began the arduous task of freeing him from prison.

Within the last week, Wyatt Caparaso and Donna Wright met at a campground in St. Augustine. Both were lured there. Donna had received a phone call from someone claiming to be an illegal migrant who needed help, while Wyatt had received a message through his campus mail promising him information about Erik Hoyle. While at the campsite, Donna supposedly attacked Wyatt, who shot her. According to Wyatt, he was then attacked by adolescent shooters hidden in the woods. I still didn't know whether to believe Wyatt's account.

Shortly after shooting Donna Wright, Wyatt disappeared and was found murdered in his parents' barn. We knew he was murdered, but we didn't have any suspects or leads.

Erik Hoyle was then released from prison. He went to his former wife's house, where I pepper sprayed him. He was then murdered in his bed-and breakfast. The suicide notes at both crime scenes gave me reason to believe he was murdered by the same person or persons who killed Wyatt Caparaso. Brittany Ashbury's mom and his ex-wife's new husband might have wanted him dead, but they had no real connection to Wyatt.

Once I had the details written down, I stepped back from the board and crossed my arms. Then I reconsidered and wrote that someone—maybe the same person I was investigating for Hoyle and Wyatt's murders—attacked me in my home.

For a few moments, I studied the timeline. At first, I thought I had wasted ten minutes, but then I noticed something. Wyatt Caparaso had disappeared for almost two days after he shot Donna Wright and before he was found dead in his barn. With everything else going on, I hadn't given that much thought. I had no idea where he had been during that period. He hadn't used his credit cards, and he hadn't called his parents or his lawyer...he just disappeared.

At this point, everything in this investigation had significance. I went back to my office, grabbed my purse, firearm, and keys, and then locked the building before getting into my Volvo. Wyatt had been a healthy, well-adjusted young man. He had a girlfriend and friends. Somebody had to know where he went.

I drove to the college and stopped by the public safety office. Rusty Peterson sat behind the front desk and agreed to help me find Lily Tidwell and Parker Jeffries. We walked to a classroom building near the campus center and took the stairs to the third floor, where Rusty knocked on the closed classroom door. A second after that, we stepped inside.

The professor looked almost flustered. The class was small. Parker wasn't inside. Rusty cleared his throat.

"Sorry for interrupting, Doc," he said, "but have you seen Parker Jeffries?"

The professor shook her head.

"He's not in today. He wasn't in Friday's class, either. When you find him, let him know I'm interested in talking to him. He's missed enough class that I'm worried about his ability to catch up."

Rusty nodded and looked at the students. There were eight of them, most of whom were young men in their late teens to early twenties.

"Anybody else seen Parker lately?"

A few of the students shook their heads. One in the back cleared his throat.

"He's not on campus," he said. "We're in the same fraternity. He and Lily disappeared."

"Lily Tidwell?" I asked. The student nodded. I squeezed my jaw tight. This was a problem. I had three bodies on the ground in St. Augustine lately. Missing college students worried me. "If you see either of them again, have them contact Officer Peterson in public safety."

The students nodded, and Rusty apologized to the professor again for interrupting her class. Then we stepped into the hallway.

"Lily should be in a biology lab," said Rusty. "We can go there or her house."

"Bio lab," I said. "Maybe she told her professor she'd be absent. Sometimes young women are more responsible than young men."

Rusty nodded.

"That is often true."

We walked across campus to the science building, a four-story modern facility with classrooms and labs and even a planetarium. It was a beautiful building, but, as expected, Lily wasn't in. She hadn't told her teacher to expect her absence, either. Afterward, we went by the house Lily, Parker, and Wyatt had rented. The windows and doors were locked and intact, and nobody answered our knock. The driveway was empty.

With three bodies on the ground so far—Wyatt, Donna, and Erik Hoyle—Parker and Lily's absences left me nervous.

"If these two kids show up, call me," I said.

Rusty furrowed his brow.

"You think they're a threat to the campus community?"

I looked toward the house and shook my head.

"No. More likely than anything, they're already dead."

Rusty drew in a breath through his nose, his eyes absent.

"I hope you're wrong."

"Me, too," I said. "I'll write this up at my station and request that my boss put out an APB on them."

He nodded, and we drove back to the public safety office. Before leaving, I asked Rusty for the missing students' emergency contact information, which he dutifully supplied. I thanked him and drove back downtown. When I got back to my office, I contacted Parker Jeffries's parents. Parker hadn't made it home, nor had he contacted them to say he was going somewhere else. I didn't sigh or make a noise, but I grimaced. They must have heard something in my voice because Parker's father swore.

"Wyatt Caparaso is dead. Is my son dead, too, now?"

I shook my head.

"I have no reason to believe that," I said. "The College's Director of Public Safety and I went to the house Parker was renting, and the windows and doors were locked tight. I didn't see any signs of violence or struggle."

"Then where is he?"

I shook my head.

"I don't know, sir," I said. "I'm going to call the parents of another student. Then, I'll contact my superior. We'll issue a bulletin so every police officer in Missouri knows to look for Parker. We'll do our best to find him. It's important to emphasize that I haven't seen any sign that anyone's hurt your son. It's entirely possible that he just needed some time alone after losing his friend Wyatt."

Mr. Jeffries went quiet.

"I hope you're right," he said, his voice soft. I thanked him for taking the call and asked him to call me if he heard from Parker. After that, I called Lily Tidwell's family. Her mom answered immediately.

"Afternoon, Mrs. Tidwell," I said. "My name is Joe Court, and I work for the state highway patrol. Do you know where your daughter Lily is, by chance?"

Tidwell paused.

"She's at school. Waterford College. Why? Is she in trouble?"

"No," I said, shaking my head. "Can I ask when you last spoke to her?"

"Last night," she said. "We talk every Sunday night. It's my husband's favorite part of the weekend."

My breath became shallower.

"And you spoke to her last night, and she was at school?"

Tidwell hesitated.

"Yes. Is something wrong?"

"Can you contact her for me?" I asked. "A friend of hers is missing. We thought the two might be together."

"Okay," she said. "I'll hang up here and call you back on the landline."

"That's fine," I said. She hung up. About five minutes later, my phone rang again, so I answered.

"I've been texting her," said Tidwell. "She says she's fine and that she's at school."

"Ask her to call you," I said.

She sighed.

"Are you sure this is necessary?"

"Yeah," I said. "Tell her that you need to hear her voice because you miss her. Tell her that Wyatt Caparaso's death has made you nervous."

Tidwell's voice grew low.

"Wyatt's dead?"

I grimaced.

"Yeah."

She went quiet, but I heard her breathe.

"Lily must be devastated," she said. "She loved him. She talked about marrying him."

"I'm sorry. I assumed Lily would have told you," I said, wondering just why she hadn't told her. "You talked to her last night on the phone, and she didn't mention Wyatt's death?"

"It was a quick conversation," she said. "She has exams upcoming, so she couldn't talk long."

I blinked and grabbed a notepad.

"Did she seem stressed?"

"She's always stressed before exams," she said. "That's why she's done so well in school. The stress helps her focus."

Something was wrong here.

"Ask her to call you," I said. "I need to hear her voice."

This time, Tidwell didn't hesitate. She texted her daughter, and we waited about a minute before the reply came.

"Lily says she's at the library and can't talk."

I nodded and pushed back from the desk.

"Tell her to stay at the library," I said. "I'm on my way."

"What's going on? Is my daughter okay?"

"I don't know," I said. "I've got to go."

I hung up and stood. As I walked toward my car, I called Rusty Peterson. He promised to send officers to the library to find Lily. He also asked if we needed to shut the campus down again. I said no, mostly because I didn't think Lily was actually on campus. As I drove toward campus, I switched my cell phone to speaker and called Lily's mother again.

"Hey, this is Joe Court again. What kind of phone does Lily have?"

"Why does that matter?"

I squeezed my jaw tight before answering, so I wouldn't snap at her too harshly.

"It determines the best way to track it," I said. "What kind of phone does she have?"

"An iPhone," said Tidwell. "If you need to track her, it's got an app on it. Our daughter's an adult, so we haven't used it since high school."

I flashed my lights and honked my horn at a pickup in front of me to get him out of my way, but he didn't seem in a hurry to do me any favors.

"Use it," I said. "This is an emergency."

Tidwell went quiet for another moment, presumably as she opened the app.

"Her phone's off," she said. "Why would she turn her phone off?"

"Does your app show the location history?" I asked. "Does it show where she was yesterday, for instance?"

"No. It's an app for finding her in an emergency, not tracking her movements."

"Damn," I said, squeezing my jaw tight. I reached the outskirts of the campus and turned through the gate. The area was both bucolic and unnerving.

"Why would Lily turn off her phone if she knew I needed to talk to her?" asked Tidwell.

"I don't know," I said, trying not to floor the accelerator through a busy college campus. I reached the academic buildings and parked in front of the library behind a public safety SUV.

"What is going on? What happened to Wyatt? How did he die?"

I sighed and started toward the library's front door.

"I'm sorry, but this isn't the time to have this conversation."

As I walked, one of the front doors opened, and a public safety officer named Austin Reich stepped out.

"She's not here," he said. "I called in the night shift early. They're on their way. If she's on campus, we'll find her."

"Good," I said, holding my thumb over the microphone on my phone. "Keep me informed."

He agreed and started jogging toward his SUV to coordinate the search. Mrs. Tidwell was crying.

"Where's my daughter?"

"I don't know, ma'am," I said. "I'm doing what I can to find her right now."

"My husband and I are coming down," she said. "We'll be there in five hours."

I started to tell her I needed her at home, but she hung up before I could. I swore to myself, looked around, and found a wrought iron bench beside a weeping cherry tree on the library's front lawn. There, I sat and called Lieutenant Cognata.

"Hey, boss," I said. "This is Joe Court. I need some help in St. Augustine. I just found out Wyatt Caparaso's roommate and girlfriend are missing and have been for several days. Both Parker Jeffries's parents and Lily Tidwell's parents are on their way." I paused and gave the lieutenant a moment to catch up. "I hate to say it, but I think we're going to find some bodies pretty soon."

Chapter 38

Lieutenant Cognata had questions, but I didn't have many answers. When I told her what had happened, I focused on Lily Tidwell. People would understand if she and Parker had run away together to escape the stresses of losing Wyatt. Everybody would need time away to heal after losing a loved one.

Instead, Lily had disappeared and lied to her parents about her whereabouts. When caught in that lie, she stopped all communication. That worried me.

She was legally an adult, so she could leave college and clear her head without telling anyone. Her parents loved her, though, and she, by all appearances, loved them. It was out of character for her to disappear without telling them. Parker had a loving relationship with his parents, too. Even if he needed time alone, he would have called them first. Nobody would have blamed them for needing time away.

"This is a missing person's case," said Cognata. "We have no reason to think Lily and Parker are dead."

"Except for the deaths of Wyatt Caparaso, Erik Hoyle, and Donna Wright."

Cognata made a soft, low noise.

"We deal with evidence, not speculation," she said. "We'll put out APBs on Lily and Parker's vehicles, we'll contact hospitals, and we'll share their pictures in briefings. Since Parker's been missing and nonresponsive for over twenty-four hours, you can pull his credit reports to see if he's used a credit card lately."

"I'd like to get both of their cell records, too," I said.

"I'll have Detective Atherton put together a search warrant affidavit."

I thanked her and let her get to work. Then I called Rusty Peterson and told him I needed to talk to the girls in Lily's sorority. Rusty was in his car, driving back to the school, but he said he'd arrange it as soon as he arrived. For the next few minutes, I sat, wrote notes, and waited. Eventually, Austin Reich knocked on my window. I stepped out of the car.

"You found anything?" I asked.

"No," he said, "but the boss is at Lily Tidwell's sorority with the house mom. They're waiting for you."

"And where is that?"

He gave me directions, so I got back in my car and drove. It wasn't far, and I parked behind Peterson's SUV out front. Lily's sorority occupied a massive, three-story brick mansion with a white portico in front. The boxwoods along the home's foundation were trimmed and neat, as was the lawn.

I hurried to the double front doors, which Rusty opened before I could knock. The lobby was clean, but staid and dull. It reminded me of a funeral home. There were couches grouped in several seating areas. In the back corner, I saw a table with four chairs around it, suitable for playing cards.

Rusty stood beside an elderly woman just inside the door. I nodded hello to them both.

"Are the girls ready?" I asked. The elderly woman nodded.

"I'm Mrs. Engels," she said. "The girls are in their rooms, and they know Lily is missing. You can talk to them upstairs or in the lobby. It's up to you."

"Bring them down here," I said. "We'll use the card table in the corner. I'm probably going to talk to everyone in the house."

Mrs. Engels nodded and said she'd start bringing her girls down, while Rusty and I went to the card table. I set my phone on the table to record our conversations, and Rusty put on glasses and set a yellow legal pad and pen on the table. Within two minutes, the first coed entered the lobby. Three minutes after that, we wished her well. She was a sophomore and one of fifty-four girls who lived in that sorority house. She barely knew Lily except to say hello.

The next interviewee knew Lily better than our first young woman, but she had no idea where Lily had gone and hadn't seen her leave. She was concerned and sad and hoped Lily was well, but she couldn't help us. And that was how most of our interviews went until we met Abby Brewer. She was a junior and had curly brunette hair and freckles. Lily was her Big Sister in the sorority, which meant Lily was something of a mentor to her. The moment Abby sat down, I knew this interview would be different.

"Lily was pregnant."

Rusty straightened. I raised my eyebrows. We hadn't even asked a question. I covered my mouth for a moment and tried to hide my brief surprise.

"She wasn't far along," she said. "She wasn't showing."

This did change things. I nodded and considered my next question.

"How'd she feel about the pregnancy?" I asked.

"Scared," said Abby, her voice low. "You can't tell anybody. I'm the only one who knows."

I drew in a breath.

"Okay," I said. "How else did she feel? Was she sad? Was she depressed? Did she talk about hurting herself?"

Abby shook her head and looked at the table.

"She was okay. She was figuring things out. There's a clinic in Illinois. It's just across the river from St. Louis. I told her we could go there, but Lily hadn't decided. She hadn't even told Parker."

Rusty nodded, but I furrowed my brow.

"Wait a second. Why would Lily tell Parker? She was Wyatt Caparaso's girlfriend, right?"

Abby looked at the table but said nothing. I leaned forward and lowered my voice.

"Am I wrong?" I asked. "Were Lily and Parker together?"

Abby shook her head. It was so slight I almost missed it.

"Lily loved Wyatt. She wanted to marry him."

"Was she carrying Parker's baby?" I asked.

Abby nodded. Again, it was a slight movement. I drummed my fingers on the table, considering.

"If Lily was with Wyatt, how did Parker get her pregnant? And don't just say they slept together. I know the mechanics. I want to know how it happened."

Abby didn't respond.

"Did Lily and Parker often sleep with other people?" I asked.

She shook her head.

"It was a mistake. Lily had a bad day, and Wyatt was gone. Parker was there. She felt awful about it."

I gently pushed back from the table, giving myself a moment to think. The pregnancy was unexpected news, but I didn't know if it changed anything. If Wyatt had known that the girl he loved had slept with and become impregnated by his very close friend, he might have killed himself, but in my experience, he would have been more likely to kill Lily or Parker.

"Did Lily care about Parker?" I asked.

Abby, once more, reverted to silence.

"I need you to answer, Ms. Brewer," I said, my voice soft. "Lily and Parker's sex lives don't matter here. Their safety is my only priority. By talking to me, you're protecting your friend. You're not betraying her confidence or besmirching Wyatt's memory. You're doing your job as Lily's friend."

I let the silence drag on. Abby started crying. Then she shook her head.

"Lily doesn't trust Parker."

I straightened.

"Why did Lily not trust Parker?"

"She thought he took advantage of her when they slept together."

I glanced at Rusty. He focused on Lily. We were getting somewhere.

"I can step away, Ms. Brewer," he said. "You can talk to Detective Court alone if that's more comfortable. I can bring in a social worker, too, if you'd like. I know a woman in town who'd be happy to talk to you. She's really easy to talk to."

Abby glanced at him and shook her head.

"I'm fine."

"Did Parker rape Lily?" I asked.

Abby blinked and stared at the table.

"Lily was really drunk when they hooked up. He should have known better."

I nodded and considered my question.

"Was she sober enough to consent?"

"I don't know."

"Would she have talked to anyone else about this?" I asked. "Maybe her mom or another friend?"

Abby shook her head again.

"She didn't tell anybody. She didn't even tell Wyatt. He would have killed Parker. He had a gun. Nobody was supposed to know that, but the police made him nervous."

I gave myself a moment to unpack that.

"Why did the police make him nervous?"

"Because of the articles he wrote," she said. "He was going to be a journalist. His articles were going to free an innocent man from prison. That was his senior project. Most of us just write a paper. He showed the world that the local cops here were dirty. If they're willing to send an innocent man to prison, what would stop them from killing the college student who proved they were corrupt?"

Delgado wouldn't have killed anybody, I didn't think, but he wouldn't have been happy, either. As a police officer, he had an awful lot of power. He could have ruined Wyatt's life with a phone call. More and more, I was glad the state had shut my department down. Shane Fox was a racist who had immediately joined the Church of the White Steeple, Delgado had been an asshole, Sergeant Bob Reitz and Detective Marcus Washington had helped Dave Skelton keep Skelton's son out of prison for murder...St. Augustine was better off without us.

I squeezed my jaw tight before speaking.

"I'm going to change the subject," I said. "Did Lily ever mention the name Erik Hoyle?"

"No, but I've heard of him. He was Wyatt's interest, not hers, but everybody's read Wyatt's articles."

I nodded.

"Has Lily contacted you lately?" I asked.

"Not since Wyatt died. She went underground."

"Has she ever done that before?" I asked.

Abby shook her head. I reached into my purse for my wallet and pulled out a business card.

"This card has my information on it," I said. "If you hear from Lily, call me. Day or night, it doesn't matter. Okay?"

She took the card and nodded.

"Before you go, miss," said Rusty, "can I ask you a quick question?"

Abby nodded.

"I'm the Director of Public Safety here at Waterford. I'm a licensed police officer, just like Detective Court here. That means I can investigate crime and make arrests. I'm here to keep students safe. That's my only goal. You said Lily and Parker had a sexual encounter, and you're not sure whether it was consensual. Does Parker have a reputation for that?"

It was a good question, and I appreciated Rusty for asking it. Abby shook her head.

"No," she said. "I always thought he seemed like a nice guy. He had a girlfriend who went to Georgetown, but they broke up."

"Do the girls in your sorority talk about that kind of thing?" I asked. Abby narrowed her eyes and lowered her chin. She looked confused, so I clarified. "If a girl in your sorority was dating someone who got handsy with his girl-friends, would somebody warn her?"

She understood and nodded emphatically.

"Oh, yeah," she said. "We keep a list of the jerks."

Rusty looked up from his paper.

"And was Parker on that list?"

She shook her head.

"No."

"Great," he said, glancing at me. "Do you have anything else?"

I shook my head. Rusty thanked her for her time, and she left. Once she was gone, I lowered my voice.

"What do you think? You know the students here."

Rusty considered.

"I think she was honest and forthright," he said. "We're a college campus. Every college has assholes, but Parker's never hit our radar. I'll never discount a young woman's account of events, but it sounds like it'd be out of character for Parker to rape his best friend's girlfriend."

"Plenty of people do plenty of awful things when they're drunk," I said.

"That is certainly true," said Rusty.

Unfortunately, I didn't know where that left us. Wyatt may have had motive to kill Parker, but he was dead long before Parker went missing. Lily might have had motive to kill Parker, too. Or maybe Wyatt and Hoyle's killer had gone after Parker and Lily, thinking they knew something about him.

Every piece of evidence I uncovered led me to one inescapable conclusion: I didn't know a damn thing about this case.

"We've got a lot of officers looking for these two," I said. "Whether Parker assaulted Lily or not is irrelevant to that search. We need to find them before somebody dies."

Rusty nodded as if that made sense. He seemed confident in my abilities. I wished I had the first idea of where to look.

Chapter 39

Hunter Collins loved a girl once, but it didn't work out. He hadn't expected to fall for another, but fall he had. Lisa Burke would be his last romance. She felt right, nestled against his side, his arm around her shoulder as the two lay in bed, their clothes strewn about the floor, the room dark. Hunter hadn't expected to come to her house and carry her into her bedroom. As busy as he had been lately with his Church's special projects, he hadn't expected to see her at all. It made moments like this even sweeter.

"I love you, Ms. Lisa," he said. "I'm glad you're in my life."

"That makes two of us," she said, softly. "It would be awful lonely here without you. Then again, it'd probably be safer for you if you weren't here. I suspect Daddy would kill you if he knew what we were up to."

Hunter chuckled.

"Your dad's a grown man. I'm pretty sure he knows what we're up to."

She laughed and patted his chest.

"He loves you like a son," she said. "I think he's glad we're together."

Hunter brought his hand up to hers.

"Let's not talk about him," he said. "I've been working enough lately."

"Yeah. Enough work," she said. "I'm glad you had some free time."

They stayed like that for another few, perfect minutes. Then his phone rang. Hunter's shoulders sagged, and he could feel some of the energy leave his body.

"You don't have to answer," Lisa whispered. "We deserve some time to ourselves."

He gently squeezed her shoulder and then kissed her forehead.

"I wish that were true," he said before swinging his legs off the bed. He put on boxer shorts and carried the phone to the living room. "I'm here."

"We need you at the Church, son," said Burke. "You with Lisa?"

"I am."

"Then kiss her goodbye and tell her you love her," he said. "We've got work to do."

Hunter rubbed his nose, wishing he had brought his shirt.

"Should I be worried?" he asked.

Burke paused.

"We all make sacrifices," he said. "I'm in the meeting-house."

"So we're talking dirty work," said Hunter, nodding. "Give me fifteen minutes. I'll be there."

"Come unarmed. The full Council is in session. No weapons allowed."

"Sure," said Hunter, sighing. "I'll be there."

Burke agreed and hung up. Hunter had talked to Damon hundreds of times since he and Lisa had started dating. Never once had Burke suggested Hunter kiss his future bride and tell her he loved her. Whatever he had going on tonight, it was dangerous. He wondered if that meant they were moving their timeline up.

He went back in the bedroom. Lisa sighed as he began picking up his clothes.

"You're going to work, aren't you?"

"Yeah," said Hunter.

She pulled the blanket down, exposing her breasts.

"You sure I can't entice you to stay?"

He looked at her and drank in the imagery.

"I'll be back," he said. "I love you."

Hunter must have put more into his tone than he intended because she covered herself again and swallowed.

"He's got you doing something tonight, doesn't he?" she asked. "Something ugly."

"That'd be my guess," he said.

The blanket rose and fell as Lisa breathed. Hunter pulled his shirt over his head.

"Promise me you'll make it back safely," she said. He held her gaze.

"I promise I'll do my best," he said. "That's all I can ever promise. The world's a scary place sometimes. The good guys don't always win."

She nodded.

"You get hurt, I'll never forgive you," she said.

"I won't let anybody hurt me," he said, smiling. "Stay naked. It'll give me something to look forward to."

She laughed.

"I can't promise the world," she said, "but I can promise that I'll always be naked beneath my clothes for you."

"That's good enough for me," he said, winking. He told her he loved her again before leaving. The drive to the Church was easy. Sarah and Mary Knapp were working the front gate. They opened it, let him through, and closed it after him. Presumably, they called the boss to announce his arrival, too. His truck cruised over the packed gravel road. The Church had power from the main grid as well as backup generators, but they needed better lighting. The road looked like a cave.

A few minutes later, Hunter parked beside the meetinghouse. The Church's administrative buildings and sanctuary were dark, most of the staff having gone home for the evening. Few lights illuminated the meetinghouse. He stepped out and pulled the front door open. Burke stood in the lobby, waiting for him.

"Come on in, son," he said. "The Elders are in session."

Hunter hesitated.

"It's a full session?" he asked.

"Clarke's not here, but everybody else is," he said. "Come on. This won't take long. You tell us what we need to know, and then you'll go on your date or whatever you were doing with Lisa tonight."

Hunter nodded. Like most religious organizations, the Church of the White Steeple was hierarchical. Michael Clarke was the spiritual leader, but the Council of Elders conducted the business of the Church. Clarke could overrule the Council on certain matters, but when the Council spoke, the community listened. Hunter's heart started beating faster. This was unusual.

He followed Burke down the hall to the Council Chamber. When the Church designed the meetinghouse, they had kept the future in mind. The Council Chamber had seats for forty Church members and a moon-shaped wooden desk at the front, similar to City Council chambers in city halls all over the country. A wooden podium faced the Council, allowing community members a voice in the governance of their Church.

Four of the most respected men of Hunter's community watched as he and Elder Burke walked down the center aisle to that podium. Burke patted Hunter on the shoulder and walked to his spot behind the big desk. John Decicco and Matt Gould, two of Hunter's soldiers, sat in the gallery. They wouldn't meet Hunter's eyes. It was unusual for the Council to have guards. That didn't bode well. Hunter turned to face the collective.

"Gentlemen," he said. "I didn't think the Council met on Monday nights. And without Michael Clarke. What's going on?"

"These proceedings aren't for the reverend's gentle nature," said Donald Bagby, a longtime Church Elder. "We're here to talk about your project, and your recent mistakes."

Hunter placed his hands on the podium and focused on Damon Burke.

"And what mistakes are those?" he asked. Burke shuffled in his seat and looked away.

"You brought a world of hurt on us," said Brian Petty. At fifty, Brian was a recent addition to the Church's Council. He had joined only after his father had died. Hunter barely knew him, but his father had been reliable. "Damon told us about your project at the Wright's farm and about the detective. Don't you think you should have requested the entire Council's opinion before plotting to blow up a federal building using Church funding?"

"No," said Hunter.

"That's your defense?" asked Petty. "No?"

"I've got plenty to say," said Hunter. "You just don't want to hear it."

Petty rolled his eyes.

"Why don't you try us?"

"Fine," said Hunter. "I've seen the world. I've seen things you haven't. You'd see our Church and our movement picked apart, all so you could have a fancy office and money from Michael Clarke's ministry. I'm not interested in table scraps. Maybe you don't care now. You have a lot to lose. And maybe you're right. But I look at this Council, and I see atrophy and weakness. I see old men more interested in past exploits than the fight for our future."

"You went after a police officer," said Petty. "That endangers all of us. Detective Court'll come after us now. And she's not just a regular cop, either. She's the most vicious cop in that department."

"Vicious," said Hunter, lowering his chin. He paused. "You're not the only person I know who's described her as vicious."

"Whatever you want to say about her," said Damon, "she's a problem."

Hunter swept his gaze across the Council members and shook his head.

"You gentlemen sit up here behind this desk and pronounce judgment on others, but you don't understand the world. We're in a war. They are coming after us. And make no mistake about our enemy's capabilities: they are crafty, intelligent, and devious. They're going after our children in schools, indoctrinating them in false ideologies and forcing them to read filth. They hate us so much, down in Texas, they're letting dangerous gang members flood across our border to rape and kill white women and their families. They want to replace us.

"Do you men need a history lesson? April 19, 1993. The federal government took honest-to-God tanks to a church in Waco, Texas and burned the men and women inside to death. Almost eighty people died. That included twenty-five children and two pregnant women. And what was their crime? Worshipping God? The government says the Branch Dividians had guns, but so what? Guns are legal. Last I checked, mass murder was not. If you think that can't happen here, you are dead wrong."

Some of the Elders shifted. A few looked at Damon. Others looked at Bagby.

"We know the stories," said Bagby. "And we know the rightness of our cause. We don't need you to remind us of who we are."

"Why am I here?" asked Hunter, crossing his arms.

Elder Mark Rose, the longest-serving member of the Council, leaned forward.

"You brought a devil to our doorstep, son," he said, his voice hoarse with age. "This detective ain't stupid, but she made you look stupid in front of our whole Church. Michael Clarke had to come to your rescue."

"Am I on trial here?" asked Hunter. "Is that what's going on? Am I supposed to justify every decision I made? Because if it is, that's fine. You just let me know. I made a judgment call. Joe Court's a dog with a bone. Somebody needed to put her down. I didn't ask for your permission because I didn't have three weeks to sit through a meeting while you folks talked."

"She's a cop," said Bagby. "Her station's shut down, but no detective works alone. She's got reports, partners, evidence. You haven't left us with a choice, Hunter."

"So you're going to turn me in to save yourselves?" he asked.

The Council went quiet. They glanced at each other. Then Damon cleared his throat.

"I'm sorry, son," he said. "The vote was three to two. Your mission's going to go forward. Shane Fox will take the lead. He's up for the job. I'll take care of Lisa. Don't worry about her."

"So that's how it is," said Hunter, nodding, his voice soft as the realization struck him. "Do I at least get the satisfaction of knowing who voted against me?"

"The proceedings of this Council are closed," said Damon. "I'm truly sorry, son. John, Matt, take Hunter outside. We'll take him to the caves at the Wright's farm. Nobody'll hear us there."

Hunter closed his eyes and squeezed his jaw tight.

"Cheeks, Goldie, this Council plans to kill me. Who voted to let me live?"

"Mr. Rose and Mr. Petty," said a voice behind Hunter. Something inside Hunter went cold. He made his decision and looked at Damon.

"Three to two," he said. "You were the deciding vote. You voted for my death."

Damon said nothing, so Hunter closed his eyes. This Council had never understood Hunter or his work. Now, it was too late. He allowed his voice to soften.

"Broken arrow."

It was a code phrase used to signal that an American position was being overrun and to request all available combat aircraft to strike enemy positions. John Decicco had spent twelve years in the Army. He had gone to war in places few Americans knew existed. Matt Gould was a former active duty Marine with deployments in Iraq and Afghanistan. They understood the world. They had trained beside Hunter for years. The Council never should have used them as its guards.

The shots were immediate and rapid. After emptying the magazines of their pistols into the Council members, the two men reloaded, walked toward the desk, and fired additional shots at point-blank range into the back of the Elders' skulls to ensure the job was done.

It was a waste.

"Cheeks," said Hunter, "can I borrow your pistol? I came in unarmed at Damon's request."

"Of course," he said. Hunter thanked him, took the weapon from his outstretched hand, and left the room. His two soldiers followed. Outside, the night seemed almost eerily quiet after the cacophony of shots. Shane Fox stood by Hunter's truck.

"You shouldn't have talked."

Shane looked almost confused. Then he held up his hands.

"I didn't mean—"

Hunter squeezed the trigger six times, striking Shane in the chest with each shot. The former police officer fell straight to the ground. Hunter fired twice more into the back of his skull before handing the pistol to his friend.

"Goldie, get on the radio. We're shutting the farm down. Civilians are to stay indoors. I need a full security team out here. Cheeks, I need you to go to the supply barn. We need six body bags and some bleach. I'm going to visit Michael Clarke. It's time to see where his loyalties lie."

Chapter 40

A fter interviewing thirty-four young women in Lily Tidwell's sorority, I drove back to my station, compiled notes, and checked in with Lieutenant Cognata. She had sent photographs of Parker Jeffries and Lily Tidwell to every highway patrol station in the state, and every trooper on patrol knew to look for their vehicles. A team of administrative officers had also begun calling hospitals throughout the region, but nothing had turned up so far. We were doing what we could, not that it amounted to much.

After the call, I texted Shelby to see if she and Preston were home. She invited me right over. I didn't stay long, but I hugged them both and picked up Roy. The night was cold enough that my breath became frost as I walked back to my Volvo. Roy didn't seem to mind. I think he was glad to see me. We drove downtown and walked around the neighborhood before going to my office. I stayed for three hours, writing notes and reading through reports.

At about eleven, I started yawning. My house was still a crime scene, so I couldn't go there. Only two hotels in town allowed dogs, and I didn't want to pay for the nice one or stay in the crappy one. Instead, I fed him dinner from the small bag of dog food I kept in my office and grabbed blankets and a pillow from our jail cells. Then I slept on the couch. It wasn't the best night's sleep in the world, but it beat staying in the car.

The next morning, I showered in the locker room. I didn't look great, but I didn't care. I fed Roy, ate a granola bar, and then took him for a long walk. As we walked, I tried to order my thoughts and create a schedule of things to do. I had crimes throughout Missouri to investigate, but little was in my control. Lieutenant Cognata was handling Lily Tidwell and Parker Jeffries as well as the death of Erik Hoyle. A detective in Blue Springs was investigating Wyatt Caparaso. Detective Atherton was investigating—or had finished investigating—Donna Wright. And someone named Detective Griffin was investigating the person or persons who tried to kill me.

Every officer investigating every crime was fine at his or her job and could probably solve most cases. The problem here was that our investigation sprawled across multiple jurisdictions and crimes. Everything, though, was connected to Wyatt Caparaso. He sprung Hoyle from prison, he killed Donna Wright, and he lived with Parker and loved Lily.

Roy and I passed old, familiar buildings, and I felt my frustration rise with each step. It didn't make sense. Wyatt got Hoyle out of prison, but so what? People get released from prison every day. In this case, Hoyle was exonerated, forcing me to open my investigation into Brittany Ashbury, but even that shouldn't have mattered. Since Hoyle didn't kill Brittany, someone else did. I could imagine her real killer panicking, but why would he go after Hoyle after his release? Why would he draw attention to the case by killing Wyatt? He should have left town.

There were gaping pieces of my puzzle, and I had no way to fill them. Worse, the more I dawdled, the more this case spread. I had three confirmed dead people and two missing college students. I didn't even know if our killer was done. That was unacceptable. I refused to sit around and wait for more bodies.

Unfortunately, I didn't know what the hell else to do.

Roy and I walked for half an hour before I returned to my station. When I arrived, a man in gray chinos and a navy cable-knit sweater sat on the front steps. He stood when he saw me. I almost turned around and kept walking, but I suspected he'd stick around and wait. I rubbed my eyes, wound Roy's leash around my hand, and started toward the front door. Kyle Pennington stood and walked toward me. He had a plant.

I ignored him and unlocked the door.

"Can I have a moment, Ms. Court?" he asked.

I glanced at him and shook my head.

"No. The last time you were here, you accused me of taking advantage of your aunt, who you barely knew and who thought so little of you that she never mentioned you nor had pictures of you anywhere in her house. You've used up any indulgence I might have otherwise given you."

"My family's relationship to Susanne was complicated."

I flicked my eyes up and down him and shook my head.

"You ignored her. That's not complicated. She was a wonderful, kind, intelligent woman. If you had made an effort, she would have welcomed you into her life. But you didn't. She had no one in her life but me. That's sad. She deserved better than what she had. If you couldn't spare a moment for Susanne, I can't spare one for you."

He nodded and stepped back.

"I understand."

"Good. If you'll excuse me," I said. I pulled open the door and stepped inside. Roy followed and yawned. The heavy door shut behind me, and I closed my eyes. Muscles all over my body seemed to ache. I had enough stress. I didn't need to add my deceased friend's family to it.

Roy and I started upstairs when my cell phone began to buzz. It wasn't a phone call; instead, it was a reminder of a meeting I had that morning with the St. Augustine County Charter Commission. I sat on the steps and rubbed my eyes. Roy walked to the second-floor landing, where he had more stable footing and sat down, his head between his paws. I looked at him.

"You worried about me, buddy?"

He raised his eyebrows but didn't lift his head.

"I'm okay," I said. "I'll make coffee, and then we'll head out. The blowhards need us."

He didn't understand, of course, but he popped to his feet as I stood up. I made a pot of coffee, poured half into a travel mug, and headed out. At the courthouse, I made small talk with a few commission members before sitting. My coffee tasted lousy, but it was hot and had caffeine.

At this point, with our new charter written, the Charter Commission was conducting regular county business, the same as the County Council used to. The charter the commission had produced seemed well written. It had checks and balances as well as rules of change. Once the electorate approved it, we'd start to rebuild. We'd hold elections for a new sheriff and other county officers, too. I just had to hold on.

Once everyone showed up, we called the meeting to order. Everything was formalized and recorded for posterity in case there were issues. Once roll was taken, a representative from the county's Department of Health came forward and requested permission to destroy public health records from the early 1980s. It seemed reasonable, so that passed without issue.

After that, a representative from the county's Department of Procurement requested permission to dispose of obsolete computer equipment. We agreed on the condition that the department recycle everything they could. I started to drift off after that. Roy snored beside me.

Then, the acting director of the St. Augustine County Department of Planning stepped to the podium to discuss a zoning issue relating to a 9,000-acre tract that was currently zoned agricultural. The planning department had received a development proposal from Pennington Investments that outlined an ambitious plan to create a solar farm and battery solution for long-term energy storage.

I sat straighter and squeezed my jaw tight.

That's why Pennington had come to St. Augustine. It wasn't about his aunt; it was about money. I should have figured. Pennington stood from the gallery and walked to the podium. He nodded to everyone, but his eyes lingered on me for a moment. I wanted to glare at him, but I tried to play it cool.

He pulled the microphone toward him.

"Morning. Thanks for seeing me. I'm Kyle Pennington. My family has roots in St. Augustine that go back generations. Unfortunately, that history hasn't always been pleasant. My great-uncle, Stanley Pennington, raped and murdered a young woman at a summer camp well before I was born. Instead of arresting him, the sheriff and a county councillor named Darren Rogers covered up the crime. I'm not here to debate or discuss the past, but I am sorry for it. I'm also ashamed. I didn't know that history until recently. Now that I know, it's clear that my family has an obligation to this town that goes beyond anything I could propose."

He looked at me.

"I hope you can overlook my family's failures and any failures of my own to consider what my company is proposing."

I leaned forward, my voice stern.

"And what are you proposing?"

My position on the commission was advisory, so I had no right to speak. Still, nobody corrected me.

"My company, working alongside the Department of Energy and a number of private investors, has signed contracts to purchase 9,000 contiguous acres overlooking the Mississippi River, including the property on which Ross Kelly Farms sits. On this property, we will create a combined solar array and wind farm capable of producing almost six hundred megawatts of power. That's enough electricity to power approximately half a million homes.

"In addition, we have a grant from the federal Department of Energy to build a hydroelectric battery. We will construct a 12,000-acre-foot reservoir on property once owned by Ross Kelly Farms. Over a thousand feet below that property, we will build a power generation station near the Mississippi River. When in need, water will pass through a tunnel system built into the hillside, turning vertical shaft, air-cooled turbines and producing electricity, which we can send to St. Louis and the surrounding area.

"My engineers tell me our reservoir system will have a storage capacity in excess of ten gigawatt hours. When demand is low, we will utilize renewable energy to pump water from our reservoir near the Mississippi River to our elevated reservoir. When demand is high, we will release water from our upper reservoir into our lower reservoir, thereby turning our generators and creating electricity. It will enable us to send reliable, renewable energy to the local grid without the highs and lows associated with wind and solar power."

The members went quiet.

"That's quite a project," said Jerry Baker. He started to say something else, but then caught himself and closed his eyes. "You have funding for this? This isn't just a pipe dream?"

Pennington considered.

"This is not a pipe dream. Construction will take years and will create thousands of highly paid construction jobs. Once the system is in operation, we'll employ several hundred engineers, technicians, and administrators."

The commission members wanted to ask questions, but Pennington held up his hands before they could.

"I'm not going to lie to you. This is a hard project. I'm not asking for tax breaks, and I'm not asking you to take anyone's property. My teams have already negotiated with the required stakeholders. We're ready to move, but we need the county's guarantee that you won't stand in our way. We have the federal and state governments on our side. We need yours, too."

I crossed my arms.

"What do you get out of this?" I asked. "You'll forgive me for saying the Pennington name doesn't carry the same weight in this part of the world it once did."

"Money," he said. "If this works in St. Augustine, my team will move on projects in a half dozen other locations. The geography of St. Augustine County fits our needs, allowing the area to become our proof of concept. That my family once lived here is a happy coincidence. This is a multi-generational project. We'll plant trees not knowing if we'll ever sit under their shade. Our children, grandchildren, and great-grandchildren will, though. For me, that's enough. I hope it is for you, too."

The commission went quiet again. The members looked at each other. Then Jerry Baker leaned forward again.

"I'm not sure that we have the authority to help," he said. "Without a working government, we can't make the promises you need."

"I understand," said Pennington. "I'm here to break the ice. My company is in the very early stages of a project. We invite everyone to speak to our engineers, lawyers, public relations team, builders, project managers... really anyone on my staff."

Gina Ellington, a real estate attorney, cleared her voice.

"What kind of investment do you plan to make?"

"At least two billion dollars over the next fifteen years."

"And you have that much capital?" she asked.

Pennington nodded.

"Grant money, but yes. This is a public-private partnership. If we pull this off, everybody will win. This is not new technology. It's been successfully done in Wales in the

United Kingdom and here in the US on Lake Michigan. If there's any innovation in our plan, it's the combination of renewable energy and an elevated lake battery. This is proven technology. It works.

"The project will take decades. We'll have more meetings. In the meantime, thank you for having me. My team will be in touch with each of you to answer questions."

Pennington stepped back. The proposal sounded great, but I knew St. Augustine. Pennington thought he could ram his project through with charm, but it would blow up in his face soon enough. Hopefully, it wouldn't take out too many of our county residents, too.

That was for the future, though. I had to focus on the present. I had two missing college students and three bodies on the ground. I had work enough.

Chapter 41

Once the meeting ended, I checked my phone to find two missed calls, both from the same unfamiliar number. As Roy and I walked back to the station, I called it back.

"Hey, this is Joe Court," I said. "I'm returning your phone call."

"Thank you for calling, Detective. This is Ed Pruett. You were out at my farm a couple years back about some exploding mailboxes."

I remembered the case if not the name. St. Augustine didn't get too many calls about explosives, and those we did get tended to involve kids shooting fireworks. The exploding mailboxes involved bored high school kids, empty two-liter bottles, and dry ice. The exploding mailboxes scared people, but because the kids worked at night, no civilians got hurt checking their mail. Instead, the case solved itself when a bottle blew up in one of the kids' hands. He lost three fingers, a whole lot of skin, and a college baseball scholarship.

"That was quite a while ago, Mr. Pruett," I said. "What can I do for you?"

"My dog and I were out for a walk this morning on the back forty, and we smelled smoke and burning plastic. I thought somebody might have dumped their garbage and lit it on fire, but it was a car."

I sped up to a jog.

"Was anybody inside?"

"I couldn't tell," he said. "The inside's all melted."

I asked him for his address, which he provided. Then I told him Roy and I would be over soon. We jogged the rest of the way to my station. Pennington's plant was outside the front door. He must have dropped it off. If we had a trash can nearby, I probably would have thrown it away. Instead, I ignored it, made sure the door was still locked, and hurried to my Volvo. We drove out to Pruett's farm and parked in his long gravel driveway in front of an old farmhouse. Mr. Pruett—Ed, as he requested I call him—drove Roy and me out to the car on a green utility vehicle.

The car was a BMW sedan, and it was a charred mess. The air reeked of gasoline. I asked Ed to hold Roy's leash as I stepped toward the vehicle. The metal radiated heat, but the flames had died back. The windows were broken. I flashed a light inside. The central console had melted, and the seats had caught fire as well. There were no bodies inside, thankfully. I stepped back and snapped a picture of the license plate before calling Lieutenant Cognata.

"Hey," I said. "This is Joe Court. I'm in St. Augustine County at the farm of a man named Ed Pruett. He and his dog found Parker Jeffries's BMW this morning. It's been doused with an accelerant—possibly gasoline—and lit on fire. The windows are broken, but I can't see any bodies. I haven't opened the trunk. Can you get me some forensic techs?"

Cognata sighed.

"We are expending a lot of resources on St. Augustine," she said. "Kind of wonder if my bosses knew what we were stepping into when we agreed to help out."

"If it makes you feel any better, I don't think the attorney general gave them much of a choice," I said. "When they shut down my department, they didn't seem to be in the negotiating mood."

She sighed again.

"I don't mean any offense, Joe, but I hope I never hear your name again after this. Things break around you."

I had heard similar things before. Hearing it voiced again didn't bother me much.

"You going to send me some help?"

"Of course," she said. "What's your feeling on this?"

I looked at the car and swept my gaze over the surrounding area. The surroundings were so rural that the car had burned beside the road all night, and nobody reported it.

"I've worked a couple of cases involving burned vehicles. In one, a guy torched his ex-wife's car to let her know he could get to her. We caught him and sent him to prison. Another case involved drunk, stupid teenagers who lit their car on fire and tried to pee the fire out. One kid burned his penis. Another had third-degree burns on his hands. Most of the time, when I've worked burned vehicles, it's because somebody wanted to destroy evidence."

I paused.

"This was planned," I said. "Our arsonist drove to the middle of nowhere, burned it, and left. This wasn't stupid teenagers, either. They do stupid things close to home. I think our arsonist was trying to hide something. This might be a murder scene."

Cognata promised to get people out to me as soon as possible. I thanked her, hung up, and looked at Mr. Pruett.

"You run cattle, right?" I asked. He nodded. "Anybody ever steal your cattle?"

"No, ma'am," he said. "We're careful around here."

"You have cameras?"

He shook his head.

"Not out here," he said. "I keep some on the chicken coops because something's been scaring them lately, but I can't afford to have surveillance cameras everywhere."

"Are your cameras at the chicken coop pointed in this direction?"

"They can't see over the hill," he said.

It made sense, so I nodded.

"You have any dogs to keep coyotes away?"

"Dudley, Borris, and Natasha," he said. "They're Anatolian shepherds."

I nodded again and considered.

"Would your dogs have barked if they saw somebody torching a car?"

"Yep."

I nodded once more. His dogs should have barked last night.

"Is there anyone they don't bark at?"

"Me and the boys. My wife. They see us, they come running because they think we'll give them treats. They're good dogs. If they see an intruder at night, they're liable to tear him apart, but to us, they're family."

I scratched my head. This wasn't making sense.

"What kind of training do they have?"

"Like formal training?" he asked, lowering his chin. I nodded. "Basic obedience. They're well-bred livestock guardians. Most of what they do is instinctual. They teach each other how to live together and hunt."

"So they've never had guard dog training," I said. He nodded. It was an important point. A trained guard dog wouldn't have allowed anyone onto the property without alerting the property owner. A lot of domesticated dogs, though, could be subdued with enough treats. You give them enough freeze-dried chicken, they'll think you're the greatest human ever.

CHRIS CULVER

I thanked Mr. Pruett and warned him that we had troopers incoming. He agreed to go back to his house and direct them out here. That gave me a few minutes to snap pictures of the vehicle and organize my thoughts.

About ten minutes later, my phone rang. I was roping off the scene with yellow crime scene tape to remind everyone to stay away from the car until the forensics team cleared it. Normally, I would have sent the call to voice mail, but it was Julia Green, my adoptive mom. We used to talk often, but we had both been so busy lately, our calls had been few and far between. I missed her.

"Mom, hey," I said, pinching the phone between my shoulder and ear. "Can I call you back in an hour? I'm at a crime scene."

"Your dad and I are in St. Augustine at the shelter. You're not here."

I closed my eyes and stopped.

"Oh, yeah, sorry," I said. "I moved. Roy and I live in a little place near my station. Linda needed the space above the garage for a full-time employee. The shelter kept growing and growing. They needed more help." I paused. "Why are you in town?"

"Because I got a call from Travis Kosen. He said you were attacked and sent to the hospital. I tried calling, but your phone kept going straight to voice mail. I panicked, I guess. Sorry."

A tight feeling began spreading over my chest. I put the crime scene tape down and sighed.

"No, I'm sorry," I said. "I've been busy. And I'm okay. I was attacked. Roy and I may have interrupted a robbery. They hit me in the head and ran. My neighbor found me, but I'm okay. I have a hard head."

My dad said something in the background, but I couldn't understand. Then Mom got back on the phone.

"Your dad asked when you moved."

I grimaced and felt my cheeks grow warm.

"It's been a few months," I said. "I meant to tell you, but, you know... everybody's busy. Audrey's getting married and having a baby, Dylan's... Dylan. I haven't talked to Ian in probably six months. Everything changes, right? I'm rolling with the punches. I had planned to send pictures when I had a permanent place."

"I'm sorry we haven't visited."

"It's fine," I said. "Don't worry about it. Things happen, you know? You just get wrapped up in your life and lose track of everything else."

Mom went quiet.

"You're my daughter. I don't want to lose track of you," she said. "I've almost lost you before, and I don't want to let it happen again."

My throat tightened, and I spoke without thinking.

"Maybe you and Dad could try calling some."

Mom went quiet.

"We deserve that," she said, her voice low.

"Are you guys at the shelter now?" Mom said they were. "Go to Able's Diner and get a milkshake. I'm at a crime scene, but as soon as I get somebody out here, I'll meet you there. I'll just tell my boss I'm dizzy. My traumatic brain injury might as well get me something."

"I'm sorry you were hurt," said Mom. She paused. "We'll get a milkshake. Then I want to talk."

"I'll be there as soon as I can," I said. Mom said she loved me. It felt better to hear than I had expected. I said I loved her, hung up, and leaned against my Volvo. As I waited for the highway patrol to arrive, I swore aloud. Mom was helping Audrey plan her wedding and driving her to and from doctor's appointments. Dad was trying to figure out his life in a big city. The last time we spoke—which was months ago—he told me he didn't feel like he fit in there.

It was easy to drift through life. Relationships took work. You had to put in the time. You had to let yourself be vulnerable. Growing up, I had never let myself form those emotional attachments. I had loved my biological mother, and I think she had loved me. She wasn't a fit parent, though. In the foster care system, relationships were transactional. You occasionally hugged your foster mother for comfort, she hugged you for whatever she needed, and then you both moved on.

Life afterward, the life I was living now, I didn't understand. It was complicated and hard. My sister Audrey flitted through life without a care in the world. For her, life was like a dance. She loved it and had fun. For me, life was something to endure. One day, I hoped it'd get easier. For now, I'd do what I could to make it through the day.

CHAPTER 42

The first highway patrol trooper arrived about ten minutes after I hung up with Mom. A uniformed sergeant arrived shortly after that. They took over, and I drove to Able's. Mom and Dad had a booth by the window. Both had milkshakes, but it didn't look as if they were enjoying them. When they saw me, they both stood and hugged me.

Mom asked whether I had lost weight, and I probably had. My diet hadn't been great lately. It was hard to fit in time for nutritious meals. Sometimes it was easier to grab a protein bar and keep your head down at work. Dad wanted to talk about my house. He said my neighborhood didn't sound safe—and he was right. I was the first attempted murder, but there had been break-ins. If I stayed in the area, I told Dad I'd look into getting an alarm.

After that, Mom finally took a sip of her milkshake, and we settled into an uneasy silence. Dad rested his hands on the table.

"It's quieter than it once was," he said. "You used to have to fight for a seat."

"Yeah," I said. "The county's fallen on rough times. Unemployment's up, tourism is down. The whole place is falling apart, but we're going to pull through. Our Charter Commission's put together a new county charter with appropriate checks and balances. We had a bunch of law professors come in and help. Once that passes, we'll have a real government again that can start putting the pieces back in place. We'll be okay."

Mom and Dad didn't look convinced. I looked at the table.

"There's even a proposal to build a power station here," I said. "It's all green energy. I can't say much about it yet, but it'll pump billions into the local economy and should bring in thousands of jobs. The developer's a guy named Kyle Pennington. He's Susanne Pennington's nephew."

"Well, that's good," said Mom.

"Yep," I said, nodding. "It's all peaches and cream here. The future's bright."

I smiled. Mom tried to smile in return, but it almost looked pained.

"Travis told me you work with the highway patrol now."

I nodded and raised my eyebrows.

"Sort of," I said. "I'm a reserve officer. The attorney general dissolved our department because we didn't have enough officers to maintain safe staffing levels, but I don't think he wanted to lose everyone. For the moment, I'm a civilian employee with the highway patrol. My job is to keep the lights on in our station until we reconstitute the department. Then we'll rebuild from the ground up. Everybody else has moved on to other jobs or retired."

Mom reached across the table to my hand. I forced myself to smile.

"It's not bad, really. I get free coffee, and we've got a great gym," I said. "The highway patrol emptied out the armory, but, at last count, I had almost a million staples at my disposal. Roy and I are living the dream."

Dad nodded. Mom kept her hand on mine. I let her keep it there. We didn't talk for a while.

"You guys want to get some dinner?" I asked, finally. "We can get takeout and eat it later. Or I can make you tacos at home. I'll show you around town."

"You don't need to cook," Mom said. "We'll get sandwiches. We can do whatever you need."

So we got dinner, and I drove them around town. They had visited before, so I didn't show them the town and county as it was. I drove them by places and explained what it would be one day. We went by the waterfront, and I told them about the proposed casino. We drove past Ross Kelly Farms, and I told them about Pennington's proposal. Then we drove past Shelby and Preston Cain's place, and I told them about the budding literary artist in our midst.

I tried to keep things light. When we got back to my place, I swore to myself when I realized it was still a crime scene. Mom said they'd go to a hotel, but I called Lieutenant

Cognata and asked if they had completed their investigation. She said yes, so I just cut the seal and opened the front door.

Blood covered the linoleum in the entryway. Bloody footprints led across the carpet. I tried to stop Mom and Dad from coming in, but they were right behind me. Mom covered her mouth. Dad put a hand on my shoulder and pulled me in for a hug.

"I'm fine, really," I said. "I was just a little dizzy afterward. The doctors said I was okay. Scalp wounds bleed a lot, apparently. You should see my shirt. It was like a prop from a horror movie. Everything's fine, though. The doctors wouldn't have released me from the hospital if I wasn't fine."

Dad didn't let go, though. Mom put a hand on my back. I could hear her breathe.

"I'm fine, guys," I said, feeling my throat go tight. My knees felt weak. "Everything's under control."

I didn't realize I was crying until Dad led me to the couch. My hands balled into fists on his sweater.

"It's fine," I said again, trying to convince myself when even my body knew it was bullshit. "I'm fine."

Mom rubbed my back. I waited for them to leave me alone, but they didn't. So I sat there, and I cried. I was thirty years old, and I was crying like a teenager who got her heart broken, but I didn't care. Then, after a few minutes, I stopped and rubbed my eyes.

"Sorry. I didn't mean for that to happen."

Neither of my parents said anything, so I pushed myself away from Dad and walked to the kitchen for paper towels and Clorox spray. I couldn't clean everything, but I started to wipe down the linoleum by the front door. For a moment, I worked in silence. Then I felt Mom's hand on my shoulder.

"Can you talk to us, honey?"

I looked at her and shrugged.

"There's nothing to say," I said. "My world fell apart. My friends left, I lost my home, and I lost my job. Then somebody attacked me. Roy saved my life. I'm dealing with everything the best I can."

Dad knelt beside me and took the Clorox from me.

"Let me take over," he said. "You go sit with your mom."

He seemed insistent, so I handed him the cleaning supplies and sat beside my mom on the couch. Neither of us said anything. I just sat beside her and felt less alone than I had before. Roy stayed beside my dad on the floor and showed him every tennis ball we had in the house. After cleaning the linoleum, they went for a walk. Some days, I wondered if my dog liked my dad more than me. Then again, I also wondered whether my dad was half dog. It would have explained a lot.

"We're going to get a golden retriever," said Mom. "Your dad doesn't know it yet, but we're on a breeder's waitlist for a puppy."

"Can you keep a puppy in your condo?" I asked. Mom shook her head.

"We're looking at moving back to Missouri. We need a house. Doug wants a garden. I need more space. Audrey and PJ will move, too. Chicago's great, but it's not home."

"That sounds nice."

Mom and I sat and talked for a while. Mostly, Mom listened without interrupting me. Dad and Roy came back about half an hour after they left. He was holding the plant Pennington had tried to give me.

"Found this by the station," he said. "I didn't think it'd make it through the night outside. It's a peace plant."

I glanced at the plant, and then I glanced at my dad.

"Some guy tried to give it to me."

Dad held it up and looked at it.

"It's a healthy plant," he said. "You don't have to like the giver to enjoy the gift."

I closed my eyes and shook my head.

"Put it on the table," I said. "I don't want to think about the giver."

Mom raised an eyebrow.

"It's a peace plant," she said. "Sounds like somebody was trying to be nice."

I rolled my eyes.

"He wasn't being nice," I said. "He treated me badly, and I called him out. Now he's trying to get in my good graces because I'm on the Charter Commission. He wants our help with a project."

Mom leaned forward.

"It's from that Pennington guy, isn't it?" she asked.

I forced my lips to flatten and shook my head.

"Mom, I know how your brain works. Don't go there."

"Kyle Pennington, billionaire investor, insulted you, and apologized with a plant. You refused. Is he handsome?"

I kept my expression flat.

"I asked you not to go there."

"Is he cute?"

I sighed and rolled my eyes.

"My life isn't a romance novel, and I don't think he's a billionaire. He's using federal grants to pay for the project."

Dad coughed to get Mom's attention. When she looked at him, he showed her his cell phone. She immediately sat straighter.

"Whoa," she said, taking Dad's phone and turning it to me to show me a picture of Pennington. "That's the guy? And he's rich? Jeez. I sure wouldn't kick him out of bed."

"Dad's right behind you, Mom," I said. "He can hear you."

She handed Dad the phone. He shrugged.

"It's fair," he said. "I wouldn't blame her."

"We're not having this conversation," I said. "He's a jerk."

"That's what the women in your mother's favorite romance novels say," said Dad. "They still sleep together by the halfway point."

I stood up and brushed my hands together as if I were washing them.

"Nope, nope, nope," I said. "You've both used up all your words tonight. I'm finding you a hotel."

Mom laughed.

"We're done," she said. "We won't say anything else. And if you'd rather we stay in a hotel, we will. We didn't actually announce we were coming, so you're probably not prepared for guests."

I didn't have to think. I just shook my head.

"Stay," I said. "If you want to."

Dad knelt beside Roy to pet him. The dog licked his face.

"If we're going to stay, we're going to need food. I don't know about my friend here, but I'm starving."

I stood up from the couch.

"Roy always thinks he's starving," I said. "I'll feed him. There are paper plates on top of the refrigerator and beer in the fridge."

I fed the dog while Mom and Dad got dinner together. We laughed and talked about Audrey and PJ and Dylan and their neighbors in Chicago. I tried to keep the conversation light. At ten, everybody went to bed. Mom and Dad stayed in the guest bedroom. Roy wanted to stay with Dad, but I kept him in my room.

For the first time since I had rented it, my house felt like home.

Chapter 43

Roy got up the next morning as soon as my dad stepped out of the guest bedroom. If I didn't know better, I'd say he was waiting for his friend. They went for a walk, while I stayed in bed and fell back asleep. When I woke up again, I smelled coffee and cinnamon. I rolled out of bed and grabbed a bathrobe before stepping into the hallway. Mom was reading on her phone in the living room, while Roy sat beside Dad on the ground, stone asleep. Dad smiled when he saw me.

"I went by the grocery," he said. "There are cinnamon rolls in the oven and coffee in the pot."

I walked to the kitchen and picked up the bag of coffee.

"Name brand. Fancy," I said. "The stuff I drink at work comes in a big sack and looks like fertilizer."

"How is work?" asked Mom. "Are you doing okay with the closure?"

I grunted and sat at my breakfast table.

"Once they shut down the station, I thought things would slow down. Instead, I'm working on multiple separate but probably related homicides and trying to find two missing college students. It's been hard."

"That's a lot," said Mom. "Have you got help?"

"Theoretically, but my help isn't helpful," I said. "A woman named Donna Wright died here in St. Augustine. There are a ton of open questions about her death, but we've got a confession, so the detective assigned to the case closed the investigation. Then Donna Wright's killer was murdered in Blue Springs, Missouri. Supposedly, he hanged himself, but the scene was staged. It was a murder. Then a man named Erik Hoyle was released from prison. He was murdered, too. He supposedly overdosed on sleeping pills, but the pills were jammed into his throat after his death. Finally, two kids—the roommate and girlfriend of Donna Wright's killer—went missing. Different investigators are assigned to each part of the case, and they're all so focused on their individual roles that nobody understands the big picture."

Mom put down her coffee cup.

"That's hard," she said. Mom had spent her entire career with the St. Louis County Police Department before retiring. She knew how to run a complex investigation. She also knew enough not to step on another police officer's investigation. Dad, however, had no such qualms.

"You want the opinion of a complete amateur who likes mystery novels?"

Mom started to hold up a hand to stop him, but I shook my head.

"Sure. I can talk it out," I said. "I'm working alone now. Roy's my sounding board, and he keeps his opinions to himself."

Dad nodded, and mom sipped her coffee. I told them about my case from the moment I met Wyatt Caparaso at Waterford College to the finding of Parker Jeffries's BMW in Ed Pruett's field. I had hoped that by laying it out in one coherent narrative that I'd see a connection I had missed before, but I didn't. I talked for almost twenty minutes. When I finished, I pushed back from the table.

"What do you think?" I asked.

"It sounds like a tough case," Mom said. "Anytime you add another agency, you're adding complexity—especially if they don't have protocols in place for communicating. If you were closer to St. Louis, I'd suggest you kick it up to their major case squad. They're good at these kinds of sprawling investigations."

I shook my head.

"Even when we had a department, St. Augustine was ineligible. They're too far from us."

Dad furrowed his brow.

"Who's Donna Wright?" he asked.

"She's the young woman whose body was found in a tent here in St. Augustine. Wyatt Caparaso shot her."

Dad shook his head and leaned forward.

"I remember," he said, "but I can't figure out how she's involved with this. Everybody else makes sense. You've got

Brittany Ashbury. She was murdered, which is awful. Erik Hoyle was wrongfully convicted of her murder. That's awful, too. Wyatt Caparaso helped get Erik Hoyle out of prison, so he's connected. Then he was murdered. Parker Jeffries and Lily Tidwell have connections to Wyatt Caparaso. They're missing, but you found Parker's car. Donna Wright isn't connected to anybody. She's the odd one out. You said someone lured her to the campground where she was shot, just like they lured Wyatt. Why her of all people?"

I shrugged and shook my head.

"I don't know, Dad," I said. "Sometimes people just get unlucky. Sometimes the world sucks and good people die for no reason whatsoever. It's not like the books. I wish it were."

Dad nodded and looked down. I stood and touched his shoulder.

"It's a good thought, Dad, but there's no silver bullet here," I said, walking past him to the coffeemaker.

Mom joined me in the kitchen.

"You okay, hon?" she asked. I nodded.

"Yeah. I'm fine," I said. Then I sighed and shook my head. "No, that's a lie. I'm not okay. I'm angry, and I'm frustrated. I ruined Erik Hoyle's life. I took him from his wife, his kids, his entire life. And now he's dead. I can't fix that, and I can't follow up because my department was so riddled with corruption that the state decided it was better to shut it down than continue and rebuild. I'm all that's left. I'm the last survivor. And you know the worst part of it? I don't know if I deserve to be.

"I think I should just move on. I became a cop because it matters to me, because I wanted to help people who needed it. I didn't help Erik Hoyle or his family, though. It makes me wonder how many innocent people I've sent to prison. I've killed people at work, too. I've shot people. How many of them are dead and didn't deserve it?"

Dad stood from the table to stand beside me. He said nothing, but it was always comforting to have him near.

"That's a lot to unpack," said Mom. I nodded and closed my eyes.

"Sorry," I said. "I shouldn't have said anything."

"I'm glad you said something. You needed to say something. I know a counselor who sees police officers. You're not the only person to feel that way. A counselor can help."

I shook my head and chuckled.

"I don't have time for therapy. I barely have time to sleep anymore."

"What can your mom and I do to help?" Dad asked. "We've been busy in Chicago with your sister and PJ, but you are our daughter. We love you, and we want to support you."

I glanced.

"Your first step should probably be to teach PJ and Audrey to use prophylactics," I said. "I hear they're highly effective at preventing pregnancy."

Mom gave me a weak smile.

"I'm not going to let you deflect an uncomfortable situation with humor anymore. You're not going to push us away, either."

I swallowed a lump in my throat.

"I don't know what to do. Everything I try just seems to blow up. I'm angry, and I'm sad, and I'm overwhelmed. My friends are gone, I've lost two homes now, my parents moved away, my sister's pregnant and engaged, and I've barely got a job. My assignment with the highway patrol is temporary. If the county can't get its act together and get a charter passed, I don't know what I'm going to do. I'm sick to my stomach at night, and my best isn't good enough anymore.

"The attorney general didn't say it, but I shut this place down. I started the investigation into the old County Council. I dug that hole. And I'm the person who forced Bob Reitz and Marcus Washington out. If I hadn't forced them out, I'd probably still be Detective Court. I destroyed this entire county."

Mom and Dad both shook their heads.

"You didn't force anybody to do anything," said Mom. "That burden you're carrying isn't yours to bear."

I nodded and licked my lips.

"Even if you're right, it doesn't matter," I said. "I'm the only one left to clean up, and every time I stop working, something else breaks."

Dad put a hand on my elbow.

"And none of that is your fault. You did your job. You made good choices with the information you had. You did the right thing. Erik Hoyle's imprisonment isn't your fault."

"It wouldn't have happened if not for me, though," I said. "Nothing anyone says will change that. I have to live with that."

They seemed to agree with that because they stopped asking questions. Mom and Dad stayed for another hour, but they had a long drive home, and they wanted to make it before dark. At ten, I hugged them tight and told them I loved them. Their departure was more awkward than I had hoped for, but we were family. I'd see them again.

Afterward, I sat on the floor in my living room beside the couch. Roy snuggled up beside me. He was warm and solid. I couldn't say that about many things in my life. Realistically, I should have gone into work. I should have called Lieutenant Cognata to see if she and her team had gotten anywhere on Parker Jeffries's car. There were a dozen tasks with my name on them. I didn't care, though. For just a little while, I needed to sit with my dog and catch my breath.

CHAPTER 44

Roy and I stayed in the living room for about twenty minutes. Then he farted and left. Some days, I felt like I was living with a frat boy. It didn't matter. I needed to get ready for work.

I showered and dressed for the day. As I drank the rest of the coffee my father had brewed, I realized Dad was right: Donna Wright was the odd person out in my investigation. She didn't make sense. Everyone else I investigated had some kind of connection. Donna Wright didn't. Wyatt Caparaso said someone had lured him to that campground. There, Donna Wright attacked him. He shot her and escaped, but not before some young people fired at him.

I had assumed Wyatt was making up a story to convince me not to charge him with murder, but what if he was telling me the truth? What if Donna had lured him out there to kill him? She lived on a compound with a couple of young teenagers. In cities, relatively few teenagers could shoot well, but in St. Augustine, guns were everywhere. A lot of families hunted deer, wild turkey, and other animals for food. Hunting was a part of many rural children's lives, the same way playing recreational soccer may have been part of a ten-year-old's life in the suburbs.

I had tried to investigate the note that lured Wyatt to the campground, but he said he had destroyed it. Donna could have written it and dropped it off at the school. Waterford wasn't a huge campus, but it probably had two or three hundred faculty members and another two to three hundred non-teaching staff members. On top of that, parents and alumni likely visited daily. She would have blended in.

Donna had the means and opportunity to lure Wyatt to the campground, and her children could have shot at him. Did she have the motive, though? That, I couldn't say.

Before leaving the house, I grabbed my phone and texted my dad.

You were right. Donna Wright is important.

Dad texted back and said he loved me. I'd never get too old to hear that.

Roy and I walked into work. It was an overcast, cool day. A drizzle had turned the concrete, brick, and limestone of St. Augustine's buildings into darker, almost more ominous versions of themselves. Few cars drove past, and no pedestrians greeted us. Upon reaching the office, I turned off the alarm and started pacing in the lobby, thinking. Roy lay on the cool terrazzo marble floor beside the front desk.

The Wrights lived on a farm near the Mississippi River. The family farmed the property, but they had other jobs, too. Donna Wright had been a therapist. She also spoke Spanish well enough to communicate with the immigrants who lived at Nuevo Pueblo. She and her family provided them with blankets, toiletries, clothes, and other things newly arrived, impoverished immigrants might need. When those immigrants needed sanctuary and escape, the Wrights provided it. They were good people—so they said.

No matter what else, ICE had them under surveillance. They had installed at least one trail camera on the Wright's farm. I suspected there were more. Trail cameras were cheap. If they were wireless, Homeland Security special agents wouldn't even have to physically visit them to swap out memory cards. They'd only have to drive past, make a wireless connection, and download the video.

Donna Wright helped people with problems. She knew how to talk to people. Based on the information I had, Wyatt would have had no reason to desire her death. No one would. She seemed like a good person, but she—and her family—had secrets. I needed to uncover them.

I went to my office and searched through my files until I found the number for Whitney Ashbury, Brittany Ashbury's mom. She answered on the third ring.

"Ms. Ashbury, this is Joe Court. I'm sorry to bother you, but I'm investigating your daughter's murder, and I wanted to ask you a question: have you ever heard the name Donna Wright?"

"My daughter was murdered by Erik Hoyle. He's dead now. You said so. I don't want to talk anymore."

"I understand," I said, speaking quickly before she could hang up. "I'm just trying to cover my bases. Have you heard the name Donna Wright? Ms. Wright was a therapist. Did you or your daughter go to therapy?"

"I don't know her," she said. "You don't need to call me again, Ms. Court."

She hung up before I could respond. So that didn't get me anywhere. I left the office and went back to the main lobby. Roy yawned when he saw me, but then put his head down. I had worked him pretty hard lately. Big dogs like him slept twelve or fourteen hours a day, and he hadn't received anywhere near that lately. He needed his rest.

I started pacing and thinking again.

The Wright family took in illegal migrants and helped them escape. I had already been to Nuevo Pueblo, but the place had been abandoned—probably because Kyle Pennington and his investment group had purchased the property from Ross Kelly Farms. Without the poultry processing plant, the company had likely released its workforce without severance.

Those men and women had little money and few resources. Still, I hadn't seen them on the street. Someone was taking care of them.

I hesitated before grabbing my phone. Then I dialed a familiar number. It rang a handful of times before a cheery woman answered.

"Joe Court," said Linda, the director of the Erin Court Home for Women. When I founded the shelter, I had anticipated playing an active role in its development, if not its day-to-day business. Linda Armus had other ideas. They did great work, and I shouldn't have minded, but it stung. I had provided the seed capital and building to house the clients. Linda provided the direction. Then my biological father stepped in and gave them so much money they didn't need me or anything I had to offer. I was just the landlord now. "How can I help you?"

"I need a favor, and you're not going to like it. I wouldn't call you if I had other options. Ross Kelly Farms is shutting down Nuevo Pueblo."

Linda paused.

"I've heard," she said. "We've been working with some of their former employees."

"Good, I'm glad," I said. "I worried they'd slip through the cracks."

Linda sighed.

"They have," she said. "It's been difficult. We try to provide services to everyone regardless of immigration status, but people afraid of being deported are oftentimes afraid of asking for help, even from groups like ours."

"You'll do your best. That's all anyone can ask for," I said. "I won't ask for details, but if I can help, let me know."

"Thank you," she said before pausing. "What's this favor I won't like?"

"I'm investigating the murder of a woman named Donna Wright. She was a licensed clinical social worker and provided therapy services. Her family also helped migrants at Nuevo Pueblo. Donna's killer is dead, but before he died, he claimed someone had set him up. I think someone set Donna up as well."

"Okay," said Linda. "I don't know how I can help, though. When the families in our care need a therapist, we bring them in, but Donna's not one of ours."

I nodded and leaned against the front desk.

"You've helped families from Nuevo Pueblo recently."

"We have, but I don't appreciate where this conversation is headed," said Linda, her voice low.

"I don't either," I said, "but I've got a whole bunch of dead people, and every door I try to open gets slammed shut in my face. Have you heard any rumors or whispers about wrongdoing at Nuevo Pueblo, or anything involving Donna Wright?"

"I can't tell you anything my clients have told me," she said. "I'm an administrator at the shelter, but I'm a licensed clinical social worker. Even if I wanted to tell you something, I couldn't unless they were threatening themselves or someone else."

I covered my mouth with my hand before speaking.

"Is there something you'd like to tell me but can't?"

She went quiet for a moment.

"The Wright family isn't the hero in this story. I don't know Donna. I've never met her, but I doubt the apple fell too far from the tree."

I straightened.

"Can you be more explicit?"

"I've already told you more than I probably should have," she said.

"Thank you, Linda," I said. "I owe you one."

"No, we're not doing favors for each other. When I agreed to run this shelter, I knew you were a police officer. I wish that didn't matter, but it does. I'd prefer if you didn't call me again."

I furrowed my brow.

"Excuse me?"

"My job is to provide the ladies in my shelter the comfort and support they need to rebuild their lives. It's hard to do that if they think I'll relay everything they tell me to you. I'm going to contact our board and tell them that you are withdrawing from any association with our organization."

I shook my head.

"You wouldn't have an organization without me."

"That's part of what makes this hard," she said. "Your heart's in the right place, but we can't work with you. If this shelter matters to you, leave us alone."

"We're both trying to help people. We're not on different sides."

"From the perspective of the families in my shelter, we are on different sides. Your job is to send people to jail. That scares them. These people have not lived perfect lives. They come with baggage. If they're scared that I'm going to share the things they tell me with you, they won't talk to me, and I can't give them the help they need. Whether that's fair, I can't say. It's reality, though, and we have to deal with reality. I'm sorry."

I swallowed hard.

"I'm sorry, too," I said. "Thank you for your candor. Good luck."

I didn't need to hear a response, so I hung up before she could give one. It felt like she had just slapped me. I had become a cop to help people, and I had created that shelter to help people. The two things went together naturally. Cops helped people when they most needed help.

I had believed that since a police officer picked me up off the bathroom floor of a grocery store after my biological mother overdosed on heroin. That uniformed officer—I never even learned his name—had wrapped me in a blanket as gently as if I were his own kid, and he had made me feel safe. He didn't know me, but he stayed with me when I most needed someone.

I had fought my entire adult life to live up to that moment. I wanted to help people the way that officer had helped me.

Whether he knew it or not, he had given me hope I never had before. Some days, I fell short, but I did my best. I sacrificed and fought and tried.

I hadn't considered that those sacrifices and sleepless nights, all the losses I had endured because of my badge, had made me the villain in so many people's lives.

I put the phone down and rubbed my eyes. One day very soon, I'd process this conversation. I'd add its contents to the well of melancholy in my gut, and it would become a part of me. It would hurt. That wasn't for now, though.

I had work to do.

CHAPTER 45

I f Linda believed the Wrights were dirty, they were dirty. Unfortunately, without more information, that didn't help me one iota. It did, however, make Wyatt Caparaso's story more plausible. Maybe they did lure him there, maybe Donna Wright did attack him, and maybe her children did shoot at him. The question is why. What threat could he have posed?

I had been pacing through the lobby, but now I started walking through the building, letting my mind wander as my legs carried me up the steps and to the long hallway on the second floor.

Wyatt Caparaso was a journalism student. He wrote for his college's newspaper and had even broken a big story about Erik Hoyle, one that led to Hoyle's release from prison. That would have been a remarkable achievement for any college student and had likely opened doors to his future career. What if he wasn't done, though?

The Wrights owned a farm. They allegedly provided sustenance for migrants at Nuevo Pueblo. They must have done more than that, though, because the Department of Homeland Security had them under surveillance, which meant Homeland Security agents had convinced a judge that the agency had probable cause to believe the Wrights had committed a serious crime. Presumably, the Wrights didn't know about Homeland Security's surveillance. But what if Wyatt did? What if he learned the Wrights were smuggling migrants or using migrants to smuggle drugs or guns or committing some other crime and threatened to write about it?

In that case, the Wrights had good reason to want him dead. If he seriously threatened them, they very well might lure him to a remote campground, where Donna could attack him and where her kids could finish the job if she failed. After killing Wyatt, it would make sense for them to attack those close to him, believing Wyatt might have told them about the crime he was investigating.

The theory fit loosely, but my speculation had problems, too. First, I didn't have any evidence. Second, it didn't explain Erik Hoyle. The evidence—particularly the suicide notes—indicated Wyatt and Hoyle were killed by the same people. But why? Wyatt Caparaso had an interest in Erik Hoyle, but the Wrights shouldn't have cared.

Nothing fit or made sense. I had hoped to find a missing piece that would explain the puzzle, but instead, I found more missing pieces everywhere I turned. As I walked down the second-floor hallway, Roy came sauntering up the stairs. When he saw me, he lay down by my office, his mouth open and a contented look on his face. He had already gone for a walk today, but he would have enjoyed a trip to the park. As much as I wanted to take him, I needed to focus.

I needed information, which I wouldn't get sitting around. We found Parker Jeffries's BMW about a mile from the Wright's farm. Parker and Lily had cared about Wyatt Caparaso, so maybe the Wrights killed them in revenge for the death of Donna Wright. It was a stretch, but I had nothing else.

If Parker had driven anywhere near the Wright's property, the trail cameras the Department of Homeland Security had hidden would show his car. Unfortunately, they'd never share that footage with me. Realistically, I could probably go to the property, find the cameras, copy their hard drives, and then bring the cameras back without getting caught, but nothing I found would be admissible in court.

If, however, I visited with the property owner's permission and found the cameras, I should be okay. I'd piss off everybody at Homeland Security, but I had multiple murders to solve. If the information on those cameras could help me solve multiple murder cases, it'd be worth it. If I couldn't find information on them, they'd never even know. It wasn't as if they considered their investigation into the Wrights a high-priority case. If they did, they'd have put in cameras that allowed them to monitor the farm live.

At least that's what I told myself.

I went to the office but left my door open for Roy. Then I started searching through my notepad until I found one that held my interview notes with William Wright, Donna Wright's father-in-law. He had lied about the family, but I could still use him.

Before calling, I opened an app on my phone that would record my conversation in case Wright later said we hadn't spoken. Then I called the number he had given me when we last spoke and waited through five rings for a voice to answer. The voice was high and thin. It was a child. I asked to speak to William Wright, and they told me to wait. A few minutes later, William Wright answered.

"Mr. Wright, this is Joe Court," I said. "We spoke a few days ago about your daughter-in-law and your family's activities rescuing migrants from Nuevo Pueblo."

He paused.

"What do you want, Detective?" he asked.

"Help," I said. "I don't know if you've heard, but Ross Kelly Farms and Nuevo Pueblo are shutting down. We're going to have a couple hundred migrant families in need of services very soon. Because of your family's unique position and the help you've given them in the past, some of those families are likely to call your family for assistance."

"It's already started," he said. "We're doing what we can."

"I'm glad to hear that," I said. "I think I can help you with something, though. The trail camera your grandsons found... it belongs to Immigration and Customs Enforcement. It wasn't the only one, either. There are more. The migrants who come to your farm for help have nowhere else to go. I don't want them picked up by ICE."

He grunted.

"Thank you for your call," he said. "When my boys come home from work, we'll take care of them."

"You don't have time," I said. "The cameras are on your property. If you give me permission, I'll remove them."

"You'd do that for us, huh?" he asked.

"I'd do that because ICE pissed me off," I said. "When I returned their camera last time, they arrested me and accused me of theft. This time, I'm sending them to a reporter in St. Louis. I don't like it when assholes abuse their authority or arrest innocent people for administrative crimes."

He chuckled.

"Hell hath no fury," said William. "You have my permission to come and piss off the government, young lady."

"Thank you," I said, breathing easier. "I'm on my way."

William hung up, and I played back the recording of our phone call. I had lied, but I hadn't entrapped him. This was fine.

I grabbed Roy's leash, and he dutifully hopped to his feet. We took a quick walk so he could go to the restroom, and then we drove toward the Wright's farm. Since I had just talked to William, I didn't bother going by the main house. Instead, I parked just off the main road, hooked Roy's leash to his collar, and stepped out of the car. I was taking a risk by coming here, but I wasn't getting anywhere by sitting on the sidelines. It was time to step out of my comfort zone.

I wrapped Roy's leash around my hand and pulled out my phone. Something—I presumed a camera—was broadcasting a weak wireless signal. I walked about twenty feet to my left and then forty feet to my right to see if the connection grew stronger. Then I stepped twenty feet back and forty feet forward. By doing that and measuring the strength of the signal, I got a direction. Southeast.

I headed through the woods. Roy had experience navigating deep woods, so he knew where to put his feet to avoid tripping, but he had a hard time with the leash. I tried to keep an eye on him and an eye on my phone so I could see the varying signal strengths from the camera, but we kept running into trees. It slowed us down.

Eventually, though, I found my first camera. It had a clear view of the family's barn but was unobtrusively small. I snapped pictures of the tree and the camera on it before unhooking the device and walking it back to my Volvo.

William Wright wouldn't knowingly let me see anything incriminating, but he had given me permission to walk the property. So Roy and I started walking again. This time, I started walking toward the house I had seen on my previous visit. I'd need a search warrant to enter the building, but if I happened to hear Parker Jeffries or Lily Tidwell shouting, I'd have extenuating circumstances. I could do what I needed to do to save their lives.

About halfway to our destination, Roy stopped walking. His body was rigid, and he stuck his tail in the air. I stopped midstep and watched. Then he darted to the right until the leash went taut. He hadn't reacted like this on our last visit. I paused.

"What do you smell, buddy?"

He, of course, didn't answer, so I unwound the leash from my hand. Then, hesitantly, I unbuttoned the strap that held my pistol in its holster.

"Find the blood," I said. "Find it."

Roy pulled hard. He wouldn't have done this for a dead deer or other animal. Roy was a cadaver dog, and he smelled the body of a human being. We headed deeper into the woods until we hit a trail. Roy kept his nose down and pulled me along but then stopped when we reached a chain-link fence. Gray stone towered in front of us, forming a hillside as tall as a three-story building. A stream ran out of a half-round opening in the cliffside. The opening was tall enough that I could stand upright and black enough that it made my heart race just staring at it.

A cave made a good place to stash a body. Roy wanted to go inside, but I was a little less enthusiastic.

"You're sure there's a body in there?"

He barked, not that he could understand me. He was just excited. I sighed and opened the chain-link fence's gate, and we stepped inside. I hadn't brought a flashlight, so I used my phone and ducked low, even though the mouth of the cave was at least an inch or two above my head. The mouth of the cave opened into a cavern. Someone had placed six bodies in a row on the ground. All six had multiple gunshot wounds to the torso and at least one in the skull. They were executed. Five of the bodies, I didn't recognize, but one I did.

Shane Fox had two bullet wounds to the head and several to the body. He was as dead as anybody I had ever seen. I pulled my weapon from its holster and hurried out of the cave. The instant I had a cell signal, I called Lieutenant Cognata.

"Lieutenant, this is Joe Court. I'm at a farm in St. Augustine. I just found six bodies, including one of a former St. Augustine sheriff's deputy. Send everybody we've got to the coordinates I'm about to give you. And bring a tactical team. We're going to be arresting the homeowner and his family, and I'm not sure they're going to go willingly."

CHAPTER 46

I t turned out to be easier to apprehend William Wright than I had expected. As Roy and I walked back toward my Volvo to wait for help, Wright came toward us. He looked almost jovial.

"I found a camera," he said. "It's pretty high in the tree, but I can get you a ladder."

I slipped my hand to the holster on my hip. Instantly, he stiffened.

"Are you armed, Mr. Wright?"

"Should I be?" he asked.

"Are you armed?"

He considered and then shook his head.

"If you're lying to me, my dog's going to bite you. Then I'm going to shoot you."

His shoulders fell, and his jowls drooped.

"You found the mushrooms, didn't you?"

I raised my eyebrows.

"I found six bodies in a cave. My colleagues are on their way," I said. "What mushrooms?"

He slowly put his hands in the air.

"I'm going to exercise my right to remain silent."

"Good call," I said. I didn't have handcuffs or zip ties on me, so I made him stay where we were. A few moments later, Roy started howling, which meant he had heard a siren somewhere in the distance. My backup arrived slowly at first and then in spurts until we had almost twenty officers on-site. A highway patrol major and captain arrived as well. I didn't know either of them, but they took charge. When they saw the bodies in the cave, they both called me over. The chain-link fence and closed nature of the cave nicely controlled the crime scene.

Both men crossed their arms as we spoke.

"Okay, Ms. Court," said the major. "I talked to your lieutenant this morning. She said you've been doing some interesting work in town—especially for one of our reserve officers. Now you've found six bodies in a cave. What the hell is going on?"

"Nothing good," I said.

"Mr. Wright refused to speak to us except to say we're illegally trespassing on his property," said the captain. He closed his eyes. "I'm guessing you don't have a search warrant."

"I don't, but Mr. Wright gave me permission to search the property. While here, my cadaver dog smelled a body. I followed his signals to the cave, where I found the bodies. The gate was shut but not locked."

"I don't suppose Wright gave you that permission in writing," said the major. I shook my head.

"It came during a phone conversation, which I recorded. I didn't expect to find these bodies."

"Whose bodies did you expect to find?" asked the captain, lowering his chin. I looked over my shoulder to the cave.

"Lily Tidwell and Parker Jeffries. Instead, I found this cave."

The two men went quiet. Then the major looked at me.

"When you write a report to explain all this, it had better be thorough."

"It always is," I said.

"Then get back to your station and start writing," he said. "I want context that explains all this...mess."

I nodded and gave them each my business card in case they needed to get in touch with me. When I got back to the car, I realized I still had one of Homeland Security's cameras. Realistically, I probably should have told the bosses about it. The moment I did that, though, this already complicated investigation would explode. Nobody needed that just yet. I'd contact the US Attorney's Office in a day or two, but for now, I could keep it quiet.

Roy and I drove back to my station, where I spent the next hour writing a report. I had already written everything down in scattered reports, but I tried to include an overview of my entire investigation in one relatively short document so my colleagues could understand what was going on without devoting an entire day to reading.

Then I focused on the camera. Nothing it had filmed was classified, and it could still help an investigation. Someone had murdered those men and shoved them in the cave. That someone could have walked in front of the camera's lens carrying a body. So I opened the camera's back plate to get the serial and model numbers. Then I spent a few minutes reading its instruction manual online so I could learn how to connect to it.

It sounded easy enough, and since I had taken inventory of the second-floor supply closet, I happened to know where we kept thirty-one three-foot USB-C cables. I grabbed one, connected the camera to my computer, and downloaded the app. Within two minutes, I had the footage in front of me. It was a video of a big barn with beige metal siding, a gravel road in front, and a big sliding door. And that was it. Leaves skittered across the ground, and trees swayed, but it wasn't the most exciting video ever.

I sped it up until people came on scene. At seven this morning, Connor Wright drove a pickup toward the barn, threw square bales of hay in the back from inside, and drove away. At a little before eleven, a gray cat crossed the field of vision. I thought that'd be it for excitement, but then something curious happened. At noon, four pickup trucks pulled to a stop around the barn. Men got out and opened the sliding door. Then a red-and-black armored truck reversed into the field of view. It couldn't fit inside the barn, so it stopped two or three feet away.

I didn't recognize the armored vehicle's driver, but Hunter Collins hopped out of one of the trucks. He and the armored truck's driver spoke for an extended period of time while men in the barn rolled gray fifty-five-gallon drums toward the vehicle. I couldn't see things well, but a tractor equipped with a forklift helped put the drums inside the armored car.

This was Hunter and his CAP team minus one member: Shane Fox, who was dead in a nearby cave. At one time, I would have grieved for Shane. I still felt bad for his family. For him, though...he made his choices. It was hard to feel a lot of sympathy for a man who threw his lot in with murderous racists. As best I could tell, Hunter and his team didn't dump any bodies, but they loaded the truck for an hour. Then, for two additional hours, two other men worked inside the cargo hold.

Then they left in a hurry.

Since I didn't know any of the officers currently working the cave murders, I called Lieutenant Cognata. She picked up quickly and sighed.

"No more bodies, please."

I shook my head.

"I'm not calling about the bodies, but I think I know who killed them. Are you investigating the cave murders?"

"No, but I'm in town," she said.

"Someone needs to pick up Hunter Collins. He's a member of the Church of the White Steeple, and he runs something they call their Citizen Action Patrol. It's a vigilante group. He's heavily armed and well trained, and I suspect he and his group killed everybody in the cave. Shane Fox, one of the victims I've identified, worked for him. I've got video of Hunter at the farm at noon today, and he was loading up something from the main barn. I'd like you to call your team and find out what they've got there."

She paused and clicked her tongue.

"I'll call in an APB for Hunter Collins. Can the barn wait?"

"Hunter and his men were loading fifty-five-gallon barrels into an armored car," I said. "The barrels themselves were so heavy they had to use a tractor. Altogether, the barrels made the truck drop several inches. Maybe they're moving maple syrup, but I doubt it. You can make a lot of nasty stuff and store it in barrels."

"You thinking drugs?" she asked.

"I don't know. That's why you're going to send somebody to the barn. Maybe they left things behind. Maybe you'll find a meth lab there. I don't know. We should find out."

She paused.

"I hate this town."

"Some days, I'm not a fan of it, either," I said. "Do your job."

I hung up and closed my eyes, half expecting her to call back immediately to lecture me. Thankfully, she didn't. I grabbed my phone and took the dog outside so he could use the restroom. Before we returned, my phone rang. The caller ID was blocked, which meant it was possibly law enforcement. I answered.

"Yeah, this is Joe Court."

"Tell me everything you know about this truck and what you saw on video."

I didn't recognize the man's voice, but he sounded strained.

"Lieutenant Cognata give you my number?"

"Yeah. Tell me about the truck and video. Now."

"It was a surveillance video. It showed an armored truck, four pickups, seven men, and an awful lot of rifles at and around the barn. Most looked like AR-15s or variations thereof."

The guy's breath sounded ragged.

"Are you all right?" I asked.

"How much stuff did they load in the truck?"

I shook my head. He was nervous. That made me nervous.

"It was hard to see," I said. "They moved a lot of barrels and took their time."

"Where is it going?" he asked. "I don't care how you know. I don't care if you're involved. I don't care if you're conducting an illegal investigation. You tell me where it's going, you get a free pass for anything you might have done."

My heart started beating fast.

"I don't know," I said. "What'd you find?"

"Hydrazine racing fuel and prilled ammonium nitrate," he said. "Mixed, they make a fuel oil bomb."

My hands started trembling. The world seemed to disappear around me.

"Damn."

"You know these people, Officer," he said. "Where would they go? You know the shooter. Hunter Collins. Where would he go?"

I forced myself to think.

"Schools, sporting events, malls, shopping centers," I said, stammering. "St. Louis has a professional soccer team. Are they playing?"

Apparently, I was on speakerphone because other people started talking quickly, suggesting places Hunter and his crew might go. Most weren't local. Even with a thousand officers, we couldn't search everywhere they suggested. We needed to narrow this down.

"They're in an armored car," I said. "If they wanted to carry the biggest bomb they could, they would have rented a big box truck. The armored car itself has to be important."

The group went quiet. A woman said they might have been preparing a last stand. The armored car would allow them to fight longer. It made some sense, but it didn't sit right with me. I shook my head.

"If this was a last stand, they'd do it at their compound in St. Augustine. They've got bunkers and supplies. It's not that. What if the armored car isn't for protection? What if it's for blending in? Armored cars can go places moving trucks can't. One came to our station monthly to pick up drugs and take them to St. Louis so the DEA could destroy them."

That got them talking again. Somebody said they had seen an armored car at the Galleria Mall in St. Louis. Someone else said they had seen one outside Ballpark Village by Busch Stadium. The conversation wasn't getting us anywhere, but I knew someone who knew Hunter better than anyone else.

"I'm going to call you back," I said. "I need to talk to somebody."

Everybody was talking at once, so I doubted they had even heard me. I hung up and dialed Sophie's number.

"Joe, hey," she said, her voice a whisper. "Can I call you back? I'm at Church. Something has happened. My brother's people have us locked down pretty tight. You guys going to raid us or something?"

"No," I said. "Your brother's got a giant bomb and an armored truck. What's he going to blow up?"

Sophie drew in a breath.

"This is for real?"

"Yeah," I said. "He killed Shane Fox and a bunch of old men, too. Where's he taking his bomb?"

"The Federal Reserve Bank in St. Louis. You can't kill the beast, but if you take his money, you'll hurt him bad. He's talked about it for years. I never thought he was serious."

I squeezed my fists tight.

"Thanks, Sophie, you're the best."

I hung up. I couldn't call the major or captain back because I didn't have their numbers. Instead, I called Lieutenant Cognata. She answered right away. I spoke before she could.

"He's likely hitting the Federal Reserve Bank in St. Louis. Call your boss and tell him."

I hung up. The instant the phone call ended, my adrenaline crashed, and every ounce of strength I felt faded. My butt hit the concrete hard, and I covered my face with my hand, my heart pounding so hard my ribs hurt. Then I closed my eyes and squeezed my trembling fingers tight, hoping I wasn't already too late.

CHAPTER 47

Roy and I stayed outside for a moment until I caught my breath. My head throbbed, and I felt dizzy. My vision became hazy, like I was seeing the world through smudged glass. Some of that was adrenaline fading and my blood pressure returning to normal, but some of it was the residual effects of my concussion. My doctors had warned me to take it easy. I probably shouldn't have even been exercising yet, let alone hurrying through the woods, climbing into a cave, and exerting myself.

I had done my part. My partners needed to do theirs.

I patted Roy's side. He looked at me and licked his nose and seemed to grin.

"I think we did okay," I said, my heart still beating fast. I took deep breaths. The haze left my vision, and my dizziness subsided. I felt better. My phone beeped. It was Sophie. She had sent me a text message, asking what was going on. I texted her and told her to sit tight. I'd keep her posted when I had information.

After a few minutes, Roy and I went inside, and I searched through the supply closet for a police radio. Missouri's public responders operated a public safety radio channel that allowed approved agencies across the state to communicate in emergency situations. I tapped into that and listened. So many officers and dispatchers were speaking and coordinating movements that it was hard to follow. It was clear they hadn't found Hunter, though.

Then everything kicked off at once when a police helicopter spotted a red-and-black armored car heading north on I-55 in the St. George neighborhood in St. Louis. It was a suburban part of town with small businesses just off the interstate. The highway patrol, in tandem with the St. Louis County and City police departments, began redirecting traffic.

The police set up a roadblock a quarter mile from the bridge that crossed the River Des Peres, a drainage channel that carried stormwater through town and into the Mississippi River. From the radio communication, they had roughly a hundred officers on-site and considerably more in the surrounding area. Three police helicopters and dozens of drones hovered nearby. Hunter and his men weren't going anywhere—certainly not to their destination.

Marked police SUVs surrounded the armored truck, boxing it in. Then they started slowing a good distance before the roadblock. It sounded as if the armored truck was cooperating initially, but then it rammed an SUV. Officers tried conducting a PIT maneuver, where they strike the vehicle in the rear quarter panel to force it to spin out, but the armored truck was too heavy, and the SUVs were too light.

The highway patrol had redirected traffic, but several dozen motorists had slipped through their net and were caught immobile behind the roadblock. As the armored truck barreled toward them, officers started clearing as many motorists out of their vehicles as they could. The civilians ran toward the River Des Peres bridge, where the reinforced concrete barriers would provide some protection.

At the last minute, officers deployed spike strips across the interstate. Neither the armored truck nor the pickups that followed had a chance to swerve. The spikes shredded their tires. Hunter's men stopped. A few jumped out of their pickups. The armored truck, however, kept moving. It veered right, hit the embankment alongside the road, and rolled off the interstate. Then it stopped on the grass.

The gunfire started almost immediately. So many officers yelled simultaneously that I couldn't keep up. And then, in seconds, it was over. Officers started screaming for ambulances and paramedics. Hunter's men had a lot of guns, but they faced a police force with overwhelming numbers. It became a last stand, after all. I hoped we didn't have too many casualties, but I suspected we did. The good guys may have stopped the bad guys, but nobody won. I turned the radio off and slumped behind the front desk.

Then I looked at Roy. He was shifting his weight from his left side to his right. Then he saw me and whined.

"What's going on?" I asked. "We just went outside."

He whined again. Then he barked at me.

"You do not bark at me," I said, shaking my head. "You know better than that."

He whined again. Then, once more, he barked. I sighed.

"Your belly bothering you?" I asked, standing up. "Come on. We'll go out."

I grabbed his leash from the counter, but when I went to hook it to his collar, he darted away. I furrowed my brow.

"What is with you today?"

He cocked his head to the side. Roy, like most Chesapeake Bay retrievers, had big floppy ears. They didn't pop up like a German shepherd's, but they still rose. He had heard something. I started toward him, and he darted away. He wasn't moving toward the front door. Instead, he was headed toward the staircase.

"You want to show me something?"

He barked, almost sounding happy.

"Okay, let's go," I said, wondering whether we had an animal downstairs. That hadn't happened since the station's renovation, but critters could crawl through pretty tiny holes. If we had mice, it was better to remove them before they reproduced.

The basement was clean and neat. It reminded me of a hospital. The contractors had installed big ceramic tiles on the floor. It was supposed to look like stone, but it wasn't. The surface had grit so it wouldn't become slippery. The walls were white drywall. In the past, I would have seen officers going to the gym and locker rooms, evidence technicians walking between the lab and vault, and clerks in the evidence room. It would have been lively and bright. Now, with only every third overhead light on, it was gloomy.

A cold draft blew in from the left. I hurried toward it. The exterior door nearest the evidence vault was open. That should have been locked.

I walked to the door, removing my pistol from its holster, my heart beating fast once more. The steel door was undamaged, but someone had drilled into the deadbolt, destroying the screws that held it together. With the screws damaged, the lock fell apart, exposing its innards. A drill sat outside on the ground. Roy must have heard it.

I swore under my breath. This was a very serious problem. Before I could stop him, Roy bounded off into the darkness. I clenched my jaw before speaking.

"Roy, get back here," I said, my voice barely above a whisper. I listened and thought I heard his nails on the floor, but they weren't coming toward me. "Roy. Come here."

Roy was usually pretty good about listening, so he probably didn't hear me. I gripped my pistol tightly and started heading down the hall, hoping my footsteps weren't too loud. When I turned the corner, I saw Roy sitting outside the women's locker room, his tail wagging as he stared at the door.

"Get over here," I said, gesturing furiously toward him. He lumbered to his feet and then hurried. He grinned at me, seemingly proud of himself. "Don't you do that again."

His tail stopped wagging, and he tilted his head to the left and right, confused.

"Butthead," I said, reaching down to pet his neck and cheek. Then I focused ahead of me and raised my voice. "Police officer. If you can hear me, step into the hallway with your hands above your head."

Nobody moved. I repeated the command but nobody stepped into the hall.

I crept forward. Because of Roy, I knew the bad guy's location. He didn't know that, though. It gave me an advantage, but only if I could preserve his ignorance. I pounded on the door of the crime lab.

"Police. Anybody in there?"

The door was locked. I had a key, but I didn't bother opening it. I did the same for the gym and actually stuck my head inside. I skipped the supply closet, men's locker room, and basement break room and stopped outside the women's locker room.

If the bad guy had been monitoring my movements, he probably thought I was outside another door. The switch for the hallway lights was just overhead, so I flicked those off. No light spilled from beneath the locker room's door. My would-be ambusher wanted it dark. Fine by me. I slipped off my jacket and knelt low.

Sophie had warned me about her brother and his men. Hunter had been a soldier. He knew how to set an ambush. I could use that. I closed my eyes and adjusted my grip on my pistol. Hunter had attacked me at home; I was convinced of that now. I hadn't expected him. This time, I was prepared.

Let this work.

I knelt low and counted to three before throwing the door open. It smashed into the wall. Roy vaulted through the doorway, barking and growling. I tossed my jacket to the left. It hit the lockers with a soft rustle and a clank of the metal zipper striking the metal lockers. A dark figure fired toward the noise. I squeezed my pistol's trigger six times at his muzzle flash.

Something thudded to the ground.

"Roy, heel," I said. The dog stopped barking and ran back to me as I flicked the light switch. Hunter Collins lay on the ground about twenty feet in front of me. His black shirt glistened with fresh blood. At least four of my six shots had hit his chest. He wasn't breathing. I kicked a black pistol out of his hands and checked his neck for a pulse. He was dead.

I sat down on a bench nearby and allowed my adrenaline to fade. Then I looked at Hunter. He was young and dead. I shouldn't have been glad, but he had hurt a lot of people, me included.

What a waste of a life.

Chapter 48

T he next couple of weeks passed quicker than I had
expected, mostly because I was barely able to sit down.
Hunter and his CAP team had loaded their armored vehicle
with tons of explosives. If they had gotten it into place,
it would have taken out half a city block and potentially
murdered thousands—including a number of children on
school field trips. We stopped their plan, but it came at a cost.
Eight police officers were shot on the interstate, one fatally.
The city gave his family a somber parade downtown.

Four members of Hunter's CAP team died on the interstate in St. Louis, and Hunter himself died in my building's basement. Before they died, though, Hunter and his
team murdered Shane Fox and five members of his Church's
Council of Elders. Hunter thought God had given him a
glorious mission that would only end with the dissolution
of the US government or his death. He got what he wanted,
I guess.

Once the full extent of Hunter's plans became known,
every federal government agency in the world descended

on St. Augustine. Because my station was mostly empty, it became the de facto headquarters of the investigation. Each agency commandeered a different conference room, jealously guarded their turf, and refused to cooperate with anybody else. It was amazingly petty and stupid, almost like we had our own miniature version of Congress just down the hall from me.

By interrogating the survivors, subpoenaing financial records, and interviewing every member of the Church of the White Steeple ad nauseum, we eventually learned a few things about the bombing and murders that precipitated it.

This mess, so we learned after interviewing dozens of Church members and reviewing hundreds of pages of Church files, had started almost ten years ago. I was in college at the University of Missouri-St. Louis, studying biology and considering whether I should go to medical school or follow in my mother's footsteps and become a police officer. In St. Augustine, the Church of the White Steeple was struggling to pay off a series of loans its founder Richard Clarke had taken out to purchase property for his long-running, racist ministry.

The Reverend Richard Clarke and Church elders Damon Burke, Donald Bagby, and Mark Rose brainstormed and came up with a permanent solution to the Church's financial problems: Medicare fraud. They thought the US government was a cancer on the American people, so they had no moral qualms stealing from it, and, with a large population of immigrants of questionable legal status nearby at Nuevo Pueblo, they had no problems finding people who could help pull the fraud off. They created the Rural Missouri Health Clinic in an old house left to the Church by a former member.

Clarke and his friends paid longtime Church members, the Wright family, a significant sum of money to establish ties to the workforce at Nuevo Pueblo. Because their property bordered the town, they already had contact with the immigrants. Now, instead of chasing them off their property at gunpoint, the Wrights brought them blankets, food, toiletries, and cell phones. They also encouraged them to use the Church of the White Steeple's newly established clinic for their medical needs.

At the clinic, nurse practitioners, physician's assistants, and a doctor provided reasonable care for minor illnesses and issues. For these issues, they billed Medicaid and Medicare. For each actual service the clinic provided, they billed for several more they didn't. Patients with a sprained ankle or rash might incur charges for diagnostic evaluations for much more serious injuries. Through the clinic, the Church of the White Steeple stole millions while simultaneously winning the gratitude of the people they exploited.

If anyone at Nuevo Pueblo complained, the Wrights sold them to human traffickers. There was a global market for cheap labor. Because the workforce at Nuevo Pueblo was largely undocumented, disappearances were an accepted part of life. Those same human traffickers had surrounded me and chased me from Nuevo Pueblo during my investigation. ICE didn't know who they were, but they had a bead on them.

The Church and Wright families profited highly until a young man named Joaquin Herrera started asking questions he ought not have asked. The Herrera family lived a stable, middle-class life in St. Augustine. Since he had grown up speaking Spanish and English, Joaquin had friends from all walks of life, including a few at Nuevo Pueblo. When those friends suggested he could get Xanax easily at the rural clinic, he did. He pretended to live in Nuevo Pueblo and speak only Spanish. The clinic provided a false name, social security number, and address, and billed the government on his behalf for services befitting someone with severe abdominal pain.

Joaquin wasn't stupid. He knew what was going on and told his girlfriend, Brittany Ashbury. They planned to contact the IRS, believing they'd get a share of any money the IRS recovered. Unknown to Joaquin, his new girlfriend, Brittany, still loved her ex-boyfriend, Hunter. She told Hunter everything, hoping to impress him enough that the two of them could report the fraud together and cut Joaquin out.

Hunter was a member of the Church of the White Steeple, but Brittany didn't realize the Church operated the clinic. Acting under orders, a group of Hunter's friends abducted

Joaquin. They held him inside a run-down home in St. Louis until the appointed time and then shot him full of heroin. He overdosed and died.

Our details of Hunter and Brittany were fuzzy, so we had to speculate. We knew that Brittany loved him. While Hunter's friends held Joaquin captive, we believe Hunter and Brittany met behind her hardware store, got high on psychedelic mushrooms, and had sex—probably consensual. He then slipped her a Rohypnol and shot her.

Hunter and his friends seemed to believe that the frame was clear and obvious. They wanted us to believe that Joaquin raped and murdered his girlfriend and then killed himself in St. Louis. If they had killed Joaquin in St. Augustine, and if Detective Delgado had done his job, we might have come to that conclusion. Instead, we hounded, cajoled, and threatened Erik Hoyle until he confessed. Then we sent him to prison.

The situation hadn't worked out as Hunter Collins had expected, but he had still eliminated a threat to his Church. The clinic continued its work, the Wrights continued their work, and all the morally bankrupt bastards profited.

Then, years later, Wyatt Caparaso entered the scene. Wyatt was ambitious and curious. Brittany Ashbury was beautiful, young, innocent, and dead. Erik Hoyle looked like the perfect conniving, evil villain, but he wasn't evil, and he wasn't a murderous rapist. He was an innocent man, and we had sent him to prison.

Hoyle became Wyatt's project. He wrote articles and dozens of letters. He contacted attorneys across the country. A few encouraged him, but none agreed to take on the case. Then an associate of Brian Carlisle's passed him a college newspaper, and Carlisle saw an opportunity. He took the case pro bono and fought hard to free his new client. Erik Hoyle's release must have seemed inevitable.

Then something weird happened: Donna Wright contacted Hunter Collins and said that someone had called and threatened to expose her family's dealings at Nuevo Pueblo. Donna was to meet this mystery caller at a campground and give him money. Hunter thought he could take care of the problem. He went to the campground with Donna, thinking he could kill the blackmailer and end the threat. Unfortunately, when they got to the camp site, they found Wyatt Caparaso. He was armed and shot Donna. Hunter's men returned fire, but they missed. Everyone ran.

It was a bad break with terrible timing.

Hunter and his men were planning an operation to consolidate their power over the Church and strike a blow to the US government. Donna Wright's death became a threat to the entire project. Her family wanted revenge, so Hunter and his CAP team killed Wyatt Caparaso. Caparaso had clear ties to Erik Hoyle, so they killed him, too. They tried to make both deaths look like suicides, but they weren't good at it. They tried to kill me, for good measure, but they failed.

Hunter's failure to kill me became a problem for the Church. The elders met and decided to dispatch him and replace him with Shane Fox. Unfortunately for them, Hunter had trained the Church's entire security team. They were loyal to him. Under his orders, they murdered the Council of Elders and locked the property down. Everyone was ordered to stay inside.

With everyone locked down and their enemies dead, Hunter and his crew moved up their project in St. Louis. They intended to blow up the federal building and pull back to the farm, which they thought they could defend against a significant force. In their eyes, they had become a sovereign country unto themselves. The innocent civilians in their midst provided a measure of security against armed incursion by the federal government. The ATF or FBI might move against racists who blew up a federal building, but they wouldn't risk killing children.

The gunfight on I-55 prevented all that.

The investigation was complex, tragic, and closed. I had finally found the identity of Brittany Ashbury's killer: it was Hunter Collins, a man she loved and had hoped to spend her life with. Her mom broke down upon hearing the news. Knowing that her daughter's murderer was dead provided little consolation for her loss, but at least Hunter wouldn't hurt anyone else.

Lily Tidwell and Parker Jeffries were a bright spot amidst the tragedy. They were alive and reasonably well. Erik Hoyle had been Wyatt's project, but Lily and Parker knew enough about Hoyle that they worried when he died. They suspected I had killed him and that I might go after them, too, just as I had gone after Erik Hoyle eight years ago. In their eyes, I was just another corrupt police officer in a town full of dirty and corrupt officials.

To protect themselves, they stored a week's worth of food and ran. They even burned Parker's car so we'd think they were dead. For a week, the two stayed at the Tidwell family's cabin in Fish Creek, Wisconsin, and were found only after they tried to use Lily's credit card to purchase groceries. A trooper with the Wisconsin State Patrol took them into custody, believing they were using a stolen card. As I understood it, their parents cried for hours when they found them.

Most of the people who had committed major felonies were already dead, but we arrested Connor and William Wright for various terrorism-related charges, human trafficking, aiding and abetting a felon, accessory after the fact, fraud, money laundering, and too many other felonies to count. We arrested the two surviving members of Hunter Collins's CAP team for multiple cases of murder and several dozen other major felonies. We arrested the staff at the Church's clinic. We arrested two accountants in St. Louis who helped the Church cook their books. We arrested Hunter Collins's fiancé for conspiracy and for aiding and abetting felonious acts. Lastly, we arrested several people who had worked at Ross Kelly Farms for human trafficking.

The investigation would take years to unwind fully. It started simply. Then, like a snowball rolling down hill, it grew and grew. It was over, though. For the moment, I could breathe again.

Unfortunately, even then I knew my real work had just begun.

CHAPTER 49

Three weeks after the massacre on I-55, I met Sophie in Sycamore Park. Not long ago, a young father named Joel Robinson had died in that park, trying to protect his son. I hadn't meant to meet Sophie at a crime scene, but few places in town were free of tragic memories. The key was imbuing those places with joy—as children on the playground clearly were.

Sophie and I watched the kids in silence for a moment. Her daughter was with her this time. She and Sophie had gone for a walk earlier, which had lulled her to sleep in her stroller. She moved and kicked and made little grunting noises. It was hard not to smile at her.

"She's beautiful," I said.

"Thank you," she said. "She's my darling. I never thought I'd be a mom. Now that I've got a daughter, I can't imagine being anything else. Life, sometimes, throws you a curveball."

Her voice had a familiar southern twang that slowed her speech while still seeming, somehow, elegant. It was so seamless. I didn't know how she did it.

"You and Richard Clarke weren't planning on having kids?"

Her eyes went distant as she looked over the park grounds around us. Then she leaned toward me.

"She's not Richard's. Her daddy teaches Chemistry at the University of Chicago. He's brilliant. Richard and I didn't have a romantic relationship, but he liked letting the world believe he was shagging a woman a third his age. It made him seem virile and strong, and it kept me in the good graces of my Church."

I chuckled.

"That's reassuring to hear," I said. "I had wondered about that."

We settled into silence. At one time, it would have been easy, if a touch awkward. Now, I didn't know how to characterize it.

"You've had a big couple of weeks," she said, finally. "Medicare fraud, domestic terrorism, murder, attempted murder, assault, battery. And that's just the stuff my brother did. How's your head?"

"It's fine," I said. "My doctors warned me against taking up boxing, but I don't have any scarring or other permanent damage. How are you now that your Church's leadership has been dismantled?"

She sighed and rolled her eyes.

"Busy, busy, busy," she said. "We're still figuring things out. I hate to say it, but the chaos has given us the opportunity to rethink our community's governance. Women are going to have a voice now. It's pretty exciting times. More importantly, we're taking care of our own. Nobody's going hungry. That's what matters."

"I'm sorry about your brother. I wouldn't blame you if you hated me for killing him."

She held her gaze on mine. Then she looked away.

"I can't hate you," she said. "Hunter was my brother, but I lost him a long time ago."

I crossed my arms and looked out over the grass.

"Still, I'm sorry. If I could have taken him into custody without getting hurt, I would have," I said. Sophie started to speak, but I continued. "Truth be told, ever since Donna Wright died, I've felt like a pin at a bowling alley. A ball hits me, and I go flying into one set of pins. Then another pin hits me, and I go flying in another direction."

"I can imagine," said Sophie. "I've read the news stories. You just call to catch up? If so, I'm glad."

I looked down and shook my head.

"I called because we need to talk."

She raised her eyebrows, a bemused look on her face.

"This sounds serious."

"It is," I said, nodding. "For the past three weeks, I've been reviewing work conducted by half a dozen agencies to figure out what happened with your brother and your Church and Wyatt Caparaso and Erik Hoyle and everything else. The FBI ran a background check on you. I've read it."

Sophie straightened.

"Okay," she said, nodding. "You're making me nervous, Joe."

I inhaled through my nose to keep myself calm.

"You are a patient, intelligent woman," I said. "From the day I met you, I formed this idea of you as an old-fashioned southern belle. I thought your Church forced you to be with Richard Clarke. But nobody's ever forced you to do anything, have they?"

She considered me before speaking.

"I'm not Wonder Woman, Joe. Plenty of people have forced me to do things I didn't want to do. That's life, unfortunately."

I nodded.

"You went to Vanderbilt as an undergraduate and then the University of Rochester for a PhD program in political science. You studied heresthetics. It's the science of political manipulation. I tried to read a paper you wrote, but I didn't get very far. It was outside my expertise."

"I'm flattered you even tried," she said, smiling. When she spoke, her voice was smooth and confident. It was a teacher's voice. "As far as my field of study, it's not necessarily about manipulation. It's simpler than it seems. We live in a world full of rules. Some are written down, some aren't. We've got rules about how to talk during a City Council meeting, we've got rules about how close to stand to someone to make them feel comfortable—or uncomfortable, we've got rules about all kinds of things. I've spent my life studying those rules so I can make them more efficient—and so I can change them to produce the kinds of results I want. That's it. Nothing exciting in that."

"Your southern accent's gone," I said.

She shrugged.

"It was an affectation designed to lower people's expectations of me," she said. "People look at me and see a blonde, pretty girl and hear that southern accent and dismiss me. They think I'm an idiot. You'd be amazed at how quickly you're ignored when people think they're smarter than you. Then, you can work without them bothering you."

"I'm sorry if I ever ignored you, and I've never thought I was smarter than you."

She reached across the divide between us to rub my shoulder.

"You never ignored me, disrespected me, or made me feel inferior," she said. "I've always liked that about you."

"I've tried not to be a dick," I said. She chuckled before scooting closer to me and putting her head on my shoulder.

"I guess the cat's out of the bag now. I'm as smart as you are. You don't know how long it's been since I've been able to have a normal conversation with someone. Everywhere I go at home, I have to tread carefully so I don't reveal too much. I'm glad I can be honest with you. You're a friend."

Hearing her call me a friend was almost bittersweet.

"I wish we could be friends, but that can't happen. I think you know that, too."

She nodded but said nothing.

"My investigation started when a young man named Wyatt Caparaso went into the public safety office at Waterford College wearing a bloody shirt and carrying a pistol. He said he shot a woman after she attacked him. He also said several children shot rifles at him. I now know those children were under the tutelage of your brother. The victim was Donna Wright. You know the Wright family. They're members of your Church."

She crossed her arms.

"I know the family."

"You also know Wyatt Caparaso. I interviewed his former girlfriend and roommate. They didn't refer to you by name, but Parker Jeffries called you 'the hot blonde chick from that crazy church.'"

Sophie chuckled softly.

"Hot blonde chick from that crazy church could describe anyone, Joe."

I smiled but mostly ignored the quip.

"Both Parker and Lily told me you had contacted Wyatt eighteen months ago about Erik Hoyle. I assumed Wyatt had found Erik on his own, but you tipped him off. You wanted Erik to go free. Why?"

Sophie sighed and considered.

"I didn't know or care about Erik. I was interested in my brother. He deserved to go to prison. He murdered a girl he loved because Damon Clarke told him to. If he did that to her, he'd kill anybody. I didn't want him in my community. I would have gone to the police, but I didn't trust your colleagues. Who would I have talked to? You? You would have listened, but then you'd be forced to pass it on to George Delgado or somebody else. They'd ignore me. So I went to a student journalist. He got the ball rolling. The lawyers and court system did the rest."

For a few moments, neither of us spoke. Then I cleared my throat.

"According to Donna's father-in-law, Donna got a phone call that threatened to expose the family's dealings at Nuevo Pueblo unless a family representative dropped fifty thousand dollars cash at the campground. Wyatt Caparaso received a note that said someone had information about Erik Hoyle. The campground was their meeting point. They were both lured to that campground at the same time."

Sophie straightened.

"So somebody set them up," she said.

"You did," I said, nodding. "I can't prove that, but it was you. You knew Donna, so you knew there'd be violence. You knew I'd investigate because I'm the only police officer in town, and I don't let things go. According to my old colleagues, I'm like a dog with a bone. You knew I'd investigate Donna Wright and learn about her family's activities at Nuevo Pueblo and their connections to your church. You also knew I'd investigate Wyatt and discover his connection to Erik Hoyle and Brittany Ashbury. It'd bring Brittany—and your brother—to the forefront of my attention."

"I love your imagination, Joe," she said. "You must think I'm truly devious to have coordinated all this."

"You adopted a southern accent and pretended to be an ignorant farm girl for years so people would underestimate you."

She tilted her head to the side.

"Touché, I suppose."

"You're not a bad person," I said. "You think you're doing the right thing."

She blinked.

"That is a weird, backhanded compliment," she said. "I kind of feel like you're going to insult me now."

"No," I said. "When you visited me at work, you warned me about your brother and your Church. You said there was a cold war you worried would become hot. Your Church was split. Michael Clarke wanted to take his racist ideology mainstream, your brother believed the federal government was evil and would sweep through and take the Church's children, and regular folks just wanted to live."

She considered.

"We're a community with diverse political and social beliefs," she said. "We're not a cult, and we don't have purity tests. Community members are allowed to come and go and express themselves."

"Your brother was using Church funding to build explosives and stockpile weaponry."

"And he's dead now," said Sophie. "You killed him."

"Not before he killed your Church's entire governing body. It was a clean sweep. No cold war anymore," I said. "You know what the best part about investigating your Church is? The paperwork. You guys take it seriously."

Sophie said nothing.

"The Church elders took meticulous notes of every Council meeting," I said. "Before they were all murdered, they met to discuss your brother's attack on me. You requested that meeting."

She blinked and looked away.

"You're my friend. He tried to kill you. I couldn't stand for that, so I called on my Church to punish him. Is that wrong?"

"Misguided, maybe, but not wrong. Instead of punishing Hunter, his security team killed your Church's entire leadership structure," I said. "You expected that, though, didn't you?"

"I can't tell the future, Joe."

"But you expected violence," I said. "You requested security at your home, didn't you?"

She closed her eyes and said nothing. I pulled a notepad from my purse and flipped through pages until I found the one I wanted.

"Donald Bagby, one of the Elders, kept the logs," I said. "You made a formal complaint against your brother and requested security in case he tried to retaliate."

She sighed and closed her eyes.

"I did. Where is this going, Joe?"

"You requested four specific security team members. Why them?"

She frowned.

"Because they were good men. I've known them for years and knew I could trust them."

"I'm glad you had people you could trust to keep you safe," I said. "The Council wasn't so lucky, were they? By removing those four men most loyal to the Church from the security rotation, the men most loyal to your brother became the security team at his trial. Instead of punishing Hunter, they killed everybody. Then they died in St. Louis while trying to blow up a bank."

Sophie's eyes had a coldness to them I hadn't seen before.

"Funny how fate punishes the wicked, isn't it?"

I squeezed my jaw tight.

"You moved everybody around you like they were chess pieces," I said. "I'm just curious how far this goes. Did you engineer the attack on me, too?"

She tilted her head to the side and furrowed her brow.

"Of course not," she said.

"You used me," I said, allowing the full measure of my anger into my voice.

"People use each other every day," she said. "I'm sorry for what happened to you—truly I am—but cut the self-righteousness. Don't forget who you called when you needed to find my brother. Without me, you'd have an awfully big hole in downtown St. Louis."

I squeezed my jaw tight before standing and looking at her.

"You got what you wanted, I guess," I said. "Your brother's gone, his CAP team is gone, the Elders are gone, we shut down the fraudulent clinic your Church ran, and we've ended your influence at Nuevo Pueblo. You ended your Church's civil war by decapitating your opponent's entire command structure. It was smart. Is Michael Clarke going to die soon, too?"

She raised her eyebrows as if she were shocked.

"I certainly hope not. He's a good preacher. Every organization needs a pretty face in public."

I drew in a breath through my nose.

"You risked an awful lot of people getting hurt to get what you wanted. Your brother had eighteen thousand pounds of explosives stuffed into a truck. He would have killed hundreds if he had reached the bank."

She considered and narrowed her eyes at me.

"He didn't. Think about this for a minute. I didn't know Hunter's plan, but what if I did? What could I have done? Called you? What would you have done?"

"I would have done my job. I would have followed the rules, secured search warrants, put together a team. We would have made arrests. Nobody would have died."

When she turned to me, her eyes were soft, almost pleading.

"You would have died, Joe. You and everyone who came after Hunter. My brother was a soldier. I don't think you understand that. His security team were soldiers. They trained forty hours a week to defend that farm. They would have shot you and your entire search team with fifty-caliber rifles from half a mile away. You wouldn't have stood a chance. Then his CAP team would have closed the gates and activated claymore mines along the driveway and throughout the woods to prevent anyone else from coming after him.

"You are so smart, but you don't understand the world, Joe. It is cruel and cold, and sometimes it needs someone just as cruel and cold to control it. Now, my brother and his followers are gone. The ATF came in and raided his armory. They confiscated hundreds of firearms and millions of rounds of ammunition. The FBI froze our Church's finances. We're no longer a threat to anyone. Do you understand what that means? My Church can become a community. I don't have to put my daughter to sleep in a reinforced-concrete bunker. I don't have to worry that the federal government will raid my home. Is that so wrong?"

I shook my head.

"As admirable as the goal was, Wyatt Caparaso is dead. That didn't have to happen. Erik Hoyle is dead. That didn't have to happen," I said. "If you had come to me, we could have come up with a plan. Nobody needed to die."

"Do you even have a badge anymore, Joe?" she asked. "If I had come to you, my brother and his people would have killed us both. And I'm sorry for everybody my brother killed. For his actions, he is now enjoying hell's full assortment of amenities. If I did anything—and I'm not admitting that I did—I used the tools at my disposal to keep the people I love safe. You would have done the same."

I wanted to shout, but I couldn't sustain the anger. Instead, I sat down beside her and went quiet.

"I'm sorry you got hurt," she said. "And I'm sorry any of this happened. I really wish we could have been real friends."

I nodded.

"Me, too."

For a few minutes, we stayed there. Then I sighed, stood, and started walking away.

"There's something else we need to talk about," she said. I turned and nodded to her.

"There's nothing else to say," I said.

"Unfortunately, there is. The county charter your commission put together is good," she said, "but it's not going to pass."

I crossed my arms.

"Are you working against it?"

"I don't have to. My PhD is in political science. The people whose votes you're trying to secure don't have time to care about the structures of government. They care about their grocery bills and their reduced hours at The Chicken Shack. Your commission is trying to sell this thing based on its long-term benefits to people so worried about their next paycheck they can't plan past next week. They're paranoid about people coming in and taking the little they have. To them, no government is the best option."

I put my hands on my hips.

"What do you suggest?"

"If you had asked earlier, we could have knocked on doors. We could have changed some minds."

"Maybe we could have," I said. "Little late now."

She smiled.

"For what it's worth, you've got my vote. I want you to become sheriff or even county executive, but the members of my Church need a better reason to care. They don't know you, and they don't trust the government."

I squeezed my jaw tight before speaking, trying to keep my anger out of my voice.

"They trust you."

She raised her eyebrows and nodded.

"They do. With my brother and the Elders gone, I could swing the whole election if I wanted. My Church forms a voting block with over five hundred members. They'll follow Michael Clarke. Clarke follows me."

I rubbed my eyes.

"Your help is going to cost me, isn't it?"

"It will. I have to think of my community. If you want our support, you'll pay. You don't have a choice."

Unfortunately, she was probably right.

"See you around, Sophie," I said. "Hug your daughter for me."

"I will, Joe," she said. "Good luck."

Chapter 50

After meeting with Sophie, I went back to my station. We no longer had a custodial staff, and the federal and state agencies who had briefly made my station their local headquarters had left the place a mess. I had been vacuuming and cleaning, but I hadn't cleaned everywhere yet. I wasn't in a hurry, either. The building could wait.

My stomach felt gurgly, and a heavy weight seemed to have begun pressing down on me. I felt ill almost. Sophie may have purged her Church of its more extreme elements, but a hateful, paranoid core still remained. Long term, I didn't know how to deal with that. The short term looked no better.

Roy was with Preston and Shelby. He rarely misbehaved, but he was a big dog, and he had made some of the federal agents nervous. I missed having him with me, but he was having fun on the farm. For the day, I was alone.

I went to my office and pulled up the website the Charter Commission had authorized. It had our proposed charter as well as explanations of what everything meant and how it'd fund the schools and other organizations in the county. A lawyer could spend hours on that website learning about the newly proposed St. Augustine. Our constituents weren't lawyers with free time, though. They were grocery store workers, laborers at construction sites, farm workers...they were the working poor who put on their shoes every morning and came home exhausted every evening.

Sophie was right. The men and women whose votes we most needed didn't have time to read and understand everything. Unfortunately, it was too late now. We had a vote coming up—one we couldn't afford to lose.

I closed the website, pushed back from my desk, and started walking toward the break room—one of the few rooms I had actually cleaned—for a cup of coffee. As I poured, a voice called out from downstairs.

"Hello?"

I recognized the voice. I grimaced, sighed, and took my coffee to the lobby to find Kyle Pennington. As had been the case every time I had seen him, he was so handsome he almost looked pretty. Today, he wore gray slacks and a white Oxford shirt that he had left open at the collar. I nodded to him.

"Can I help you?"

"I just came by to check on my plant," he said. "And you."

I walked to the front desk and leaned against the counter so we could talk without shouting across a lobby.

"Your peace plant is healthy and well."

"How are you?" he asked.

"Healthy and well," I said, forcing myself to smile.

He shifted on his feet.

"I'm glad."

For a moment, neither of us spoke. I sipped my coffee, preferring to hide behind it than speak. He looked down. I thought he'd say something, but then he straightened.

"Okay, then," he said. "You sound busy. Thanks for your time, and sorry to interrupt."

He turned to leave. I almost let him go. This was Pennington's third visit. The first time, he had yelled. The second time, he had apologized. I didn't know what he wanted now, but he probably didn't deserve my scorn.

"Do you want a cup of coffee?" I asked. "It's terrible."

He stopped and looked at me, his eyebrow quirked as he blinked.

"That's a strange offer."

"I'm a strange person," I said. He smiled and looked down.

"Can we still talk even if I decline your terrible coffee?"

I sipped my drink and considered.

"I suppose so, but you don't know what you're missing without giving it a shot."

"Based on your endorsement earlier, I think I'd rather live in ignorance."

I shrugged and continued to lean against the counter. He cleared his throat.

"I told my mother about you. I also told her what I said to you. She told me to apologize."

I raised my eyebrows.

"Do you always do what your mother says?"

"Most mothers tend to be wise beyond their years," he said. "I take her advice seriously. In this case, it wasn't just her advice that convinced me I was wrong. Mom and Susanne didn't talk on the phone often, but they wrote letters. My aunt loved you. She didn't visit us in California because she thought it was more important to stay with you. She declined my mother's invitations to Christmas and Thanksgiving because Susanne wanted to stay here with you. She said you were her sister. Mom thought you'd be older. We didn't know you were a young woman. When I saw you, I made assumptions, and they were wrong. I'm sorry."

I swallowed hard and tried to keep my expression neutral even as I could feel myself wavering.

"You had a dog on my last visit," he said. "Was that Roger? Susanne said he was the finest animal she had ever met."

I shook my head.

"No," I said. "That was Roy. Roger's been gone for some time."

"I'm sorry," he said. He gave me a meek smile before looking toward the door. "Thank you for caring for my aunt. I'm going to head out now. I won't bother you again."

I nodded, and he turned to leave. I almost let him go again. Then I thought about all the work our Charter Commission had done. I didn't have many allies in St. Augustine. I couldn't afford to let one walk out the door.

"Wait," I said. "Are you serious that you're here to help people?"

He turned and considered.

"My company is here because we see an opportunity," he said. "My investors and I have a commercially viable business plan that will make us money. I pushed for St. Augustine because my power plant will be a net positive for the community in the long term. The area deserves that."

The answer may have been honest, but it didn't get my blood pumping.

"Net positive for the community," I said. "That's what you want to hear."

He shrugged.

"That's an honest answer. If you wanted bluster, I'd give you my PR manager's phone number. I know what we're asking St. Augustine to do, and it's a big ask. We'll bring in jobs—potentially thousands—but we're going to change the complexion of this town. Change is hard. For some people, it's too hard. So, it'll be a net positive in the long term. In the short term, we have a challenge ahead of us. That's just how it is."

I drew in a breath.

"Thank you for your honesty. In the spirit of honesty, the vote for our charter might not be favorable. If that happens, you won't get the zoning permissions or anything else for your project. You should consider your Plan B. St. Augustine's not the place it once was."

Pennington crossed his arms.

"We have backup plans, but answer this: are you going to give up on St. Augustine?"

I shook my head.

"Of course not. It's my home."

"And you'll fight for it?" he asked, lowering his chin.

"Yes. Of course."

He considered that and nodded.

"Then I won't give up, either."

I shook my head.

"No. That's not how you run a multi-billion-dollar initiative. You need to conduct feasibility studies and have actuaries analyze the risk. You need professionals. If you rely on me, you're going to fail."

"Does that mean you plan to fail?"

"No, but I can't solve every problem. I can't make guarantees."

Pennington considered me.

"Nobody can make guarantees. Everybody who does is trying to sell you something. My partners will ask me to hire consultants and consider other sites—which we will—but I trust you."

Again, I shook my head.

"You don't know me, Mr. Pennington."

"True," he said, nodding. "I don't know you, but I know what you've done around here. You could have cashed in like Darren Rogers and left, but you didn't. You sent the bad guys to jail. My aunt gave you property and a house worth millions. You sold everything, bought a defunct bed-and-breakfast and started a battered women's shelter. You then purchased a second building to house more families in need. Either you're running such a sophisticated con that I can't see it, or you're a genuinely good, genuinely capable person trying to do her best. I lean toward the latter, and I'll take your efforts against an entire firm of consultants and lawyers."

I raised my eyebrows.

"You're placing an awfully big bet on a stranger."

"Maybe," he said. "Win or lose, I'm putting my money where it has its best chance of success."

I tilted my head to the side.

"So no pressure," I said.

"Maybe a little pressure," he said, winking. "Good luck, Ms. Court. I'll see you around."

"See you around."

He left. For a moment, I watched the door in case he returned. Then I went to my office. I had brought his peace plant into my office a few days prior, thinking I needed a little greenery. I had neglected it since then, so I took it to the bathroom and watered it. Then I carried it to the lobby and placed it on the front desk for everyone to see. It deserved better than I had given it.

A lot of things deserved better than they had received. Me, my town, my department, my old colleagues, Sophie... Pennington was right. Nobody could guarantee you future success. It was easy to guarantee failure, though. You just had to stop trying.

Hope was a powerful, fragile thing. It could lift the heaviest load, but hope without a foundation was merely a dream. You couldn't build on it. Pennington, so it seemed, had placed his hope in St. Augustine. More than that, he had placed it in me. I didn't know whether our county charter would pass, whether our community would thrive again, or whether my station would reopen.

The future was nebulous, but I felt hopeful. The future didn't feel so bleak. Sophie would fight for her community, Pennington would fight for his project, the casino company would fight for their hotel and convention center... I'd fight for everyone who couldn't fight for themselves. Even if I didn't succeed, I'd work until I couldn't work anymore. If people needed hope, that's what I'd give them. I'd do the best I could. Because this was my home.

I wasn't going anywhere.

Free Joe Court Novella

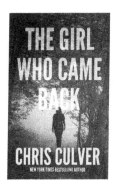

You know what the best part of being an author is? Goofing off while my spouse is at work and my kids are at school. You know what the second part is? Interacting with my readers.

About once a month, I write a newsletter about my books, writing process, research, and funny events from my life. I also include information about sales and discounts. I try to make it fun.

As if hearing from me on a regular basis wasn't enough, if you join, you get a FREE Joe Court novella. The story is a lot of fun, and it's available exclusively to readers on my mailing list. You won't get it anywhere else. If you're interested, sign up here:

http://www.chrisculver.com/magnet.html

CHRIS CULVER

Stay in touch with Chris Culver

As much as I enjoy writing, I like hearing from readers even more. If you want to keep up with my world, there are a couple of ways you can do that.

First and easiest, I've got a mailing list. If you join, you'll receive an email whenever I have a new novel out or when I run sales. You can join that by going to this address: http://www.indiecrime.com/mailinglist.html

If my mailing list doesn't appeal to you, you can also connect with me on Facebook here:

http://www.facebook.com/ChrisCulverbooks

And you can always email me at chris@indiecrime.com. I love receiving email!

About the Author

Chris Culver is the *New York Times* bestselling author of the Ash Rashid series and other novels. After graduate school, Chris taught courses in ethics and comparative religion at a small liberal arts university in southern Arkansas. While there and when he really should have been grading exams, he wrote *The Abbey*, which spent sixteen weeks on the *New York Times* bestsellers list and introduced the world to Detective Ash Rashid.

Chris has been a storyteller since he was a kid, but he decided to write crime fiction after picking up a dog-eared, coffee-stained paperback copy of Mickey Spillane's *I, the Jury* in a library book sale. Many years later, his wife, despite considerable effort, still can't stop him from bringing more orphan books home. He lives with his family near St. Louis.